MRS ZHIVAGO
of QUEEN'S PARK

Mrs Zhivago of Queen's Park

OLIVIA LICHTENSTEIN

First published in Great Britain in 2007 by Orion Books,
an imprint of The Orion Publishing Group Ltd
Orion House, 5 Upper Saint Martin's Lane
London, WC2H 9EA

1 3 5 7 9 10 8 6 4 2

A CIP catalogue record for this book is
available from the British Library.

ISBN-13: 978 0 7528 7629 0 (hardback)
978 0 7528 8645 9 (export trade paperback)
ISBN-10: 0 7528 7629 5 (hardback)
0 7528 8645 2 (export trade paperback)

Typeset by Deltatype Ltd, Birkenhead, Merseyside

Printed in Great Britain by Clays Ltd, St Ives plc

The Orion Publishing Group's policy is to use papers that
are natural, renewable and recyclable products and made
from wood grown in sustainable forests. The logging and
manufacturing processes are expected to conform to the
environmental regulations of the country of origin.

www.orionbooks.co.uk

For my father, Edwin
March 1923 – March 2004

So they were married
To be the more together
And found they were never again so much together,
Divided by the morning tea,
By the evening paper,
By children and tradesmen's bills.

Louis MacNeice, Les Sylphides

Marriage may be compared to a cage: the birds outside despair to get in and those within despair to get out.

Michel de Montaigne, Essays

Happy families are all alike; every unhappy family is unhappy in its own way.

Leo Tolstoy, Anna Karenina

Chloe Zhivago, aged thirteen, carefully folded a sheet of writing paper decorated with psychedelic swirls in various shades of pink. On it she and her best friend, Ruthie Zimmer, had written: 'To Help the Work of Future Historians and Archaeologists. This box contains important clues to the lives of two girls in the 1970s.' They placed the letter in a tartan biscuit tin which contained a plum-coloured Biba lipstick; a copy of Jackie *Magazine; odd pieces of broken jewellery; letters they had written to each other and a contract of eternal friendship signed in their blood. Once they had sellotaped the tin shut, they dug a deep hole at the bottom of Chloe's garden and buried the box in the earth. The two girls stood solemnly in front of the freshly turned earth, their heads bowed as they mourned a future that would, one day, no longer contain them. Later, they sat indoors watching the rain fall and having a race with two raindrops that were running down the windowpane: one was Chloe's, the other, Ruthie's. 'What are you going to do when you grow up?' Ruthie asked Chloe. 'Get a good job, fall in love, have children and live happily ever after,' Chloe answered.*

This is it then, the bit that came after 'living happily ever after ...'

Chapter One

I'd been fine when I'd got up that morning. Quite chirpy really. Not even irritated when I couldn't find the kettle because my husband Greg had hidden it. It's the very things that so charm you about a man when you first meet him that subsequently cause you such intense exasperation. Greg's uncle had got Alzheimer's when he was thirty-two and, as a result, Greg had developed a pathological fear of his memory deteriorating and had set himself little memory tests from an early age. 'The brain's a muscle just like any other and needs exercising,' he says. Absolutely fine for him, but irritating for the rest of us, who don't feel that remembering where you hid the kettle from yourself is a major and necessary triumph in the muscle-taut memory stakes. But that morning I remember whistling as I hunted for it and giving an exultant and good-humoured cheer when I finally unearthed it in the drum of the washing machine.

Greg remained oblivious; sitting at the kitchen table scratching out yet another furious letter in his illegible doctor's handwriting, using the quill pen I had jokingly given him some years before with which to write his many letters of complaint. (I was surprised that he didn't write on parchment, use a wax seal and get a liveried footman to deliver his missives by hand.) This current letter was to the council about a parking fine.

'Ha, Chloe, listen to this,' he said. 'I'm demanding a reply from the councillor himself.' He stood up, held the letter as far from himself as his arm would reach – vanity forbade the use of reading glasses and concomitant recognition of middle-age – cleared his throat and, using the special voice he reserved for officialdom, read: 'Upon examining the legislation, I am astonished to learn that the London Borough of Brent, or its agents, appears to be attempting to extort money from me in an unlawful manner. Please find enclosed an extract of the Bill of Rights Act 1689, enacted and formally entered into Statute following the Declaration of Rights 1689. I draw your attention to the following section: *That all grants and promises of fines and forfeitures of particular persons before conviction are illegal and void.*' He looked up at me, delighted with himself, like a dog that has brought a far-flung stick back in record time to lay at his master's feet. He reached for a slice of toast, which he spread carefully with a thin layer of cholesterol-busting Benecol.

'What does that mean then? That they can't enforce parking fines at all without convicting you of a crime?'

'Precisely,' he said, giving a smug little smile as he left the room. 'First you have to be found guilty in a court.'

Leo, our fifteen-year-old son, made a lightning kitchen raid before our eyes, during the course of which he successfully snatched a chocolate bar from a tin that was supposed to be hidden in a top cupboard, swigged orange juice from a carton in the fridge, and left before anyone could shout at him. Bea, the Czech au pair, gave a characteristic scowl at the space he had briefly occupied before shrugging and returning to her careful task of assembling a platter of exotic fruits that I had bought specifically for that night's supper. I said nothing, assuming it was for my twelve-year-old daughter, Kitty, who had recently announced that she was on a health kick and, as every parent knows, nothing and no one should stand in the way of any child who voluntarily eats fresh fruit and vegetables.

Just then Kitty came in carrying a plate of half finished instant mashed potato.

'I've got a tummy ache,' she said.

'I'm not surprised, eating that processed rubbish. What happened to the new health regime?' I answered unsympathetically. I realised then that the exotic fruit platter must be intended for none other than Bea's own stomach. Sure enough, Bea settled herself comfortably at the table while I tried not to watch as she ate slice after slice of expensive mango, papaya and guava delicately with a knife and fork. The sun was shining and I was determined to preserve my good mood. So with only the merest tightening of the jaw, I emptied the dishwasher and brushed Kitty's hair. Really, everything was fine until I saw my third patient of the day.

I'm a psychotherapist and our Queen's Park house has a separate basement flat where I see my patients. 'Most people put their nice harmless old mothers at the bottom of their houses, not a bunch of self-pitying whingers who bore on about their problems,' says Greg. The idea that Greg is able to put the words *nice* and *harmless* anywhere near the word *mother* is, in the light of his own female parent, frankly risible. Moreover, my 'self-pitying whingers' helped see him through the last few years of medical school. But, being a GP, he doesn't really have much patience for any sort of illness, and especially not those that have no obvious physical characteristics. The notion that people can feel better and happier by talking to a trained therapist causes him to roll his eyes in exasperated disbelief. 'Why don't they just talk to their friends instead of to a complete stranger like you?' We discuss my work as little as possible.

That morning I'd said goodbye to Furious Frank, who has a little anger management problem we've been working on, and I was enjoying the ten minutes between patients by looking out the window and watching feet crunch autumn leaves as they passed. Summer was over but I didn't feel my usual desolation in the face of the impending season of mists.

The doorbell rang with a familiar nagging insistence. It was Gloomy Gina, who has been coming to see me for five years. ('Do you think they know about the names you give them?' my friend Ruthie recently asked me. 'Of course not,' I'd answered, 'you're the only other person who knows. It's my gallows humour, just an affectionate shorthand for differentiating between them.')

I hadn't always been so cynical. At twenty-eight, I'd been the youngest person to qualify at the British Association of Psychotherapists and had always been dedicated to my work. Just lately though, the gloss seemed to have faded and I often felt I was only going through the motions.

Gina is rarely able to see the good side of a person or a situation and makes me feel like Pollyanna in comparison. She'd been much happier recently as she was soon to marry and hadn't yet found much wrong with her fiancé, Jim, although God knows she'd tried. By her standards, she'd been positively jubilant for the past three months. That day though, her pretty face had a pre-Jim look about it. Something was up.

'I've been thinking,' she began. Always a bad start with Gina. 'This is it. I'll never sleep with another man again. I'll never know that excitement and mystery of discovering someone for the first time, of having that first kiss, of waking up together full of the wonder of newness.'

I wanted to say, 'Don't be silly, he could die, you might get divorced, you could have an affair,' but I didn't. Instead, I suddenly realised, 'Oh my God, I've never thought of it like that.' In that instant, like a painful and unexpected blow to the head, the seed of betrayal took root in my own breast.

I'm afraid I barely listened to anything Gina said for the rest of that session. I even felt a twinge of guilt when I took her cheque, but only the slightest twinge; after all, she gets her money's worth with all her after-hours phone calls and midnight panic attacks. Instead, I sat there nodding absently and staring at the wall behind her. The streaky bubbling smears of the earth's oozings that were rising damply up my basement wall mirrored my mood of growing unease perfectly. The day, which only moments before had felt bright and full of promise, now felt cloudy and damp. The sun had gone in.

Never again to feel the first kiss of a new lover? What was that e. e. cummings poem, something about liking your body when it's with someone else's, the thrill of 'under me you so quite new'? I've always rather loved e. e., initially because he died the day and year I was born, 3 September, 1962, which for an adolescent is a spooky coincidence, full of mystical significance. I felt we must have had a unique spiritual connection. For a while, I even thought that as his soul left his body at 1.15 a.m., the time of his death, it flew directly into mine as I opened my mouth to take my first breath at 3.23 a.m. Just over two hours seemed about the right amount of time for a soul to travel from East Coast America to Chalk Farm in London.

Mainly I admired cummings because he was naughty enough to ignore capitals and muck around with grammar, something I was never able to get away with at my *Grammar* School. I tried it, obviously, in my 'the soul of e. e. cummings lives on in me and I'm going to be the world's greatest living poetess' phase. But Miss Titworth our English teacher was a stickler for punctuation. She even made us verbally punctuate our spoken English. 'Miss Titworth comma please may I be excused question mark.' This was the source of hours of witty schoolgirl repartee over crafty fags in the cloakroom. 'Miss Titworth comma, how much are your tits worth question mark.'

But now, sitting in my consulting room, all I could think was, 'Is this it question mark.' Forever and ever, the same old same old? After Gina left, I went upstairs and straight to the fridge, gloomily surveying the contents and grazing on pieces of cheese and cold meat like a sheep with attention deficit disorder. I needed something to fill the gaping abyss of the bleak, unchanging future I faced. Of course, I should know better, 'food isn't love' and all that, but just as all dentists don't have perfect teeth, neither do all psychotherapists have perfect psyches. Kitty came in and caught me guiltily sucking Philadelphia cheese from an index finger that had clearly scooped it directly from the tub, and swigging orange juice straight from the carton. Both my children have been taught that these two crimes carry a custodial sentence.

'You're always bloody telling us not to do that,' she protested.

'You weren't meant to see me and don't say bloody,' I responded feebly. 'Anyhow, why aren't you at school?' She did that sighing and rolling eyes thing that I thought was only supposed to happen after puberty when you are suddenly struck by the overwhelming stupidity of your parents. She was still meant to be at the stage where I could do no wrong and her adoration was unequivocal.

'I told you I had a tummy ache this morning,' she said accusingly, 'but you *made* me go to school and I was sick, so Bea had to come and pick me up.' Bea had been rather pointedly and not altogether silently hovering outside the kitchen door; now she came in and shot me a reproachful look.

'Thank you, Bea. Didn't you tell Dad you had a tummy ache?' I asked, deftly trying to pass the buck. 'I mean he is a doctor.

'Mum, you know you have to have your head actually hanging off your body before Daddy will take any notice at all.'

'Poor baby.' I took Kitty in my arms and held her.

I loved being a mother from the first moment I held my babies. Even now, I often lull myself to sleep at night by replaying their births in my head like a treasured movie. I loved the sweet milky smell of them and wore them close to my heart on my breast, like a precious brooch, for as long as they were small enough. I loved that part of them at the nape of the neck that you had to bury your nose into to kiss; I still do. I loved stuffing whole tiny newborn feet into my mouth. Kitty continues to let me nibble on her limbs and cover her with kisses and Leo is unusually accommodating for a fifteen-year-old as long as no one else is watching. I tease them both by telling them that I long ago made them sign contracts where they undertook to suffer my kisses and cuddles irrespective of their age and in perpetuity.

I'm a respecter of contracts. Call me old-fashioned, but I'd meant it seventeen years ago when I had made my wedding vows to Mr Grumpy, their father, promising to forsake all others and be faithful to him as long as we both shall live. I've had the odd little dalliance, a few stolen kisses, but never seriously contemplated infidelity. Recently, though, I'd found myself flirting with my only single male friends who are dyed-in-the-wool homosexuals.

'What's wrong with us girls?' I bleat occasionally.

'You're just not, well, furry enough.'

'We can be if we don't wax our legs and upper lips,' I protest.

But now, with Gina's words on the finality of never sleeping with another man ever again ringing in my head, I felt as though I was gasping for air. What was I to do? Was Greg the only man I would ever have sex with? But could I really imagine having a lover? I'd rather assumed that you weren't allowed to take your clothes off in front of a stranger once you were over forty. Surely it's against the law on grounds of common decency. It's fine for your husband to see you naked if absolutely necessary. After all, the less-than-taut, post-childbirth body is his fault, so there's a kind of perverse pleasure to be gained in parading it in front of him, the very act a silent scream of *Look what you've done to my body, you bastard.* But someone new, that would be, well ... the word 'impossible' springs to mind.

'You find me interesting, don't you?' Ruthie asked me later as we reclined like Romans on her sofa and ate lunch.

'Course, or we wouldn't be celebrating our thirty-second year as friends. Why?' I popped the last bite of a salmon and cream cheese bagel into my mouth.

'It's just that whenever I say anything to him, Richard sighs and closes his eyes.'

'Ah, HHATT,' I pronounced sagely.

This is our shorthand; it makes text messaging so much faster and allows us to tell each other how we're feeling without fear of prying eyes. It came about after I'd had a particularly bad fight with Greg when he had spent an entire weekend shouting at the children and me. I tapped out my message: *My husband is a cunt.* But I sent it to Greg instead of to Ruthie. When I realised what I'd done, my heart raced and I felt like a child caught making 'V' signs at the teacher. I had to bluff it out by sending Greg another one: *Only joking, darling. What do you want for supper?* Luckily I pulled it off. After that, acronyms seemed a safer route, hence HHATT – Hating Husband All The Time.

Ruthie yawned and stretched. That's how I always think of her, yawning and stretching in a smudged, sleepy sort of way, like a cat rousing itself briefly to change position in front of the fire. At work she's sharp, pressed, businesslike efficiency, but I know her secret; she's always longing to go and have a little lie-down. She has a beautiful heart-shaped face, a Marilyn Monroe of a body and liquid brown eyes. When she was younger, boys wanted to stab each other to win her affections. Irresistibly, she is unconscious of her allure and wears it as comfortably and absent-mindedly as a favourite, and slightly grubby, towelling robe.

We met on our first day at grammar school, when we were initially nudged into friendship by being seated at adjoining desks. Our surnames began with the same letter, Chloe Zhivago and Ruthie Zimmer. Hers used to be Zimmerman but the border guards found it unnecessarily long and dropped a syllable somewhere along the route when her father walked from Germany to England to escape the Nazis. Ruthie was a better Jew than me and knew stuff. For, in spite of the fact that I'm a psychotherapist, make fantastic chicken soup and do all that soul food business, I'm fundamentally ignorant about Judaism. It's not surprising really: I remember asking Dad once what the Chanukah candles signified and he looked at me with bemusement and said, 'Do you know darling, I have absolutely no idea.'

'What sort of a Jewish father are you?' I asked.

'A very bad one,' he smiled, 'but I can hold a tune.' (My father Bertie composes musicals for the West End stage.)

Mum would have known but pretended not to; since marrying Dad she'd rejected her religious upbringing and the only holiday we celebrated was Christmas. So, I'd gone off to ask Ruthie. Apparently, thousands of years ago, oil was needed for the candelabrum in the Temple, which was supposed to burn throughout the night every night. But there was only enough oil to burn for one day. Inexplicably, it burned for eight days. So they declared an eight-day festival to commemorate it. It's a bit like the loaves and the fishes feeding everyone really. Every religion needs its miracles. We used to joke that it was also like the miracle of Stevie Brick who, when we were fifteen, managed to get off with four of us in the same evening at three different parties. Anyhow, since then I have always consulted Ruthie on matters Jewish when the need arises.

We'd made each other into the sisters neither of us had and vowed to live as close to each other as possible and have our children at the same time. We'd succeeded in doing both. Ruthie was just the other side of Queen's Park and we could have communicated by semaphore from our roofs if either of us had had the ability or the desire. Instead, we phoned and texted constantly and bumped into each other often in the course of going about our local business, quite apart from our many proper scheduled meetings. Her children, Atlas, and Sephy (Persephone), are best friends with Leo and Kitty and the same ages. Her husband Richard is a Classicist and Ruthie felt since he had had so little say in so much of their life, it would have been churlish of her to begrudge him naming the children. Atlas was a small, fine-boned child. You couldn't imagine anyone less physically capable of bearing on his shoulders the pillars that kept heaven and earth apart, but he did have the air of someone who wore the weight of the world heavily. Like his Greek counterpart, he was passionately interested in science and astrology and spent his evenings perched precariously on the rooftop of their house, often with Leo, peering through a telescope and pointing out the stars and the planets. (Ruthie's Jewish mother's instincts were in conflict: on the one hand, joy at having a son who pursued knowledge, on the other anxiety that he may fall to his death in his quest for it. The solution? A sturdy iron railing that circumvented the roof was installed at considerable expense.) For her part, Sephy was an unlikely Queen of the Underworld. She was a joyful, fairy princess of a child, just like my Kitty and when they both left the room, it felt as bleak and barren as if they'd returned to Hades, heralding the onset of Winter. In choosing your child's name, to some extent you are influencing their destiny and personalities. That's why I'd gone for strong names like Leo and Katherine – the names of former Emperors and Empresses – no one was going to push my kids around.

'When did you last have sex?' I asked Ruthie.

'With Richard? Don't be disgusting, he's my husband.'

'I know what you mean.' I munched on a hot green pepper, enjoying the way it made my eyes smart. 'We haven't done it for so long that the very notion of bumping and grinding in the marital bed feels inappropriate and obscene. Thank God we both had so much sex before marriage, there's bugger-all after.'

'Do you think it was like that for our mothers? Maybe the fact that they saved themselves meant that they had lots as married women?' Ruthie reached for an olive and nibbled at it, she'd hardly eaten a thing. 'Perhaps we should just ditch the husbands and set up a lesbian commune,' she suggested.

'In principle, that's an excellent idea. One slight hitch, we're not actually lesbians.'

'I know,' said Ruthie regretfully. 'Pity. How about a commune with a separate wired-off area for men, then? We could go and play with them when the fancy took us?'

'A men pen?' I mused. 'Actually,' I said, Gina's words still ringing in my ears, 'I was thinking I might take a lover, purely for reasons of weight loss – you know how new sex makes the pounds drop off?' I pinched at more than an inch around my midriff.

'No one could blame either of us for having an affair, no woman can be expected to live a life with so little sex, it's a human rights issue really,' Ruthie said as she dipped the tip of a finger into a bowl of hummus. 'The real problem is that the only sex there is after marriage is with other people.' She looked at me appraisingly and added, 'If you do have an affair though, make sure you remember the rule.'

Ruthie is the editor of *Smart Magazine – Beauty and Brains for Today's Woman* and frequently uses me under a variety of pseudonyms for her case studies. She has written or edited articles on virtually every subject imaginable and is the fount of all knowledge. I studied her; she was dressed in her professional uniform: Issey Miyake. She never wore anything else for work. (His clothes, made up of thousands of little knife-edged pleats, always make me feel rather nervous. Does someone have to sit there folding and folding like a lunatic in Bedlam with obsessive-compulsive disorder?)

'What rule, O wise and pleated one?' I asked.

'*Never have an affair with anyone who has less to lose by its disclosure than you do.*' Very clever and absolutely obvious if you stop to think about it. It was all I could do to prevent myself from surreptitiously jotting it down like an over-zealous student.

'You'll have to have an affair for both of us,' she added. 'I could never let anyone other than Richard see my untidy, ever-increasing middle-aged breasts.'

I looked at her breasts; they did seem bigger.

'You know how ears and noses never stop growing?' she went on. 'Well, my breasts are just the same, they don't seem to know when to call it a day.'

'At least you have breasts, mine never really started growing and now they're like small empty socks.'

Ruthie laughed, 'Go on, you were always the adventurous one, then I can have an affair vicariously.'

'As usual, I have to do all the work. Things really haven't changed much since the days you used to copy my Latin homework.'

'I know darling, you've always been so much better than me at actually doing things; I just write about other people doing them.'

We both laughed knowing the important and equal nature of the symbiosis that bound us.

'Did you know that seventy percent of men and thirty percent of women commit adultery?' Ruthie said.

'It's about time women caught up then,' I commented wryly.

I hadn't really meant it, the *Shed Those Unwanted Pounds the Fun Way – Shag a Man Who Isn't Your Husband Diet*. I'd just wanted to roll the words around my tongue, taste the idea and say it out loud. It had felt like so long since I'd had any fun; life was full of being a wife, a mother and a psychotherapist and here I was, suddenly in my forties, with no time to feel carefree and full of joy. I could see why the forties were the Decade of Divorce; everyone was bolting in terror in a last bid for freedom from the drudgery of responsibility and obligation. As I was leaving Ruthie's, I nearly collided with a woman who was dragging a crying toddler and pushing a howling baby in a pram. When I looked closer, I saw that tears were trickling down the mother's weary face too. That love and marriage, horse and carriage song started playing ironically in my head. It was now one of those drizzly, grey London days when the damp snacks greedily on your bones and you think that you'll never see the sun again. I felt depression nudging at my gut.

By the time I'd walked home, I was feeling increasingly rueful about my life. What had happened to the flurry of passion and whole weekends in bed that Greg and I had once shared? I asked Greg when he came back from work. He was looking for some chocolate he'd hidden from himself earlier.

'Don't be silly, that honeymoon period can't last for ever, you'd never get anything done.'

'But don't you miss it, darling, don't you wish we were still like that?'

'No, there's too much to do; kids, work, books to read, films to watch. Ah, here it is,' he beamed with satisfaction as he pulled a chocolate bar from behind one of the many recipe books that looked about to tumble from their over-stuffed shelf. 'Want some?' (He wilfully refuses to discuss his diet's strange bedfellows of Benecol and chocolate).

'Why not?' I answered bitterly, thinking, 'I can always burn the calories off adulterously.'

Greg went off to the living room greeting Leo with a cheerful 'Yo Rasta man, I and I have learnt our lesson with the weed.' This arose from the small matter of a confiscated matchbox full of grass that Greg had found as he was trying to reclaim stolen designer boxer-shorts from his son's wardrobe. Greg is no stranger to the weed himself; he'd sniffed it ostentatiously and said, 'looks like good gear, might have to smoke it myself.' Ever since, we'd had the Rasta joke, amusing initially, but we were ten days in and it was wearing thin.

Leo shuffled into the kitchen, almost visibly cocooned in the cloud of disgruntlement that had become his constant companion over the past two years. A bizarre physical change overcomes boys on their thirteenth birthday. Overnight their heads, which they previously had no trouble supporting, become too heavy for their necks and their speech, once clear, becomes indistinct. That once upright, chatty and articulate son becomes a slouching mumbler.

'Have you done your homework, darling?' I asked.

'Mmmf, mrumf,' he answered.

'Pardon?'

'Yes, yes, whatever,' he enunciated with exaggerated clarity.

I threw the rest of the chocolate bar away; the self-loathing that accompanied every mouthful was too much to bear. Besides, perhaps I should at least try diet and exercise before resorting to adultery. I decided to flirt with Greg and seduce him. That's what you're meant to do, that's what I always tell my patients anyhow. Rediscover each other, put the romance back in the marriage, go out on dates with each other, do things together, make the time to talk and enjoy each other. Who's to say a relationship with another man would be any different? After the honeymoon of the first two years, it would probably settle into what I had now. Was it worth the lies, the deceit, and the risk to everyone's happiness for a couple of years of good sex? (Although, in my case, it didn't even have to be good; just sex would do.)

I could hear the television in the living room and through the doorway saw Greg slumped on the sofa, his mouth slightly open, as he watched the weather forecast with an intensity more usually seen on the face of a hungry infant at his mother's breast. I took off all my clothes and undulated sinuously in front of him to see if he would notice. He waved me aside before pointing at the television, 'Very nice darling, but, you know, the weather ...' It is his favourite programme, but still. At that point the telephone rang. It was one of Greg's regular patients, Mrs Meagan, or 'Me Again' as she is known, on account of the frequency of her calls. God knows how she'd managed to get hold of our ex-directory number; I think Mr Meagan works for BT or the Police or is a thief or something. Normally I field these calls, Greg hates ill people at the best of times and hypochondriacs are his bêtest of noirs. But now, after my bitter rejection, I said sweetly, 'Yes, Mrs Meagan, of course, he's right here' and, wearing only my high heels, harrumphed out of the room neatly colliding with Leo as he slouched up the stairs. He took one look at me, shuddered and said very clearly, 'Urgh, naked parent! That's like really bad for my psychosexual development Mum.'

I spent the rest of the evening sulkily sewing a felt elephant badly for something or the other that Kitty was doing at school while she told me all about Henry VI and his eight wives or Henry VIII and his six wives – *yes, yes, whatever*. Is this my life? Whatever happened to me and how did I get here?

Chapter Two

Grandpa Rabbi Neeman's Recipe for a Happy Marriage

250g love
250g humour
250g sexual attraction
500ml admiration and respect for one another
500g intellectual parity
1 small pinch of in-laws, unless to your taste, in which case add more
1 reasonable budget

A generous dash of team work
4 tsp. readiness to admit fault
250g quick and easy apology
250g each confidence and encouragement
1 large or several small interests or hobbies in common
250g delight in each other
Separate bathrooms (budget permitting)

Sift all ingredients and remove any lumps of jealousy, accounting of wrongs, grudge-bearing, point scoring, temper or accusation. Stir in frequent portions of healthy and satisfying marital sex. Pour into generous servings of love and bake over many years in the steady warmth of affection, mutual respect and desire.

That night I had my recurring contact lens anxiety dream. It comes in various forms; this version was the one where I tried to insert an enormous contact lens into my eye. It was simply too big and wouldn't go in, but I kept on trying. I was confused: I wear these lenses every day, why did they no longer fit? The lens in question had extra flaps on the side, like those sanitary towels with wings that you're meant to tuck round your knickers. The flappy bits were supposed to fit onto the white of your eyeball, but try as I might, I couldn't get them in. It was a relief to wake up. I glanced over at Greg, who was snoring less gently than he imagines, next to me. What did it mean? I always examine dreams; it's the Jungian in me. They make us think about our lives and are our subconscious's way of talking to us. Mine was clearly telling me that I was anxious. Perhaps it was also trying to tell me that Greg didn't fit me any more? Maybe, day after day for seventeen years he had, but now he no longer did? A few hours before, when we'd got into bed, I'd rubbed my foot up and down Greg's calf, our marital Morse code to signal the desire for sex. I knew he was still awake, but he'd deepened his breathing to pretend he was already asleep, grunted and turned over with his back to me, leaving a lonely ocean of white sheet between our two bodies. The lack of response from him couldn't help but make me feel unloved and unlovely.

It was four a.m. It's always four a.m. when I wake up anxious and alert in a sleeping house. I got out of bed, went into Kitty's room, and sat in the chintz-covered nursing chair that she insists on keeping by her bed. I love to watch her sleep. Asleep she looks like a baby again; her features soft and contented; her arm carelessly flung across her chest, her long, dark lashes sweeping damply across her cheek and her mouth slightly open. She has a particularly beautiful mouth, full and red, ripe like succulent fruit and full of the promise of the sensual young woman she is soon to become. I wanted to kiss her but resisted. Instead, I laid a hand gently on her chest to feel the rise and fall of her breathing. When she and Leo were babies, I used to put a finger under their noses to check they were still alive. Sometimes their infant breath was too soft to detect and I would accidentally wake them with my fearful prodding. I remembered all those nights I would sit in this same chair, breast-feeding – first Leo, and then a few years later, Kitty – in the middle of the night. I used to feel that I was the only person awake in the world and was at pains to be silent and keep my babies from crying so that we wouldn't wake Greg. He would be in a terrible ill humour all day if he didn't get enough sleep at night.

Now Kitty stirred and said mysteriously, 'Four chestnuts and a badger's tail.' Everyone in this house talks in his or her sleep except me. Greg especially is given to loud biblical pronouncements that wake me up. Is he dreaming that he is Jesus? This is his biggest fear, that he will suddenly see the Light. He's made me promise to shoot him if he is born again and gets religion.

I made my way downstairs. In response, the house creaked, groaned and turned over in its sleep. I looked around me, at my life, the clutter of it. Coats in a jumble in the hall, shoes scattered on the stairs. Fetching and carrying, that was what life amounted to: picking something up from one place and putting it in another, then later picking it up from there and putting it somewhere else. Every available surface was full of *stuff*. Items seemed to mate with each other and reproduce at a terrifying rate. Odd socks gathered in gangs and had parties with empty coffee cups, carelessly discarded items of clothing and endless pieces of paper. Sometimes, the clutter threatens to overwhelm me. What if I just walked out the door and never returned? Drove to the airport, took the first plane to somewhere and started a whole new life? Occasionally, I liked to examine this idea, roll it round in my head and taste it before rejecting it, because I could never seriously contemplate it. The thought of leaving Leo and Kitty behind made me feel ill, literally physically ill, a dull nauseous ache in the core of my being.

When I was a child my father would bring me hot milk after a bad dream or if I couldn't sleep. He would sit with me while I drank it, stroking my forehead and smoothing my eyebrows with his thumb. He'd sing me his latest song, one he was still writing and which no one else had yet heard. Sometimes it would just be a phrase or two and he'd sing it over and over, more and more softly until I fell asleep. I loved those Daddy and Chloe nights, when he made the world safe for me. These days the only time I ever drink milk is in the middle of the night. I heated some now and curled up, hugging the mug as I lay on the sofa trying to examine my unease. I must have dozed because the kitsch clock that my brother Sammy had given us sounded six times, a small pink pig snorting its way out of the hatch where a cuckoo should be. I picked up the phone and dialled.

'Daddy?'

'Who is this please?'

'Which other woman calls you Daddy?'

'We won't go into that now,' he laughed.

'It's Chloe,' I said, playing along.

'It's true, I used to have a daughter called Chloe, but I haven't heard from her for a very long time.'

'I spoke to you three days ago.'

'Three days multiplied by a Jewish Father is three months as you well know.'

'Are you awake?'

'I am now.'

He was anyway; I knew he would be. He's always up and at his piano by six.

'Hold on, darling,' he said, 'I just have to get the birds out of my head and onto paper before they fly away.'

My father has songs in his head the way the rest of us have thoughts. When I was little, I used to imagine that his head was full of birds which, when he opened his mouth, would fly out singing and he had to capture them. And I was certain that when he did he glued them down on paper, because the little black notes that he inked onto his manuscript looked just like tiny blackbirds perching on telegraph wires. When the birds were ready to come out, Dad would get agitated and didn't like to talk until he'd got them all neatly stuck down. So I held on patiently for a few minutes.

'There, all down. What gets you up so early, Chloe?'

'Thinking. Dad, do you think you can be happily married to one person for the rest of your life?'

I listened to the clock tick in the quiet early morning and waited for him to answer.

'I think relationships change like everything else. There were times when I thought I couldn't stand another minute with your mother, then the week after I'd feel that life would be impossible without her. Sometimes you're happy, sometimes not. Lust is instant, but love takes a long time to grow. Mark Twain said, 'No man or woman really knows what perfect love is until they have been married a quarter of a century'. Maybe you haven't been married long enough.'

Among all the things I loved my father for, and there were many, I loved his ability to encapsulate the issue at hand with a quotation; he had one for every occasion.

'Aren't you happy, darling?' he asked.

'It's not so much that Dad, it's just that everything seems to have settled into this monotonous continuum. It's as though everything that's exciting has already happened, and now it'll just be the same for ever and ever and there's nothing left to look forward to.'

I could hear the plaintive, petulant child in my voice but it in no way weakened the intensity of my feelings.

'It's your age, Chlo, you know? You've married the man and had the kids and now what? I remember feeling it in my forties too.'

'What did you do?'

There was a long pause. I looked out of the window and saw that it was raining in the blue dawn light. I could hear the swish of wet tyres on asphalt as cars passed with increasing frequency. The world was rubbing its eyes and coming to life. A new day. But how new would it be and how much would it be merely a repetition of the old day that was yesterday?

I waited. Dad cleared his throat on the other end of the phone.

'Well, Chlo, I wouldn't recommend it, but I had an affair.'

I was silent as an old half-forgotten memory rose unbidden at his answer: The phone ringing, a stream of angry words, the phone being slammed down, my mother red-eyed and tearful, shouting in hoarse whispers from behind closed doors. My father away suddenly for a few days, 'to see a performance of one of his shows in Leeds.' I must have been about twelve, uncomprehending, but aware that divorce was – if not on the cards – at least under discussion. With the egocentricity of a child, all I could think was 'will I be allowed to live with my Daddy?'

'God, did Mum know?'

'Only later,' Dad said. 'Let me wait till I see you and I'll explain.'

My mother was the youngest of four, the much-wanted, pampered only daughter who came, just as all hope was almost lost, after three brothers. They were so pleased to have a girl in the family, a daughter, that they only ever called her Girlie. Actually, that's all anyone ever called her, or was allowed to call her. Her real name was Gertrude. Gertrude Neeman. 'It makes me sound like a plump matron with thick ankles,' she complained. She was a beautiful child who, as family lore had it, emerged from the womb with abundant dark curls and long dancer's legs. She started dancing as soon as she could walk and won a scholarship to the Royal Ballet School at the age of eight. Her parents, who came from generations of learned, Talmudic Jews, her father a Rabbi, her mother a teacher, could tolerate the dancing when it was classical and qualified as 'art.' They found it less easy to cope when she left the Royal Ballet and leapt to the freedom of the West End stage's 'racy musicals.' And their horror knew no bounds when she fell in love with and married my father, who was ten years older than her and composed the very musicals that had lured her from her true artistic purpose. The fact that his parents were in the 'schmata business' and had a dress shop was yet another black mark against him.

'We are book Jews, that our daughter should marry a money Jew; pah!' they said. 'At least he is actually Jewish,' Girlie retorted.

They turned pale. A week later, they were back to patting her cheek and telling her how beautiful she was. She was their miracle, their gift from God, how could they stay angry with a face like that?

Girlie was a rare and quixotic creature and everyone always told me how lucky I was that she was my mother. But she wasn't terribly motherly, not a 'sit down and let me give you something to eat, my darling' sort of a mother, and at an early age our roles had become blurred and confused. By the time I was a teenager I felt I was the responsible adult and she the moody, tyrannical and depressive child. I would come home from school, turn my key in the door and sniff the air apprehensively. I could tell by some subtle odour whether or not all was well in my mother's world, and therefore in mine. All families have their own smell, a subliminal aroma that speaks of familiarity but not necessarily of contentment. I could sniff out my mother's ill humour or distress at twenty paces. She would lie in her bed in the darkness, her voice a lifeless monotone, while I tiptoed around the house fearful of making matters worse and tried to dispel her mood by tempting her with food or drink. All my offerings would be rebuffed: 'I suppose you want me to get fat,' she would complain, 'that's what you want isn't it, a fat mummy sort of mother?' She was probably right; I did want a mummy sort of mother, not the unpredictable and disappointed woman who was hiding in the dark. Her mood could change in an instant. If the doorbell rang, she would hurry out of bed, put on her make-up and make her entrance, ready to perform and to dazzle, her former misery forgotten in her delight at unexpected guests. It was as if she ceased to exist away from the glare of the spotlight. Her dancing days long over, friends and acquaintances were now her audience. Without them, she withered; her family was not enough to sustain her.

This neediness certainly put me off show business and turned me firmly to books. I'd inherited my mother's dancer's legs but not the desire to show them – or any other part of me – off, and observing Girlie in the grip of her dark moods made me vow never to fall prey to depression. It became something of a phobia for me. The vain hope that I could become mistress of my own mind kicked rather than pushed me towards psychotherapy.

I made my way back to bed. Through the window, I could see the Pigeon Lady in the yellow glow of a nearby street lamp, waging her usual war against the pigeons. Sometimes she talked to them as though to close friends, often she appeared to quarrel with them. It was as though the birds had said something particularly offensive and she had to persuade them of their error. Again and again she rushed at them, shouting and admonishing them, her carrier bags and her wild grey hair flying, her coat pulled tightly around her tall thin body. Two of the birds remained impervious to her cries. They stood side by side on the pavement, one seeming to shield the other with its wing as they pecked companionably at the ground together. A third pigeon whooshed between them, pushing them apart. It seemed to me that that was what I had done to my parents: by being my father's favourite, I had destroyed their unity and wrenched them asunder. I remembered all those nights that I left my brother Sammy alone in our room and crept into our parents' bed, forcing my determined way into the middle. I would dig my small heels into my mother's thighs and push her a little further away so that I could take my rightful place next to my father. Then I would rest my victorious head on his chest.

I loved the smell of him, his expensive Givenchy cologne that was made especially for him in a little place just off the Place de la Concorde in Paris, where he also went twice a year to buy his socks: thin, black and made of silk. My father has always been a dandy, immaculately dressed, whatever the occasion. He carries a spare tie in his pocket at all times, in case the worst should happen: a stain on the one he is wearing. I wasn't surprised to learn that he had had an affair; he was too charming, too ebullient and too affectionate to be contained by marriage. I suppose, somewhere, I must have known it, and read the currents of the tension that flowed between him and my mother. After a few days, he returned from 'Leeds' and normal family life was resumed. In any case, I think my mother felt he had already betrayed her long before by falling so deeply in love with me, his little girl. But then, she had my brother to love.

Over the next few days I couldn't stop thinking about Dad's affair and what it might be like to have one myself. When Greg wasn't at work, he was spending much of his time writing more furious letters to the council and scouring the Internet for legal precedents that would support his newly declared war on parking fines. The rest of the time he was on the phone to his new friends: fellow parking fine warriors. There was a nationwide network of them with their own website, bonded like brothers by their common purpose.

'It's all very well fining people who obstruct the road or park in resident permit areas,' Greg said, at the end of a long exposition over dinner one night, 'but now they're doing it purely for revenue and they must be punished.' He had no other topic of conversation and the children and I gave him a wide berth. We could only hope he would tire of it eventually.

The universe seemed to be screaming adultery at me. When one afternoon a patient cancelled and I treated myself to some illicit daytime television, the theme of the Jerry Springer show was *My*

Partner's a Cheater. There they all were, black, white, fat, thin, cheating away to their hearts' content and looking rather smug about it. Jerry summed up the programme sanctimoniously: 'The person you really cheat is yourself. What sort of a relationship is it if you're not being honest?'

'An exciting one,' I said aloud as I threw down the remote in disgust and left the room. Everywhere I looked I saw lovers walking along together, their bodies as close as possible, kissing on street corners and holding each other's faces lovingly. Women's magazines in the newsagent round the corner assaulted me with their adulterous headlines: *Falling in Love With a Man Who Isn't Your Husband*; *My Husband and Lover Both Live with Me*; *My Affair Brought Us Closer*. On the street outside our house, the Pigeon Lady shouted incongruously at me, 'Go find yourself a fancy man why don't you, you're all the same.' I found myself looking at men again, really looking in an 'up for it' sort of way – and some of them started looking back. The invisibility pill that I had unwittingly swallowed with my fortieth birthday seemed, temporarily at least, to have lost its power.

Chapter Three

Sariputra's Cactus Salsa

1 bunch fresh coriander
1 large (780g) can Italian peeled
  plum tomatoes
2 large (400g) cans marinated
  cactus (or fresh if you can find
  it)
900g fresh tomatoes
3 lemons

1 or 2 bunches spring onions
2 large red onions
4 small hot red or green chillies
6 – 8 cloves of garlic
1 tsp. salt
1 tsp. freshly ground black pepper
2 large tbsp. olive oil

Open can of tomatoes and mash in a large bowl. Dice strained cactus, fresh tomatoes, onions and spring onions, and add. Finely chop coriander leaves and chillies and add along with the juice of the lemons, the garlic, which you should crush, the salt, pepper and olive oil. Mix everything together and leave to mature for a few hours.
Serve with fish, chicken or meat to add flavour.
Or, blend briefly to make a finer mixture and use as a dip for tortilla chips.

'I thought happily ever after would be more satisfying than this, didn't you?' Ruthie said. We were in one of our habitual haunts, the café in Queen's Park. She looked tired and seemed to have a perpetual cold these days. When I asked her what the matter was, she said that work was getting her down.

'Mmm,' I said, 'but maybe, just maybe, it is possible to have a different life. You know, a life full of love and passion, to talk and have someone listen, to stroke and be stroked, to have someone gaze into your eyes and tell you that they love you, to look in their eyes and find everything you need there.'

'Oh Chlo, you're a hopeless romantic,' she said, pushing her food around her plate like an anorexic pretending to eat. 'By the way,' she said suddenly, 'Happy Birthday.'

'It's not my birthday.' I looked at her in confusion.

'I know. It's just that Lou hasn't spoken to me for weeks because I forgot her birthday, so now I'm wishing everyone happy birthday whenever I talk to them; that way they won't get cross when I forget on the day. Anyway,' she went on, 'Lou's got other things to worry about now since she and James split up.'

I was horrified. Lou and James had been together for twenty years; they'd married before any of us and had had children as quickly as they could, four of them, one after the other, boy, girl, boy, girl. They actually liked each other, laughed at each other's jokes and talked; real proper conversations, not mere business meetings about whose turn it was to call the plumber or get the car fixed. Lou's hand was always fluttering affectionately around James, smoothing his hair, tracing the curve of his jaw. James noticed what Lou wore and liked to shop with her, pulling the clothes that he knew would suit her off racks and holding them against her. We always joked that he was a gay man trapped in a straight man's body. They were the standard bearers for the rest of us: Mr and Mrs Happily Married, living proof that it was possible to live happily ever after. Their union was essential to the ecology of everyone else's relationships. How could they split up? They had always seemed to stand together in marital harmony like two strong oak trees flourishing under the same sun, their roots intertwined beneath the ground, their presence untroubled by the passing of years. There'd been the odd creak, or metaphorical shedding of a small branch, but no one could have imagined this would lead to a felling of the tree itself. Until now.

'What? How? When?' the words tumbled out of me. 'I can't believe you haven't told me about this.'

'I forgot ... like birthdays. They're having a trial separation, they feel they need to start dating again or something, that they've been taking each other for granted.'

'If they can't stay together, what hope is there for the rest of us?' I muttered.

'True,' said Ruthie, 'but you never know what goes on behind closed doors; I always thought all that lovey-dovey stuff in public was a bit suspicious, you know, a sign that nothing much was actually going on between the sheets.'

'Nothing much is going on between our respective sheets, but we're still with our husbands,' I said.

'Did you know that lack of sex is actually grounds for divorce?'

'But we're nice Jewish girls who will do all we can to keep the family together, remember?' I said.

'Of course, but if we were religious and really were in celibate marriages we could go to the Rabbi who might well sanction a divorce. Jews are big on sex and intimacy and the Torah actually obligates the husband to meet the sexual needs of his wife. Some texts even suggest that a man must bring his wife to orgasm first.'

'Very clever people, Jews, I've always said so.' I finished my coffee and was silent for a few moments; something she'd said was bothering me. 'Just hold it right there,' I said. 'What's all this "if we really were in celibate marriages" stuff? Ruthie, have you been having sex with your husband?' I asked sternly.

'Not really,' Ruthie answered. 'You know, just the normal twice a month thing.'

'That is positively rampant in my book.'

Ruthie looked at me.

'Two hundred and forty-five days,' I said.

'What do you mean?'

'Since Greg and I had sex, two hundred and forty-five days. It was a drunken shag last New Year's eve. I think that means I'm officially a virgin again.'

'I can't believe you haven't told me this before.'

'I couldn't bring myself to.'

'Have you talked to him about it?'

'I've tried to, but he says everything's fine; we're both busy and just going through a bit of a no sex phase. It's no big deal as far as he's concerned.'

'At what point does a phase become a permanent state of be- ing?' Ruthie looked at me as if I was a recently discovered example of a rare species. 'It'd make a good feature, *Women in Celibate Marriages Speak Out.*'

'Cheers, well you know where to come for copy.' I looked at my watch. 'Christ, on that bombshell, I must dash.'

I hadn't realised Ruthie's definition of no sex was sex twice a month. Her shock at my revelation made me realise Greg and I really did have a problem. That's what happens sometimes when you say things out loud.

I only just made it back in time for my three o'clock. Gentleman Joe is American and used to be a stripper with the Chippendales, 'Before they were all gay,' he repeatedly assured me. Gentleman Joe was his stage name and after he'd come clean about his col- ourful past, three years into therapy, I could never think of him as anything else. He was gorgeous: olive skin, floppy black hair, eyebrows like luxurious furry caterpillars and lashes so long and heavy it was a wonder that he could keep his eyes open at all. He had commitment issues and a deep and abiding disappointment in the female species: he couldn't get a single one of them to commit to him and become his wife. Joe was a serial fiancé; his brides-to-be always ditched him as soon as they came within sniffing distance of the altar. 'What is it with these British broads,' he complained, 'they all cheat, every single one of them. You think that you're in an exclusive relationship and then off they go, with some "chap" who went to school with their brother or something.'

'Have you considered dating another nationality, a fellow American perhaps?' I suggested mildly.

'Nah, American women are too needy.'

'Pot. Kettle. Black,' I thought. 'Hmm, you know Joe, perhaps you should just stop looking for marriage and it will happen all on its own. Do you think you might be attracted to women who are unavailable to you?'

He was an anomaly, the proverbial exception that makes the rule, a Jewish man who wanted to settle down, but then he *was* forty-four and his Chippendale heyday had been in the Eighties. Stripping? What kind of job was *that* for a nice Jewish boy?

I'd never really been able to have a serious relationship with a Jewish man. I must have an in-built incest taboo about it; Jewish men are just too much like family. I knew they'd send food back in restaurants, answer a question with a question, secretly lust over icy blonde *shiksas,* and that we'd wind up more interested in eating cake and chatting in bed than having wild tempestuous sex. I did have a Jewish boyfriend once – and the sex was even quite tempestuous until the day we were doing it in front of a mirror and simultaneously realised how similar our reflections were. It felt like I was going out with my brother and much as I love Sammy, I have no desire to sleep with him.

Sammy is two years younger than me and lives in a tepee in the Alpujarras in Spain. He's got a Buddhist name now, Sariputra, which means Child of a Spring Nightingale. We call him Sari, which if you mumble it, sounds pretty much like Sammy. That keeps everyone happy. He used to be a musician, and was on the road to success in an R & B band, but then our mother died and after we'd numbly buried her ashes in my garden and planted a cherry tree above them, Sammy ran away to North Carolina to live with the Cherokee Indians. 'It's a matriarchal society,' he said before he left. He was grief-stricken. We all were; we felt betrayed, bereft and bewildered. Mum didn't like getting older and at fifty-five she'd simply decided not to. She'd gone to sleep and never woken up – no one knew what caused her death – the post mortem didn't reveal anything. She might just as well have said, 'Right, well I'm off, I've had enough of you all.' (I couldn't help feeling that she'd done it on purpose, just to be the centre of attention once again. Not so much making an entrance, which she so used to relish, as an exit.) Sammy lived the Cherokee life for five years and wouldn't talk to me or to Dad. As a matter of fact, he wouldn't talk to anyone at all. 'Peace may be found in silence,' he finally explained when he set up tepee in Spain, embraced Buddhism and got back in touch. 'I seek to walk a gentle path on this planet.'

'Yes, and a bloody uncomfortable one too,' I'd retorted as I'd hugged him fiercely, feeling that my heart would burst with pain and joy. Secretly, I love his tepee, the woody, smoky smell and the simplicity of his existence. Over the years it's become a sort of haven for me, a place to which I can escape and taste a different life. I go at least four times a year, usually with the children and sometimes with Greg. He's cut six windows into the canvas walls, complete with glass panes and wooden frames, an innovation he's immensely proud of. 'No native American thought of that did he?' When we were children, we insisted on sharing a room and would lie in our beds in the morning looking through the skylight at the clouds. We called it 'animals in the sky'. One of us would make out the shape of an animal and the other had to find it.

'Unicorn,' Sammy had said as we lay on a mountaintop on my last trip to Spain, lazily dipping tortilla chips into cactus salsa, his trademark dish (those years with the Cherokee Indians hadn't been for nothing).

'Are mythical creatures allowed?' I'd asked, competitively scouring the sparse puffballs above.

'Is that a sensible question to ask a man who lives in a tepee?'

I'd hugged him, inhaling the sheer brotherliness of him and loving how his sense of irony about himself was still intact. Kitty and Leo play animals in the sky too and call Sammy Uncle Bonkers. He takes them trekking through the mountains and tells them about the grandmother they never knew.

Mum died twelve years ago and I'm still furious with her for leaving me with a three-year-old, a swollen pregnant belly and no mother to help me. Greg's mother doesn't count. We don't see her often enough and when we do, we wish we hadn't. Most children go through a phase of worrying about whether they were adopted: Greg used to hope that he was. He felt he'd turned up in the wrong family, an uninvited guest at a party that was not to his taste. He looked nothing like his brothers and sisters and had nothing in common with any of them. They were all fair-haired and brown-eyed – his hair was jet black and his eyes blue. They were Irish Methodists and no alcohol was allowed in the house except for Baileys, which for some reason had been declared a non-alcoholic drink and was consumed by the crate load at family gatherings. Aunts and uncles would grow flushed and fulsome, and emotional renditions of 'Danny Boy' would swell the air. These were Greg's few happy childhood memories.

His father, the one person approaching an ally in this family of strangers, had long since relinquished his own membership when Greg was eight by going to America; ostensibly to see if it was a suitable place for them to move. He was never heard from again, and his face was painstakingly excised from all early family photographs, which were displayed prominently on every available surface. Greg remembered his mother sitting night after night snipping away at a pile of photographs with a pair of sharp nail scissors. He'd managed to rescue a few of his father's severed heads when she wasn't looking and has kept them in his wallet to this day – his only memento. No one was allowed to mention his father's name, and life was neatly divided into two sections: B.E. – Before the Event, and A.E. – After the Event. Edie, Greg's mother, had spent the years A.E. with an expression of distaste as though there were a bad smell permanently under her nose. When Leo was born, Greg had said, with all the relief of a drowning man who has found dry land, 'At last I've got a family that I like.'

I felt tired. Sometimes my patients drained me. Usually it was when I wasn't feeling robust and was unable to stop their lives seeping into mine. I went upstairs and found Greg bustling about in the kitchen, peering inside drawers and cupboards, slamming doors and growing increasingly exasperated. His hair was standing on end like a toilet brush and he was wearing Kitty's flamenco apron in vivid red with yellow spots. It suited him. With his right hand he was miming the action of the object he sought, an incantation to abracadabra the item into being.

'Soup ladle?' I guessed. 'Top left hand drawer, unless you have hidden it from yourself.'

'Taste,' he said, proffering hot soup. 'Hmm, well, mmm?' he nodded impatiently.

'Delicious, darling, but ...'

'But what, what, it's perfect!'

Greg has spent all the years of our marriage in self-declared chicken soup combat with me, an unspoken challenge that by the time the marriage ends, whether by divorce or one of our deaths, he will have emerged the chicken soup victor. He's a good cook – it's one of the reasons I married him – and has his own repertoire but is obsessed with the need to prove that you don't have to be Jewish to make Jewish Chicken Soup. His soup is good, near perfect even, but less authentic and aromatic than my own and he hasn't quite mastered the correct consistency of the *kneidlach*, the dumplings.

As a Jew, I am genetically programmed to respond to news of friends' or relatives' misfortunes by going straight to the kitchen and making soup. This gene can, it turns out, be transferred by marriage: this is what Jewish women do to their non-Jewish husbands – irrevocably and osmotically we turn them into Jews. If Dad's not feeling well, Greg is now as likely as I am to hurry round with chicken soup: Jewish Penicillin, the known cure for all ills from heartache to cancer. This latest challenge means that I will have to make defensive chicken soup as soon as I can, to take up the gauntlet he has flung before me and prove, once again, my supremacy in this realm.

'I can't do it tonight,' I said irritably, 'I'm going to FF's thing, aren't you coming?'

Greg shuddered, 'I would rather eat a stew of poisonous snakes. I'm going to watch telly in bed and read up on the Road Traffic Act of 1991.' He nodded towards his steaming pan of soup; 'I win then.'

'Your misanthropy is becoming an illness. I'll make my soup tomorrow and we will settle this once and for all by putting both our soups to the test of a wider audience.'

'Fine, let the public decide whose is the best,' he said.

I flounced out of the kitchen. I'm a great fan of flouncing, and Kitty and I practise together to see who can look the haughtiest as we toss our heads, turn on our heels and exit rooms. Kitty, who had come in and heard the last of this, was standing by the fridge. She discreetly gave me the thumbs up as I whisked past her. (She can already shrivel a teenage boy at twenty paces with her narrow-eyed contemptuous glance and barely audible snort of displeasure.) I winked at her, beckoning her to follow me.

'Help me dress,' I said.

She took the stairs two at a time. If she's my dolly, then I too am hers and she likes to lay prospective outfits out on the floor for me so that we can see how they look. Blouses, skirts or trousers, tights and shoes, belts, bracelets and scarves; bodiless and spread-eagled on the carpet they remind me of the cut-out outfits that used to be printed on the back of *Bunty*, the ones with paper tabs that bent around your cardboard doll to transform her from workaday girl to party girl.

My Famous Friend Lizzie, known to her friends only as FF, is having a party to celebrate the publication of her latest book *Celibacy: Learning to Love the Essence of Self*. She'd somehow managed to make celibacy seem cool instead of the guilty secret it was for me, but then she wasn't actually married at the moment. I peered despairingly into my wardrobe which offered only two choices: reassuring, cardigan 'shrink' wear, or outmoded 'fuck me' clothes, with a few obligatory grungy t-shirts and jogging bottoms in between. It took Kitty longer than usual to find something that she and I agreed on, and we settled for a short black skirt, red shirt casually unbuttoned to reveal cleavage (such as it was), black jacket and red high heels. By the time I'd showered, moisturised (different creams for different body parts, it's a wonder one manages to leave the house at all) and done my make-up, I was running late.

Greg was in the living room doing embarrassing dancing to *Top of the Pops* while Kitty and Leo cringed on a sofa. 'One of the great pleasures of being a parent,' Greg always said, 'is being able to take revenge for the embarrassments of your own childhood.' Air guitar, pointless pointing, ill co-ordinated movements, little leaps and contorted facial expressions all contributed to his exquisite display of parental torture. The children were beside themselves. I joined in with hip gyrations for their added mortification and kissed Greg goodbye. As ever, he patted me heartily on the back.

'I'm not a horse,' I said. He proffered a hen's bottom of a mouth for a kiss.

'Nor am I your maiden aunt.'

I opened the front door, breathed in the chill night air and felt freedom course through my veins, as a prisoner must, allowed out on leave for good behaviour.

Chapter Four

Recipe for Trouble (anon)

1 part sexually neglected woman
1 part dissatisfied, questing, exotic
  man
2 parts need of adventure

1 dash all done up and out on
  their own
3 drops heady scent of desire

Mix together and wait for results ...
(Stand well back as can sometimes explode).

Famous Friend's party was in full flow by the time I got there. It was in one of those trendy Soho media joints; the kind of place where the queue for the loo is longer than the queue at the bar due to people's urgent need repeatedly to powder their noses. I've never understood the lure of cocaine. I tried it a couple of times and felt that I was snorting anxiety and depression in powder form. Since I have more than enough of both, it seemed a pointless exercise. I was already on the sartorial spiral of shame as I walked through the door, tugging at my too-short skirt, trying to hide my lack of cleavage and generally feeling all wrong and far too Eighties. Why is it that we all get stuck in some sort of time warp of our youth, our 'hottest' moment, frozen in a time that has become for us forever synonymous with looking sexy?

London's literati were draped about chattering, drinking and inhaling faux workingman's fodder of tiny fish and chips and miniature sausages. FF's book was everywhere, and she herself was unmissable in a bright-red shift dress with No Entry signs embroidered in white over the breast and genital area. Suddenly I felt rather better about my own attire. FF has an uncanny knack of capturing the zeitgeist, which, coupled with the best contact book in London and great personal beauty, had catapulted her to fame with her first book, *How to be a Geisha*, published just as the post-feminist era was dawning. She'd been at school with Ruthie and me and our friendship, although fundamentally warm, was shot through with a certain amount of envy, like the letters in a stick of rock. Ruthie had phoned me earlier and said that she wasn't feeling generous enough to play the part of fawning acolyte; she was a bit sleepy and dying to lie down with a book. Could I do it for both of us and she owed me one. 'You owe me about twenty,' I retorted, but she'd already sent loud smacking kisses down the phone and was gone. I sent her a text saying if she didn't come I would terminate the contract of eternal friendship we had signed in blood and buried in the garden thirty years before.

FF swooped like an exotic red bird to air kiss me.

'Hello darling. I want you to meet David, he's got such an interesting relationship with his father.'

That's the trouble with being a psychotherapist; everyone you meet wants their pound of flesh, an instant slot-machine-pouring-cash kind of answer to all their troubles. In the days when Greg still came with me to parties, we had a secret game: *How Much Could You Have Earned This Evening?* Many of those we encountered would either ask him for medical advice, or me for psychological guidance. We would convene in a corner of the room after having gone the first round.

'I'm up to five hundred guineas,' Greg would mutter. 'You see that woman over there? She's having fertility problems and thinks her husband has a low sperm count but he won't go to be tested.'

'See the chap to the left of her?' I might have countered. 'He's full of rage because his mother wouldn't make him pancakes for breakfast when he was five.'

It's not so much fun now that Greg has eschewed the human race; I have to do the therapy anyhow, but without the thrill of the game. I braced myself, turned to David, trying to look interested as he told me how his father never once told me he loved him in all the time he was growing up. He had rather a cute Hugh

Grant-ish haircut though. Sexual abstinence and thoughts of adultery had mixed a heady cocktail and my hormones seemed to have taken on a life of their own. To my horror, I realised that my long dormant flirting muscles were twitching into life.

'And then, when I was six ...' David was saying.

I stifled a yawn as I recognised that we were about to travel the entire road of his psychological development year by year, each imagined slight, each moment of rejection, every nook and cranny, no stone unturned. No amount of cuteness could sustain my interest under these circumstances. I looked past him and saw that Ruthie had just arrived. I surreptitiously SOS'd her with my eyes. She waved gaily, made strangling signs with her hands and moved away. She was punishing me for making her come at all.

'I can't remember him ever taking me to the park to kick a ball,' David was saying. Over his left shoulder a tall striking man with exquisite cheekbones came into focus. 'Who's that?' I hissed at FF who had just joined us. Cheekbones was now staring intently at me.

'Oh, that's Ivan.'

'Shagmeister?'

'Don't think so. From what I hear, just married to a rather plain publisher called Becky.'

'Hmm,' I glanced over covertly.

So far everything seemed in accordance with Ruthie's Rule. What was happening to me? I was starting to feel like Tintin's dog, Snowy, who, when faced with a choice between good and evil, has a bad black dog on one shoulder and an angelic white one on the other. The black dog urges him on to acts of perfidy, the white points him towards the path of righteousness. My black dog was clearly in the ascendant. I found myself returning Ivan's gaze with fluttery, under-the-eyelashes glances – it seems this flirting business is like the proverbial riding a bike. Within moments, he was by my side thrusting a card into my hand.

'Here is my phone number,' he said, 'I am Ivan' (he pronounced it 'Eevahn'), 'you must phone me. I never usually do this, but I have to get to know you.'

I laughed politely as I offered my hand. (Why is it that the charming, ice-cube tinkling laugh of one's youth seems to become a deep-throated witch's cackle as one grows older?)

'You may call me Vanya for short, and when we are better friends, Van'ka,' he continued.

I hooted unbecomingly.

'Yes, yes, I know this is very funny in English.' I blushed.

'No,' he said so vehemently that I jumped. 'I don't trust you to phone. Give me your number.'

'Shall we have a round of conversation before I do?' I suggested coquettishly.

He was from St Petersburg and looked like a Count straight out of a Tolstoy novel: tall, dark, and with those chiselled, high cheekbones that brought the Russian steppe to mind. He was really right up my *Strasse*, or rather the *Strasse* I used to inhabit in my single days.

'You know, when I left Russia, it was still Soviet times,' he said. 'I wanted so much to leave and finally I got out. All those years I felt like a bird in a cage, flapping my wings futilely, eager for the freedom of flight. Then when I got here, suddenly there was no cage, but I discovered I could no longer fly. My wings had been clipped.'

'I'm married with two children, Leo, fifteen and Kitty, twelve,' I blurted out.

'I also am married,' his smile was a little sad at its edges, 'but, you know, sometimes ...'

'Yes, I know.' And I do. Sometimes ... Ivan was terribly alluring, with a suggestion of something tragic about him, a little residue perhaps of the brutality of Soviet rule. I felt weak and destabilised by a barely remembered sensation. It was the steady pulse of sexual desire – an altogether unfamiliar emotion after so many years of holy matrimony. What was it about him that touched me so? My own need to *feel* again? The sense of a man's interest in me? A rare feeling of being looked properly in the eyes and listened to? I couldn't stop staring at his hands. They were the hands of a pianist or a surgeon, long tapering fingers, combining strength with delicacy. As I spoke, he tilted his head slightly to one side, his beautiful hands held as though in prayer, the fingers interlocking, save the index fingers which he held against his lips like a small church steeple. I imagined those hands stroking my face, moving down to my body. The cuffs of his shirt fell back slightly to reveal black-haired forearms. I wondered about the hair on the rest of his body and blushed for already imagining him naked. His mouth was full, his eyes a piercing blue. My favourite combination – dark hair and blue eyes. Just like Greg. Oh God.

I gave him my number. How could I not, after the bird and wings story? All of a sudden I wanted to leave. I felt dizzy with possibility, and scared too. So I grabbed my coat and was making my exit when FF stopped me, waving tickets under my nose.

'Tickets to Frou-Frou darling, it's soon to be the hottest late-night show in town.'

She is the queen of the freebie, and from the age of fourteen could wangle free passes to pop concerts, even when people like The Who or 'Reggie' (Elton John to you and me) were playing. Now that she's rich and successful in her own right, she still likes nothing better than a freebie.

'No thanks FF, I'm off.'

'Come on, it'll be fun and afterwards we can go to the First Night party, my name's on the door.'

'Of course it is,' I said and I moved away quickly before she could bend me to her will. She has an extraordinary ability to make people do what she wants.

I looked around and saw that Boring David had Ruthie *pinned and wriggling* up against a wall. She looked panic stricken.

'We have to go,' I said taking her arm, smiling briefly at David and leading her to the safety of the door.

'I love you,' she whispered, 'always have and always will. I won't have a word said against you, not by anyone, ever.'

'Yes, well you don't deserve me. I'm a much nicer person than you. You didn't help me out earlier, next time you're on your own.'

I was pleased she hadn't noticed me talking to Ivan. I wanted to keep our meeting to myself for now. Speaking about it would have meant recognising the beginning of something and, at this point, I wasn't prepared to do that even to myself.

Once home, I walked through the silent, sleeping house. A shadowy figure made me jump. It was Leo.

'Grumph a fiver, yeah, like wanna you know, with the guys tomorra.'

Which is adolescent speak for 'Could I possibly have five pounds, mother, the chaps and I want to go out tomorrow night.' Filled with guilt at the adulterous thoughts simmering in my head, I paid the parental toll. I removed my make-up – I always do because it is a truth universally acknowledged that you will burn in the fires of hell if you don't – and crept into bed beside my snoring husband.

'And they came forth in their multitudes and lo! the antibiotics were shared between them,' he muttered in his sleep. Bizarrely, so used am I to sharing all news and views with him, I had to restrain myself from waking Greg to tell him my latest delicious bit of gossip; that I'd just met a wonderful and exotic man.

I woke up with a sense of excitement and luxuriated in memories of the night before, parcelling them out for myself like a child might an illicit bar of chocolate eaten just before dinner. My sense of well-being was quickly diminished by the harsh reality that is the school day routine. Bea was moving around the kitchen in that irritatingly languorous way she has in the morning when everyone needs to *hurry*. I stumbled in, blindly feeling for the kettle.

'Greg, kettle,' I snapped.

'*Voilà!*' he beamed, producing it with a flourish from the top of the fridge like a rabbit from a hat.

'Could you perhaps exercise your memory on the things that only you require rather than items that are for collective use and save us the fucking Tommy Cooper act in the morning?' I snapped.

'Mummy!' Kitty scolded from behind a cereal box.

I squinted at the clock on the wall. 'Give it a rest, Kitty, I didn't know the swearing police reported for bloody duty at 07.45 hours.'

Kitty pushed her head far enough over the edge of the cereal box to roll her eyes. 'Someone's a bit grumpy this morning. Did you get drunk last night?'

'I see the drinking police are here too,' I muttered. 'Actually,

I had one glass of champagne and I have a witness prepared to testify under oath.'

Bea was smiling. This was as unusual a sight as watching an orthodox Jew set up a picnic table beside the Wailing Wall and tuck into a plate of pork sausages.

'You all right, Bea?' I asked.

'Yes, yes, today I am very happy. My friend Zuzi she come today from Czech Republic. Is okay she staying with me in my room for few days until she find job?' Bea held my eyes in that age-old, unblinking glare of the warrior au pair. It was a look known to and feared by all working mothers. Louder than words, it conveyed 'You say yes to whatever I want or I'm out of here, and you, lady, are fucked.' I know defeat when I see it.

'Yes, Bea, of course. A little bit more warning would have been nice and it mustn't be for too long.'

Greg whispered, 'Well, that's telling her' into my ear as he pushed past.

'Is Leo up?' I asked.

'I wake him five time already,' said Bea. 'Seven o'clock, ten past seven, twenty past seven, half past seven ...'

'Thanks, Bea, I'm getting the picture. Could you wake him for the sixth time; that generally seems to be the one that works?'

I pushed my way through the barricade of cereal boxes that Kitty had built around herself. She's entering that excessively self-conscious stage associated with the first surges of oestrogen and doesn't like anyone to watch her while she eats. I brushed her hair, trying to work my way through the knots as gently as I could.

'Ow,' she squealed predictably, 'you're doing it on purpose, you're just trying to hurt me.'

'You're right, that's why I endured nine months of pregnancy and agonisingly painful childbirth, just to get my own back on you by brushing your hair.'

A disgruntled crouching shape shuffled into the kitchen, grunting and snuffling its way to the fridge. Leo was up at last.

'Morning Darling,' I said.

'*What?*' snapped Leo as if I'd interrupted him.

'I can't find any clean socks,' Greg shouted from upstairs.

'Marvellous, now I'm the bloody sock curator too,' I said.

I hate mornings: the whole getting up, getting everyone else up, getting them ready for school, getting myself ready ... My mobile phone bleeped. 'Now what?' I grumbled. 'Will no one leave me alone?' I snatched it up and opened the message. *I am thinking about you. You are very beautiful. Ivan.*

It was a beautiful day. The sky was a crisp autumnal blue, the trees were alive with pinks, reds and browns, leaves were falling gently in the breeze and conkers lay on the pavement gleaming like jewels, their hedgehog casings flung aside like picnickers' discarded sandwich wrappers. I picked one up and felt its hard smoothness under my thumb; it was big and strong and had all the makings of a conker-fight winner, a good twenty-fiver. The Pigeon Lady shouted after me, 'Very pleased with yourself today Mrs Madam, aren't you?' Well, yes, as a matter of fact I was rather. I hurried to the café to meet Ruthie for a quick coffee before my first patient.

'Bloody hell, you look good,' she said when she saw me. 'You are positively glowing. So who was that man last night?'

'Which man?' I said coyly.

'They look quite good up there against the blue sky, don't they?'

'What do?'

'The pigs on horseback, flying. For God's sake Chlo, you might just as well have "fuck me" tattooed on your forehead.'

'That bad?'

She nodded. 'Now come on, give.'

So I told her about Ivan. I felt like a swooning Shakespearean maiden in love for the first time. The mere uttering of the loved one's name made my face flush with warmth. I had no appetite for my croissant and sipped peakily at my cappuccino like a child with a fever.

'For God's sake be careful, Chlo,' said Ruthie. 'You've got a lot to lose.'

'I haven't done anything yet. I haven't even answered his text message. Look, I know this is all classic mid-life crisis stuff. Woman in her forties needs to prove she's still attractive; it's not all over; there's life in the old girl yet. But it's just nice to have met someone who finds me interesting and beautiful.'

'Well, just because he does, it doesn't mean that you have to sleep with him. You should work out why you're not sleeping with your husband instead.'

'You should be the therapist, Ruthie.'

'All those books, all that analysing. No thanks. Anyhow, I only care about my friends and family. I have no need to heal the world like you do.'

'So what should I do?'

'Nothing. Just do nothing.'

'You're right.'

Walking back home, I texted him, 'I liked meeting you too.' I sent it and immediately wished I hadn't. How articulate, *I liked meeting you too*. I was out of practice. I didn't know how to do this anymore. I wasn't even quite sure what 'this' was.

FF was waiting outside my door with her daughter, Jessie. Me and Mini Me, identically dressed in long skirts and tight little tops that accentuated their perfect breasts, tiny waists and flat stomachs. But the long skirts hid a secret: heavy legs and thick ankles, burgeoning in Jessie's case, well established in FF's. This was her secret flaw, her area of less-than-perfection. She hid it well, but we girls who had been to school with her used secretly to call her 'tree trunks' and offer silent thanks to some unseen deity who had given her this cross to bear. It allowed us to look a little more charitably upon her absurd beauty. She easily escaped the mini skirt by taking the hippy route of long skirt and billowing flared trousers, and then quickly embraced feminism, not so much for its ideology but for its fashion: Doc Martens and dungarees hid a multitude of sins.

Jessie never looked very happy, her face a somewhat off-centre copy of her mother's. Looking at them together was like doing a test to identify what makes one thing beautiful and another plain. Jessie had the seeds of beauty within her, but not yet the talent or temperament to make them flower. Now and then, a rare smile would bring her face to life, but this just seemed to highlight her troubled nature. I recognised the look – it had been mine as a child – it was the look of a child forced into the role of 'friend' and 'confidante' at too early an age when she longs simply to be a daughter, with all the requisite cosiness and nurture. At thirteen, Jessie already had a sense of the overwhelming burdens of the world, a place of sorrow, double-dealing and thwarted expectation. We had an understanding, Jessie and I. My role was to feed her, spoil her, ask her all about school and her friends, and never to tell her how I was or what I was doing.

'There you are, darling,' said FF, 'we've been waiting ages. I rang the bell and heard giggles, but no one answered.'

'That's odd.' I peered through the letterbox and spied an unknown suitcase in the hall and heard muffled sounds from the living room. I rang the bell.

'Haven't you got a key, Chloe? It is your house,' Jessie looked at me quizzically.

'Yes, of course, quite right, my house, I live here.' This Ivan business had got me all mixed up. I fumbled around in my handbag. Ruthie had told me once that three per cent of a woman's life is spent with her hands in a bag trying to locate a ringing phone, a set of keys or some other piece of essential equipment. Those accumulated minutes would probably add up to several weeks that could be spent far more profitably – weeks that could be devoted to wonderful, illicit sex with a glorious new lover, for example.

'You all right, Chlo?' said FF, looking at me curiously.

'Keys, yes, here they are,' I said brightly as I opened the door and tripped over the suitcase in the hall.

'Didn't you hear the doorbell?' I asked Bea crossly as she emerged from the living room, looking oddly flushed.

'No, I was talking with my Zuzi. We have so many things to talk about.' I had never seen Bea looking so happy in the two years she had been with us. Her heavy-featured face, characterised by an almost permanent scowl, had lightened and looked contented. A pretty redhead appeared at her side.

'Ah,' I said, 'you must be Zuzi and this must be your case?' I rubbed my shin ruefully.

'Thank you for to allow me to come to live in your house,' Zuzi said, wrinkling a small freckled nose in a manner that someone had clearly once told her was adorable. I threw a look of alarm at Bea who stared back at me impassively. I reassured myself that this was a mere linguistic error; 'stay for a couple of days' and 'live' were no doubt served by the same verb in Czech. I took FF and Jessie off to the kitchen.

'I met someone last night after you'd gone,' FF said excitedly, once we were settled at the kitchen table, a cup of builder's tea in my hand, and of fennel herbal tea in hers – very good for lymphatic drainage apparently.

'Jeremy, Jeremy, Jeremy. I never realised what a lovely name that is. He's a fabulous shag.'

It all became clear, FF had pulled and had rushed round to tell me all about it.

'Jessie,' I warned, indicating Jessie's presence with a tilt of the head.

'Oh, don't worry darling, Jessie and I are the bestest of best, I tell her everything. We're bosom buds, aren't we darling?'

Jessie assented wearily.

'Sweetheart, go upstairs and see if you can find a book or something in Kitty's room. Too boring for you here with us,' I said.

'I've got some of my own here,' Jessie said, tapping the heavy bag she'd eased onto her shoulder. Jessie's visits were frequent and each time she came, she seemed to leave more of her things in the spare room.

I turned to FF. 'What happened to *Celibacy: Learning to Love the Essence of Self?*' I asked.

'Don't you see, it's because I love myself that I can now love another,' said FF. 'Well, maybe not love, but certainly fuck the arse off.'

She's always had this habit of giving too much sexual information. The face of an angel, the mouth of a fishwife. I'm told it can be very alluring to men; that old cook in the kitchen, whore in the bedroom stuff. But here she was being a whore in my kitchen. The detail is just that bit off-putting, a little too close to a gynaecologist's textbook and not the kind of stuff you want to know about a friend. For the next hour, I was subjected to a blow-by-blow (yes indeed) account of their night of passion. It was enough to put a girl off sex, which given my current febrile state was no bad thing.

'His penis is absolutely splendid,' she was saying, 'about this long,' she measured out an improbable length with her two hands, 'and nice and thick. I really hate those long thin ones, don't you?'

'I can't remember,' I said. 'I can barely remember what a penis looks like, much less what it's for.'

'Anyhow,' she continued, ignoring my comments, 'it's given me the idea for my next book, *Back in the Saddle: Embracing Your Sexuality*. Fabulous, don't you think?'

FF was very serious about her work and approached it with the solemnity of an Oxbridge don on the brink of some new scientific discovery. I doubt whether Crick and Watson were as pleased with themselves when they discovered the double helix as she is when writing one of her self-help books. Her books were her very own DNA, each one a new and vital piece of the jigsaw puzzle that formed her picture of what it meant to be a human being, and more specifically to be her in all her wondrousness. And it was all her own made-up nonsense, with no scientific, sociological or psychotherapeutic basis. She hadn't spent years in therapy as I had when I was training, reading Freud and Jung and delving into my own psyche as well as those of others.

Now, she was flushed with excitement at the brilliance of her new project and, when excited, she had this annoying habit of jiggling her leg up and down as she talked which always made me want to smack her and send her to her room. As always, I wondered why I put up with FF and her self-centred nonsense. We were bound by the past, by shared history and my sense of loyalty, my credo of 'once a friend, always a friend.' Also, if I were honest, I enjoyed the patina of glamour that I acquired through association with this famous, beautiful and somewhat absurd woman. There was something seductive and hypnotic about being in the presence of beauty; some Keatsian truth that compelled you to sit and stare in the belief that you would be warmed and aesthetically enriched by the association. Not all beauty has this effect. FF's ex, Jessie's father, was an absurdly handsome actor who had changed his name from Eric to Helvetica, believing it to be the name of a beautiful Greek God. He and FF had bathed in the pool of their reflected beauty, like Narcissus. (Now, he *was* Greek). Eric/Helvetica was very good in the role of lovesick swain, but not up to the demands of playing dutiful husband and father. I felt sure that if I were to ask him what he did for a living, he would reply, 'I am handsome,' as if that were sufficient. He was *professionally handsome*. I've never found the type attractive, there's something oddly asexual – too mannequin-like – about male perfection; in fact, you wouldn't be surprised to find a mound of pink plastic where the genitals of a perfectly formed man should be.

In any event, Eric, or Swissy, as we somewhat unkindly called him, wasn't around long. He collected beautiful women like trophies, and had he been a barbarian would doubtless have exhibited them like the stags' heads found on the walls of hunting lodges. FF had tired of him just as fast, although the marriage was fruitful in giving birth both to Jessie and to FF's first book *How to be a Geisha: The Fundaments and Principles of a Successful Marriage,* which told us all how to be the perfect wife. Always make his dinner and never refuse him a blow-job, was pretty much what it boiled down to, but FF somehow managed to make it last three hundred and fifty pages, with pictures. It was a publishing sensation and now she could do no wrong. 'See,' she had said when the book came out, 'not just pretty, clever too.' That was her Achilles heel, the fear that she was nothing more than just a pretty face.

'So, just as I was about to come, he stuck his finger up my bum. I had the most amazing orgasm,' she went on. Out of the corner of my eye, I saw Greg on the kitchen threshold. On hearing the 'O' word, he grimaced, executed a sort of mid-air, soundless pirouette and crept away backwards, his hands held out to me in mute entreaty not to give him away. Poor thing, he'd just popped back from the surgery hoping for a spot of lunch. A minute later, my phone bleeped *text me when coast is clear*. Greg is squeamish about hearing the details of other people's sexual exploits.

'You know how I only really like one-night stands?'

'When you're not being celibate you mean?'

'Yes.' The irony escaped her. 'Well, last night was so good, I think I might have to shag Jeremy again, although not exclusively, obviously. I've got a bit of catching up to do.' She paused, gave an exaggerated sigh of contentment and said, 'Oh Chlo, I so love it here in your kitchen, you and me together, sharing everything just as we've always done. And isn't it lovely that we'll always be friends? I just don't know what I'd do without you. You know how Jessie adores you too.'

It was always the same. Just as you thought you couldn't take another moment of it, FF would bathe you in her golden light and make you feel special and wanted and ... trapped in a friendship with no hope of escape.

Once she'd gone, I felt deflated. Her sexual adventure had somehow tainted any thought of one of my own and the prospect of an affair with Ivan now seemed faintly distasteful. I sat at the table, staring at a sticky patch of jam left over from breakfast. A fly found this treat and set about spitting all over it in that nasty fly-like way. It was soon joined by another who, shunning the delicacy, jumped on top of the first fly. The Birds and the Bees and the frickin' Fli-eeze. Two flies fucking. It reminded me of that silly schoolboy joke about a Native American boy who wants to know why his sister is called Running Deer. His father explains that the custom is to name a new baby after the first thing you see after its birth. 'Why do you ask, Two Dogs Fucking?' You know the one? Hilarious. Yes, my mood was clearly ruined.

'I suppose she's forgotten me again,' said Jessie, who'd just come into the room.

'No, angel, of course not,' I lied swiftly. 'She's gone to get you some clothes so you can stay the night. Why aren't you at school?'

'Mum was too busy shagging to wake me up, so by the time we all got up it was really late and there didn't seem much point. I don't need any clothes; I've got enough in my room ... I mean ... the *spare* room here.'

It was lucky really that FF had stopped at one child. Lucky for me mainly: Jessie stayed over so often she was fast becoming my third child. Fortunately I loved her so I didn't mind. For her part, FF couldn't bear to repeat the utter agony of childbirth which, of course, had been far, far worse for her than for anyone in the history of womankind. Naturally her periods were terrible too; they'd always been absolute agony and had usually necessitated a day off school. These are the kind of women that give the rest of us a bad name.

I left the room to phone FF discreetly and tell her to bring some clothes over for Jessie without revealing that she had, in the glow of newly-sated sexual passion, in fact forgotten her. I bumped into a shadowy figure lurking in the stairwell.

'Has she gone?' Greg hissed.

'Yes, just a few minutes ago.'

'I'm starving and I've got to get back to the surgery now. Bugger. Where did she go?'

'To have her pubic hair shaved in the shape of a heart for the delectation of her new lover.'

'Bit old hat,' Greg commented. 'Mary Quant did that in the sixties for her husband.'

Greg is a mine of extraordinary and trivial information. Although it's not really that astonishing since it's yet another way he can flex the memory muscle. It's quite useful, especially when you're struggling to remember who had a hit, say, with '1,2,3' (Len Barry in 1965).

'Name of Quant's husband?' I shot out now.

'Alexander Plunkett-Green,' he answered.

'I'll make you a sandwich to take with you,' I said admiringly.

Greg had gone back to the surgery, chicken, avocado and tomato sandwich in hand (olive oil, no butter – bad for his cholesterol); I'd put FF in the picture about her motherly duties and Jessie was reading to Janet the cat. Kitty had chosen the cat's name; she'd wanted her to have a proper name, not a silly cat name that no human would answer to. So she was Janet, not Spoofie or Paws or Fifi, but Janet Zhivago McTernan (she had both my surname and Greg's just like the children) and she had a complicated human psychological disorder to match her name. Janet was anorexic and it was all we could do to make her eat enough food to stay alive. On the few occasions she did eat, she would gorge herself on massive portions of food and then be found quietly sicking it all up in a discreet corner of the garden. Mike the vet was a frequent visitor to the house and had made Janet his special case study. His latest theory was that since Janet thought she was a teenage girl, she should be treated like one. So, Jessie was reading *Fat is a Feminist Issue* to her while Janet lay on her lap sneaking surreptitious glances at herself in the small mirror beside them. What did she see there? An image disfigured by her dysmorphia into a cat of gargantuan proportions, or the small rather too-thin cat that she actually was?

I felt vaguely depressed, the elation of the early morning soured by subsequent events. I looked at myself in the mirror and a tired-looking middle-aged woman stared back at me. Who was she? I didn't recognise her at all, I'd been looking for the face of a young girl. That's what happens, one minute you're young, juicy, full of sexual power, with your life ahead of you; the next, you're sliding inexorably into old age, your flesh loosening like the elastic on a pair of old school gym knickers.

Hearing a sort of mewling noise coming from upstairs, I went to investigate. The sounds led me to Bea's door and I peeked in to see her head bobbing enthusiastically between Zuzi's parted thighs like a cat lapping at a bowl of milk. Well, not our cat obviously, but any normal cat. A memory flashed: me at the age of eleven; I had been woken by a bad dream, and had crept to my parents' room for comfort. As I neared their door, I heard strange breathing noises and peeking in saw them spread-eagled across the bed. I had stood in the doorway rocking silently with horrified and embarrassed laughter. I did the same now and tiptoed away. Everyone, it seemed, was at it except me. My phone bleeped, and the words winking at me sent a treacherous jolt of pleasure through me: *I am thinking only about you and about how I must see you again. Ivan.*

Chapter Five

Chloe Zhivago's Jewish Penicillin
The Ultimate Chicken Soup with Dumplings

For the stock:
One fresh boiling chicken
1 stick celery
1 peeled carrot

2 bay leaves
4 black peppercorns
1 peeled and quartered onion
1 handful fresh parsley

Place all ingredients in a large pot and cover with cold water. Bring to the boil, and then reduce to simmer for two and a half hours.

Remove the chicken and reserve, strain the broth and discard the vegetables. Leave broth to cool and skim off fat. I find the stock can be a bit watery, so, for extra oomph, add a couple of dessertspoons of Telma chicken stock (it comes in powdered form).

While stock is simmering prepare the *kneidlach* (Jewish dumplings).

Grandma Bella's Kneidlach

1 egg
25g secret ingredient
6 tbsp. soup stock
75g medium matzo meal

25g ground almonds
1 tbsp. chopped parsley or
    coriander
Salt and pepper to taste

Beat the egg into a mixing bowl, add and whisk in the secret ingredient. As you whisk, add the soup stock, the matzo meal, the salt and pepper, and parsley or coriander. You should have a firm but malleable mixture. Leave to chill in the fridge for an hour (it doesn't matter if it's longer). Then roll into small balls. This quantity makes 15 walnut-sized balls.

Add kneidlach balls to your stock with:
2 peeled and sliced carrots
1 washed and sliced leek
Your boiled and reserved chicken torn into pieces – all skin and bones removed
salt and pepper to taste.
Return pan to heat and simmer for 40 minutes. Serve with a sprinkle of fresh parsley.
Serves 6 – 8.
Proven to cure guilt, remorse and all major illnesses.

Greg was intensely amused by the lesbotic antics of the au pair. In fact, he was positively titivated by it, but then nothing excites men more than the prospect of a little girl-on-girl action.

'It's all very well,' I said, 'but she's settled in, put a framed photo of her dog next to her side of the bed and shows no signs of leaving.'

'What kind of dog? A big licky sort of one?'

'Don't be disgusting.'

'Who exactly was doing what to whom again?' he asked.

'For God's sake!'

I was making chicken soup, Dad was coming for supper and Sammy had teepeed into town. Greg had insisted that this was the perfect occasion for the Chicken Soup Tournament. Both his and my soup would be served and the winner declared by independent arbitration after blind tasting. He had been adding secret ingredients to his, hunching his body over the brew, much like a child shielding his homework to stop the person sitting next to him from copying. I made a sticker which read TOP SECRET and stuck it on Greg's soup pot while he was happily engrossed in his weekly task of examining all the 'use by' dates on everything in the larder and bowling offending expirees into the rubbish bin in a long arching throw that would have done justice to Glenn McGrath.

I hadn't answered Ivan's text yet. I felt poised at a crossroads, in need of a wise man to point me in the right direction. Of course, it didn't take a biblical stranger with long flowing hair and silver beard to tell me what was right. But I felt so bored with my life, with my job, with myself; so in need of a Big Adventure and painfully aware that this might be my last chance. Knowing how lucky you are compared with others doesn't stop you from aching for something more. Furthermore, it seemed a bit rude not to answer Ivan at all. *Perhaps we'll meet at another of FF's parties in the future.* There. Polite and friendly and not suggesting intimate meetings *à deux*. I was just about to send it when the devil entered my body and made my fingers tap out *I can't stop thinking about you and would like to see you too.*

'You didn't tell me that Lou and James had split up,' said Greg.

I jumped, my finger springing guiltily off the 'send' button. 'Forgot. Who told you?'

'I bumped into James in the park with a young woman he introduced as his girlfriend.'

So much for trial separation.

'What, *Man Leaves Wife for Younger Woman*? Gosh, I don't think I've ever heard of that before,' I said. (I'm prepared to admit that the sarcasm was a bit rich from someone who'd just sent the twenty-first century equivalent of a billet-doux to an admirer.)

'Funny, I thought those two were so happy,' Greg said.

'What about us, are we happy?'

'Hmm, course we are. Now where did I put the teabags?' He stood with his eyes closed, like a game show contestant trying to recall the prizes on a conveyor belt in order to win them. 'Of course, in the mop bucket.' Looking very pleased with himself, he went to retrieve them. Endearing, I grant you, but just the tiniest bit irritating after seventeen years.

Bea and Zuzi came into the kitchen, bathed head to toe in post-coital glow.

'We will be staying for the supper and the chicken soup

examination,' Bea announced, 'then I will to take my Zuzi to a club in the London.'

I shrugged agreement half-heartedly. While all my own years in therapy had taught me that I had 'boundary issues', I still hadn't learnt how to deal with them. Professionally, I more or less kept my boundaries clearly demarcated, but personally, they were about as effective as a chastity belt with a broken lock.

'Righto,' said Greg to Bea, 'the more the merrier. I need a few non-partisan testers, you know, people who aren't actually Chloe's blood relatives with a vested interest in her winning the contest.'

Kitty, who was off school again with a cold, was sitting in a corner with Janet trying to coax her to eat.

'Leo and I are just as much your blood relatives as Mummy's,' she said.

'You do know what *blind* testing means?' I said irritably. 'No one will actually know whose soup is whose.'

Kitty got up, pirouetted to the cutlery drawer and started laying the table. She had inherited her grandmother's showing-off gene. Simple acts are transformed into showstoppers: face-washing and teeth-brushing become a small ballet about a young beautiful princess who wakes up, prettily rubbing her eyes, stretching and going about her ablutions. The miming and the dancing often supersede the activity in hand and so Kitty often performs the tasks themselves in a perfunctory manner.

Just the other day I had watched her dancing in a Ballet School show, the tears running down my cheeks; not just a delicate moistening of the eyes, but great shuddering sobs shook me. I've always been like this watching my children perform and can never understand how other mothers remain dry-eyed. Leo, aged five, playing third shepherd from the left in the school nativity play was, for me, a six-tissue experience. There's something about watching your child on stage, separate from you, that I find unbearably moving. Watching Kitty perform, I wept at her talent, lost in admiration and wonder at her ability to do something that I couldn't. Although each of us is an individual, we are also the sum of the individuals who have preceded us, the solution to the equation formed by our ancestry. Kitty was a culmination of the dancing talent in the family; it had taken generations to hone the art and for it to find full and complete expression in her. How proud my mother would have been to see Kitty dance. As I watched I could see flashes of my mother in her, in the tilt of the head, and the sweep of an arm.

'*Battement frappé, pas de bourré,*' Kitty mouthed as she danced the setting of the table.

'So Zuzi, how's the job hunting going?' I asked in the bright tones of someone pretending that the answer to their question is a matter of complete indifference to them.

'Is good. I have found the job in the restaurant.'

'Excellent. Do they give you a room too?'

'No, I prefer to stay here with my Bea. She say this make her happy and if she happy then also you happy and your family happy.' She smiled and, throwing Bea a coquettish glance added, 'and I too, of course, happy.'

Bea looked me in the eye, unflinchingly, daring me to say something.

'Which one you prefer? Smiling Bea or crying Bea?' she asked, smiling exaggeratedly and then pulling her mouth down into a cartoon of misery. She looked different; her mono-brow was gone, neatly plucked to extinction, doubtless due to the affectionate ministrations of Zuzi. She had also taken to wearing a tie, a nod perhaps to her role as the male in this relationship. (Why did some lesbians need to pretend to be men, and why did their partners need them to? If Zuzi wanted a man, there were any number who would surely have been willing.) The tie looked familiar – it was one I had bought Leo for his birthday. My boundary fence had not merely been vaulted, it was lying in pieces.

'Well, we'll see,' I muttered, beaten, 'just for a little while then.'

Across the room, Greg raised his eyebrows at me and wiggled his tongue lewdly. 'I'm off to get changed for evening surgery. See you later and don't touch my soup.' I followed him upstairs, tripping over a solitary shoe lying in silent reproach. Its partner, long lost, had been hidden somewhere by Greg. He had unique feet; the little toe on each permanently hitched a ride on top of the fourth as though too lazy to take part in the standing and walking business itself. As a child, Greg had been embarrassed about this minor deformity and had developed a shoe habit to compensate.

He was Queen's Park's answer to Imelda: the owner of fifty-one pairs of shoes. He bought them in charity shops throughout the land, all still in mint condition. 'My dead men's shoes,' he called them cheerfully. I found it odd that he was prepared to walk in other men's shoes and felt haunted by the stories these shoes could tell. Leo, who had inherited his father's feet (it's a boy thing apparently) was wholly unconcerned by his affliction.

As soon as Greg had gone, I checked my mobile to see whether Ivan had replied, but my inbox was empty. 'It's probably for the best,' I reasoned. 'I must pull myself together, I'm a grown woman with a career; I'm a mother and a wife.' Scrolling through my phone, I noticed that I hadn't sent my message to Ivan after all; Greg's talk of Lou and James had interrupted me just as I was about to. As my finger hovered uncertainly above my fate, the phone rang.

'Hello,' I said too eagerly.

'Darling, FF here,' said her brusque, self-assured voice.

'Oh, hi.' Disappointment overwhelmed me.

'You all right, Angel? You sound like you've taken a job as receptionist in an undertaker's. Are you chicken-souping tonight?' she bulldozed on without waiting for an answer as to my wellbeing or otherwise. 'I thought I'd come and join you, my nutritionist says it provides the correct fuel mix for my body.' What was she, a fucking car or something? ''Bout eight, but I can't stay too long, I've got to go on somewhere after, private art celeb thingy.'

I tried to tell her it was a family supper, not a general free-for-all, but for some reason, it's impossible to say 'no' to FF. The word starts to form; the tongue gets ready to do its job on the roof of the mouth behind the teeth and then, before you know it, as though you have been overtaken by an irresistible force, it relaxes across the back molars and the word 'yes' pops out. I comfort myself with the thought that in bygone times she would have been burned at the stake as a witch for her ability to bend people to her will.

'OK sweetie, must dash, there'll be two of us,' she hung up. *She* was the one that had rung *me* but, as ever, her haste left me feeling rebuffed, as if I were somehow detaining her from a more important task.

It was 4.50 p.m. 'Fuck, God's Gift!' I rushed down to the basement and got there just before the doorbell rang. No time to text Ivan. This was officially A Good Thing. Enough of this nonsense. So, you saw some guy at a party, so he liked you, so you liked him. (Not only was I thinking like a fifteen-year-old, my syntax had become that of one too. Whatever.) I smoothed down my hair, caught it in a scrunchie, appeased my residual-food-particle-in-teeth phobia by quickly grimacing in the mirror, and opened the door.

God's Gift swaggered in, holding my hand and looking me in the eye just that little bit too long. I had thought this was classic transference – shrink-as-object-of-desire stuff – until I got to know him better and realised that he thought everyone he met was dying to fuck him. It's true that he was exceptionally handsome and equally true that no one realised this more than he. He came in through the narrow hallway, past the mirror into whose loving gaze he briefly lost himself while sucking in his stomach. Flicking at an imaginary bit of fluff on his immaculate suit, he worked his lips in that odd, slightly camp way he had. It was as if he were barely able to restrain himself from puckering up and covering his own body in kisses or self-inflicted love bites. God's Gift ran a television production company, made famous less for the quality of the programmes it produced than for the young, long-limbed, full-mouthed girls it employed: blow-up porn dolls made flesh. The only other man working there apart from God's Gift was his PA, Baz.

'I can't have girls working too closely with me,' God's Gift had told me early on, 'they fall in love and the whole thing gets messy. Mind you, between you and me, I think Baz has a bit of a thing for me too.'

'But I thought he was dating a supermodel,' I protested.

'Well,' God's Gift said, leaning forward conspiratorially, 'there's something in the way he looks at me.' God's Gift came to therapy less to discover and understand himself than to 'understand what it is about me that makes women fall for me. I want to learn to deal with it better and break fewer hearts.'

His real problem was self-delusion; he had little more than a nodding acquaintance with reality.

'So,' I said, as we settled into our respective armchairs, 'what's been happening with you this week?'

'Same old story,' he said with a heavy sigh. 'There's a new girl in the office and she's been giving me the come-on all week.'

'What exactly has she said to you?'

'First day, she told me she liked my shirt. Next day, she asked me if she could get me a coffee. Classic symptoms.' He shook his head as though in sorrow at the irresistible pull of his sexual magnetism.

'Is it possible that she just liked your shirt? And that as a new employee she thought it appropriate to offer you coffee?' I reasoned.

God's Gift sat back, held up his hands, tilting his head back slightly and raising his eyebrows as if to say, 'Who can resist this?' Although good-looking and well dressed, he did nothing for me. He had an irritating habit of twitching his jacket collar up with his fingers, which he did now while shaking his head sadly. 'Please don't take this the wrong way, but you're a woman.'

I bit my tongue to stop myself shouting out, 'Thanks for the breaking news pal, and here I've spent the last forty odd years thinking I was a man.' Instead, I nodded and silently invited him to tell me more.

'You see,' he continued, 'men know when women like them. They just do, and God knows, I should know.'

I was feeling quite pleased I hadn't texted Ivan back. God's Gift was putting me off the whole damn sex; he was condensed man, poisoned by testosterone and turned into a parody. Nor was his self-love as harmless as it might seem: he harassed the girls who worked for him, convinced that they invited his attentions, and then coerced them into acquiescence. However handsome, he was in his forties and therefore invisible to most twenty-year-old girls, but, with their toes just barely on the first rung of the precarious TV ladder, they were ill-equipped to rebuff his advances. I was trying to help him, but the cure for both his delusion and his habit of sexual harassment was, it seemed, still some way off.

I was running late and I still had to make my *kneidlach*, the matzo balls for my soup. I couldn't make them while Greg was watching.

This was the lethal weapon in my Jewish cookery armoury. It all boiled down to this one essential constituent, my secret ingredient: To make matzo balls with the right consistency, fluffy and chewy at the same time, you needed *schmaltz*. I kept mine in a jar hidden at the back of the fridge. Greg would pick it up from time to time asking what an old jar of fat was doing cluttering up the fridge, little realising that this was the obstacle that lay between him and chicken soup supremacy. *Schmaltz* is rendered chicken fat; you boil the fat to sizzle away any old bits of chicken still hanging about and then you strain the clear chicken fat through muslin to remove any remaining dark particles. Once you have mined this liquid gold, you fold it into the matzo meal mixture in the time-honoured tradition of Eastern European Jews for ultimate dumpling perfection. The matzo balls, correctly made, then infuse the soup itself with a particular flavour. Now what non-Jew can be expected to know or understand this? It's the sort of thing you have to learn at a grandmother's knee, as I did at mine.

Grandma Bella, my father's mother, was born in Vilnius, the capital of Lithuania. She had come to England as a young girl in the summer of 1917, as the revolution fired its opening shots in nearby Russia. She brought with her her elderly parents (she had been a late addition to the family), a Yiddish-English dictionary and a jar of *schmaltz*. Somehow they made their way through war-torn Europe and thereafter, in gratitude for their safe passage and to add flavour to food eaten away from home, she always carried this talisman in her handbag. Her sturdy brown Gladstone bag with two handles and a zip across its worn belly was an Aladdin's cave of treasure to a small child: a lipstick in its own ornate golden holder complete with small mirror; jewelled powder compacts; hair combs; faded sepia family photographs of white-bearded, serious-faced men and full-bosomed, demure matrons and finally, carefully wrapped in a plastic bag to avoid spillage, the jar of *schmaltz*, which she would whip out, open and, using a small bone-handled knife she always carried, she would slather the golden fat onto a piece of bread and push bite-sized pieces into my small child's mouth.

She looked just as a grandmother should, which was comforting to a child whose mother didn't look much like a mother. Small, plump, soft and white-haired, she had that prettiness that some elderly women retain, a fond memory of their youthful selves etched nostalgically onto their features; age had not dimmed her astonishingly turquoise eyes, *Bella mit die shayne oigen*, Bella with the beautiful eyes, was her nickname. My father had inherited her eyes. They were also her legacy to me, although mine were a little less bright than the original, as though they had faded through replication.

Her plumpness irritated her but she couldn't resist the foods that caused it. In a vain attempt to counteract their effect on her waistline, she would eat each mouthful with a face twisted into an expression of distaste as if to inform both the world and herself that there was no pleasure to be gained from it. I remember her spooning potato salad, wet with mayonnaise and gleaming with the emerald of its salted cucumber, into her mouth and wrinkling her nose in apparent revulsion. As she helped herself to another portion, seemingly against her will, she would shake her head and tut-tut her disgust.

When I turned thirteen, the age when Jewish boys become men, she took me by the hand, saying, 'It's time.' We marked my important rite of passage into womanhood in her kitchen, where she taught me the art of chicken soup with *kneidlach* while telling me stories of her life 'back home' and how she'd met Grandpa at English classes for Jewish immigrants in a small library in London's East End. (He'd arrived in London a month before her from Oryol in Russia).

I felt the pleasurable texture of the matzo meal against my fingertips and could hear Grandma Bella's soft voice in my ear, 'Gentle, gentle, make like you crumble autumn leaves with your fingers, not like you pack a snowball.'

'Yo mother fucker, you my bitch, you my ho.' I was jolted from my reverie; Leo was home. He sauntered into the kitchen, singing along to his iPod.

'Leo,' I admonished.

'Yo, Mamma,' he shook a hand, balled into a fist; index and little fingers extended and grabbed his crotch with his other hand. A hip-hop king in school clothing. I was about to remind him that he was not black and did not in fact live in a New York ghetto, when

I had a vision of myself at his age – bright pink hair and wearing a tattered ball-gown from the 1890s. Since the advent of the Great God iPod, conversation with Leo had become increasingly difficult. Extraterrestrials, visiting earth for the first time, would be forgiven for assuming that humans were connected to some power source by means of the white earplugs with long white wires snaking their way to a battery-like device in their pockets. Those of us without the trailing wires were perhaps the masters and mistresses of these slave iPodians. Through their wires, we issued instructions and controlled their actions. Although it didn't seem to be working now as I tried to tell Leo to change and wash.

He shook his head and shouted, 'I can't hear you.'

I unplugged him. 'You don't have to shout. Supper's in an hour, Grandpa and Uncle Bonkers are coming.'

'Cool,' he said, 'Fuck you man, fuck you.'

'Pardon?' But it was no use. He was plugged in again and making his way out of the room on the balls of his feet, with a funny little half hop between each step.

The house was alive with the sounds of early evening: the TV blared, the children argued, Bea giggled with her Zuzi and Greg shouted down the phone to someone who had made him angry. 'No,' I could hear him say, 'I'm afraid I can't bring it in next week as it will be too late. Why? Because I will have picked the computer up and smashed it through the window and it will be lying in the middle of the road where it will have been run over by passing cars and shattered into a thousand small pieces, that's why.' He slammed the phone into its cradle. I waited. He came down the stairs and held the broken and now useless phone out to me. Wordlessly I took it, opened a cupboard and handed him a new one. We were stocked up for the next few months or so; there were five new phones in the cupboard. It had become a contest between us to see who could spend the least on a phone; Greg was winning with a 50p phone bought on eBay. His emotional temperature could be measured in telephones. The best we'd ever had was a one-phone year, the worst, a twenty-niner. That was in the year Leo was born, when Greg, struggling to come to terms with fatherhood, was sleep-deprived and overwhelmed by responsibility. Me? I just turned my rage at his unreasonable behaviour inwards, where it roared and crackled like a dragon that has set itself on fire by chasing its own tail. Home, sweet home. I went off to have a bath before the soup kitchen opened.

Chapter Six

Greg's Wild Mushroom Risotto and Salade Frisée aux Lardons

6 tbsp. olive oil
1 large onion, chopped
2 cloves garlic, minced
2 cups Arborio rice
4 cups assorted fresh wild mushrooms (shiitake, oyster, portabello), cleaned and roughly chopped
2 oz dried porcini mushrooms soaked for 30 minutes in a cup of warm water. Strain and reserve the soaking water. Dry and chop the mushrooms
1 cup dry white wine
7-8 cups hot chicken or vegetable stock (use the mushroom water to make up stock)
1 oz unsalted butter
1 cup grated parmesan cheese
1/4 cup chopped flat parsley
salt and pepper

In a large heavy-based saucepan, sauté the chopped onion in the olive oil. When it begins to brown, add the garlic and the rice and stir until the rice is coated. Add the white wine and, stirring all the while, cook until absorbed. Now add the hot chicken or vegetable stock, a ladle at a time, stirring every few minutes until the liquid is absorbed. After about 15 minutes, add the chopped porcini mushrooms.

When the rice is *al dente* and all the stock has been added, throw in the fresh wild mushrooms. After a few more minutes, remove from the heat, add salt and pepper, the cup of grated parmesan cheese, the butter and the chopped parsley. The cooking process takes about half an hour and the trick is to ensure that the mixture remains wet and creamy.

For the salad:
Wash a head of frisée lettuce and tear into small pieces in a bowl. In a frying pan, cook the lardons: small pieces of thick cut bacon, often sold ready-chopped (or I like to use small chunks of Spanish *jamon serrano* when available). When browned, add the lardons and the juices to the frisée. Dress with olive oil, fresh lemon juice and pepper (the lardons add enough salt) and serve. Serves four as a main course.

'Somebody get that!' I yelled. The doorbell rang again. 'Bugger, I'll get it myself.'

Greg was responsible for the rest of the evening meal and was in the kitchen making his wild mushroom risotto with salade frisée aux lardons. I'd fallen asleep in the bath and hurried to the door, skin wrinkled by over-immersion, a towel wrapped around still wet hair, another around my body, both coloured that off-putting grey symptomatic of the washing techniques of the careless au pair. I opened the door to FF. A man was standing next to her, his back to me, pointing his key at a car parked in the street outside and pushing a button to check that he'd locked it. There was something familiar about the angle of his head. I greeted them. He turned around. It was Ivan.

My astonishment and pleasure at seeing him on my threshold were quickly replaced by horror at my appearance and the question, *what the fuck is he doing with FF?* This last I only just managed to stop myself from uttering out loud. And why did FF have to be fifteen minutes early for the first time in her life? I'd said eight o'clock. My heart was beating so fast that I was surprised it didn't leap out of my throat to lie throbbing pinkly on the floor between us as I said, 'Come in, come in,' in a chummy, expansive way. 'Go on down to the kitchen, I'll just be a sec.'

Typical, I raged as I flung clothes out of my wardrobe. *FF must have known I liked him and now she's back in the saddle she's nabbed him. It's always the same, that's exactly what she did with Matt Salmon in 1975.* Then I remembered two things. One: I was married. Two: my husband was actually on the premises and probably shaking hands and making polite conversation with Ivan right now. Three: I was no longer in the third form. (Yes, yes, I know that's three things). At the back of the cupboard I found a little black dress I thought Bea had lost; a stalwart, dependable lycra friend who pulled me in and pushed me out in all the right places. I sprayed Vivienne Westwood's *Boudoir* into the air and walked through the mist (a little trick my mother once taught me), ran a comb through my hair, mascara'd my eyes, glossed my lips, prepared my mirror face, nodded grudging acceptance at my reflection and made my way down to the kitchen with unseemly haste.

En route, I opened the door to Sammy and Dad who had been ringing the bell unnoticed for some time. Sammy, newly arrived from Spain and here to stay for a while, was holding a *Patta Negra* (dry-cured ham, particularly delicious to secular Jews, who enjoy pork more than most Christians) strapped to a *Jamonera* (the wooden rack invented by Spaniards for holding a pork leg in just the right position for easy slicing). He was brandishing a scary-looking knife like a pirate.

'Acorn-fed. Delicious,' he announced. 'Got it in Seville.'

'How do you do,' my father said, proffering his hand, 'I'm your father.'

I kissed him. 'Aren't you the man I spoke to this morning? You could phone me yourself sometimes too, you know.'

'Don't want to pester you, darling.' He looked at Sammy and me together and beamed. 'What wonderful children I have.'

In the kitchen we found, and joined, the assembled company who were already seated solemnly at the table. There were the four of us; Bea and Zuzi; Dad and Sammy; FF and Ivan and Nick the Vet, who'd decided to stay for supper to see whether eating with us could inform his treatment of Janet. I loved having everyone round the table, eating my food; my compulsion to feed people was the most Jewish thing about me. Kitty had been put in charge of organising the tasting. In front of each person were two bowls labelled A and B and two spoons. Beside each bowl was a piece of paper and a pencil and, in the centre of the table, Leo's former piggy bank acted as a ballot box. Kitty had dressed the centre of the table with small furry yellow chicks, former Easter cake adornments she had found lying forgotten in a drawer. Greg stood at the head of the table like a conductor on the brink of an overture. At his signal, we each picked up a spoon and drank first from Bowl A and then from Bowl B.

'Are we allowed to taste them again?' asked Dad, keen to offer a reasoned empirical response to the experiment in hand.

'Yes,' said Greg, 'just make sure you use the correct spoon with the correct bowl.' Matzo balls were rolled around tongues, soup was sucked from spoons, considering and exploratory noises were made, lips were licked and votes were cast. Ivan didn't seem at all surprised by the bizarre ritual. He caught my eye, glanced sideways at FF and shrugged apologetically. I was struck once again by how attractive he was and had to struggle to remain calm.

Kitty had appointed herself ballot keeper and now danced the extraction of the tightly folded pieces of paper from the piggy bank, fluttering each expressively through the air before laboriously smoothing it out on the table.

'For God's sake Kitty, you don't have to make everything such a bloody drama,' Leo complained. 'Stop doing a bloody ballet and just count the bloody things.'

Undeterred, she laid the ballot papers out on the table in a row. Each bore a single letter: B. Greg tried to laugh it off, but I could tell that he was really quite upset.

'Why, why?' he muttered, his hand covering his face in despair. Dad patted him on the back in a 'there there' sort of fashion. I tried to kiss him.

'I don't want your pity,' he said in that brave, jokey tone people use when they're not really joking. He held his hand up to ward me off, his eyes drawn to something on the floor. I followed his gaze to find that salt had been ground further into his humiliating wound. A smaller Bowl A and Bowl B had been laid out for Janet the cat. Bowl B was empty, Bowl A untouched.

'Well at least we now know that Janet will eat chicken soup,' I said brightly, trying to gloss over his public defeat.

Nick was writing furiously in a notebook, his pointy beard bobbing up and down in excitement. 'She needs to be treated as one of the family,' he was saying. 'She needs to eat what you eat with you.'

'Eureka!' I said.

As I was serving the next course which, in an attempt to appease his humiliation, I took pains to point out had been prepared by Greg, I saw him stuffing one of my matzo balls into a specimen jar from the surgery. The cat's problems may have been improving, but Greg had been driven to the limits of endurance. Only science could save him now; he had obviously decided to send a sample to the lab to solve the mystery once and for all.

'Let me help,' said Ivan, leaving the table and coming up to join me by the oven. He lowered his voice, 'I'm so sorry Chloe, I didn't know we were coming to your house. I didn't want to come out with FF at all, but for some reason she persuaded me.'

'She's a witch,' I said, 'she bends you to her will.'

'Yes, that's exactly what it felt like, but it seemed too ridiculous to say it. Anyhow, I don't want to embarrass you in your own home, but, I would very much like to see you again.' His hand started on a journey towards my face. He looked at it in surprise and drew it back like a child caught stealing from his mother's purse. 'On our own,' he added quietly.

'Where's your wife?'

'She's gone away for a week or two.' He shrugged, 'We just need a little break, some time to think.'

Hmm, trial separation. How did this square with The Rule? I'd have to check with Ruthie.

He scribbled something on a piece of paper and gave it to me. 'You have to work this out,' he said enigmatically.

Tvoi sup – chudo, kak i ty. Ponedel'nik v shest' chasov, 23 Potter Lein

'What is it,' I asked, 'a riddle?'

'Find someone who speaks Russian. They will help you.' He smiled and our eyes held each other's faces as though memorising their contours. For a moment, he stood just a little too close. He smelt heavenly, of soap and of some other scent all his own and yet somehow familiar to me. Everyone has his or her own odour with the power to attract or repel, just as families have their own smell. Our *eau familiale* hit you as you walked through the door and was notable by its absence when we'd been away and someone else had been staying in our house. Leo had always had particularly well-developed olfactory powers; he could name the owner of any item merely by sniffing it. Out of the corner of my eye, I saw him doing it now as he picked up a scarf that had fallen on the floor, sniffed it and silently hung it over the back of Dad's chair.

I sat down at the table next to Ivan.

'Mm, this is delicious risotto,' I said.

Everyone made appreciative noises and praised Greg for his culinary skills.

'Don't patronise me,' he said, still smarting from his earlier defeat.

I could feel the heat from Ivan's body beside me. It seemed as if our surroundings had blurred and the sound of everyone's voices excitedly chatting and laughing had become little more than a distant rumble. Ivan's hands stood out in sharp relief as they went about the business of eating, and his lips, teeth and tongue came into sharp focus as he chewed. I wanted to kiss him and feel his mouth on my face, his hands on my body.

'Chloe ... *Chloe*.' I heard a familiar voice calling me as though from a great distance and then a face gradually came into focus beside me. Greg was looking at me quizzically. 'I have to go and make a house call. Bloody Mrs Meagan – she thinks she's having a heart attack. She's been into the surgery three times this week. I'm sure it's nothing, but her husband is very insistent.'

'Fine, okay then, yes indeed.' I snapped back to reality from the warmth of my unfaithful imaginings.

'We must go too Chlo, darling,' said FF. She stood, smoothing her hands down her body. Her chemically enhanced blonde hair was caught up into an instant facelift in the form of a tight high ponytail that somehow succeeded in looking more chic than Chav. 'Come on, Ivan.'

Ivan began to remonstrate, 'No, I think I will stay ...' nonetheless he got up, meekly pulled on his coat and followed her out, a lamb to the slaughter.

Sammy and the kids had abandoned us for the television upstairs, Bea and Zuzi had giggled their way into the night and Nick the Vet had said his goodbyes, muttering 'astonishing, truly astonishing' as he went. Dad was humming, his hands moving in silent conversation with himself as they often did and his feet tapping to the music that played continuously inside his head.

'Tell me about the affair, Dad.'

He sighed, poured us each another glass of wine and turned to face me.

'You remember Jürgen Geber.' It was a statement, not a question.

Geber had been a part of our mythology for as long as I could remember. The story of how he and Dad met was a family fable that Sammy and I begged Dad to repeat at every opportunity. In 1943, Dad had joined the army. Aged only sixteen, he'd changed the date on his passport, forged his father's signature and, leaving a note explaining his actions, had crept from his parents' sleeping house one night to join the Fifth Armoured Division for training. A year later he found himself in Italy, the radio operator of an armoured tank. He said morse code was a music all of its own and he picked it up very quickly. It was July the fifteenth, the sky blue and cloudless, and Dad and his five tank mates were lying on their backs in a wood near Sienna, a welcome lull in their life as soldiers. They were enjoying a few moments of the careless relaxation that young men deserve, smoking and exchanging stories of their home lives, the girls they had known and loved and the ones they hoped still to meet.

Bonded by their common purpose, they would never have met at home, far less become friends. Jimmy, Bertie's closest tank mate, was a brickie from Croydon whose idea of a joke was to raise his leg like a dog and fart as loud as he could. The fact that he could sing like Frank Sinatra and had an irrepressibly cheerful nature had endeared him to Bertie and the two of them would sing and dance sequences from *Las Vegas Nights* to amuse the others. The afternoon was made even more magical by the normality lent to the scene by the buzzing and humming of myriad insects, quietly going about their business of supping nectar from one sparse wild flower to the next. One of the men got up, walked a few yards from the others, unbuttoned his flies and peed in a great stream that arced over his companions and landed just the other side of them. The others applauded his skill, then, bathed by the sun's warmth and lulled by the hypnotic buzzing of the insects, they fell asleep. All except Bertie who, enjoying the freedom of movement after confinement in a tank for so long, stretched, and wandered off into the woods on business that necessitated privacy for a man of his fastidious disposition. He squatted above the dry earth, feeling the soft, warm breeze on his naked haunches.

When he was done he walked further into the woods, relishing his rare privacy after months in the company of rowdy soldiers. Lost in thought, his head was, as always, full of the music that rushed in to take the place of silence and solitude. He must have walked for quite some time; the sky was growing dark and he realised that he had reached that Hansel and Gretel moment of no return. Tiring, he sat under a tree for a few moments to order the melodies that were taking shape in his head and to decide on his next course of action. He must have fallen asleep, as the next thing he felt was the ice of a rifle's muzzle against the back of his head. 'I remember thinking quite clearly: so this is how it ends for me, before it's barely begun. I felt a sort of distant sorrow as if I was watching someone else, rather than myself.' Turning his head slowly, he met the eyes of a German soldier of a similar age, the terror in his eyes an exact reflection of Bertie's own. Both young men were trembling; the German's finger shook on the trigger. His eyes never leaving Bertie's face, he muttered over and over again like an incantation *'Der Sohn einer Mutter,'* before finally flinging his gun aside and bursting into tears. 'We were little boys, two little boys, frightened, alone and far from home,' Bertie used to tell us. Bertie took his own rifle and ceremoniously placed it next to the German's. He held out his hand and introduced himself as if they were meeting at a cocktail party.

'Private Bertie Zhivago, Fifth Armoured Division.'

'Jürgen Geber, Second Division, German army,' the German shook Bertie's hand politely.

By dint of Bertie's broken Yiddish and Jürgen's schoolboy English, they took their first steps on a journey of kinship that was to last until Jürgen's untimely death in 1973.

'I couldn't kill you,' Geber said as they sat, shoulder to shoulder in the shade of a tree, sharing a cigarette, 'all I could think was that like me, you were a mother's son, *Der Sohn einer Mutter,* it would have been like killing myself and the only thing I could see was my mother's face when I left for the war. She held me close and I felt how small she was, how fragile, as if I could snap her with a hug. She looked at me intently as though she were taking a photograph of my face with her eyes.'

Physically, they were strangely alike, short and well-built with dark, wavy hair and blue eyes. Jürgen had become detached from his regiment as he took cover from enemy fire. For the next two days, the two of them hid together in the forest. They survived on rabbits, which they shot and skinned inexpertly before cooking over an open fire of their making. Lying back after these charred and somewhat furry feasts, they shared their histories.

'I didn't want to join the army, I was forced to,' said Jürgen. 'What is this impulse to die for your country whatever it stands for? Nationalism is a bad thing, it teaches you to hate and then it teaches you that this hatred is a good thing. They tell us lies about Jews and compare them to rats and show us pictures of rats being exterminated. You tell me you are a Jew, but I see you are a man like me. We are all people in this world, people with hope and fear, people who want to give love and to receive it. Those who led us into this war are villains, but they do not wear their villainy on their faces, they hide it in their hearts and their minds and take it out to use to their advantage when they choose.'

The similarity in thought of the two young men made a nonsense of war. Bertie could just as easily have been born Jürgen and Jürgen, Bertie. What throw of the dice determined who we were and where we lived? Those two days in the forest changed their lives forever; they learnt to look for the truth and commonality in their fellow man and to think for themselves. Too frightened to commit each other's addresses to paper lest they be found and accused of spying or collaboration, Bertie composed a little rhyme for each of them to memorise. They parted company on the evening of their second day together. Bertie heard later that Jürgen had shot himself in the leg in order to get invalided out of the war. After several months in a military hospital, he was sent back home. For his part, Bertie took another day to find his way back to his tank. He had left his mates dozing peaceably by the tank, and he found them now, frozen forever in the still of that July afternoon, shot dead as they slept.

How must it feel for a seventeen-year-old to find the dead bodies of his young companions? Bertie felt terrible guilt that he had been spared, coupled with incredulity that the need to perform a trivial bodily function had saved his life. He sat on a rock and wept. Realising his own possible danger, the instinct for self-preservation took over. He made his way to the tank and radioed for help, then he collected the few personal effects of each of his comrades, determined to deliver them himself to their relatives when and if he got home. As he waited for assistance, he sat behind the tank, out of view of his friends' dead bodies and sang quietly to himself:

> Jürgen with an umlaut
> Geber with a G
> Lives on Friedrichstrasse
> In apartment C
> Building number eighty
> In Berlin, Germany

He realised that Jürgen's regiment had probably been responsible for the death of his friends and was struck by the bitter irony of fate which holds each of us in its teasing grasp. Safely home at the war's conclusion, Jürgen and Bertie stayed in contact and traced the trajectory of each other's lives with letters and photographs. But they never met again, each fearful of destroying the magical quality of those two days together. Jürgen became a painter and managed to escape from his home in East Berlin to the West of the city just days before the wall went up in 1961. Bertie became a composer. As children, Sammy and I had sung *Jürgen with an umlaut, Geber with a G* the way other children sang *Twinkle, twinkle little star.*

Dad leant towards me and took my hand. 'Now let me tell you the rest of that story,' he said. I must have looked surprised because Dad patted my hand soothingly and smiled. He told me how, in the autumn of 1973, Jürgen's widow, Helga, had travelled to London with the sad news of Jürgen's death from cancer and to give Dad one of Jürgen's paintings. It was of a young man in uniform, lying asleep beneath a tree; it was Bertie as Jürgen had first seen him all those years ago in that Italian forest, astonishing in its detail and verisimilitude. I knew the picture well; it hung on the wall in Dad's study, next to a photograph of Sammy and me wearing the bright, shining faces of well-loved children. Dad was drawn to Helga as if to the young man he had once been in that forest far from home, and they quickly became lovers. United by grief, they recaptured their youth and kept Jürgen alive in their urgent love-making. Helga was Jewish; Jürgen had joked to Bertie that this had been his way of making amends for the misdeeds of his countrymen. His gesture of defiance, while alienating his relatives, was no hardship, for Helga was a beauty. When Dad met her, she was a tall redhead in her early forties, and with her full bosom and generous lips, she reminded him of Rita Hayworth. Her English was perfect, with that slight precision and clipping of the vowels that betrayed her native tongue.

'We meet in Paris four times a year,' said Dad.

'Still?'

'Yes, still. For the past thirty years. I love her. Loving Jürgen's widow is my way of thanking him for saving my life all those years ago. *Geber,* it means 'to give' you know. Without Jürgen's giving there'd be no me, no you, no Sammy.'

'And Mum?'

Dad got up and walked to the window, looking out into the darkness of the garden. He sighed, his warm breath leaving a mist against the window's cold glass and he ran a hand through his hair. It was still thick and wavy, but had faded to white with the passing of the years. This is what ageing does, it bleeds the colour from you, softening and blurring your edges until you fade away and disappear altogether.

'She found out. I'm afraid I was so caught up in Helga that I wasn't very discreet. It caused her terrible pain and I swore to give Helga up. I tried, but I couldn't. Mum believed I had, formally forgave me and took her revenge by having her own affair. Tit-for-tat was always your mother's way. I can't say I blame her.'

My own recent turmoil felt trite. Here I was, wanting to shag some bloke I'd met at a party, and here was Dad bubbling in a fiery cauldron of life, love, honour and death. His life felt epic, mine merely mundane.

I was touched by his story and saw my father, as children rarely do, as an individual, a man with memories that did not include me, a person in his own right, with his own life and secrets. This perception of his separateness somehow made me feel even closer to him.

'Why don't you and Helga live together now?' I asked

'We have our own lives in our own countries,' said Dad, 'but more than that, we don't want to tarnish our time together with the detail of day-to-day life. It suits us this way. The writer Helen Rowland said, "After a few years of marriage, a man can look right at a woman without seeing her and a woman can see right through a man without looking at him." I never want that to happen with Helga and me.'

We heard the front door opening above and Greg's voice as he returned from his house visit.

'I must go,' said Dad, kissing me as he always did, once on the lips, once on the nose and once on the forehead. I parcelled leftovers in Tupperware for him to take home – I hated to think of him cooking and eating alone, and now that I knew about him and Helga, I found myself wishing that they lived together. He took my hand and held it in both of his.

'Just because *he* wants you, doesn't mean you have to give yourself to him,' he said.

I flushed, realising that he was talking about Ivan and wondering whether it had been that obvious to everyone.

'That's pretty much what Ruthie said.'

'Smart girl that Ruthie, I've always said so.'

Chapter Seven

Mutton Dressed as Lamb

1 woman over the age of forty	1 part Mango
1 wallet full of cash and/or credit cards	1 part Zara
1 part Top Shop	Dash each, Accessorize and cosmetics

Mix woman with Top Shop, Mango and Zara. Allow selection of age-inappropriate apparel. Decorate with costume jewellery from Accessorize and paint with cosmetics. When ready, steal furtive and insecure glances in mirrors, shop windows and the eyes of those you meet (especially men).

Banging noises woke me early the following morning. Exploring the source, I found Sammy noisily hammering tent pegs into the garden lawn. His hair fell in untidy curls over his face and he looked invigorated by the exertion.

'Too stuffy in the house,' he said, 'I couldn't sleep with the central heating. OK if Kitty, Leo and I sleep here for a few days?'

I patted his shoulder, went back inside and wearily started clearing up the devastation that had been the previous night's meal. Amongst the crumpled-up ballot papers I found Ivan's riddle. I'd carelessly left it lying on the table; clearly I had a thing or two to learn about duplicity. My resolution – made as I fell asleep the night before – to forget all about Ivan was quickly discarded as I racked my brains to think of someone who spoke Russian.

Later, between patients, I almost collided with the Pigeon Lady as I turned out of the front path into the street. 'Watch this one, ladies,' she said to the pigeons that hopped and flapped around her feet. 'She's heading for trouble.' She held out her hand to me. I took it; it was surprisingly soft, white and delicate. She pulled me towards her and studied my face closely. 'Just as I thought,' she murmured enigmatically. She turned, and in a flurry of wings and footsteps, she and the birds made their way briskly down the street. I felt unnerved and strangely exposed and stood watching long after she and the birds had disappeared from sight.

'Of course, the delicatessen!' I remembered the Volga, a Russian shop on nearby Salusbury Road. I cut through the park. The playground was empty save for a mother and her small twin boys, one of whom she was pushing dispiritedly on a swing. A solitary drunk sat on a bench, can of beer in hand, swaying with closed eyes to the beat of a tune only he could hear. Most of the trees were bare now, and moved skeletally under the grey sky, their flesh stripped from their bones by the cold. I pulled my coat around me more tightly. As I passed Ruthie's house, her front door opened and a young man in leathers bounded down the front steps. I caught a brief glimpse of her as she closed the door. The man answered a ringing mobile. I heard him say, 'Be there in five' and he jumped on a motorbike and sped off down the road. Ruthie sometimes worked from home, but rarely on a Friday. Perhaps she was ill.

I'd never actually been into the Volga before although I'd peered curiously through its windows a few times. It was only a few doors from our friend Abe Green's Jewish diner where we went quite often, particularly on the nights when his brother Herbie's band was playing. The Volga was small and dim with one of those bells that gave a merry little tinkle as you pushed open the door. I walked up and down its aisle, examining the unfamiliar tins and jars with their Cyrillic writing. There were old-fashioned hand-wrapped chocolates with pictures of squirrels, loaves of heavy dark aromatic bread, a freezer full of dumplings that looked like won ton and neatly stacked bottles of vodka.

'*Chem ia mogu vam pomoch'?*' said an unsmiling man in his fifties from a corner of the shop. He sat on a stool in front of shelves untidily stacked with Russian videos and newspapers, a strange-looking cardboard tube of a cigarette hanging from his lips.

'I'm sorry, I don't speak Russian.'

'How I can help you?'

I showed him my piece of paper. He smiled and the sun came out: most of his teeth were gold. He was younger than I'd first thought, nearer to my own age, although he wore the face of a harder life. Taking the cigarette from his mouth, he plucked a flare of escaped tobacco from his lips, came closer to me and nudged me familiarly in the ribs. '*Nu-ka devushka,*' he said. 'Well, well.'

'What does it say?' I asked, at once nervous that Ivan had written something too intimate for the eyes of a stranger.

'"Your soup is a miracle, and so are you. Monday, 6 o'clock, 23 Potter Lane".' He looked at me intently, his eyes moving from the ring on my left hand to my face and it seemed to me that he grasped the situation in its entirety.

'Life is short,' he said softly. I flushed, but was saved from the need to reply by the beeping of my mobile phone. A single word glowed at me: *Well?* It was Ivan. I thanked the shopkeeper and backed out of the shop. My heart was beating with excitement and, without allowing myself time to think, I texted back: *Code cracked. See you there.* The die was cast.

Ruthie wasn't answering her house phone or her mobile, so I rang her doorbell on my way home. She didn't answer that either. It was odd and not at all like her; we made a point of being able to contact each other at any time. I felt uneasy, but since I had to hurry back to Gloomy Gina I resolved to track Ruthie down later. Gina, it seemed, was feeling better about her impending nuptials.

'It's all fine. I mean, I really love him and it's not as if I haven't slept with enough men. They're all the same anyhow. Well, Jim's not obviously, he's better than all the rest. I mean I love him. And that's all you need, right? Love is all you need.'

Clearly she had stepped inside a Beatles' song. But then, that's what happens when you're in love; every song is pregnant with meaning, every cliché startles you with the sharpness of its truth. Greg and I had had two songs: Chaka Kahn's 'Feel For You' and Stevie Wonder's 'I Just Called to Say I Love You'. Slushy I know, but they were two big hits of 1984, the year we met. I wondered what Ivan and my song might be, 'Duplicity'? I lost myself in thoughts of what to wear for our meeting on Monday. I looked at Gina, admiring her gypsy skirt, which she wore with a roll-neck jumper, wide leather belt and cowboy boots. It was a good look; maybe she'd lend me something. I opened my mouth to ask her and only just caught myself in time. I was her shrink for God's sake, not her bloody girlfriend. I was losing my grip. I've always taken pride in my job and done it well. I even have a waiting list of people keen to come under my care. I was shaken by the recent dilatory nature of my 'shrinking'. Perhaps I needed to take a few weeks off.

I said as much to Greg later after we'd tucked Kitty, Leo and Sammy up in their freezing tent and were enjoying the barely remembered comfort of a living room with a television tuned to a channel of our own choice.

'Nah, you're all right Chlo. You're better when you're working,' he said dismissively.

I searched for the words to tell him of my restlessness and longing for something more without giving my secret away. I also wanted to ask him why he no longer touched me. But before I could speak, he started telling me how Mrs Meagan had been perfectly healthy when he'd been to see her the night before.

'She's fucking bonkers if you ask me. I think I'd better refer her to one of your lot. Well, to a proper one, you know, a psychiatrist.'

It really annoyed me when he did that, rubbishing psychotherapy by only recognising psychiatry.

'Psychiatrists are medically trained doctors,' he said now, as he did all too often, with the exaggerated patience of a man used to explaining things simply to small children, 'and there is concrete evidence that drugs cure people, but it's far less certain that just sitting and talking does.'

'And so I killed him, Your Honour,' I muttered, preparing my defence at the trial for his murder as I stomped furiously off to bed. It would be Greg's fault if I did have an affair with Ivan; he would have driven me to it. Before I went to sleep, I sent Ruthie a text: *Where and how are you? Coffee in park at 11? Husband is King Cunt of Cuntsville.* I was too furious to observe the need for acronyms.

*

Kitty and Leo must have come in from the cold sometime in the night. I found them asleep, curled around each other in Kitty's bed in the morning, two orphaned puppies seeking comfort. I was still angry with Greg. 'I know what our song is now,' I thought, as I emptied the linen basket and put the washing machine on, 'After The Love Has Gone.' In silent fury, I ate four pieces of toast and marmite. 'Get out of the kitchen!' I shouted out loud to stop myself eating any more, and went to the basement to see my two Saturday morning 'earlies'. Piqued by Greg's disparaging dismissal of my chosen profession, I forced myself to concentrate. Furious Frank was my first patient. He apologised for being late and explained that it was due to his having to finish writing his letters of complaint to various government bodies in time for the first post. I was struck by how like Greg he was, and how odd it was that I'd never noticed before. He'd been keeping an anger diary, and today I found myself nodding in agreement with some of the things that made him really furious: automated choices on telephone answering lines; railways' absurd pricing systems where return fares were cheaper than singles; drivers who idled in the middle lane of motorways. I couldn't help feeling that he was right; sometimes white-hot rage is the only response.

Ruthie was queuing up for coffee when I got to the café. She looked tired. She had dark circles under her eyes, her hair was lank and she was wearing a hideous pair of fluorescent green tracksuit bottoms with a purple sweatshirt. I pointedly pulled a pair of sunglasses out of my bag and put them on. She laughed.

'Croissant, Chlo?' I shook my head as though she'd just offered me hemlock. I had fifty-four hours until I was due to meet Ivan, and after my early morning toast fiasco I'd resolved to fast until then to ensure maximum sveltness.

We made our way to the only free table. Next to us sat a father with the same twin boys I had seen in the park the day before. They were dipping sticky fingers first into a sugar bowl, then into the mug of hot chocolate in front of them, before licking their fingers and wiping them on each other's faces, hair and clothes. Simultaneously, they banged their spoons loudly on the table.

The noise the spoons made clearly did not satisfy their auditory requirements, so they were actually shouting, 'bang, bang, bang' at the tops of their voices too. 'Freddie, Charlie, stop it,' their father said, swatting at them ineffectually, as one might at a troublesome fly, with his copy of the *Financial Times*. He caught my eye and shrugged as if to say, 'Kids, eh? But what a great guy I am taking them out for my wife.' No doubt he was giving his wife a lie-in, in that self-consciously generous way peculiar to the breadwinning man with the stay-at-home wife.

This is what happens when you have children: on your arrival home from hospital with your precious bundle clasped fearfully to your bosom, you find that someone in your absence has erected a giant scoreboard in your house. All the things that you and your partner used to do unthinkingly are carefully entered onto the board – who last made a cup of tea for whom, who put on the du-vet cover, who changed the most nappies, who went shopping for food, who emptied the dishwasher ... Constant reference is made to the entries in this imaginary ledger ('I did bath-time five times last week'). Although women keep the score just as assiduously as men, men additionally demand recognition and praise for every-thing they do because they do it 'for' us. 'I'm putting the rubbish out for you,' 'Look, I've swept all the leaves in the garden for you.' Thus without doubt the man at the next table: 'I take the children out every Saturday morning for you,' never mind the fact that his wife is at home with them every day, that very same, tired-looking woman who yesterday had listlessly been pushing one of them on the swing in the playground just as she had done on countless other yesterdays and would do for as many tomorrows.

'Ruthie, you don't look your best. Are you OK?' I asked her.

'Just fed-up with work. I seem to spend all my time sorting out everyone's problems. I feel like a mother bird pushing chewed-up food into their greedy little insatiable beaks. People can't do any-thing for themselves these days. And then, if I'm not doing that, I'm trapped in pointless meetings where time stands still. I might as well be working for Shell or in a biscuit factory or something; I never seem to do any of the fun, creative stuff anymore.'

'That's what happens when you've been around a while,' I

said, 'you move into management which is pretty much the same whatever the job is.'

'I'm just so bored of it all,' said Ruthie, blowing her nose. 'Meetings with pompous people who like the sound of their own voices and start off their sentences with "this may sound a bit whacky, but what about if we ..." Or phrases like "let's do some blue sky thinking". Then some little popsy with a name like Wendee, spelt with an unnecessary amount of Es, pipes up with some trite comment in her little-girl voice and all the men look at her as if she was Einstein when really you know they're wondering how they can fuck her without their wives finding out.' She wearily pulled her hair back, shaped it into a bun and stuck a plastic knife through it to keep it in place. 'Maybe I should just chuck it all in and go freelance. The trouble is, I don't think I could be bothered to go around interviewing some bloody Z-lister who's famous for having tits that fall out of designer frocks. I'm really not sure I care about magazines at all anymore ...'

That was the trouble with growing up. You spent all those years scrambling up the ladder only to find that you didn't much like the view when you reached the top. You were left with three choices: to stay up there and admire it anyway, to slide down the big snake back to the bottom, or to find another ladder to climb.

'One last whinge and then I promise I'll stop,' Ruthie went on, 'I'm also suffering badly from HHATT. Everything about Richard is driving me mad; the way he clears his throat pompously before talking, the way he doesn't look at me when I'm talking to him, the way he never listens to me and the way he takes out his floss to clean his teeth as the *News at Ten* comes on.' She looked at me brightly. 'There, *kvetching* over.'

(*Kvetch* is a particularly useful little Yiddish word meaning to gripe or complain. I'm not entirely sure how anyone manages to get through life without it. Ruthie and I had long ago built a virtual kvechatorium, it gave us carte blanche to vomit out our complaints at any time of the day or night; the beauty of the kvechatorium was that it was always open).

On the other side of us a man and a woman our age were holding hands across the table. He was feeding her with little pieces of croissant as they giggled at some shared intimacy.

'Look at those two,' I whispered. 'Do you think they're married?'

'Oh yes,' said Ruthie, then she paused. 'Just not to each other.' She licked the froth from the rim of her cup, and added, 'So, when is *your* secret assignation?'

I kept my eyes down, busying myself by mopping up spilt coffee with a bedraggled looking tissue selected from the many that festered in my handbag.

'It's written all over you,' she said smugly.

'Monday.' It was futile to deny it, she knew me too well. 'What shall I wear?'

'Your period knickers so you don't fuck him on the first date.'

I must have looked shocked because she added, 'Don't look so guilty. You don't have to have a husband that beats you to justify your interest in another man. A total absence of sex is reason enough. But just be careful and discreet.'

I was saved from further discussion by Sephy and Kitty coming through the door in a blast of cold air and eager anticipation. Weeks ago, I had promised to take them shopping.

'Distant elephant,' I muttered to Ruthie as I went to my fate. Elephants look very small on the distant horizon, it's only when they're close that you realise just how big and overwhelming they are: I'm always saying yes to things that are weeks away, I lack the imagination to believe that the appointed day will ever dawn.

'Omigod, it was like so fun …'

'She's like such a bitch, she asked Molly and Anna to her party like right in front of me.' Kitty and Sephy were twittering in the back seat of the car, each sentence ending on a rising cadence. Too much American TV. Was it still acceptable for parents to wash their children's mouths out with soap and water, I wondered, or if not, perhaps to bang their heads together?

We rode the escalator down into what was, for them, girlie heaven, and for me the fiery depths of hell. Top Shop on a Saturday afternoon – what was I thinking? I was in the worst kind of furious ill humour, the kind when you only have yourself to blame. I left the girls to it and slumped in the café with yet another coffee and a paper I was meant to be writing on 'Understanding Adolescents' for *Psychotherapy Today*. Every now and then, Sephy and Kitty would come and twirl their gorgeous girlish bodies in front of me in this outfit or that. Looking past them, I spotted the same skirt Gina had been wearing. If she could do it, so could I. She was only a few years younger than me – well, fifteen actually. Defiantly, I gathered the ingredients of the outfit Gina had been wearing from various corners of the shop and went to try them on. A bored, gum-chewing girl stationed by the changing rooms looked me up and down. For a moment I thought she was going to call security and have me thrown off the premises for daring to try on clothes that were age-inappropriate.

She wore the lowest of hipster jeans and turned to reveal a fatly bulging bottom. Since when had builder's crack become so ubiquitously *à la mode?* I wanted to grab her by the belt hooks, pull her trousers up and shout in her ear, 'I can see your bottom.' I studied myself in the mirror. I looked rather fabulously boho, without seeming too much like the sort of woman who keeps an abundance of cats and newspapers in piles in an attic.

'I fought she woz goin' ta look a bit mutton in that lot, but it suits her, innit?' I heard the keeper of the changing room say to her colleague as she disentangled her chewing gum from her tongue piercing.

'I'm standing right here,' I said, and swept haughtily past them.

This Top Shop business was great fun; I lost myself in boots and belts, scarves and make-up. The girl at the till looked like she was going to ask to see my ID for proof that I was under twenty-one, but instead she smiled, put my purchases in a bag, and said, 'Your daughter will love these.' Sephy and Kitty were waiting impatiently by the door, their own retail appetites long-sated. I'd hidden my Top Shop swag in another bag, away from Kitty's beady eye.

'Come on Mum, we've been waiting for ages and we're really hungry.'

'When I was a child, Kitty, parents did what they wanted to do and children had to fit in.' Kitty rolled her eyes.

'Don't do that,' I said. 'I used to spend ages sitting in cars while my mother finished her boring conversations with boring people on boring pavements, or else I'd be dragged out to tea to some of their boring friends who had nothing for Sammy and me to play with, while the grown-ups talked and talked. You and Leo never do anything you don't want to do. In fact, I spend most of my time doing the things you want.'

'Like what?'

'Watching endless episodes of that crap reality TV show where couples scream and shout at each other.'

'You mean *Bit of a Barney*? Come on, Mum, you love that show; you always want to see if they're going to hit each other. That doesn't count. What else?' said Kitty.

'Watching you and Leo play computer games which all seem to be about how many people's heads you can blast off with a range of increasingly lethal weapons in the shortest time possible. It's not fair, it's never been my turn to do what *I* want to do.'

'Yeah, well I was actually the one who suggested we go to Top Shop in the first place,' said Kitty. This was, of course the fatal flaw in my argument. We were doing what she'd wanted to do in the first place.

'Time to go,' I blustered, sweeping them out the door.

'Hold it right there,' she said, 'what's in the bag?'

Damn. 'Nothing much, a few bits and pieces. Hurry up, let's go.' Luckily, at that moment, her attention was deflected by a young boy walking past.

'Très buffting,' Kitty said, giving Seph a nudge.

I must have shown my incomprehension.

'Buff, you know, fit,' she explained.

'Ah, you mean, what we in ancient times might have called *handsome*?' It was becoming clear to me that despite my new clothes, I was an old, old woman.

Chapter Eight

Ruthie Zimmer's Recipe for Adultery

1. Never have an affair with anyone who has less to lose by its disclosure than you do.
2. Never Confess: if you can't do the time, don't do the crime.
3. Tell Nobody: your friend has a friend, don't tell him.
4. Never pay by credit card.
5. Never fall in love with your lover if you don't intend to leave your husband for him.
6. Deny and lie.
7. Make sure you're strong enough to bear the guilt of deception.
8. Do not leave any visible marks.
9. Only swallow the first time and then you never have to ever again, but they always think you might. (NB: refers to all relationships with men, not only adulterous ones).
10. Never agree to a DNA test.

I woke up on Monday morning feeling a warm tingle of expectation quickly followed by a warm trickle of blood. My period had started. Typical. Now I would have to wear period knickers after all and not the whisper of erotic lace I had planned in defiance of Ruthie's advice. Women's lives are measured by the state of their knickers. Periods, absence of periods, thrush, miscarriages; it's all there in our underwear waiting to trip us up. The power of the knicker was such that I even had a lucky pair, red satin bikinis with ribbons on the side. I felt that familiar dull ache in my lower abdomen and looked down to see the unwelcome curve of the bloated menstrual stomach. 'Thanks, mate,' I said to the God I only believe in when things go wrong.

Kitty guiltily jumped away from her chest of drawers when I went into her room. 'What are you hiding?' I asked

'Nothing,' she lied. She has yet to acquire the moody secretiveness that is nature's birthday present to every thirteen-year-old. Kitty still wears her lies on her face as openly as someone on a hilltop communicating in semaphore.

I gave her my stern 'don't hide things from me' look.

'I bought a bra,' she broke down and confessed at once. Really, she'd be useless under torture.

It was small and pink with little red roses stitched around the cups. I looked at her narrow child's body with its flat chest and up at her small face; tears welled in her eyes as I took her in my arms.

'Don't be in such a rush, baby,' I said.

'Everyone else has got one and I hate being small and not having bosoms.'

'I know darling. I was the same. My first bra was a Lucky Check. We all had them; they were gingham and came in very small sizes. Mine was purple and white, a 28AA with a little triangular gap in the middle that you could slip a thumb in to pull it down.'

We used to pull our bras down ostentatiously all the time, as much to advertise their presence as to stop them from slipping up to our necks, unfettered as they were by the presence of any actual breasts. The seven stages of woman: bras, periods, exfoliation, sex, marriage, children and the menopause. Followed by an eighth stage of course, that old showstopper, death.

I kissed Kitty, told her she could keep her bra and took her to school. As usual, the other mothers by the school gate ignored me. I'm beginning to think that there is some magical power that renders me quite literally invisible as soon as I set foot in the school grounds. Either that, or I become the plump, plain girl in the playground that no one wants to play with. I see all the other mothers, laughing and chatting, cloistered in groups that allow no chink for my entry, calling to each other 'See you for coffee in our usual,' or 'Don't forget, Molly's coming to yours tonight.' It's a club I am not a member of, but I haven't yet worked out why.

'You know how you like some people and you don't like others?' Ruthie said once when we were discussing the whole issue of other children's parents and why we felt so out of place with them. I nodded.

'Well, they hate us. Why they should and why they do, I don't know. They just do.'

'But aren't we nice?'

'We're all right, but we're different. We have other stuff to worry about than whether little Jimmy's costume is ready or whether or not to make little Sophie wear a vest, as she seems to have a bit of a cough. We just do the parenting thing differently.'

'You mean our benign neglect as opposed to their precious parenting?'

'Yes, I think it threatens them. Parenting is a competition and for them to be doing it all right, we have to be doing it all wrong.'

I still wanted them to like me and kept looking for ways to ingratiate myself with them in an anxious, people-pleasing way. Perversely, to amuse myself, I also liked to count how many mothers could blank me at one go. This morning, so invisible had I become that Molly's mother actually bumped into me in her efforts to walk through me. Anna's mother had involuntarily given me the beginnings of a smile, but it had barely lifted the corners of her mouth when she remembered herself and halted it before it could embark on the long cold journey towards her eyes.

On my way back home, I saw Sammy chatting with the Pigeon Lady. They were sitting together on the stairs outside her basement flat as though they'd known each other for ages. Sammy has a talent for making friends, often with the most unlikely people. The railings were decorated with brightly coloured rags and she sat as she always did, her legs apart, like a statement, to reveal the astonishing whiteness of her pants. Perhaps her madness had spared her from the stains of normal womanly life? The image of her remained in my mind like an accusation.

'That Russkie Ivan's not really my type,' FF said when she phoned later. 'He's more the sort of dago type you used to go for.' Political correctness and FF were Johnny Foreigner to each other.

'What were you doing with him then? And what about Jeremy, Jeremy, Jeremy?'

'He's been out of town for a couple of days. A girl's got to eat.'

'So you shagged him?' I asked with affected casualness.

'Ivan? Nah, it turned out that he was married.' FF did not sleep with married men. It was her one rule, illogical in the light of her general bad behaviour, but one that I was grateful for under the circumstances. For, witch that she is, Ivan would have had no choice but to sleep with her if that is what she had decided.

'I'm seeing Jeremy tonight,' she said. 'We're going to a film première. By the way, Jessie's coming to stay with you for a few days, so can you ask Bea to pick her up with Kitty from school? Got to run, I might call by later in the week.'

'I'll be holding my breath,' I said as I put the phone down.

I had one last thing to do before I went to meet Ivan, and that was to resolve which lie to tell. I didn't want to implicate any of my friends so where could I say I was going at six o'clock on a Monday evening? I was in the bathroom putting the finishing touches to my make-up when Greg came in. The bloating had miraculously subsided and I felt slim and sexy, if a little dizzy and faint from hunger.

'You look nice, Chloe,' he said. I threw myself onto the floor in an exaggerated faint.

'Ha ha, very funny,' said Greg. 'You see, I do look at you.'

He lifted the lavatory seat to pee. I'd become so fed up with his and Leo's careless aim that I'd had a bull's-eye painted at the back of the toilet bowl. Give a boy a target and he will have to aim for it; pee-pee partout had happily become a thing of the past in our house.

Leo came in to squeeze a spot. 'You look cool, Mum,' the iPodian screamed in my ear.

'Very sexy skirt,' said Zuzi nodding approvingly as she checked her face in the bathroom mirror on her way out to work. Bea stood in the doorway and scowled at her jealously.

'Where did you get those clothes?' Kitty asked. 'You got them at Top Shop didn't you, that's what was in the bag? Honestly, you're not a teenager you know. Dad, you can't let her go out like that?'

'She looks very nice,' said Greg.

'Where are you going, Mum?' asked Kitty suspiciously, her eyes locking with mine in the mirror from where she sat on the lid of the lavatory.

'Anyone else want to come in here and join us?' I hedged, as Janet jumped up onto Kitty's lap and Sammy came in to sit on the edge of the bath where he began eating a banana. The bathroom was filling up.

'I'm going to have a drink with the editor of *Psychotherapy Today* about an article I'm writing for them. I should be back by nine.' There, it just popped out, all ready-made like a foil-wrapped lie from a box labelled *Lies for Every Occasion*. It seemed that I was naturally duplicitous after all.

I quickly did my Latin and English homework (it wasn't actually mine, but it might just as well have been), checked that Bea wouldn't forget to feed the children and left.

Anyhow, I reasoned as I walked to the tube, *I'm only having a drink with him. Just because a woman has a drink with a man doesn't mean she's having an affair.*

Raindrop was in his usual place outside the station hawking the *Big Issue*. His unique selling point was that he sang while he sold, his tuneless voice belting out 'Raindrops Keep Falling on My Head' whatever the weather. This was the extent of his repertoire. He winked recognition at me with his mournful brown eyes as I paid my guilt tax. *It won't be long till happiness steps up to greet me.* Today he seemed to be singing just for me.

Potter Lane was a dark and narrow alleyway off Beak Street, the sort of place, you couldn't help feeling, that Jack the Ripper would have been proud to call home. I pushed open the heavy oak door of Number 23 and found myself in one of the many private drinking clubs that proliferate around Soho. This one had an air of faded elegance about it: sloping floors, shabby armchairs and shelves lined with books. There were framed cartoons everywhere, hung haphazardly from floor to ceiling. Thinking that I had arrived before him, I was just about to run to the Ladies for a last check, when his head appeared round the side of a winged armchair in front of a roaring fire. He got up and came to greet me, taking my hand and pressing it to his lips with old world charm, while looking me intently in the eyes.

'What a nice place. What is this place? Why are there all these cartoons? Can anyone come here or do you have to be a member? I never knew it was here,' I was babbling. Ivan took a finger and placed it to my lips and drew me down onto a sofa. God, this man was sexy. I took a deep breath to compose myself.

'I'm nervous,' I said simply.

'I know,' he said. 'Me too.'

He was wearing a beautifully cut dark suit with a white T-shirt in place of a shirt and tie. His face was closely shaven, and for the first time I noticed a small scar that interrupted the passage of his left eyebrow. He pushed his dark hair back repeatedly with his right hand as he spoke. His hair was delicately frosted at the temples; time's way of gently tapping him on the shoulder. Leaning forward, he took a small package from the briefcase next to him and handed it to me. It was a Russian-English dictionary.

'To help you with future riddles,' he said. We settled into the business of exchanging life stories, and I found myself indulging in that cute, flirty stuff, where you offer up anecdotes that illustrate how interesting and adorable you are, rather like a chef whetting a customer's appetite with an array of tantalising *amuse-bouches*.

'Then, when I was five,' I heard myself saying, 'I decided that I was the secret love-child of royalty, abandoned on my parents' doorstep for them to raise. I used to lie awake at night waiting for my real parents to come and claim me.'

Ivan was a cartoonist, which explained why we were sitting, as I now learned, on the overstuffed sofa of the London Cartoonists' Club. He had met his wife, Becky, when he was a post-graduate student in what used to be Leningrad and is now, once again, St Petersburg. A student of Russian, she had come to study at the university for a year. Ivan used to contribute cartoons to the Soviet satirical magazine *Krokodil,* but he fell foul of the system with a cartoon depicting Brezhnev as a dog on the end of a leash being pulled along by Margaret Thatcher. 'I must have been mad to draw it, but I was becoming disillusioned with my country and no longer believed the lies they told us.'

To avoid the inevitable reprisals, he quickly married Becky and made his escape.

'When I was growing up, I wasn't one of those Russians who dreamt of coming to the West,' he explained. 'I used to feel terrible pity for anyone who wasn't a Soviet citizen. I really believed that our country was the finest in the world. Now, of course, I understand why they made it so hard for us to travel abroad: we would have seen immediately how hard our lives were by comparison and what lies we were being told.' These days he drew cartoons for *The Times* and had met FF when she asked him to illustrate her book on celibacy.

He took my hand in his, his skin warm and exciting against my own.

'Chloe, I don't want to make your life difficult. Your children are still young, mine have left home.' The terrain was growing more dangerous with each passing moment, and I almost expected a neon sign to flash danger behind his head. I nodded and looked nervously at my watch. It was 8.30. I'd have to hurry to meet my nine o'clock curfew.

'Let's have dinner later this week?' Ivan suggested, helping me into my coat. I went to kiss him on the cheek and found instead his lips on mine. I lost myself in his mouth and my whole body felt heated by his in the way a fire warms you when you've come in from the cold. It had been years since I'd felt like this, so eager for surrender and for physical intimacy, so aware how perfectly every cliché about love and attraction described my emotions. As we parted, I saw my desire reflected in his eyes and he pressed a piece of paper into my hand, with the squiggles that, while not yet understood, were becoming familiar: *Ty mne ochen' i ochen' nravish'sia. Prikhodi ko mne na uzhin, v piatnitsu v vosem' chasov, 125 Sankt Peterburg Pleiz.*

I couldn't wait to get on the tube and use my new dictionary to decipher the note although it quickly proved hopeless. I'd have to go back to my man in the Volga. I was no longer merely poised on the edge of a precipice; my toes were now dangling dangerously over it.

And if this ain't love ... why does it feel so good? I hummed as I made my way onto the platform. Then, in the way moods so often do, mine suddenly plummeted from elation to a feeling of flatness. In the carriage I saw a couple arguing in what sounded like Portuguese. Although I couldn't understand them, their bodies told their story well enough. She had shrunk into the corner of her seat away from him, while he leaned into her body, pleading and asking for forgiveness. She stared out of the window into the blackness outside, her eyes cold and unyielding and her physical removal from him echoing the distance between them that seemed to increase with the steady movement of the train. His voice grew louder as his pleas went unheeded, and at the next station he left the train. Her eyes followed him, her neck craning forward for a final glimpse as we pulled away, and then she turned her face once more to the cold glass where I could see the reflection of tears as they travelled down her cheeks. It starts with a kiss and ends with this.

I thought of how Greg and I first met. It was a cold November night in 1984. I had recently been chucked by my university boyfriend Geoff, after three years together, and was still at that stage of wanting to look at old photographs of the two of us as I held a damp tissue prettily to my eyes and wallowed in self-pity and the intermittent alcoholism that so often attends lost love. In truth, I was suffering more from injured pride than a wounded heart; I had long grown bored of Geoff, but the bastard had got in first and ended the relationship. My friends were tiring of my Ancient Mariner's tale of woe, and FF, who was occasionally sleeping with a jazz saxophonist, had bossed me into going with her to Ronnie Scott's. I hated jazz, especially the free-form stuff that was being played that night, which sounded like the buzzing of a roomful of furious flies. I was making my way out of the hot, smoky room when I noticed Greg standing by the bar with a pint of beer, hair long and shaggy, jeans black and tight. He had long legs, a dimple in the middle of his left cheek and a small muscular bottom. We'd started talking in that loud, above the sound of the music sort of way.

'I always thought I was the abandoned love-child of royalty,' I was shouting when a passing waitress shushed us.

'Let's get out of here,' said Greg, grabbing my hand and leading me into the rain. We discovered that we both loved walking in the rain and we'd got soaked, pausing only to kiss in doorways until the need for privacy drove us back to his flat where we made love all through the night.

'I've never felt such passion,' he had said, lying beside me during a brief intermission. 'I always hoped that one day I might.'

He'd felt so right, and I'd rested my head on his chest as if I had finally arrived home. We'd stayed in bed for a week, the curtains drawn, only escaping to the kitchen to hunt and gather the food that one or the other of us would bring back to bed on a tray.

Eventually – regretfully – we'd had to get up and take up the reins of our lives. I was doing my post-graduate training at the time and undergoing therapy with a Mr Jolly, by name but not by nature. (I'd first encountered him in early adolescence, when I had been packed off to see him by my parents. It was the year that Grandma Bella died, and I had been having anxiety attacks and weeping hysterically every time my father left the house. On my first visit, Mr Jolly sat me on a small chair in front of a small Formica table and laid out page after page of inkblots; I weighed my responses, 'butterfly', 'monster with horns', 'two people kissing', calculating how disturbed I wanted him to think I was. Later, I drew a picture of a man on the moon. 'Ah,' he nodded wisely, 'Daddy moon going to Mummy moon to make babies.' I remember thinking, but not saying, 'No, you idiot. It's a man on the moon. If Mum and Dad want to fuck, they can do it at home.' So, after this unpromising beginning to our relationship, it was something of an irony to find, all those years later, that he had been assigned to me when I began training as a psychotherapist).

'Just because something is familiar, it does not necessarily make it a good thing,' he had said when Greg and I were in the first flush, his voice rolling around his vowels as though he were savouring a boiled sweet. He peered irritatingly at me over small horn-rimmed spectacles, his highly polished shoes neatly side-by-side as if their spaces had been meticulously measured and marked out. 'Mummy shoe and Daddy shoe lying next to each other to make babies,' I thought viciously. I decided I hated him. *He* was familiar, and definitely not a good thing. So I sacked him and took up with Mrs Kleinman, who suited me far better. Greg and I married three years later.

Coming out of the station, I bumped into Lou. She was holding two bottles of wine, which she quickly hid in a bag when she caught sight of me. We'd spoken on the phone since her break-up with James, but this was the first time I'd actually seen her. In accordance with the rules governing the behaviour of women who have just come out of a relationship, she had cut and radically restyled her hair.

'You think you've got it all and then you find that you've got nothing,' she said twisting a ring round and round her little finger. 'I feel like I've lost everything.'

I don't know about everything, but she'd certainly lost weight, that was for sure. She looked fantastic – well her body did, her face didn't look so good. Forget Atkins, the separation diet should be marketed as the world's most successful. For this reason alone, I felt tempted to rush home and tell Greg that he was history.

'The worst of it is that it's such a bloody cliché. Maree even looks like me, or like I looked twenty years ago. I didn't know he'd met someone else. I thought we were just going to give each other some space,' Lou continued. I hugged her not knowing what to say.

'You will feel better, Lou,' I said. 'You just need time. Who knows, this may be nothing more than a blip.'

'He's moved in with her and bought a motorbike. Arsehole. We had a life together, Chloe, it may not have been perfect, but it was ours.'

'How are the kids?'

'Filled with fury,' she shrugged. 'Why did he have to ruin everything? Why couldn't he just have had his bit on the side and kept quiet about it?'

I left her outside the house that had once been her home and had now become her prison, chaining her to the past; each book, each picture, each coffee mug a reminder of the life she and James had shared, each of their four children a living embodiment of what their love had created.

*

93

'The thing is,' Ruthie said sagely, when I met her for a quick lunch the following day, 'people always feel an absurd need to confess, as if offloading their guilt and making it someone else's misery somehow makes it all all right. If you want to be unfaithful, shut up and live with the consequences. Never Confess: *if you can't do the time, don't do the crime.*'

We'd been discussing Lou and James.

'Is that Rule Number Two?' I asked.

She laughed. 'Perhaps I should write a little handbook? Rule Two leads directly onto Rule Three.'

'Which is?'

'Tell Nobody. Actually there's a Jewish proverb that says it better: *Your friend has a friend, don't tell him.*'

'You don't count, do you? Not telling you something would be like not telling myself.'

In fact, I hadn't told her much about my drink with Ivan. I was trying to be strong and to resist him. It wasn't easy, I couldn't stop thinking about him and his latest text had read *I can't wait to hold you in my arms.*

Greg had been in good humour when I'd come home the night before.

'I've snookered them,' he'd said, waving a letter about parking fines in my face, 'the council, they don't know what to do, they know the law's against them.'

When we were in bed, I'd started trying to discuss our lack of a sex life and to have a proper conversation rather than the impersonal communication more common to business partners: *Have you spoken to the builder? Can you remember to phone the dentist?* But I quickly realised, by the change in his breathing, that he had fallen asleep. 'And I sayeth unto you,' he muttered, gave a loud snore and fell silent.

Chapter Nine

Volodya's Siberian Pel'meni

2 cups flour	250g beef
1 cup milk or water	250g pork
1/2 tsp. salt	1 onion
1 tbsp. vegetable oil	salt, pepper
3 eggs	

Grind beef and pork in food mixer. Then add chopped onion, salt and pepper. To make the mixture more tender and juicy, add a bit of milk. Reserve. Mix flour with eggs, milk, salt and oil until a soft dough forms. Knead on floured surface until dough is elastic. Take some dough and make a 'sausage' (1 inch in diameter). Divide into pieces (1 inch thick). Roll each piece so that they are 1/16 inch thick. Take a glass or a cup (2 inches in diameter) and make rounds from the dough. Fill each round with 1 teaspoon of the mincemeat, fold into half-moons. Pinch edges together and connect the opposite sides. Pel'meni can be kept frozen and cooked later or cooked immediately. To cook pel'meni, boil a large pan of salted water. Carefully drop pel'meni into boiling water. Boil for 20 minutes, stirring occasionally. Serve with butter, sour cream or vinegar.

Volodya, my new friend who ran the Volga, had given up trying to teach me the Russian alphabet and was explaining how to make Siberian *pel'meni* instead. These were the beef and pork-filled, won ton dumpling lookalikes I had seen in his freezer on my first visit.

'At our home in Tomsk,' he said, 'all the women get together and make hundreds of *pel'meni* at the end of the summer. When I was a child, my mother used to lift me onto a chair, give me a steaming glass of tea and a spoonful of jam and leave me while they worked. I would sit there sipping my tea while I listened to their gossip and their songs, their faces flushed from their labour as they competed to see who could make the most *pel'meni*. Then they would wrap them in paper and store them in the snow; our whole back yard was a freezer in winter. If you were hungry, you could just grab a handful, boil them in hot water, and eat them with sour cream or vinegar. Delicious. Here, take these home and try them.'

He wrapped a packet up for me and popped them into a string bag, saying, 'Of course, they're better when you make them yourself.'

'It's funny how every culture has a dumpling,' I remarked.

'They're comforting and filling aren't they? Soul food.'

'Eating can be so comforting,' I said, remembering how Grandma Bella would pop delicious morsels in my mouth as she patted me. 'My daughter Kitty calls it "eating your feelings".'

I'd had a shock when I'd come into his shop earlier as I'd found Volodya drinking tea with Bea and Zuzi, the three of them grouped round a small table at the back arguing with each other in their accented English.

'I didn't know you knew each other,' I'd said, taken aback.

'We are working to improve Czech-Russian relations,' Volodya said smiling, 'we do this by shouting at each other about the books we have read.'

'This is our Club of the Books,' Bea explained.

'Yes,' said Volodya, 'we are having a quarrel about *Anna Karenina*.' He pointed a finger at Zuzi, 'She says that Anna deserved to die for betraying her husband, but I think people can become helpless in the face of passion and everyone must take love where they can find it.'

'You Russians, always so full of the hot head and the passion this and the passion that,' Zuzi protested, her pretty face flushed with anger. 'This passion, it hurt the other people.'

'Anna Karenina's mistake was not to keep her love for Vronsky a secret. She could have quietly had her affair without hurting anyone,' I found myself joining in. Volodya looked at me knowingly.

'Anyway,' he said, 'we have finished this book.' He picked up a book on the table in front of him, 'Now we start to read this one.'

It was *Doctor Zhivago*. How appropriate.

'Surely you've all read that before?' I asked. (When I was eighteen, I'd spent a summer immersed in the Russian classics, burning with a teenage compulsion to find the answers to life's big questions and to find my roots. For obvious reasons, *Doctor Zhivago* was first on my list).

'I haven't,' said Volodya, 'and they pretend that they haven't just like they pretend they don't understand Russian.' He looked at them tauntingly and added, '*Na samom dele, vy vse ponimaete.*'

Bea and Zuzi scowled at him.

'What was that?' I asked.

'He say, *In fact, you understand everything,*' said Zuzi, realising as she said it that she'd rather proved his point. She made a small clicking sound of annoyance.

'Really, none of us have read the *Doctor Zhivago*,' said Bea, 'so please don't to tell us what happens.' She took Zuzi's arm and they left. It was clear that Zuzi was firmly established not only in my house, but in the neighbourhood too.

'Have you got another note for me to translate?' Volodya asked after they'd gone. 'Don't worry,' he added, seeing my worried expression, 'I do not gossip.'

'I'm sorry to ask you again, Volodya.'

'Nonsense, we Russians like nothing better than a conspiracy.' He looked at Ivan's note and laughed.

'What does it say?'

'*I like you very, very much. Supper at my house, 8 o'clock, Friday, 125 St Petersburgh Place.* Watch out Chloe, Russian men will do anything to get what they want, especially when it comes to love.'

'I wonder what he'll cook,' I mused. Then it occurred to me that dinner itself was hardly the point; if I went, I would sleep with him.

In a *carpe diem* moment, I texted Ivan agreeing to dinner. With less than two days to go, I had to get my preparations under way. My first stop was at Absolutely Gorgeous on the High Street for vigorous exfoliation. There were four or five other women sitting in the reception area, all in early middle age. We were fighting the good fight to preserve our waning beauty, but I wondered if that was the only reason we were there. The definition of a good husband used to be one that 'left you alone', but what had once been a compliment had today become a complaint and now, starved of physical affection, we had to resort to paying for massages and facials just so that someone would touch us, knowing all the while what a poor substitute it was for the intimate touch of a man who truly desires you, and whom you in turn desire. When beauty treatments were no longer enough, the next step was to take a lover.

My beauty therapist had a strong South African accent and wore a tight white uniform with a badge on her left breast that announced her as 'Jacquee'. She had an irritating habit of saying 'Is it?' quite indiscriminately in response to everything I said.

'Could you do my eyebrows too?'

'Is it?'

I kept words to a minimum and nodded when she asked me if I wanted the special bikini wax, without understanding that this meant a 'Brazilian'. She wiped me down briskly, as a nappy-changing mother would a baby, poured hot wax over my most intimate parts, and tore off almost every last hair *down there,* leaving me with a mere landing strip down the centre. 'Is it?' I was too taken aback to scream with the pain and submitted silently to her further ministrations – eyebrow-plucking, leg-waxing and the like. I felt like a chicken, plucked and ready for the pot. Thank God my skin had a day or two to vent its fiery redness and return to its usual winter yellow.

I was looking forward to a little lie-down to recover from the trauma, but found FF and Jessie in the kitchen at home. FF opened the fridge, scoured the contents and, without taking anything, closed the door and sat down. We all have a compulsive need to check one another's fridges; it's something we've been doing for the past thirty-odd years. In the early days, we would wolf down the contents with the abandon of young girls who were still growing. Now that we no longer wanted to grow, we took scant vicarious pleasure in simply feasting with our eyes.

'You look nice, darling,' I said to Jessie, who had a new top and looked less haunted than usual.

'Never mind her, look at me,' said FF, pushing Jessie aside to bring herself into my line of vision. 'Don't I look fabulous? I've had the fat sucked out of my bum and put into my lips and cheeks.'

Her mouth was pouted into an artificial O. It looked like the sort of mouth that would only be happy if it had a large penis positioned between its lips. But, I reasoned, this was probably the look she was after, now that she was so determinedly back in the saddle with Jeremy.

'Mmm, very good,' I said dutifully. 'But doesn't the fat-sucking mean you're off games with Jeremy?'

'No, no,' she answered, 'they're very clever these days, I've got just two little incisions, one on each buttock that I can easily cover with crotchless panties.'

I was sorry I'd asked.

'I'm off to my room,' said Jessie hastily, 'I mean, upstairs,' she corrected. The spare room might just as well be called her room. In the past week she'd spent most nights in it, and each time she came she carefully unpacked the bag she'd brought with her so that the cupboards and drawers were now filled with her belongings. A few days before, I'd found her and Sammy sitting on the bed bent over a colour chart; he'd offered to repaint the room for her. They hadn't thought to ask if I minded, and it hadn't occurred to me that they should until some time later. How could I expect others to observe my boundaries when I was barely aware of them myself?

FF droned on about cellular therapy, some new procedure she was considering where they grow your own cells in a lab and inject them back, returning you to the full glory of your former youth.

'You really must go to Rasa Rastumfari,' FF was saying. 'In fact, I'll buy you a session with him for your birthday. He's from Afghanistan and has a two-year waiting list.'

'Why, will he move my fat around my body?' I feigned interest.

'He's the world's leading expert on colonic irrigation. Just absolutely the best. Once you've been to him, you're clean as a whistle inside and out, it's a crime not to have anal sex.'

'Sounds like quite a good reason not to go to him,' I said. 'Anyway,' I added, 'it actually *was* a crime to have anal sex before 1967.'

'You're such a prude,' she said. Her eyes took on the dreamy cast of reminiscence, 'Last night, Jeremy was just about to penetrate me when ...'

I put my fingers in my ears and sang loudly to block out the intimate details. FF swatted me with her copy of *Celebrity Today*, which she had cleverly folded to ensure that I could see her full-page picture.

'You look different, Chloe? What have you done?' she appraised me curiously.

I blushed; even FF had noticed the glow of anticipated adultery that illuminated me. Fortunately, it didn't take long for her to bring the conversation back to herself.

I could hardly sleep that night; the child's excitement the night before Christmas mingled with the adult's anxiety before he or she does wrong. I lay there, my own version of 'Aquarius' playing on a loop in my head as Greg slept fitfully beside me:

This is the dawning of the day of Adultery
The day of Adultery

And sure enough, a few hours later, the Day dawned. I locked myself in the bathroom and carefully examined my bikini area. The redness had mostly subsided and I looked more or less normal, if a little bald. It was lucky my husband was so uninterested in my naked body; a more attentive man might have wondered what I was up to. I looked critically at my face and unscrewed a jar of eye cream (ounce for ounce the same price as gold). The top slipped from my fingers and onto the floor. As I scrabbled about for it on my hands and knees, I pulled various items from under a small cupboard: a runaway sock, three biros, two balls of fluff, a button and ... a box of GrayAway. The box's retro '50s design showed a red-lipsticked woman looking admiringly at a man with sleek black hair.

Use GrayAway to restore your natural hair colour and become the man you once were. This melanin substitution preparation will give you your youth back in one easy step: no gloves, no dyes, no bother. Stop Old Father Time dead in his tracks and feel young and in control again.

I'd discovered Greg's secret. It seemed I wasn't the only one having a mid-life crisis. Who would have thought that my no-nonsense husband would be unwilling to go grey? Was melanin the source of his potency and desire just as Samson's hair had been the source of his legendary strength? Was the loss of melanin the reason he'd lost interest in sex? I carefully put the box back where I had found it.

Later, as Greg had one new, bright-red, dead man's shoe out the door on his way to the surgery, I told him that I had an evening conference at the Royal College of Psychotherapists, the lie slipping out as smoothly as honey off a spoon. 'I might be quite late,' I added for good measure, quite awed by my own wickedness.

Furious Frank brought in a box of his correspondence with the gas board to justify why he'd punched the gas man when he'd visited the day before. It was a complicated but familiar tale of appointments made and missed and bills over-paid and not refunded.

'I have been driven beyond the limits of human endurance. Anyone else would have done the same,' he said.

He was facing criminal charges for attempted assault, which only served to make him all the more furious.

Gentleman Joe spent most of his session in tears. 'I just want to settle down with a nice woman and have children,' he said, 'is that so much to ask?'

I felt so sorry for him that I almost considered the ethics of setting him up with a single girlfriend who'd spent the last twenty years searching for and failing to find Mr Right. I tried to suggest gently that it was better not to have too overt an agenda when it came to relationships; prospective partners could smell the heady fumes of desperation and ran from the odour as if from anthrax.

I was just about to go and get ready when Dad phoned to tell me there was going to be a gala evening at the Royal Albert Hall in his honour.

'That's fantastic Dad, I'm so proud of you.'

'It must be because they think I'm about to pop off,' he said brightly.

I searched around fearfully for some wood to touch; I couldn't find any so I touched both hands to my head instead (in our family this had been decreed an appropriate 'wood' substitute for the purposes of seeing off evil spirits and safeguarding good fortune). I hated it when Dad joked about death.

'Helga will be coming over for it. Maybe you and she can get to know each other a little?'

'I'd really like that, Dad. I can't believe you've kept her secret for so long.'

'What's happening with that Russian fellow?' he countered.

'Nothing,' I lied.

'Ha, you can't fool me. According to Shakespeare, I'm a wise father.'

'What do you mean?'

'He said, "It is a wise father that knows his own child".'

By way of answer, I sang him my version of 'Aquarius'.

I'd decided on jeans. I didn't want it to look as though I was trying too hard. The fact that I had bought the jeans specially and that they had cost a shocking £150 is neither here nor there. What with the beautician's bill and all the new clothes, this adultery business was proving rather pricey. And I hadn't even done the adultery part yet. It would be stupid now not to get my money's worth, but I was still wrestling with my conscience. Should I or shouldn't I? I'd tried playing Ick-Ack-Ock with myself, but quickly realised that your right hand does actually know if your left hand is planning to make an entrance as rock, paper or scissors. Greg and I usually did the best of five; if the stakes were really high, we'd been known to do the best of twenty-one. We made both major and minor decisions this way and had signed a declaration years ago that the outcome of Ick-Ack-Ock could never, under any circumstances, be contested. It was how we'd come to live in Queen's Park, have two children and even why Greg had once spent a week with only half a moustache.

Kitty was at a friend's for tea, so I managed to leave the house without her scrutiny although Sammy, who was sitting on the front wall looking at the night sky, watched me as I got into my car and gave me a mock wolf whistle. St Petersburgh Place is off Moscow Road in Bayswater. I thought it was rather clever that Ivan had found a way to pretend he was still in Russia, but wasn't sure whether I would have chosen to live in London Road in Moscow, supposing one existed. But then I'd always felt stateless and liked to think home was wherever I chose to hang my hat. I noticed that the former Russian Orthodox Church on Moscow Road had been appropriated by the Greeks to become an Orthodox Greek Cathedral. It was Byzantium all over again. It was a wonder the street hadn't been renamed Athens Road.

All too quickly, I found myself at Ivan's dark green front door. I could barely breathe, my heart was pounding and it seemed likely that I would be sick. Could anything that made one feel this bad possibly be a good thing? I ran back down the few steps that led to the street, begged a cigarette from a passing smoker and walked back and forth outside Ivan's house while I smoked it. I'd given up when I was pregnant with Kitty and the unfamiliar rush of nicotine went straight to my head. It felt like meeting an old friend after a long absence, but after a few more puffs I remembered that this friend was false. Grinding the stub into the pavement, I had to go and find a newsagent's to buy the mints that this fall from grace necessitated.

My mobile rang. It was Kitty; she'd just got home.

'I don't feel well, Mummy,' she said, illness making an infant of her. 'My head aches and I feel sick.'

'Does your neck hurt? What about your eyes when you look at the light? Any rashes on your body?' The cloud of meningitis, which claimed lives with the stealth and silence of a professional hit man, hovered menacingly.

'No, that's all fine. But my tummy aches. When are you coming home?'

'Not till later. Where's Daddy? Let me talk to him and he'll look after you.'

Greg promised that he would be sympathetic and caring; in other words, he would treat Kitty like a daughter and not like a patient.

The green door rose once again between my future and me. I rang the bell. Ivan answered, wearing a dressing gown. It was silk and paisley, the sort that you see in shops like Harrods and expect *gentlemen* to wear while reading the paper over breakfast served to them by a butler. I noticed that he had beautiful feet, unlike Greg's idiosyncratic trotters. I pulled my jacket around my body and felt shocked by his presumption. Couldn't he at least have started the evening fully dressed? We both knew the score here, but it might have been a little more polite to pretend that the outcome of our meeting had not been so fully resolved before it even began. I turned and ran. I could hear his voice calling after me.

'Wait, Chloe,' and then his footsteps as he ran barefoot to catch me up. 'Why are you running away?'

'Dressing gown,' I said, pointing.

'So? Did I run away when you answered the door to me wearing a towel?' He was hopping up and down to escape the freezing cold of the paving stones.

'That was different, I wasn't expecting you.'

'Look, I'm sorry. I fell asleep after my bath. I intended to greet you fully dressed. Now will you come back in, sit down and have a drink, while I go off and get dressed?'

Meekly, I followed him back into the house. He led me into a high-ceilinged living room where a bottle of vodka was chilling in an ice bucket. A large Persian carpet hung on one wall and others were lined with books and Ivan's cartoons. Heavy midnight-blue velvet curtains were drawn against the night and a fire crackled in the grate. It was a scene set for seduction.

'You've done this before,' I accused.

'I'm forty-nine, Chloe. This may shock you, but I'm not a virgin.'

'Go on, go and get dressed.' I shooed him away as he drew in close to me. When he'd gone, I felt lonely and wished I hadn't.

I walked around the room, picking things up and putting them down, a dog turning round and round before it is able to settle. I hadn't expected to be especially interested in Becky. Her main function as far as I was concerned was simply to exist in order to fulfil the criteria of Rule One. Now, I was overwhelmed by the need to know everything about her. Was she thinner than me, prettier, taller or shorter, older or younger? A photograph on the mantelpiece had some of the answers. I studiously avoided looking at the two teenagers in the picture and focused instead on the small woman who stared out at me. She had the appearance of someone whose good looks had been nothing more than the fleeting gift of youth. The passing of the years had faded any former bloom and left an ordinary looking woman with a faint air of disappointment. Hair brown, eyes hazel, figure unremarkable. Next to her stood a slightly younger Ivan. By contrast, in that irritating way in which men improve with age, he was even more attractive today than he had been then, his lines adding character to his face and giving him that sexy lived-in look that I found so irresistible.

I felt his hands on my shoulders as he turned me to face him. His outfit still retained a distinctly temporary air: stone-coloured chinos, a T-shirt with Bob Dylan on the front and no shoes. He handed me a shot-glass of icy vodka and raised his own towards me in a toast.

'Let's drink Russian style. The first toast is to *znakomstvo*, to acquaintance, or in our case to getting to know each other better.' He held my eyes with his in a way that made me feel he was touching my naked body with his own. 'Here take this,' he said handing me a small piece of black bread.

'First drink the vodka, then sniff the bread hard before you eat it.'

It had a pungent aroma that soothed the fire of the vodka and filled my senses with exhilarating warmth. Ivan had it sent over from Moscow. 'You can buy it here, but they never get the flavour or the consistency quite right.' We settled on a sofa in front of the fire.

'The next toast is *za krasivykh zhenshchin*, to beautiful women and to one in particular. You.'

He pushed my hair away from my face and the way he looked

at me made me blush like a girl on the brink of her first kiss. I could smell something delicious: he had clearly cooked dinner, but it was quite apparent that we would not be eating it. We were destined to feast hungrily on each other instead.

He touched me; his finger softly outlined the curve of my cheek and came to rest on my lips as though gently advising me to remain silent. He followed the contour of my mouth and lifted my chin as he bent to kiss me. I inhaled him, the exciting and unfamiliar smell of a man whose body I did not yet know. My heart pounded with a mixture of guilt, betrayal and excitement. God he smelled good; musky and male like forbidden fruit. His lips were soft and he kissed beautifully. (A bad kisser, I have found, nearly always equals a bad fuck. All too often in my misspent youth, I had continued the seemingly unbreakable line from bad kissing to bad fucking out of politeness: if you backed out after the kiss, you might be labelled that worst of all things, a prick tease.) My whole body went into our kiss, arching into him and trying to get as close to him as possible. I wanted to burrow my way into his body. I love a man who knows how to undress a woman. No clumsy elbows in the eyes, or hair caught in zips and buttons. Ivan whisked every stitch of clothing off me in moments. For the first time in seventeen years, I found myself completely and alarmingly naked in front of a man who was not my husband. Next, he slowly removed every item of the jewellery I wore as part of my daily armour: rings, bracelets, watch, earrings, even the delicate chain around my neck; all had to come off.

'Jewellery represents the chains of the other men who have known you,' he said, 'and I want you for my own, unfettered by your past.'

'How do you know I didn't buy it for myself?'

'Did you?'

'No.'

I was too shy to meet his eyes as I began to undress him. My fingers shook as I unbuttoned his trousers, and then desire took over as I felt his warm skin. He bent his head to my breast and I was lost, free-falling in pure sensation. I wrapped my body around his, the smoothness of my skin rubbing pleasurably against the hairy hardness of his. His mouth worked its way down my body. At last, all the busy, noisy voices inside my head fell silent as I gave myself up to sensation. I existed only in the moment, kissing and being kissed, whispering, touching and exploring the new territory of him with my hands, my skin and my mouth. He laughed out loud as he came and I tightened my legs around his waist, wanting to keep him inside me forever.

Afterwards, we lay in each other's arms in that contented lazy afterglow that I had not experienced for so long.

'You're just as I imagined you would be,' Ivan said later, as he meticulously peeled an apple with a small bone-handled knife and fed me slivers. It reminded me of the one Grandma Bella used to spread *schmaltz* on bread. (He'd forgotten to turn the oven off and dinner had burnt hours before).

'What do you mean?'

'Soft, silky and sexy. I want to make love to you all night.'

We must have dozed off, but no unruly sun came through the curtains to call on us; instead the deafening siren and blue lights of a police car startled me. I looked at my watch. It was two a.m. Ivan lay sleeping beside me. The fire was almost out, save for a few glowing embers, an echo of the flickering remnants of passion spent.

'The word for passion and the word for suffering have the same root in Russian,' Ivan had told me earlier.

I hoped that the one did not necessarily follow the other, although if I didn't get home soon, some suffering looked likely. I gathered my clothes from where they had fallen and made my way silently into the night, leaving a soft kiss on Ivan's sleeping shoulder.

I was filled with a voluptuous sense of my own being, full to the brim of having touched and been touched. The physical intimacy of my encounter with Ivan had opened something up in me and left me vulnerable. I realised how long I had kept myself separate and locked away, boiling around inside my own head, my body little more than my brain's vessel. I became aware of how hurt I was by Greg's physical neglect of me. *It's no surprise I've ended up in another man's bed*, I thought, justifying my behaviour to myself.

It was so much easier and less painful to lay the blame at someone else's door. I hurried to my car, got in and quickly drove home.

I rehearsed excuses for my inexcusable lateness. I had met an old girlfriend, we had gone back to her place; talked for hours and lost track of the time. Would that do? As I drove past, I could see the Pigeon Lady looking out of her window; a lamp illuminating her white face and long grey hair. She seemed to shake her head, and as I drove on she turned, drew the curtain and faded from sight. I felt I was her naughty child, late arriving home and she, my mother, anxiously waiting. My own house was in darkness, sleeping. I felt changed by the experience of infidelity, a stranger, as if I had forfeited my place here in this house kept warm by the lie of a happy family. I found Sammy sitting cross-legged and motionless, meditating on the living room floor, his eyes closed, his breathing deep and steady. I sat opposite him and watched. He opened his eyes slowly and looked at me without saying anything. After a few moments, he got up quietly, took my hand and led me off to the kitchen.

'Where have you been, Chlo?'

I started with the whole conference-running-into-old-friend thing, but he wasn't buying it. He shook his head. 'You see, that's why I've never married. I just don't think human beings can be monogamous. Not in our society anyway, it's the hundredth Monkey Syndrome.'

'What do you mean?'

'Well, you know how individual cells make up one human body?' I nodded. 'We are also, each of us, individual cells in the body of humanity. So whatever we think or do individually affects all of us. *You* know this stuff, Chloe, it's what Jung calls Collective Consciousness, a 'oneness' we're all part of.'

'Yes, but I still don't see what it's got to do with monkeys or with monogamy.'

'The hundredth Monkey Syndrome is a spontaneous leap of collective consciousness which is achieved when a critical mass point is reached.'

'Meaning?'

Sammy folded his legs under him and leaned towards me

intently, his story-teller face close to mine.

'In the 1950s, there were these monkeys on a small island off the coast of Japan. For years, they couldn't eat a certain type of sweet potato without getting sick; they were too sandy. Then, one of the monkeys worked out that if you washed the potato before you ate it, it wouldn't make you ill. Before long, all the other monkeys on the island were washing the potato. Soon, other monkeys from other islands around the world who had no contact with the original potato-washing monkeys started doing the same thing. So the theory was that after the hundredth monkey on the original island began washing the potatoes before eating them, a critical mass was reached and the collective consciousness of monkeys everywhere was affected. In the same way, no one respects their marriage vows anymore. It seems to me that once the hundredth couple broke them and slept with other people, it became inevitable that everyone else would do the same.'

'Blimey, that's quite a theory.'

'So you see, it really matters what every individual does because it can affect the behaviour of everyone everywhere. Gandhi said, "You must be the change you wish to see in the world". I don't want to marry because I'm not sure I would be capable of keeping my marriage vows.'

'But surely the point is that if you married and were faithful and others followed suit, you could reverse the trend, it could be the hundredth Sammy Syndrome.'

'Sari,' he corrected me. He shook his head. 'The trend away from it seems too strong at the moment. Look at you, for example.'

I blushed, ashamed that my transgression was so evident to him.

'Ghandi also said, "Live as if you were to die tomorrow",' I said defensively.

'But you're looking for something in someone else, Chloe, a sense of wholeness and completeness that you can only ever hope to find in yourself.'

First Ruthie, then Dad, now Sammy: everyone it seemed was a bloody philosopher-cum-psychotherapist.

'Can't a girl just have a bit of fun?' I whined.

'This affects other people too, Chloe, not just you.'

He was right, of course. That was the trouble with growing up, getting married and having a family. You had a collective responsibility and everything you did had an effect on those around you. It didn't take a hundred monkeys, just you on your own, monkeying around, to do the damage. The even stranger thing was that knowing this wasn't enough to stop me. I felt that I'd been good and responsible for too long and I couldn't wait to see Ivan again. I peeled a banana and ate it pointedly. Sammy laughed.

'You know that whatever you do, I'll always love you,' he said.

'I know. Me too. Love you, I mean.'

Sammy was chipping away at a small piece of wood with a knife. His Spanish tepee was full of the strange creatures he had fashioned from driftwood.

'What if you are happily married?' he said suddenly.

'What do you mean?'

'Well, what if this is what a happy marriage feels like,' he held his arms open wide to embrace the kitchen, the house, my life. 'You know, here you are seeking something better, discontented with your lot, and in fact you actually have what most people are looking for.'

I shrugged, 'Happiness is in the eye – and the "I" – of the beholder. It's such a subjective thing.'

'True,' he said, looking me up and down. 'Tell you what though, objectively speaking, I can see it must have been great sex.'

'It was. Lip-smackingly good.'

He let himself out into the garden and made his way to the tent, his silhouette soon invisible in the darkness. I was tempted to join him, but the November air put me off. Instead, I showered as quietly as I could in the basement bathroom to wash the wages of sin from my body, before going upstairs where I slipped like a viper into the marital nest. What would be the outcome of my actions? At that moment, I was simply too happy to care.

Chapter Ten

Bea's Halupki
(Stuffed Cabbage Rolls)

1 head cabbage
1 1/4 lbs minced beef or lamb
salt and pepper
1 egg
1 tsp. parsley
1/2 cup chopped onion

1 clove chopped garlic
1/2 cup cooked rice
2 cans chopped tomatoes
1 tbsp. sugar
1 tbsp. vinegar
1 3/4 cups water

Boil head of cabbage 10–15 minutes. Take the leaves from the head (carefully). Mix the meat, salt and pepper, egg, parsley, garlic, onion and rice together.

Make individual balls out of the meat mixture and fold them up in cabbage leaves like a parcel.

Line the bottom of a roasting pan with some cabbage leaves. Place cabbage rolls on top with the folded edges underneath. Mix chopped tomatoes, sugar, vinegar, and water together. Pour over cabbage rolls, cover and cook on medium heat for 1 1/2 hours. Serves 4–6

God, but I felt fantastic the following morning. Not even guilt could spoil my delicious sense of inhabiting a body that had recently been put to the good use of loving. These legs, arms, lips and hands; they'd done the stuff they were meant to do. At last, they seemed to say, you've remembered what we're for. For the first time in ages, I felt my body belonged to me. I wished that

I could do one of Kitty's beautiful princesses in love, waking up and stretching dances. Instead, I hummed 'I Feel Pretty' as I made breakfast and ignored the looks of astonishment my unusual, early morning good cheer provoked.

'You've got a text message, Chloe,' said Greg, picking up my mobile.

I only just managed to restrain myself from diving on him in a rugby tackle to get it. Affecting nonchalance instead, I said, 'Pass it over, would you?' and slipped it into the safety of a pocket.

'What time did you get home last night?' Greg asked.

He – and Bea, Zuzi, Kitty and Leo – all looked up at me expectantly. Sammy paused on the threshold on his way in from the garden and Janet the cat waited poised, one paw in the air, for my answer.

'One-ish,' I lied.

'No, this is not right,' said Bea, 'I went to the kitchen at half past the one for to get me and my Zuzi a glass of the orange juice. You were not in the home at this time.'

She and Zuzi exchanged a complicit glance and a giggle as if reliving the activities that had given rise to their nocturnal thirst.

'Sorry, Torquemada, must have been sometime soon after then,' I said as I went off to the basement, eager to escape the Grand Inquisitors who had taken up residence in my kitchen.

I'm missing you. Ivan's text message seemed to caress me. I wondered how people had ever managed to have affairs before the advent of mobile phones and the Internet. Both were so perfectly suited to the needs of clandestine relationships that it was hard to imagine they had been invented for any other purpose. Information Highway, big business, ha! It was all probably down to some guy who was good at computers playing away from home.

I studied my face in the mirror. My forehead looked like a wedding banner gone awry: *Just Fucked,* it seemed to say. I looked radiant: eyes bright, cheeks rosy, and my mouth full and heavy with satisfaction. I'd come alive. I'd barely eaten for days and those stubborn seven pounds that had refused to leave my sides for years had simply melted away. Forget cellular therapy, all a girl needed was a good seeing to.

The sky had never seemed so blue nor had birds ever sung so sweetly! Walking through the park after finishing with my first patients, I saw Ruthie in the distance, standing under a tree and talking to that same young man in leathers I'd seen coming out of her house just the other day. Why wasn't she at work? Something was going on; I'd have to subject her to ruthless cross-examination later. We were all going to a Quiz Night at Kitty and Sephy's school. This was the only school event that Greg was prepared to attend as it was the perfect way for him to keep his memory on its metaphorical toes – all those trivia questions, all that general knowledge; had he managed to retain it or was incipient Alzheimer's waiting to erase all the answers, one by one, from his deteriorating brain? I'd caught him in the bath that morning, turning on the hot tap with his curious toes, as he wetly thumbed a waterlogged copy of a book entitled *Do You Know All the Answers?* If he did, I couldn't help thinking, perhaps he wouldn't mind telling me what to do about Ivan, and my life in general.

I wondered what it was that felt so unfamiliar in the kitchen that evening as I was getting ready to go out, and then I realised; it was the sight of Bea actually doing something that corresponded to her job description. She was busy making *Halupki,* a Czech speciality of stuffed cabbage, for the children's supper. Actually, it was more probably for Zuzi's supper, with the children thrown in as a hasty afterthought.

The children didn't much like it when Greg and I went out. Leo wasn't especially interested in interacting with us, but he liked to know that we were in the house and available should the mood take him, and Kitty still wanted to be put to bed. 'It's your duty as a parent to look after me,' she would say, 'so it's your duty to put me to bed.' It was hard to fault the logic, but I couldn't help feeling that I was caught in the vice-like grip of an expert manipulator, whose skill had been honed to perfection by many generations. On this occasion, we managed to slip out easily; Kitty was absorbed in choreographing The Dance of the Cabbage for Zuzi, and Leo had locked himself in the bathroom with the telephone. Although he had sworn Kitty to secrecy, she had nonetheless revealed to me that he had decided it was time he found a girlfriend. To this end, he was working his way alphabetically through all the girls in his class and phoning those he had short-listed, to interview them for the job.

Greg and I walked silently to the school. It had rained earlier and the evening cold had turned the pavement to ice. I had to hold onto his arm to stop myself from slipping. We walked in perfect step, our feet even now synchronised in a way that the rest of our bodies no longer were. In spite of our physical proximity, I felt increasingly absent mentally. This is the real problem with adultery, I realised. It wasn't so much the act of sex with another, but what that symbolised: the transference of intimacy with your husband to intimacy with someone else. That was why sex was so important to a relationship; it maintained closeness, a sense of belonging with and to each other. Without it, I'd been tempted to seek and find it elsewhere.

I beat an all-time record: six mothers blanked me before I'd even made it into the school hall.

'Congratulations,' said Ruthie when I told her. 'Hang on a minute,' she added accusingly, drawing me into a quiet corner and scrutinising me. 'You've had sex.'

I blushed.

'My God, what was it like?'

'Blissful,' I said.

'I want full chapter and verse later.'

The four of us had a table to ourselves. No one else, it seemed, wanted to be on our team. Quiz Night was a serious business and it looked like a few of the quizzees had been in far more assiduous training than Greg. I could hear the people at the next table doing a warm-up; one was asking the other questions about the current government.

'They take this so seriously,' I said, indicating the next table with a nod of my head, where the quizzee was now actually standing and doing star-jumps while shooting out staccato answers, as if this physical preparation would make him more adept at the task in hand. Ruthie whispered, 'Some of them will do anything to win.'

'Too right,' said Richard, lining up paper and pencils in front of us in his precise way.

I leaned forward conspiratorially, 'Watch out for Cheating Charles, he wanders around the room eavesdropping on everyone else's answers so that he can report back to his team.'

'I hear he's taken lip reading lessons since last year,' said Greg.

The Quiz began and soon enough, Ruthie and I grew bored and started writing each other notes and giggling just as we used to in double physics thirty years before. People at other tables were tutting and exchanging glances, so we tried to apply ourselves properly.

Globe and Jerusalem are types of what? Cheating Charles must have noted my smug expression as he watched me closely. I wrote *artichoke* on a piece of paper and showed it to the others. The next question was a cinch for Richard: *Lending her name to a famous brand, who was the Greek Goddess of Victory?* In his excitement he said *Nike* out loud. I saw that Cheating Charles had an accomplice: a man at the other side of the room who, his eyes on Richard, signalled something to Charles like a bookie at a racetrack. We'd have to be more careful. Greg came into his own with the next two questions: *What licence cost 37 pence when it was abolished in 1988?* He laughed at the ease of it and scribbled, *Dog Licence* and *What is the meaning of the word Hypocaust?* A woman at the next table glanced at me and Ruthie and, covering her mouth with her hand, whispered loudly, 'I know, I know, it's when Hitler killed all those Jews in the War.' Ruthie and I looked at each other in disbelief.

'There was a survey done where they asked American school-children if they knew what the Holocaust was, about forty per cent of them said it was a Jewish holiday,' Ruthie said loudly enough to be heard. 'At least she knows what the Holocaust was, even if she thinks it's called a hypocaust.' (Greg knew the real answer to the question, *underfloor heating*).

I knew all the answers to the cookery questions, Ruthie had celebrities covered, and between them, Greg and Richard took care of everything else. We won. Rivers of dislike flowed from all corners of the room, amassing into an ocean of swirling hatred on reaching our table. I got up to get the prize: a bottle of wine. Enemies notwithstanding, I did quite like winning after all.

Phil, the father of Kitty's friend Molly, was standing behind the trestle table. He looked me up and down. 'He's a lucky man that husband of yours, he'd better keep his eye on you.' I smiled weakly. Clearly I was radiating pheromones that seemed to be affecting those around me. Phil was balding and overweight, with a curiously unlined red face. He wore a navy blue blazer with gold buttons and a striped tie with insignia that denoted that he was a very important member of some very important club. On the weekends, according to Kitty and Sephy, who'd been to Molly's house for a sleepover once, Phil, or 'Fractions', as he'd come to be known, set Molly and her brother, Fred, extra maths homework. When they had completed it, he signed the sheets with the date and the time and marked them in red ink. Too many wrong answers meant no sweets on Sunday, the one day allocated for this special treat. Kitty and Sephy had been made to do the sheets too, since which time they had, unsurprisingly, refused further invitations. As a result, Molly had ganged up against them with Anna, another friend.

'Fractions can't take his eyes off you,' said Ruthie, coming up behind me and nodding in Phil's direction.

'I know. Have I got a sign pinned to my back saying, *Available for a bit on the side*?'

Ruthie turned me round and nodded, 'Yes, you have actually.'

She drew me into a corner. 'So how was Ivan?'

'Delicious.'

'I hope you used a condom,' Ruthie said.

I didn't answer.

'Chloe, for God's sake, you don't know where he's been apart from anything else.'

'He withdrew,' I lied.

'Yes, well you know what they call people who use the withdrawal method, don't you?'

I stared at her blankly.

'Mummy and Daddy.'

'Oh, ha ha. I'm not worried about that; my menstrual cycle is so up the spout these days, I think I'm having an early menopause.'

She looked at me sternly.

'OK, I promise, condoms from now on. I mean, if we do it again.'

'You'll do it again, all right,' said Ruthie, studying my face.

I examined hers in turn. She wasn't looking well.

'Have you got a cold?' I asked.

'No, some sort of allergy I think. I'm just going to the loo, won't be a sec.'

While she was gone, I sycophantically told Molly's mum that I *loved* her outfit. It was that safe but pretty Monsoon look, favoured by the slightly older woman. Still fashionable, but *appropriate* for a woman in her forties. Long maroon velvet skirt, matching V-necked jumper revealing the most discreet of cleavages, a co-ordinating scarf tied loosely around the neck and maroon boots with a sensible heel. It was all a little too *matchy-matchy*. Her make-up was carefully applied but understated, and her hair neatly cut and blow-dried. I looked down at my too-short denim skirt, cowboy boots and torn denim jacket. My hand went up to the pencil that was holding my hair up in a messy bun. My lips were painted bright red, my eyes heavily mascara'ed and I had a hole in my tights. Molly's mum mouthed a barely audible 'thank you' as she moved away – quickly as though fearful of catching something – and greeted Anna's mum with an effusive 'we're all having coffee at Janice's after school on Tuesday.'

I could see Greg and Richard over by the hall stage talking to Claire and Ian, the only other parents who spoke to us, because they, like us, were Johnny-no-mates. Near them, another group stood talking. One of the women was standing, anxiously, next to her husband. Every time she opened her mouth to speak, he would silence her either by saying, 'You always get it wrong, let me tell it' or by simply holding up a hand to halt her and closing his eyes in irritation. With each rebuff, she seemed to shrink into herself, as though wishing she could make herself small enough to finally disappear forever to a place where she could be shushed no longer. Observing them, I couldn't help feeling that marriage can subsume individuality, particularly when one partner is more forceful than the other. An affair sets a couple apart and allows the adulterer to reclaim herself. My encounter with Ivan made me feel liberated from Greg with my own identity intact; however, part of me longed for the *oneness* of a marriage without a secret.

Ruthie, back from the loo, laughed when I recounted my vain attempts at acceptance by Molly's mum. She was evasive when I asked her about leather man, saying that he was just a courier delivering something from work and that she'd taken to working from home when she could. It was all perfectly plausible but, although I couldn't quite put my finger on it, there was something about her manner that continued to trouble me. She seemed unusually animated and chatty and, I noticed, was drinking rather a lot.

'God it's boring here,' she said a little too loudly, 'let's go and have a drink somewhere else.' She walked over to Richard and Greg. 'Come on husbands, let's get out of here.'

Neither Richard nor Greg turned round. The curious alchemy that rendered us invisible to other mothers seemed now to have extended itself to our own husbands.

'You see,' said Ruthie turning back to me, 'he never listens to me, never.' I thought she was joking, but her tone struck an odd note. Richard must have heard it too as he turned towards her sharply, his expression a mixture of bemusement and concern.

'Why don't you ever bloody listen to me?' Ruthie asked, her voice rising to a shout. Other parents were looking over at us and, like sharks that have smelt blood, they edged closer. Richard put his arm around her.

'I do darling, you know I do,' he said quietly. He looked around nervously and tried to lead her into the corner.

'I don't know what you think you're looking at,' Ruthie yelled at a woman whose head was craned eagerly forward. 'Does your husband listen to you? Mine doesn't,' she continued without giving the woman time to answer. 'When I come home from work his head is buried in a book. He doesn't even lift his head to greet me or ask me how my day's been. If I told him I'd just been diagnosed with a terminal disease, he wouldn't bother to look up at me.' The woman quickly looked away in embarrassment and the rest of the room went quiet. Richard and I swapped more concerned glances and I put my arm around Ruthie and led her away. This time she didn't resist; just kept her head on my shoulder and cried quietly. Outside, we stood in the dark, concealed in a side doorway and listened to voices calling goodbye and car engines starting. The beam of headlights swung past us as cars began slowly to file out, their tyres crunching on the driveway's cold gravel.

'I just wish he'd listen and talk to me' Ruthie said quietly.

'Don't cry, darling, I'm here. What is it that has upset you so?' I asked.

I could see Richard and Greg standing in the main entrance, peering out into the darkness.

She shook her head. Her former animation had drained from her face leaving her exhausted. For the first time, she looked her age; disappointment does that to you.

'I'm so tired, Chlo.'

'Let's talk properly in the morning,' I said. She nodded.

We stepped out and made our way back to our husbands. Richard came towards us, took Ruthie's arm and walked her to their car.

'What was all that about?' Greg asked as we walked home.

'I'm not quite sure. The loneliness of marriage, I think.' I pressed myself against him and felt him check his reflex to move away.

'Why don't we ever have sex?' I asked quietly.

'What?' he said, pretending not to have heard me.

'Nothing,' I said.

Chapter Eleven

Greg McTernan's
Diabetic Apple Hash Cake

250g all-purpose flour
1 tsp. baking powder
1 tsp. baking soda
pinch ground cinnamon
pinch ground nutmeg
pinch salt
355ml unsweetened apple sauce

15g Splenda or other sugar
    substitute
2 eggs
1 tsp. vanilla extract
70g raisins
one dessertsp. grated hashish (or
    more, according to how stoned
    you want to be)

Preheat oven to gas mark 5/190° C. Spray an 8 x 4-inch loaf
pan with cooking spray. Sift together flour, baking powder,
baking soda, cinnamon, nutmeg and salt. Set aside. Beat the
eggs until light and add Splenda or other sugar substitute. Add
apple sauce, vanilla and hashish. Add flour mixture and beat
until smooth. Fold in raisins. Pour batter into loaf pan. Bake
for about an hour, or until a toothpick inserted into cake comes
out clean.

Next day over coffee in the park café, Ruthie said, 'We'll talk
about my behaviour last night in a minute. First I want to hear all
about Ivan. You are going to see him again, aren't you?'

'God yes, it was too delicious not to do it again.' I looked at her;
she seemed more like herself.

'Be careful,' she said, 'you're a married woman with a family.'

'Do you think anyone is really happily married, Ruthie?'

'Depends what you mean by happily,' she said.

'If this is what it's meant to be like, then that's okay, I accept it. But if it is possible to have a really happy marriage, you know, a rapturous, walking barefoot on the sands sort of marriage, then that's the one I want. I can't tolerate the thought that there is someone having that sort of marriage, and that someone isn't me.'

Ruthie put her hand on my arm, like a mother comforting an unreasonable child. She looked tired. 'I'd be happy if my husband just noticed me now and then.' We sat in silence for a few moments.

'It might be better to be married to someone who was away a lot,' I said, thinking of Dad and Helga's relationship. 'That's the best marriage; one with an absent husband. That way you don't feel sorry for yourself for not having a husband but you don't actually have to have the inconvenience of having one in the house.'

'Yes, we should have married men in the armed forces. Do you remember what John wrote in the copy of *One Hundred Years of Solitude* he gave me for my eighteenth birthday?' she asked.

I nodded. We had spent years trying and failing to make it our mantra. John was Ruthie's first proper love, ten years older and wiser than us. He had written: *If one were to look on life as a simple gift, one would perhaps be less exacting.*

'Who was that courier really?' I asked, returning to the subject of the mystery man in leather. Instinct told me he was the key to everything.

Ruthie looked at me, 'His name is Carlos.'

'Where's he from?'

'Clapham.'

'No, I mean, where are his deliveries from?' Things were beginning to crash loudly into place. 'Colombia?' I asked. How could I not have realised this sooner?

'Look, I started doing a bit of coke with some of the girls in the office to alleviate the mind-numbing tedium of the workplace. It's no big deal. Anyhow, the Ancient Egyptians used to take it.'

'What are you talking about?'

'Some Russian forensic scientist found traces of cocaine in

Egyptian mummies a few years ago, so clearly they weren't averse to a little recreational drug-taking.'

'Aren't Russians clever,' I said dreamily.

'Like the Ancient Egyptians, I've developed a bit of a taste for it, that's all.'

But it wasn't really all. She seemed grateful for the opportunity finally to confess and told me how the odd line at an office party had become almost a gram a day, starting at eight-thirty in the morning with a 'get myself to work' line followed by a 'keep myself going till coffee time' line, and so on throughout the day until bedtime.

'For God's sake, Ruthie,' I said, 'you're not meant to have a drug problem in your forties. You're meant to have one in your teens or your early twenties. I mean, I know you were always a late developer, but this is ridiculous and if you're not careful your nose will fall off.'

'I know, I know. But I seem to have created my own *Valley of the Dolls* situation. I take coke to pep myself up and escape from the dreary boredom of my life; then I'm so hyped up I can't sleep, so I have to take Xanax to calm myself down. Anyhow,' she went on, 'how about all those women in the '50s and '60s who were addicted to Valium? I'm merely continuing the noble tradition of mid-life neurosis and associated drug or alcohol addiction.'

'Yes,' I said, 'but the point about them was that they were dying from boredom because they were at home all day and couldn't find fulfilment in work. We're meant to be *having it all*.'

'So why does it so often feel like we're not having anything at all?'

I couldn't answer that, so I held out my hand to confiscate her drugs instead.

'I haven't got any,' she said, turning out her pockets.

'I'll be watching you,' I warned.

I felt destabilised by Ruthie's revelation, as if the ground were shifting ever further beneath my feet. Although I was the therapist, Ruthie had always been the one who held me steady and anchored me. I offered to go to Narcotics Anonymous with her.

'These places aren't taboo any longer,' I assured her. 'Anyone who's anyone is a member of AA or NA these days. In fact you'd be giving me the perfect excuse to go; I've been feeling rather left out.'

'That's the trouble,' said Ruthie, 'we'd probably bump into everyone we know, which makes a bit of a nonsense of the *anonymous* bit.'

Still, I knew I'd have to find a way to help her; I loved her too much to let her carry on like this.

As I walked back to work, I texted Ivan, *Can we do more kissing soon?*

Can you talk? he answered.

Yes.

He rang me immediately. I blushed when I heard his voice, my mind full of images from our time together. His dark head busy between my thighs; the gasps of pleasure that had escaped my lips. What intimate things we had done to and with each other and how little we still knew one another; pleasure threaded with embarrassment shivered up and down my spine.

'*Chudo,*' he whispered.

'What does that mean?'

'Miracle. It's my name for you.'

'Oh yes, that's what was on the first riddle. I thought my soup was the *chudo.*'

'You too. Don't you remember; *tvoi sup – chudo, kak i ty.*'

'You're rather miraculous yourself,' I said coyly. I couldn't wait to see him again.

We fell silent. What was supposed to happen next? Our initial curiosity about each other satisfied, should we now quietly return to our respective partners?

'I'm getting hard just talking to you,' said Ivan.

Quietly returning to respective partners was clearly not on the agenda. Ivan gave good dirty talk. Some of it was in Russian and therefore incomprehensible, but strangely exciting nonetheless. I love men who talk dirty; but nicely dirty with honourable intentions, not aggressively unpleasantly dirty. It's a fine line and one that Ivan, with his beautiful feet, trod perfectly.

My one-time boyfriend Gus Fallick had been the all-time master of dirty talk. His silver tongue didn't even need to touch your body: he could bring a girl to orgasm with verbal foreplay alone. It was lucky he was so good with words, as he lived in Glasgow and I was in London, so we hardly ever saw each other. I still look back on our time together as some of the best sex I've ever had. The relationship fizzled out when I went to Paris and out of ear-shot; phone calls were too expensive in those days. Last I'd heard he was married with kids, but I couldn't help hoping that he'd set himself up in business with a sex chat line, his verbal mastery available to all; it would be a shame if all that talent were wasted on one ear alone. Renewed sexual activity seemed to have reactivated my sexual memory and made me feel generous to lovers everywhere.

I went down to the basement. The only sour note to an otherwise perfect morning was God's Gift's inky presence in my appointment book. He was my first patient. He leaned back in his chair, arms clasped behind his head, legs stretched out in front of him – his goal, it seemed, was to occupy as much physical space as he could to assert his presence fully. He might just as well have peed in every corner of the room.

'Chloe,' he said, his voice self-consciously low and husky, 'how long are we going to go on fighting this thing?'

'Well, I think you're beginning to make a little progress. You just need to think more about what people are *actually* saying to you, rather than what you *think* they're saying ...'

'No, no, no, Chloe, look at me,' he leaned forward and fixed me with his eyes.

'Pardon?' I squirmed like a worm on a pin.

'We can't go on ignoring this heat between us,' he said, trying to reach for my hand. 'You're a very special lady.' The trite phrase was delivered with what can only have been intended as a heavy-lidded, smouldering glance, but resembled instead the look of someone suffering from palsy.

'I am your therapist and this is not appropriate behaviour,' I said sharply.

God's Gift had sprung out of his chair and was now kneeling by mine and trying to kiss me, his wet mouth hoovering its way onto mine. I pulled away from the force of the suction, jumped up and folded my arms across my chest. How I longed to knee him in the crotch.

'I'm afraid I don't think it's a good idea for you to come and see me any longer.'

He nodded knowingly, 'Yeah babe, we need to get outside this room and see more of each other. Know what I'm saying? Come on, you know you want me.'

'I really, really don't,' I said. But there was no persuading him. This was a man with a device in his brain that translated whatever it was that people said to him into the words that he wanted to hear. My only way out was to speak his language.

'We must fight this thing,' I agreed. 'It's better if we don't see each other any more. We have to be strong.' I promised to find him a new therapist and pushed him out the door.

Upstairs, I found Greg scrabbling through his underwear drawer looking for something, like a dog frantically spraying earth in all directions in pursuit of a buried bone.

'Found it,' he said, triumphantly holding aloft a small cling-film-wrapped trophy.

He was wearing red and white spotted boxer shorts and a T-shirt. I looked at him appraisingly. He was a handsome man, still slim with good legs, and a small muscular bum.

'What is it?'

'Hash. I confiscated it from Leo a few days ago. I'm making a hash cake.'

'Why?'

'Sammy doesn't like smoking it since he's given up cigarettes and John's coming over later.' John was an old friend of Greg's from medical school, who'd been entirely unsuited to the profession. Blood made him faint, and when they were asked to dissect frogs or mice to reveal specific arteries and veins, in between passing out he had simply diced them up as though mincing garlic. He'd left at the end of the second term and pursued a much more appropriate career as a *bon viveur*, the excesses of which had unfortunately resulted in a variety of health problems.

'You can't make a cake for John, you idiot, he's diabetic. It can't be good for your cholesterol either.'

'Which is why I'm making a low-fat Diabetic Apple Hash Cake.' Greg looked very pleased with himself. 'Put that in your chicken soup pipe and smoke it,' he added. Clearly, that defeat still stung.

'Hasn't it occurred to you that if everyone's given up smoking and is suffering from a range of diseases, it may be time to stop taking drugs?'

Greg looked mystified. 'You can't let a few minor medical problems stand in the way of a little bit of recreational drug-taking. Anyhow, marijuana is medicinal, I recommend it to some of my patients to help them manage pain.'

'So what pain do you, Sammy and John need to manage then?'

'The usual aches and pains of existential angst.'

A wave of affection for his absurdity washed over me and I hugged him, savouring his familiar smell and the safe contours of his embrace. For once he didn't pull away and he hugged me back.

'You'll have to give me the recipe,' I said.

How about tomorrow between 2pm and 4pm? I was, it seemed, perfectly capable of feeling warm affection for my husband and setting up a rendezvous with my lover. I marvelled at my own perfidy. This is how they do it, those men with double lives who maintain two families simultaneously. It was sociopathic compartmentalisation: the ability to isolate portions of your life in separate boxes in your mind without the contents of any of the boxes spilling into each other. I had never really believed that it was possible to do this and now I saw that it was. Easily. I could lock the Greg box and open the Ivan one, without breaking stride. *Can't wait to be inside you*, Ivan texted back. It's strange how a man can be inside a woman's body, but not inside her head, and how women can't be inside men at all.

Kitty and Leo were staying with friends for the night and Greg, Sammy and John had taken up residence around the kitchen table. They were halfway through having their hash cake and eating it too while laughing uproariously at something only they could understand. Thighs were being slapped, tears were rolling down cheeks, and every time one of them tried to say anything one of the others would hold their sides in a pantomime of mirth. I left them to it and was just getting ready to go out the door when FF phoned to tell me about the rapturous sex she and Jeremy had been having. Normally I would cover my ears, but on this occasion I listened, thinking that now I was back in the saddle myself, I might pick up a few tips. She always appeared to be having better sex than anyone else and made one feel like a fledgling musician plucking out her first few discordant notes on the violin, while she tucked the instrument confidently under her chin and swept her bow along it with the skill of a virtuoso.

'We were fucking, me on top; luckily, I'd tied my hair in a tight high pony tail ...'

'Wait a minute, what's this ponytail business?'

'To stop your face sagging when you lean over him, silly. You have to watch it past forty darling, when you face downwards, your whole face drips off you, like overdone meat coming off a bone.'

Ugh! Omigod (sometimes Kitty's lexicon is the only one up to the job), had I dripped my face all over Ivan? Thankfully, I seem to remember that I had buried my face in his shoulder out of shyness. What was I to do in the future? Wear a swimming cap in bed? Superglue my jowls behind my ears? The way ahead was strewn with dangerous obstacles. I ended the conversation as quickly as I could and hurried out to meet Dad.

Once a month, Dad and I would meet, just the two of us. It was a ritual we had started after Mum's death and when Sammy was in self-imposed exile. At first we used to meet in his club, a disreputable, ramshackle old place in Bloomsbury frequented by actors and musicians. I found returning to the family home after Mum's death difficult. The memories were oppressive; the ghost of our former family life seemed to bounce off the walls and reverberate. Dad must have felt it too because, after a couple of years, he sold it and moved into a light and airy flat in Primrose Hill with huge French windows. After that, we took to meeting there.

When I arrived he was in his study, papers scattered everywhere, tea and coffee cups on all available surfaces. He was pacing up and down, his face an overgrown garden: hair standing on end and eyebrows trailing down to meet eyelashes halfway. He was seventy-eight and today he looked his age. I experienced the sharp stab of anxiety I always felt whenever I contemplated the inevitable day when I would have to face life without him.

I looked at the untidy sheet music, covered with his signature blackbirds, and listened while he played me the new arrangement of one of his famous numbers. He was preparing for the gala performance of his most celebrated musical, based on Mark Twain's *The Prince and the Pauper*, which had been his favourite book as a child; he'd seen the film at the age of ten and been captivated by it. My mother was a fan of Errol Flynn, and Dad had taken her to see the film at the Everyman cinema in Hampstead three months after they'd first met in the spring of 1958. They met for tea and cakes in what was then Sherry's Patisserie on Heath Street – a few years before Louis the baker took over and renamed it eponymously. They sat in the back of the cinema as courting couples do, kissing and holding hands. As the end credits rolled, Dad got down on one knee in the aisle and asked her to marry him. Their most intimate moment made public, the auditorium had applauded them in rapturous delight. She'd rushed him to a telephone box to phone her family. 'I just casually mentioned that we might perhaps get married one day, and the next thing I know, I'm on the phone to her parents and her aunts and uncles,' Dad used to tease.

I loved to hear the tale of how my mother and father met, fell in love and married, and like all children I felt that the sole reason for their union was to make possible the miracle of my birth.

'Do you miss Mum?' it was a question I had long wanted to ask, but had been afraid to. I felt in some curious way that my mother's death had liberated my father, given him a new lease of life and allowed him to reclaim his identity. I could only guess at the guilt that would accompany such a rebirth.

'I do sometimes. I miss sharing Kitty and Leo with her and I often find myself talking to her photograph about them.'

On the wall behind him was a photograph of my mother dancing Odette in *Swan Lake* the year before she met him. She was on pointe and in arabesque, one exquisitely sculpted leg stretched out behind her, her body bent forward at an angle with her arms folded across her breast, her hands and fingers extended. Her face was framed by bird feathers and was full of that private pleasure unique to an artist who is in their moment. There is little more alluring than seeing someone do something with excellence and, apart from her obvious beauty, it was easy to see why he had fallen in love with her. On the piano below her was a photograph I had taken of Dad at Christmas five years ago. He was smiling as he watched Kitty and Leo open their Christmas presents, his expression one of great tenderness. It revealed all of the sweetness of his personality and some of its humour and warmth.

Dad followed my eyes to the pictures that framed the room.

'When you're with someone for a long time, it's hard to stop yourselves feeling like siblings, or like flatmates, isn't it?' he said.

I thought of Greg and how I knew his every nuance, the way he scratched an eyebrow when he was being serious, the way he nodded when he laughed, and how this familiarity, instead of engendering passion, bred a mixture of exasperation and affection.

'I wonder if that is the fate of every couple?' I said.

'I think you have to work hard to avoid it. It's why Helga and I have conducted our relationship as a secret affair for all these years, long after it ceased to be necessary to do so. There's no good reason why we shouldn't live together, but no good reason why we should. We've both done marriage and children, and we don't want to make our relationship something that we take for granted. The hellos and goodbyes keep it exciting and fresh; we're always so pleased to see each other.'

'That must be nice. Whereas I feel that this is my life, forever and ever, the monotony of monogamy, amen. When you're young, the future belongs to you; as you age, it's only the past that does,' I said.

'For God's sake, Chloe, you're still a young woman.'

'I can't be an astronaut anymore.'

'You've never shown the slightest interest in space travel.'

'That's not the point, the point is I couldn't be one now even if I wanted to.' I felt tears fill my eyes. 'I couldn't be a pop star either,' I added unreasonably.

'I know, darling. It's hard to come to terms with one's possibilities being limited. I'm still trying to work out what I'm going to be when I grow up, never mind acknowledging that I'm too old to do anything new.' He drew me to him in a hug and my head took its little girl place on his shoulder. I was shocked by how frail he felt.

'Have your affair if it will make you happy,' he said with the acuity of a parent who can always tell when their child has done something wrong. 'But be careful; it means you have to keep the different areas of your life separate and make sure they don't spill into each other.'

'You mean, compartmentalise?' I said, pulling back. Dad nodded. 'That's okay, I'm good at that.'

'The thing is,' he went on, 'that the secret compartments become like suburbs, areas outside your main area which is where your life is with your family. It's easy to start spending too much of your life in your green and lush suburbs and to ignore your main area, your inner city, which quickly becomes derelict because you're not doing any necessary maintenance.'

'I see what you mean, but I'm so happy in my metaphorical deck chair in my sunny suburb at the moment. Can't I just enjoy that for a little bit, *carpe diem* and all that?' Part of me couldn't quite believe that I was discussing my extra-marital affair with my father, but he was so non-judgemental and wise that it seemed perfectly natural.

Dad smiled. 'Good and decent people sometimes do things themselves that they would censor in others. It's too easy to carry on your life in modest misery in order not to offend anyone – and of course one should do all one can not to hurt others – but as the cliché goes, life is short. Sometimes, I catch sight of myself in the mirror and think "who is that old man?" before I realise that it's me. There's nothing you can do about getting old.' He put his arm round me and pulled me to him again, stroking the back of my head. 'You just have to remember that it's better than the alternative.'

'Which is what?'

'Being dead.'

Ah yes. And that, I reasoned, is absolutely the reason why I should enjoy my time with Ivan while I could. *The Grave's a fine and private place, But none I think do there embrace.*

Chapter Twelve

Volodya's Mum's Poppy Seed Roll

For the dough:

450g plain flour
pinch salt
2 tbsp. caster sugar
2 tsp. easy blend dry yeast

175ml milk
zest of 1 lemon
1 egg yolk beaten with a little
   water for a glaze

For the poppy seed filling:

150g poppy seeds
1 tbsp. sugar
2 tbsp. honey
1 tsp. butter

zest of one orange
zest of one lemon
2 egg whites

Sift flour, salt and sugar into a bowl. Mix in the easy blend dried yeast. Make a well in the centre. Meanwhile, heat milk and lemon zest in a pan with the butter until melted. Allow to cool a little then add to the dry ingredients and mix to a dough. Knead the dough on a lightly floured surface for ten minutes until smooth and elastic. Place in a clean bowl, cover with a damp tea towel and leave in a warm place to rise until doubled in size (45 – 50 minutes).

For the filling, reserve 1 tbsp. of poppy seeds. Process the rest in a blender or processor. Melt butter in a pan and add ground poppy seeds, sugar, honey, and orange and lemon zests. Cook for 1 minute over high heat. Allow to cool. When cool, add the egg whites, blending well. On a lightly floured surface, roll the dough into a long rectangle about an inch thick. Spread the filling evenly over the dough stopping an inch from one long edge and roll up, making sure that the filling is sealed inside. Place on a non-stick baking sheet, seam side down. Allow to rise for 30 minutes. Brush with the egg glaze and scatter the reserved poppy seeds on top. Bake in a preheated gas mark 5 / 190 C oven for 35 to 40 minutes. Allow to cool on a wire rack.

I was in the living room, texting Ivan to decide what time we should meet, when I felt Greg coming up behind me. I reared up, a frightened horse into whose path a snake has strayed.

'Chloe, you're as white as a sheet.'

'You gave me a fright,' I said weakly.

'You seem a bit jumpy these days. Everything okay?' He gave me an odd look that made my heart beat fast with fear. Did he suspect something?

'Fine, just a bit tired, I think.'

'Have you seen my stethoscope?'

'Why, isn't it in your bag?' He shook his head. 'Greg, where have you hidden it?'

He hung his head sheepishly, a small boy caught out doing something he knows he shouldn't.

'For God's sake, Greg, how am I supposed to know where you've put it?'

He cast his eyes around the living room and suddenly they lit up. He strode confidently to the low table on which the television stood, threw himself to the ground and reached an arm under it. 'Got it,' he said with a delight worthy of Little Jack Horner pulling out his plum.

He gave me a shrewd look. 'I know your secret,' he said.

My heart jumped and adrenalin coursed through my body. 'What secret?'

How could he have found out about Ivan? I could barely breathe as I had a clear vision of our lives collapsing: boxes being packed; the house being sold; the children in tears and it all being my own selfish fault.

'Blimey,' he said looking at me curiously, 'I didn't know you cared about chicken soup that much.'

What was he talking about?

'It's that fat in the jar in the fridge isn't it? That's your secret ingredient.' He was waving a piece of paper in my face jubilantly.

I felt badly shaken and fought to return my breathing to normal and quell the anxious rise and fall of my chest. *Schmaltz!* His lab report had revealed the presence of chicken fat in the *kneidlach*. I counted myself lucky that he couldn't send me to a lab and have me tested for the presence of another man within or upon me.

Later, Ivan and I were lying on the sofa in his living room. He was sleepy but I was wide awake. That's the difference between men and women; after orgasm, men seem to lose power and women to gain it. Becky was still away. I felt awful about sleeping with her husband in their house, but not quite awful enough not to do it. In any event, we had scrupulously avoided their bedroom, availing ourselves instead of the many other places in his house and had even congratulated ourselves on our remarkable sensitivity. I brought up Dad's analysis of relationships, how people get too comfortable with each other, too much like siblings and then prevented by incest taboo from having sex. If I'm honest, I was really trying to find out if he and Becky still did it.

'There was a book written in Russia in the late nineteenth century which described a socialist utopia,' he said. Just as Dad had a saying for every occasion, so Ivan had a book. It was down to the fact that there had been nothing to do in Soviet Russia except read. And have sex; he'd done quite a lot of that too, it being one of the few things that didn't get you into trouble with the authorities. On balance, I was pleased he had, it had made him terribly good at it.

'These kinds of books were very popular at that time,' he went on. 'Anyway, this one, by Chernyshevsky, was called *What is to be Done?*

'I thought Lenin wrote that,' I interrupted; keen to show off my erudition. (I'd read Lenin's booklet during my brief student Communist phase, when I used to sell copies of the *Socialist Worker* on the streets of Camden Town. This unpaid labour was soon replaced by a weekend job as a waitress in a cavernous bistro, which funded my increasingly serious Miss Selfridge habit. My purchases were the fruits of my labour and therefore, I reasoned, in keeping with Marxist ideology. Not long after, I graduated from university and put a deposit on my first flat, thereby giving up all pretence of communism and whole-heartedly embracing capitalism as a fully paid-up member of the property-owning classes.)

'He did, but it was Chernyshevsky's title first; Lenin deliberately used and echoed it later. Anyhow, it described a marriage of equality between a couple who agreed to respect each other's privacy. They only entered each other's rooms by invitation and reserved a third room for their meetings. I always thought there was something in that; that it might be a way to preserve the mystery and sexual interest between two people and prevent them from taking each other for granted.'

'Mmm, good idea, but you'd have to have a lot of rooms. What happened to them? Did it work?'

'Well, it got a bit complicated; she fell in love with the husband's friend and they all lived together in a *ménage à trois* for a while. Then the husband staged his own death to allow his wife to marry his friend as she loved him more.'

'Very altruistic of him. I'm afraid I can't see Greg doing that for you, but then, you're not his friend.' I thought for a moment. 'I suppose that's one of the things that makes you and me so exciting isn't it? The stolen moments and the separation from our everyday lives.'

'Maybe.' He paused. We lay in silence for a minute; he ran his hand up and down my arm making my flesh tingle. 'You know, I should never have attended my children's births,' he continued. 'I found it difficult to think of Becky sexually after that. She became a mother in my eyes and the thought of having sex with her felt inappropriate.'

'How can you say that? They were your babies too.'

'I know, I'm simply being truthful and telling you how it made me feel. Not only that, it's all that *where did you put the soap* and *can you put the cap back on the toothpaste* stuff too that erodes the mystery, isn't it? Do you know the Russian poet Mayakovsky?'

I nodded.

'He put it very well in one of his poems: *Liubovnaia lodka razbilas' o byt – Love's boat has crashed on the rock of daily trivia.*'

I found it arousing when he spoke in Russian. 'What about our boat?' I said, reaching between his legs.

'Our boat, my darling, is just setting sail,' he answered, drawing me to him and kissing me. 'I can't get enough of you,' he whispered, as he began to make love to me all over again.

I sat in the park café and watched a woman eating some bacon and eggs, one hand placed coyly in front of her mouth as she chewed, as if eating were a shameful habit that should be hidden from public view. Next to her sat a man in his sixties with thinning hair and a ponytail. It took every ounce of my self-control not to scream in his ear that he looked *ridiculous* before sawing his ponytail off with a plastic knife. I was feeling a little irritable. Ivan had had to cancel our next date as Becky had come home early, and my ill humour had spilled over into a stupid argument with Greg. Every couple dances their practiced moves of irritation and frustration in perfect step as they repeat the same argument time and time again. Ours had been of the *you're always grumpy and tired and never want to see anyone* and *you're always right and everyone else is wrong* variety. The end result was that I now hated everyone: Greg for being no fun, Ivan for cancelling our date, and Becky for coming home unexpectedly and ruining my life by getting in the way of my having sex with her husband.

Through the window, I could see Sammy and the Pigeon Lady huddled on a bench together. I wondered what they found to talk about. Sammy looked up and saw me and gestured for me to join them. I wasn't sure I was in the mood, but then something caught my eye. It was Sammy's right hand, moving up and down. I looked more closely and saw that he was playing a guitar. As far as I knew, he hadn't picked up a guitar, much less played one, since Mum died and the sight of him holding one now signified a seismic shift that I found almost unbearably moving. I was drinking the last dregs of my coffee, and putting my coat on to hurry out to them, when my mobile rang. Was it Ivan phoning to tell me that we could meet after all? A flame of hope leapt in me, then quickly flickered and died. It was Gina, in a state of agitation.

'I'm going to tell Jim the wedding's off.'

My attention was still focused on Sammy and his guitar. 'Are you?' I said absently.

'How can I be with one man for the rest of my life?'

I shifted my attention to what she was saying. 'Gina, wait until I see you. You need to think this through. This may be about fear.'

'What do you mean?'

'Your fear of commitment and your resistance to allowing yourself to be happy. Let's discuss this properly at our session later today.'

'Jim deserves someone better than me,' she said.

Finally, she promised to do nothing until we'd met. As I was leaving the café, my phone rang again. It was FF.

'Have you seen Jessie?' she asked. 'I suddenly realised that I haven't seen her for days. I thought I'd better just check that she is with you.'

'She's fine, but it might be an idea for you to phone her and talk to her.'

'I will, I've just been so busy darling, you know how it is. Come with me to Elton's White Tie and Tiara Ball? I've got an extra ticket; Jeremy can't come. It's so weird, I can't bear to be apart from him.'

'Being away from your daughter, however, causes you no problems,' I thought but didn't say. 'What is it you like so much about him?' I asked instead.

'He's terribly good at cunnilingus. You and Greg have to come for dinner soon and meet him. Must dash.' She hung up.

I shuddered slightly at the image she'd stamped in my head, turned my phone off and walked over to Sammy.

He was still on the bench with the Pigeon Lady and playing 'It Had to be You' on his guitar. She was swaying and singing along, sweetly and in tune, with a pigeon perched on her shoulder.

> For nobody else, gave me a thrill.
> With all your faults, I love you still ...

She sounded like a young woman when she sang and I caught a glimpse of what she must once have been: a young girl, a child, someone's baby. Everyone was once someone's baby, pushed out into the world from a mother's womb. Now strange, solitary and disconnected, she had become a generic 'mad woman' who roamed the streets of Queen's Park talking to pigeons. What tricks had life played on her to bring her to this point? As I approached, she shooed away the pigeons that were crowding on the bench next to her to make space for me.

'Chloe, this is Madge, Madge, Chloe,' Sammy introduced us. I'd seen her coming and going over the past ten years or so, but had never gone to the trouble of finding out her name. I felt ashamed.

'Yes, yes,' she said, 'Chloe and I are old friends, aren't we dear? But you're always so busy, busy, busy, we never have a moment for a proper conversation.'

I looked at her closely for the first time. She had astonishingly clear green, almond-shaped eyes in her careworn, lined face. They were full of sadness and longing. She must have been in her late sixties and there was something about her bearing that suggested she had once led a better, happier life. At her feet were the many carrier bags that always accompanied her. Some seemed to be full of pieces of cloth, like the ones that hung from the railings outside her flat; others carried crusts of bread for the pigeons.

'Madge used to be a textile designer,' said Sammy.

Madge nodded, her hair flapping wildly. 'I have children you know,' she said, 'a lovely little boy and girl, just like you two.'

'You're playing again,' I said to Sammy, reaching out and touching the smooth wood of his guitar.

'Yes, it's time. Madge says everyone has a duty to do the thing they're meant to do.' Madge patted Sammy's shoulder. He looked down at his fingers as though surprised to see them moving up and down the fret with such fluency after so long. 'It feels like meeting an old friend after a long absence.' He had tears in his eyes.

'Sammy's going to help me find my babies,' Madge said.

I looked at him with mild alarm. My instinct was to recoil from people who needed my help unless they were paying for my services, in which case I could be in control and conduct the relationship on clearly defined professional terms. Sammy, on the other hand, was always open to waifs and strays. He couldn't walk past a beggar without giving him the price of a cup of tea and then accompanying him to drink it, throwing in a full English breakfast and making plans to meet the following day for good measure.

'Madge hasn't seen her children for thirty-five years,' he explained.

Madge leaned back on the bench; she closed her eyes in order to replay the past more clearly and began to tell her story.

She told us how she had met her husband, Reg, when she was twenty and after a two-year courtship they had married in 1958. She was a textile designer working in a factory, he was the foreman. She was more educated than he, a grammar school girl who had gone on to Art College to study design. 'He was so handsome, all the girls wanted him. But he chose me,' she said proudly. She had given up her job when she became pregnant with their first child, a girl, born in 1962, followed by a boy in 1964. The same years that Sammy and I were born. A parallel family, in the same city, living parallel lives.

'We were happy at first,' she explained. Reg was content in his role of breadwinner and father. They lived in a small terraced house in Kilburn and she was happy enough to cook, clean and raise children. At first. When the children were both at school – Rosie was seven, Jimmy five – Madge became restless. 'If Reg had just let me go back to work, it could all have been different,' she said. But he was a working-class man who felt that a working wife was an indictment, a way of announcing to the world that he was not a proper man and that he couldn't provide for his family. Madge had too much time and too much energy. 'I was lonely. Reg would come home from work and fall asleep on the sofa in front of the television. I was alone all day and then, after the children had gone to bed, all evening too. I needed someone to talk to.' Armstrong, ('Armie'), her lover, was that someone. Not only did he listen, he talked back too. They had met when Madge had slipped and fallen on an icy pavement in Kentish Town in the winter of 1969. He had helped her up, attended to her grazed knees and taken her off for a cup of sweet tea to help with the shock. He was five years younger than she and a trained teacher, although he could only find work on the buses. Armie was from Jamaica, fresh off the boat and facing the disappointment of a country that had not lived up to its promise.

They fell in love and Madge's days became full once again, this time with secret meetings and stolen kisses. After a while, she had told Reg that she was leaving him for another man and taking the children with her. When Reg found out that Armie was black, he said that no children of his were going to live with a nig-nog, thank you very much. 'I don't know what happened then,' said Madge sadly, 'that's all I can remember. I think I was ill for a while and in hospital.' She shook her head, as if trying to mine a memory that she felt certain was inside, but couldn't quite access.

She stood up abruptly, 'I must get home, Jimmy and Rosie will be back for their tea soon.' The temporary lucidity that had enabled Madge to tell her tale appeared to evaporate and she seemed disorientated again. She fussed with her carrier bags before hurrying away, scolding the pigeons as she went for making her late.

'Poor old thing,' said Sammy. 'I have to try and find out what happened to her children for her.'

'She's about the same age as Mum would have been now,' I said.

The park was darkening. A Dalmatian and a Chihuahua ran happily alongside each other, pausing now and then to roll together in the grass. Their owners walked behind them in silence, an unlikely couple, forced into each other's company by their dogs' friendship. Elsewhere, a man wearing a neat red turban walked round and round the perimeter of the playground, as he did every day, his head bent in study over a holy book.

'You'd have thought he'd have finished that book by now,' I whispered as I nudged Sammy. We giggled like children before lapsing into silence; he strummed his guitar lovingly, at home once again.

'I'm thinking of moving back here,' he said. 'Is it okay if I stay till I find a place?'

I hugged him. 'I'd love that. Stay as long as you like.'

Madge's story had made me hum with anxiety and I was suddenly eager to see Leo and Kitty. The house was quiet and empty when I got back. I felt an unexpected need to hear Greg's voice.

'The doctor is with a patient,' said Marjorie, the surgery's receptionist when I called.

She made no concession to the fact that Greg was my husband and often wouldn't even let me see him when I came into the surgery, saying, as she pursed her perfectly lipsticked mouth and pulled her cardigan over her neat and pointed bosom, 'The doctor is busy. You'll have to take a seat and wait your turn.' I'd tried everything: killing her with kindness, extravagant Christmas presents, homemade cakes, fierce hauteur, threats of emergency, violence. Nothing worked; she might just as well have been the mother of one of Kitty's classmates.

'Marjorie, it's Chloe. Could you put me through to Greg please?' There must have been something in my voice, because for once she didn't argue and the next voice I heard was Greg's.

'"It Had To Be You", author and date?' I asked.

'Gus Kahn and Isham Jones, 1924.'

'You really are marvellous.'

'I know. Must go darling, I've got a full list this afternoon.'

The house seemed full of shadows. This is what it would feel like if we got divorced, an empty house on the days when the children were with their father. The aching loneliness of childless Wednesday nights and alternate weekends, and far worse for the divorced father who finds himself on his own most of the week. Either of us could bring about this fate on the other at any time. It takes two to have a relationship and only one to destroy it. However much one of you may want it to continue, if the other opts out, that's it, it's over.

The day was grey and a light drizzle was misting the air. Janet slipped through her cat flap and seemed to enjoy the slender ease with which she passed through it. Volodya's mother had left him copious amounts of her poppy seed roll on her recent visit from Russia and he'd given some to me as soon as she'd gone. He hated it, I loved it; it reminded me of Grandma Bella, who also used to make it, and of how she would use her handkerchief to wipe my sticky mouth, blackened by the sweet dark poppy seed jam of the filling. I had no patients until six p.m. so I cut myself a large slice and settled down with Richard and Judy for a little illicit afternoon TV. I watched their interplay with each other. They seemed so happily married; what was their secret? I wanted to write and ask them:

Dear Richard and Judy,
   You live together and work together and although you sometimes bicker, you always seem so happy and are so nice to each other. How do you do it?
Very best,
Chloe Zhivago, aged 43.
P.S. How often do you have sex?

The doorbell pierced the quiet of my solitary afternoon. Ruthie was standing outside. She looked shrunken and had deep black shadows beneath her eyes.

'Is it open?' she asked.

'The *Kvechatorium?*'

She nodded.

'Always,' I said.

'I hate my life,' she said.

I pulled her inside, made her a cup of tea and cut her some poppy seed roll. She'd lost a lot of weight and, although it may seem an oxymoron, she looked terrible.

'Which aspect of it?'

'I just can't bear going on with this feeling of waking up every morning and being unable to face what the day holds in store for me. I lie in bed and run through all the meetings I have, all the people I have to see and the prospect of getting up, bathing, washing my hair, having breakfast, leaving the house, and driving to work feels insurmountable. Then when I get there, there's that David Gibson wanker telling me "we're all on the same page" and that I should "get in the mix more". I've been taking more and more days off and I feel strung out, miserable and depressed.'

'Does Richard know how you're feeling?'

'No, he never notices anything unless it's an artefact from antiquity, which, of course, I soon will be if I go on like this. Anyhow, it doesn't matter anymore, they're making me redundant.'

'How can they make you redundant, you're the editor?'

'They're changing the remit of the magazine and saying it's a different job. I could fight it, but I think it's a blessing in disguise really; a sign that it's time for me to change my life.'

'You have to stop taking cocaine; that'll help you get back in control.'

'Did I say "Chloe, tell me like it is"? or "Chloe, give it to me straight"? No, I didn't, I came here to *kvetch* and for you to say "there there" and "poor you" in all the right places.'

'Sorry, darling.' Ruthie always retained her humour even in her darkest moments. 'Screw tea, let's have a bottle of wine,' I said, and went to the fridge where I found a bottle of champagne tucked out of sight behind some elderly vegetables. 'Even better,' I said, holding it aloft, 'now we can be a couple of desperate but posh old lushes drinking in the afternoon. I wonder how long it would take us to get from here to a park bench, or to shouting at pigeons,' I said, thinking of Madge.

'Poor her,' said Ruthie when I recounted Madge's story. 'I feel awful that I've never taken the time to talk to her. What do you think happened?'

'It must have been something terrible for her not to remember.'

We were quiet for a few moments; each of us trying to imagine what could have pushed Madge over the edge and onto the fringes of society.

'Can we go back to talking about me now?' Ruthie asked. I nodded and toasted her with my glass.

'I can't believe how hard I've worked for all these years to become an editor and how little it means to me now,' said Ruthie. 'I mean, who gives a fuck whether we lead with a story of a woman who teaches other women how to marry a millionaire, or the story of some soap star's battle against alcoholism.' She poured herself another glass of champagne, relishing the irony. 'I mean, in the great scheme of things, it's all tomorrow's chip paper. Well, actually, it isn't even that anymore; they use that white recycled stuff now, don't they?' She looked me up and down appraisingly 'You look great, Chloe. Maybe I should have an affair; as an addiction, it's clearly much better for your skin than cocaine.'

'You really, really must stop.'

'I'm going to, I promise. Tomorrow. I just need a little help getting used to this redundancy idea.' Her phone beeped. 'Oops, the eagle has landed, just popping out to meet Carlos. See you later.'

It was true. My growing obsession with Ivan was not so very different from Ruthie's cocaine habit: my affair was disturbing my equilibrium and turning me into a manic-depressive. You think you can handle it but the addiction quickly starts to get out of hand and you begin to put satisfying your craving above the other more important things in your life. I was irritable and withdrawn when I was away from Ivan, and agitated and excited when I was with him.

I'm aching for you. I will find somewhere for us to meet.

My fix had arrived by mobile phone.

The reading on my kissometer is dangerously low, please hurry, I texted back. My mood immediately lightened and I danced my way down to the basement to meet Gina.

She started to speak before she'd even sat down. Her restless energy mirrored my own. I soon found out why.

'I've slept with someone else,' she announced. 'I decided I had to get it out of my system before I married Jim.'

'So you are going to marry Jim?'

'Yes. Sorry about the panicky phone call earlier, I feel fine about it now. I realised I just needed to do this and then I'd be ready to settle down.'

'How did it make you feel?'

Her face took on the misty expression of lust recollected.

'Wonderful. I don't feel guilty about it either. I mean not really. After all, Jim and I aren't married yet.'

'Do you want to do it again?' I asked tentatively.

'No … Yes … Maybe once more.' She looked troubled. 'Damn, I do. I thought that would be it, but I do want to do it again. I'm a bad person, aren't I? You think I'm bad, I know you do.'

I shook my head. 'It doesn't matter what I think, Gina, it's what you think that matters,' I said. 'We're all good and bad, honest and dishonest, generous and mean. We're all of these things; it's how we live with that, how we manage it that counts.' I was aware I was talking as much to myself as to her.

Gina sat up in her chair, brightening. 'I've got two months left before our wedding, so it won't count if I see the other guy again.'

That was her way of justifying her *badness*, but she was merely another addict, rationalising her next fix with the promise that it would be her last. We were all the same.

'He's someone I met ages ago. There was always this attraction between us, a feeling of unfinished business. I thought I'd better finish it, the business I mean.'

'What is it about him?'

'His newness, his untrammelled paths.'

I nodded. I knew just what she meant.

'It'll be fine. I'll just get this out of the way and then I'll get married and have children and live happily ever after. Will you come to the wedding?'

It didn't feel right for me to do so, but Gina had been coming to see me for so long, and I wanted her to be happy, so I decided to break my unwritten rule. I agreed to attend the ceremony but not the reception.

'It's all your fault,' I thought unreasonably as I looked at her lovely face. 'If you hadn't planted the seed of betrayal in me, I wouldn't be sitting here in front of you, a woman with a lover and a secret life.'

'Did she hold a gun to your head?' asked an inner voice.

Chapter Thirteen

Kitty's Vengeful Chocolate Cake

For the cake:
215g chocolate (plain)   7 eggs separated
225g butter   200g ground almonds
225g caster sugar

Melt chocolate slowly and cream butter and sugar.
Add 7 egg yolks and ground almonds to butter and sugar. Add melted chocolate.
Whisk egg whites until quite stiff, then fold into the chocolate mixture.
Pour into buttered tin and bake for about 45 minutes in the middle of the oven at gas mark 4/180° C.

For the chocolate icing:
175g cooking chocolate
1/2 tsp. vanilla extract
1 cup double cream

Melt the chocolate in the top of a double boiler over medium heat. When chocolate is melted and smooth, stir in 1/2 tsp. vanilla and the cream. Whisk until well blended and silky.
Pour the icing over the cooled cake, letting it drip down the sides. Lick the bowl. Yum.

I found Kitty lying on the stairs, crying. She was in her school uniform, a small black spider with long thin limbs flung out around her in despair. She'd positioned herself so as to be able to observe her face in the mirror on the wall: sad princess crying at the injustices of life.

'What is it, baby?' I asked.

'Molly and Anna are being horrible to me. I hate them; they're such bitches.'

'Don't say that. What happened?'

'Well, you know we went to Brent Cross after school?'

I nodded. This was what young girls did; they hung around shopping malls, grown-ups in miniature, drinking coffee and window-shopping. In my day, it used to be the High Street, which, I couldn't help feeling, had more soul than a mall. (What does that mean anyway, 'in my day' as if your 'day' only lasts until a certain point and then it's over and somebody else's 'day' begins? When was this magical point? At twenty? Thirty? Wasn't it still 'my day'? I was still alive after all. Surely it's your day for as long as you can draw breath?)

'Mum, listen to me,' said Kitty, shaking my arm to reclaim my attention. 'OK, I was walking ahead of the others and then when I turned round, they'd gone, yeah? They'd run away from me and I couldn't find them. I was like running everywhere look-ing for them and I tripped and grabbed onto this girl who was like passing to stop myself falling over. She was a real chav, you know, big hoop earrings and trainers with cropped trousers. She stood in front of me and put her hands on her hips and said, "Oi, don't touch me." Then her friend saw me give her a dirty look, so she said to her, "'ere that girl just give you evils". I thought I'd better run away from them after that before they beat me up.'

Kitty had forgotten her sadness in her storytelling. She was playing every part, her voice, I was sure, a perfect mimicry of what she had heard. All of life was *material* to her.

'So then what happened; did you find the others?' I prompted.

'Oh, yes, well, I did eventually, but I was like so upset.'

I hugged her, remembering the cruelty of young girls to each other. Big girls could be just as bad, I thought, thinking about the way the mothers of these same girls behaved towards Ruthie and me.

'Everyone is always horrible to me and I've got no friends,' Kitty sobbed, burying her head in my neck. I wanted to slap Molly and Anna.

'What about Sephy, darling?'

'Sephy doesn't count, she's like my sister.'

'That's the point, sweetheart, if you've got one true friend, a real soul mate, the others don't count. They're not proper friends anyhow if they behave cruelly to you.'

'But I want Molly and Anna to be my friends too.'

One of the conditions of the girls going shopping by themselves was that they had to stay in a group. I never tired of reminding them of this. I phoned Molly's mother.

'This is Chloe, Kitty's mother.'

'Oh, hello,' she answered as if she couldn't quite recall who I was or whether we'd ever met.

I explained the situation. She gave a short, impatient laugh. 'Well, girls will be girls. I can't see what you expect me to do about it.'

The lioness within me stirred and growled, 'As far as I'm concerned, this is bullying and you should talk to Molly about it before it gets any worse.'

'Whatever,' she said and hung up. If she'd been standing in front of me, I would have torn her head off with my Big Cat's teeth.

'Bitch,' I muttered.

'Precisely,' said Kitty, overhearing me. War had been declared. Bullying had broken out across two generations. Kitty and I discussed psychological warfare. It turned out that it was Molly's birthday the next day and girls always brought a cake in on their birthdays. Molly's mum was strictly Marks and Spencer; the only dish she was capable of preparing herself, when she wasn't too busy going to the gym, was a mountain out of a molehill. Jessie, who was two years above, had come home by now, so the three of us baked an exquisite chocolate cake for Kitty to take in. Kitty rehearsed her lines: 'Oops, didn't know it was Molly's birthday, we just felt like giving the class a treat.' The custom was that bought cakes were always ignored in favour of homemade. We embroidered elaborate patterns in icing and wrote *Just Because it's Thursday* across the cake, delighted with our tactics.

'There, that should wind them up good and proper,' I said as I finished writing with a flourish.

Leo almost ruined our plan, bouncing silently into the kitchen on the balls of his feet like a burglar, and preparing to sink a large knife into the cake to cut himself a generous slice. I had to throw myself across the kitchen and unplug him from his iPod to stop him in time.

'No need to shout,' he said. 'I just want a taste.'

'It's for Kitty's school.'

'As usual, everything for Kitty,' he sighed.

I had to make him a sandwich in the shape of a gingerbread man to prove that I loved him just as much. 'Just a small one though,' I said, 'we're all going out for supper tonight, remember?'

We'd taken to going out for a meal on Wednesdays to escape Bea's sullen presence at the dinner table. For some reason, she was always at her worst mid-week. Since Zuzi's arrival and Bea's improved mood, this was no longer strictly necessary, but we'd continued anyhow and Zuzi and Bea had come to expect this weekly opportunity to have their own candlelit dinner *à deux*. The problem was that we were running out of neighbourhood restaurants. Greg was not an easy customer and had defaced most of the restaurant listings in *Eating In Your Own Back Yard*, our local restaurant guide, with a large red cross – rather, I suspect, like those that marked the doors of sixteenth-century plague victims to indicate the presence of death within. Now and again a restaurant would be rehabilitated if it was under new management, but all too often it would go the way of its predecessor and a second cross would be added to the first.

We seated ourselves in Jiminy Cricket, a new pizza joint on Willesden Lane that Ruthie and Richard had recommended. It had an irritatingly cheerful and overwritten menu: 'Try our mouth-watering Cricket Pizza, oodles of melted cheese and spicy sausage, oozing with succulent flavour.'

'I don't want anything,' said Kitty. 'I keep thinking of crickets sitting on their pizza base getting roasted alive in a hot oven.'

Greg was irritably miming a bread knife with which to butter his roll, denoting the absence of one on the table. I opted for a

Garden Salad, 'crunchy, flavoursome vegetables lovingly laid out on crisp wholesome leaves.' They should have added *with a small gleaming jewel of a bug in their centre*, because that's what I found when the salad arrived.

'Excuse me, waiter, could you call the chef over here please,' said Greg with the icy politeness he adopts when he's about to make a scene. I looked at the children and raised an eyebrow – well both eyebrows actually, I've never been able to raise just the one – as if to say 'here we go.' The chef arrived at our table, a young man with tendrils of untidy, and not quite clean, hair escaping from his chef's hat. His check trousers were tight and slightly grubby, his fingers covered in Elastoplasts.

'Could you explain to me how you make your salad?' asked Greg.

The chef looked bemused, 'Sorry?'

'You know, just talk me through the preparation of a salad.'

'Well, chop the vegetables,' he began slowly.

The children were shifting uncomfortably on their chairs in an agony of embarrassment. Greg raised his hand to warn them to remain silent. Jessie, who was still staying with us, hadn't seen Greg in action before. She looked puzzled.

'Yes,' Greg nodded at the chef.

'Wash the lettuce.'

'I beg your pardon?' said Greg, lifting his head and cocking his ears like an attentive hound that senses the fox is near.

'The lettuce,' the chef repeated slowly, shaking his head.

'Yes, but what was the word that came before lettuce?'

The chef scratched his head in a pantomime of thought, 'Um … wash, wash the lettuce.'

'Quite,' said Greg, holding up a finger for emphasis, 'the very word: wash.' He was now attentive dog turned wrathful master as he prepared to shove the chef's face into his mess and hit him on the back of his head with a rolled up newspaper. 'The washing is key wouldn't you say?' Greg said, with an unpleasant accent on the word *washing*. 'So why, might I ask, is there a bug in my wife's salad?'

His erstwhile emphatic finger now swerved to point accusingly at the offending insect, curled up in its *flavoursome* bed, happily unaware of the trouble its quiet presence was causing. The chef whisked the dish away and strode off to the kitchen, muttering imprecations in an unfamiliar language and drawing a finger across his throat in a gesture of violence that needed no translation.

I insisted that we leave after Greg's 'victory'. My youthful profession as a waitress had taught me that the chef's humiliation was likely to find retribution in spitting in our food or worse.

'Why you couldn't just tell the waiter there was a bug in the salad instead of going through that charade, I don't know,' I complained, as I hustled everyone out the door.

'They have to learn,' answered the maniac to whom I had once so foolishly plighted my troth.

We returned home starving, to find the fridge empty and Bea and Zuzi comfortably seated on the kitchen sofa, smacking their lips and patting their full bellies.

'That's it,' I shouted at Greg, 'I'm not going out to dinner with you ever again. From now on, all meals will be consumed on these premises.'

Bea looked alarmed, 'But not on the Wednesdays? This is the Bea and Zuzi night, no?'

I didn't trust myself to speak, so I followed Greg upstairs. He took down the restaurant guide and scored a large red X through Jiminy Cricket's entry, before sitting down to compose a letter to *Eating In Your Own Back Yard*. No doubt he would insist that they remove Jiminy Cricket from their listings. Stalactites and stalagmites began to form in the air around me as I froze in glacial fury and watched him as he wrote, irritatingly scratching away with the quill pen that I now wished I'd never given him. I had become the ice maiden; it would take some days for the thaw to begin. 'Oi Dad, Mum just give you evils,' Kitty said to him over her shoulder as she skipped up to bed.

Chapter Fourteen

FF's Recipe for a Dinner Party

Buy nuts and olives
Open and pour into bowls
Chill wine
Tell guests to prepare and bring the other courses

Becky's time away had convinced her that she and Ivan had to fight for their relationship and give it another chance. I was in two minds about this; it made me feel safer as it helped keep my own relationship with him under control; but at the same time I felt unreasonably jealous. Her return to the marital home presented us with a problem. We had to find new venues for our meetings and had had to resort to stolen hours in hotel bedrooms. Most hotels had rigorous rules about check-in times that didn't fit well with the needs of married lovers.

'Why aren't there any Love Hotels?' I asked Ivan. 'We may have to go and live in Japan, apparently they've got lots there.'

After a few disasters; clashes with candlewick bedspreads, not quite clean sheets, and furious, noisy humping in next-door rooms, Ivan had found a place in Bayswater aptly named Encounters that had become our own little love hotel. It was a pretty, pink, double-fronted Georgian house run, appropriately, by Georgians from Tbilisi and set back in a side street off the Bayswater Road not too far from his house.

I would stock up – for our intermissions – on goodies from the exotic food shops that lined Queensway: hummus, falafel, nuts, olives and bread; things we could eat easily with our fingers or lick off each other's. Sometimes we would spend a couple of hours there over lunchtime; now and again we managed to steal a whole afternoon. I was embarrassed by the behaviour of Mgelika, the receptionist. He gave me significant gap-toothed smiles when we checked in and shook Ivan's hand a little too vigorously as if to suggest what a virile, son of a gun he was, fucking another man's wife. He had passed our room once as we were leaving and had looked openly at the crumpled sheets just visible through the gap in the door. I'd seen him smile wolfishly while giving me an appraising look, his eyes lingering too long on my breasts. It made me feel like a whore who rented rooms by the hour. Ivan told me not to be silly and what did it matter what a stranger thought as long as we could be together.

'Don't forget Rule Four,' Ruthie said when I told her about our new love nest.

I looked at her quizzically.

'*Never pay by credit card.* It's such an easy way to get found out and so many people are so careless about it,' she warned.

There was one unanticipated and unwelcome consequence to my renewed sexual activity, which was almost as damning as a carelessly guarded credit card bill: I had developed cystitis. None of the over-the-counter products could help me, and in desperation I made an appointment to see the nurse at Greg's practice. Risky I know, but I couldn't think where else to go.

'Hello Chloe, have you come to see Greg?' Marjorie, the receptionist asked me brightly as I attempted an inconspicuous entry into the surgery. Naturally she had chosen today of all days to acknowledge that I was Greg's wife. She reached for the telephone.

'No, no, please don't bother him, I'm sure he's very busy,' I said, 'I'm just popping in to ask the nurse something.' She paused, her hand on the phone and looked at me in a way that implied she could see right into my urinary tract, before switching into receptionist mode.

'If you'd just like to take a seat, the nurse will be with you shortly.'

When my name was called, it sounded so loud that I had to stop myself from saying *shush* to the intercom system. I tiptoed along the corridor, clinging to the walls lest Greg should catch sight of me.

'You wouldn't believe how many women in their forties come in with cystitis,' the nurse seemed to shout, her voice determined to carry through the thin wall into Greg's surgery next door. 'It's an epidemic, they're all divorced women who have rediscovered sex with a vengeance. The "honeymoon disease", that's what they call it. Funny that you've got it though, you and Greg having been married for such ages and everything.' She looked at me curiously and added, 'Clearly, there's still life in the old doctor yet. Lucky old you, Henry and I haven't had sex for at least a year.' I laughed nervously and hastily scuttled out, clutching a prescription for antibiotics and terrified that she would say something to Greg.

There is nothing quite so pleasurable as lying in bed in the afternoon in the arms of a man you desire. It was a Friday, the sky was unusually blue for December and the sun, observing its short winter working hours, was making a last brief appearance before retiring for the day. Ivan was sliding a hand up and down my back and I was nuzzling into his neck, inhaling him. His long legs were entwined in mine and I could feel the heat of his thigh between mine, an area that was still throbbing pleasurably after his expert ministrations. We were experiencing those last few precious moments before we had to get up and dress and return regretfully to our real lives when, I'm afraid the L word reared its ugly head in strict contravention of Rule Five in Ruthie's book: *Never fall in love with your lover if you don't intend leaving your husband for him.*

'*Ia liubliu tebia*,' Ivan said.

'*Blu blu blah blah*, what's that mean?'

He laughed. '*Liubliu tebia*. I love you.'

'*Blu blu blah blah*, too,' I said before I could stop myself. Which wasn't the same as actually telling him that I loved him, I reasoned; I had merely spoken nonsense words to him in a language I didn't understand. Illogically, telling Ivan I loved him felt like more of a betrayal of Greg than having sex with him. Apparently it was fine to allow another man and his penis to do what they wanted with me, but saying *I love you* would banish me to purgatory. (Although, the likelihood of such a banishment was looking increasingly more of a foregone conclusion). I stopped further talk of love by kissing Ivan until it was time for us to part.

Was I falling in love? The thought terrified me. I could quite see why it was against Ruthie's rules, and beneath the terror was another feeling, one of tremendous wellbeing and I found myself humming happily as I walked to my car. Couldn't I ignore the fact that I was a married woman for a little while and simply relive the past few hours I had spent with my lover? *My lover.* I turned the words around my tongue as one might a delicious sweetmeat and felt like an irresistible woman of the world, a Mata Hari, a temptress. Chloe Zhivago, thinner and more beautiful now than she's ever been. Tra-la-la-la-la. The last *la* seemed to stick in my throat as the words that haunt every Jew in the face of happiness or pleasure rang in my head: 'It won't last'.

As I got into my car, my thoughts were interrupted by my mobile. *One more dance with you momma,* it sang to me; Leo had replaced my ring tone with one of his hip-hop numbers; fortunately it was more melodic and less violent than usual. (I panicked slightly at the thought that I must have left my phone unattended long enough for him to have been able to do so). I thought it would be Ivan calling to say goodbye again, one of us was always sure to phone or text the other after we'd been together, eager to maintain contact.

'Hello,' I said, my voice warm with the intimacy of our recent coupling.

'Just had FF on the phone,' said Greg's voice, making me start. 'She's summoned us to dinner at her place at eight o'clock next Tuesday to meet her new bloke. I tried to wriggle out of it, but somehow found myself promising her that we'd both go. Ruthie and Richard are going and so's that Russian chap, Ivan, and his wife. Apparently you're in charge of the starter and Ruthie is doing the main course.'

'And what about pudding?' I was so shocked, I couldn't think what else to say.

'She's buying a cake or something from the patisserie. You've got to hand it to her, no one else could get away with inviting people over and then getting them to bring their own dinner.'

'Do we have to go?' I panicked.

'I can't win,' said Greg. 'You're the one that's always complaining I never go anywhere. She's your friend; I thought you'd want to go.'

'No, that's fine, of course we'll go.'

After ringing off I sat in the car in a state of alarm; phrases like *chickens coming home to roost* and *people getting their just deserts* came to mind. This last seemed rather appropriate in the circumstances and I laughed hollowly at the idea that the dessert was the only thing that FF would be serving up herself.

Well now, that would be a cosy scenario, my husband and my lover around the same dinner table. It was unconscionable, but since Greg had already committed us, I quickly texted Ivan to warn him not to accept. *Too late*, he wrote back, *Becky has just got off phone from telling her we'd love to go.*

'You'll just have to brazen it out,' said Ruthie when I phoned her in panic.

'Why does it feel so awful for me to be at a dinner table with my husband and lover? I mean, I've just been in bed with my lover doing all manner of intimate things and somehow that feels sort of acceptable.'

'I think it's because if your husband knew he was your lover and knew that others knew, it would be humiliating for him, as if you were taunting him with it in public. Whereas if you're discreet and your affair is kept separate from your everyday life then it's— well, not forgivable exactly, but less unforgivable.'

'It's a minefield, isn't it? The weird thing is that I'd be pleased if they liked each other.'

'Be very careful, Chlo, you may give all sorts of stuff away without being aware of it. Body language, significant glances … People can tell things about you, sometimes things you don't yet know yourself.'

'Thanks for the reassurance,' I said wryly.

I don't know what devil got into me, but I even started feeling quite excited about the prospect; there was something about the danger of it all that made me feel alive. Suddenly I could understand why people took the risks they did; why Members of Parliament cavorted with known prostitutes, why celebrities took drugs in front of strangers. It fuelled a dangerous need to heighten experience; it turned life into an exciting game of Russian roulette, and I was lucky enough to have my own real live Russian to play it with.

On the appointed day, I sifted through my many recipe books to find something to make for a starter. *Buckwheat blinis with smoked salmon, sour cream and caviar.* Perfect.

I went to the Volga for some ingredients. Volodya was in his customary pose, leaning back in his chair, feet up on his desk, reading *Doctor Zhivago* with an unlit cigarette clamped between his teeth. He looked up at the sound of the door.

'Which bit are you up to?' I asked.

'The part where Zhivago and Lara are having their affair and Tonya hasn't yet realised what's going on.'

'That's what I've never quite understood,' I said, 'I mean, Zhivago loves Tonya so much and from a young age, so how come he falls in love with Lara?'

'It's possible to love two people at the same time,' Volodya shrugged, looking at me pointedly.

And apparently to have dinner with them at the same time too. I avoided his gaze by busying myself with searching for something in my bag.

'More riddles?' he asked.

'No, today I have actually come to spend some money. I need buckwheat and caviar.'

He sold me a tin of salmon caviar; bright orange balls that glistened, which he assured me were tastier than the usual black sturgeon eggs and much cheaper too.

'Russian love, *Russkaia liubov',* it suits you,' he said, his eyes searching my face. '*Sem'ia,* that's what's important Chloe, family.' He held me by my shoulders and turned me to him. 'Be happy, enjoy yourself, but don't ever forget that.'

It seemed no one could talk to me without urging caution or offering advice. He filled a little plastic bag with the chocolates with squirrels on them and tucked them into my hand. 'Here, take these *Belochki*, delicious with tea or coffee at the end of a meal, a little taste of home for your friend.' Leaning behind me, he dipped his hand into a small wicker basket, took out a different chocolate, unwrapped it and popped it in my mouth. It was delicious, a nut brittle covered in chocolate.

'It's called *Gril'iazh*, very popular in my country.'

'What's Russian for delicious?'

'*Vkusno*.'

'*Vkusno*,' I repeated, storing it up for an intimate moment when I could offer it to Ivan like a gift, an endearment in his native tongue.

I got home, ready to roll up my sleeves and get cracking on the blini and found FF lying on my kitchen sofa. She was wearing a neck brace.

'What happened?' I asked.

'I cricked my neck shagging Jeremy. I was on top and trying to keep my face from sagging, so I arched my back and my neck really far back to keep everything taut. I must have been a little over enthusiastic.'

'Perhaps we *femmes d'un certain age* should stick to the missionary position,' I said, trying not to laugh.

'It doesn't matter what *you* look like,' said FF, 'I mean it's only Greg, you don't have to impress him.'

'Yes, yes of course,' I replied flustered, 'but still, I have to keep him from straying off with some firm-faced young thing.' I'd nearly given myself away; I would have to be more careful.

'Why did you ask Ivan and Becky to dinner?' I asked in what I hoped was a casual tone.

'They're my new best friends and I want to ask him to do the drawings for the new book. I thought sexy cartoons of people making love would work well. Now I really have to dash,' said FF, getting up to go as if I were detaining her. 'I've got to nip down to Saigon and get my nails done.' (This was her moniker for the proliferating nail bars that were run by the Vietnamese. She called Stoke Newington, 'Istanbul' because of all the Turkish shops there; Acton was 'Tokyo' and Southall, 'New Delhi'). 'Those girls in Saigon have impossibly small bottoms,' she added, 'they make me feel enormous. Still, it's very restful and silent there, each of us is completely unintelligible to the other so there's no point talking, just what I need before tonight.' She blew me a kiss. 'See you later.'

'Can't wait,' I muttered, as I closed the door behind her.

FF lived in a large double-fronted house in an area she called West Hampstead and Greg insisted should really be called East Kilburn. It had recently become popular with the arty, muso, bohemian set who couldn't quite run to Notting Hill Gate or Primrose Hill prices. Just before we'd set out, she'd rung up and asked us to pick up the dessert on our way as she had too much to do. Going into her pristine, cement-topped kitchen (cement was the latest *dernier cri* in work surfaces apparently), it was hard to tell what it was that had kept her so busy: the only evidence that she was expecting guests were a few bowls of olives and nuts.

'I'm furious,' she announced. 'Jeremy phoned literally five minutes ago to say that he can't come. He's had to go to Cardiff; one of his producers has been arrested for assaulting someone and he has to sort it out. Honestly, the whole point of this evening was so that you could all finally get to meet him.'

I was busy comforting her, sitting her down and pouring her a drink when Ivan and Becky arrived.

Becky was smaller and prettier than her photograph had suggested, but there was a slight wetness about her mouth, which made you want to dab her with a tissue. It wasn't the moistness of sexual promise; rather a prelude to overly wet kisses. I was able to overlook this minor flaw since I wasn't planning to kiss her. I found that I took to her immediately, a possibility that I hadn't considered.

'Ivan and I are barely speaking,' she said. 'We got lost on the way here; as usual he wouldn't stop and ask anyone the way.'

'Greg's just the same,' I said. 'He would rather drive round and round for hours than face the ignominy of asking for help. Does testosterone render men incapable of asking for directions?'

'It drives me insane, and the kids too,' Becky said. 'When they were younger, they'd lean out of the car window and wave at passers-by shouting for help – "we're lost, but our father won't stop and ask for directions."'

'Did it work?'

'No, it made Ivan more determined than ever not to stop for help; he just drove faster.'

We laughed, women united by the foibles of men. Becky was friendly and funny. I'd have been furious on her behalf about her husband playing away from home if it hadn't been me he was playing with. It was a shame I couldn't just ask her if I could borrow him, as a child borrows a toy from a friend. Couldn't I just have a go on her husband? I'd promise to give him back when I was finished. *Come on, Becky, don't be mean, let's have a go on him.* That's what swinging is I suppose: having a go on other people's husbands and wives and giving them back nicely when you've finished.

FF was so busy behaving like a guest that Ruthie and I had to take charge or we'd never have been fed.

'What do you think?' I whispered to Ruthie as she helped me serve the first course. She swayed slightly as she slapped pieces of smoked salmon haphazardly on blini. She had been D.O.A. (drunk on arrival).

'He's gorgeous,' she said. 'His wife's nice too,' she added dryly.

FF's one concession to playing host was to organise the seating and she had placed Ivan next to me. It took every ounce of self-control to stop myself from intertwining calves and ankles with him under the table. Greg was sitting next to Becky and they seemed to be getting on famously.

Ruthie threw me meaningful looks over the table. She followed me as I cleared the plates.

'Rule number six,' she said, *'deny and lie.'* I looked at her questioningly. 'Unless you are actually caught *in flagrante*, deny everything.' I nodded obediently. 'Mind you,' she added, 'the way you two are looking at each other, I wouldn't be surprised if you treated everyone to a live sex show a little later.'

'Is it really that obvious?'

'To me, yes. But then, this is one of my special subjects.'

'You don't think Greg or Becky suspect?'

'No.' She paused before adding carefully, 'not yet.'

FF spent most of the evening either in another room on the phone to Jeremy or at the table in conversation with Richard about the sexual habits of the ancient world, in case there was anything she could plunder and use in her new book. The rest of us were pretty much left to fend for ourselves. After the main course (Ruthie's grilled halibut with black bean sauce and wild rice) Ruthie started a discussion about marriage. She'd added a couple more glasses of wine to the quantity she'd already drunk, in addition, no doubt, to a few little visits from her Colombian friend if her frequent trips to the bathroom were anything to judge by. Richard was watching her while twisting his lower lip between thumb and forefinger as he always does when anxious. I knew I'd have to have a serious talk with him sooner or later and betray Ruthie's secret: I couldn't see her getting back on track without his help.

'The thing is,' she was saying, 'marriages aren't meant to last as long as all of ours have. Ten years used to be about the normal length of time for a marriage. By then we women would have died in childbirth and you lot,' she waved an arm vaguely in the direction of the men round the table, 'you lot would all have died in a duel or something.'

'Perhaps I should challenge Ivan to one,' said Greg as he opened another bottle of wine. I choked on the mouthful of food I'd just taken. 'Fishbone,' I gasped, when I could speak again.

'Why me?' said Ivan calmly.

'Why not? I'm sure we can find something to fight over,' said Greg. I held my breath nervously. 'Let's see,' Greg continued. 'What, for instance, are your views on the countryside?' I relaxed and took a soothing gulp of wine from my glass; the danger had passed.

This was one of Greg's pet subjects and he loved to spar. 'Life is so dull when everyone agrees with each other all the time,' he always said.

'I love the countryside,' said Ivan.

'No, I mean foxhunting,' Greg persisted. Here we go, I thought wearily.

'Very useful way of applying Darwinian theory,' said Ivan, his eyes meeting Greg's. 'The foxes that get caught are the old and the sick.'

Off they went, back and forth. Greg held forth on the disgrace of killing for sport, Ivan waxed lyrical on the joys of hunting.

'I'm the only one here who is country born and bred.' Becky tried to make herself heard. But the men weren't interested in anyone who had real experience of the subject and their voices merely grew louder and drowned us out. Ivan interrupted Becky every time she tried to say something, just as Greg did me. She and I looked at each other and shrugged. Our husbands were more similar than I had first thought, although on balance, as I observed Ivan's relationship with Becky, I couldn't help feeling that Greg was nicer to me than he was to her. When she spoke, he looked impatient and rarely met her eyes with his own.

'It's an important part of the economic and social fabric of rural living. I'm not talking about, what do you call them, toffs, but about ordinary people whose livelihood has been connected with fox-hunting for generations,' Ivan was saying.

'All this stuff about how many jobs would be lost is beside the point,' countered Greg, 'the by-product of progress is sometimes the loss of jobs. The people affected will just have to find another way to earn a living. You have to do what's right, and fox hunting isn't right.'

'Foxes are pests, and anyhow, hunting only eliminates three percent of the fox population,' said Ivan.

'Well, why not sanction murder while you're at it; you could shoot a few human beings and say that it only eliminates a very small percentage of the human population. A death is a death,' answered Greg.

'Look,' said Ivan, pointing at FF's Siamese cat, which was curled up on a doormat, neatly illustrating that early reading sentence *the cat sat on the mat*. 'People keep cats, and they take care of any mice infestation they may have.'

'Actually,' I interrupted, 'our cat doesn't, she's anorexic.'

'Oh who cares, foxes, shmoxes,' Ruthie interrupted loudly and she started to cry in great gulping sobs that astounded us all. 'It's all so fucking irrelevant,' she said, staggering to her feet. Richard looked at me helplessly; he's not much good in a crisis, so I quickly hustled her out of the room and up to FF's bedroom so that she could lie down.

'Sorry Chlo, bit pissed,' she said as she turned over and passed out.

Ivan cornered me on the stairs on my way back down.

'Someone will see us,' I said alarmed.

He pulled me to him and I could feel him, warm against my thigh, a reminder of pleasure shared. It was almost unbearably exciting. Forget Russian roulette, this was akin to outright suicide. He put his hand down the front of my trousers and caressed me before pulling it out and slowly sucking the finger that had touched me while holding my eyes with his own. I flushed with a mixture of shock and arousal. If anyone saw us Rule six would be useless. Summoning all the self-control I could muster, I pushed past him and ran back down the stairs. FF's face appeared round the doorjamb looking quizzical. 'What have I missed?' she asked.

'Just showing Ivan where the upstairs loo is,' I shrugged casually.

As we were driving home, Greg said, 'Ivan and Becky are quite nice. I mean, Ivan's a bit fond of himself, but he's quite an interesting bloke. I might go out for a drink with him.'

I tried to hide my unease and busied myself with looking for the latest weather forecast on the car radio to deflect Greg's attention. That's all I needed, my husband and lover out for a cosy little drink together. Perhaps they'd like to discuss my performance in bed.

'Ruthie's not in great shape,' I said, changing the subject.

'Probably perimenopausal,' said Greg in that infuriating way that men have of undermining women's emotions by attributing any upset to hormonal fluctuations.

'She's only forty-three, for God's sake.'

'Lots of women start getting symptoms at your and Ruthie's age.'

'Good, well, I'll start to look forward to that then, shall I?' I said crisply.

I'd been so aroused by Ivan that I contemplated seducing Greg when he came to bed, even though it didn't seem right for Greg to finish the job that Ivan had started on the stairs earlier. I know that I wouldn't have been the first person who has thought of another man while making love to her husband, nor the last. While I was wrestling with my conscience, the sound of Greg's heavy snoring made the decision for me. I'd always thought of myself as a decent and honourable person, but I seemed to have developed a natural talent for wickedness. Was this what happened once one's toes inched over the invisible boundary that separated good behaviour from bad? The first step was not the final one, merely the beginning of the unavoidable path towards ruin; one's own and everyone else's. I lay awake for some time, searching with my treacherous, boundary-crossing feet for smooth, cool spaces in the sheets to soothe me to sleep.

'I'm so sorry,' Ruthie wailed on the phone the next morning. 'I woke up in such a spiral of shame. That's it, no more, I promise. I've erased Carlos's phone number from my mobile, my palm pilot and my computer.'

'Yes, that's all very well, but what about from your head?' Ruthie has an uncanny facility for storing phone numbers. She can still recall the phone number of Benny Tart, the first boy she kissed. (Everyone's first love seems to have a ridiculous name like Amanda Blow or Jimmy Quick).

'I will boil my head in a vat of oil to make it disappear from there too,' said Ruthie full of contrition. 'I was a bit overwrought and had already had three glasses of wine before I even got there last night. I had such a vile day at work yesterday, setting objectives for all the people who work for me. It took hours and David Gibfuck was insistent that they all had to be done and signed by the end of the day even though I'm leaving. It's such time-wasting nonsense. "What's your objective?" "To do my job well", "Oh, that's a surprise, most people put 'to do my job really badly'". It's all such bollocks; thank God I haven't got long to go. Then when I came home, Atlas was crying and when I asked him what was wrong, he told me he thinks he's gay.'

'It's probably just a phase; most boys go through it at about his age,' I said in an attempt to comfort her. 'Anyway, it could be quite nice if he was, he'll co-ordinate your accessories for you; you know, you won't be losing a son, you'll be gaining a daughter.'

'That's true,' she laughed. 'I know I'm not meant to mind, and of course in theory I don't, but all I could think when he told me was that he might get AIDS, he wouldn't ever give me any grandchildren, and one day he might be a lonely old man with no one to care for him.'

'Oh darling, you should have told me. I'm so sorry, I've been so self-obsessed with all this Ivan business. Anyway, there's no insurance for any of us against a lonely old age, straight or gay, and even if he is gay, he could still father children. Look at that gay couple that live in Manchester who've got two sets of surrogate twins. That should be a comfort.'

'I'll be fine. By the way, Ivan is very sexy, but you need to watch it.'

'I know, I'm so relieved that the evening's over; it was terribly nerve-wracking, but also exciting which made it even more worrying.'

'I'm not sure whose addiction is more dangerous, yours or mine,' she said.

Chapter Fifteen

Chloe Zhivago's recipe for Falafel

1 lb cooked, drained chickpeas
1/2 cup breadcrumbs
1 egg
1 large onion, finely chopped
2 tbsp. finely chopped parsley
1 tsp. ground cumin

1/2 tsp. ground coriander (or use
   fresh instead)
2 cloves crushed garlic
1 tsp. salt
olive oil for frying

Combine chickpeas, onion, parsley, beaten egg and spices. Mix in blender. Place in a bowl and add breadcrumbs until mixture forms a small ball without sticking to your hands.

Form chickpea dough into small balls about one inch in diameter. Flatten balls slightly and fry until golden brown on both sides. Drain falafel balls on paper towels.

Serve in pita bread with chopped tomato, cucumber, lettuce and onion and some tahini and/or chilli sauce.

'How's the girlfriend-hunting going?' I asked Leo. He was at that stage of adolescent development known as self-imposed-solitary-confinement-in-bedroom. His room looked as if it had been constructed as a film set for the bedroom of a teenage boy. The director wouldn't have needed to change a thing. There were dirty clothes in piles on the floor, bowls encrusted with the remnants of cereal, empty cups and socks on every surface. The atmosphere was pervaded by a stale doggy smell, *eau du teenage boy*. On Leo's rare appearances in other parts of the house, his ears were usually stoppered up with headphones, rendering him inaccessible.

My head had also been stoppered up recently, with the imaginings of my own secret life. When not actually with Ivan, I was usually replaying the time we had spent together on a loop. As a result, I realised I hadn't talked to Leo properly for weeks. I had become disassociated from my everyday life and spent all my time in my adulterous, leafy suburbs, just as Dad had predicted. I had become, in short, a bad wife and mother and was in danger of turning into a bad psychotherapist too. I was seeking to make amends, but my opening gambit was badly judged.

'Who told you I wanted a girlfriend? It was Kitty, wasn't it? Bitch, I told her to keep quiet about it. I'm going to get her for this,' he got up to find her and turn his threat into reality.

'No, no,' I backtracked. Damn, now I'd betrayed a confidence; 'I just thought you were probably at that age.'

'Oh, yeah, right. Look Mum, I really can't talk to you about this sort of stuff,' he said.

'Why not? I'm a girl, I know about these things.'

He looked at me disbelievingly, 'Yeah, right. Look, it's not like it was in your day.'

'This is still my day,' I muttered through clenched teeth.

Leo laughed shortly. 'Yeah, right.'

If he said that again, I might have to hit him. Affecting a casual tone, I said, 'But it is girls that you like isn't it?'

'What do you mean?'

'I mean, girls rather than boys. It's fine if it is boys, I just thought we should have a chat about it.'

'Look Mum, I know that Atlas thinks he's a poofter and good luck to him. That's fine if he is, I don't care, he's just Atlas and he's my mate whatever. But it's girls for me. Okay? End of.'

I was ashamed at how relieved I felt.

'Now if you don't mind,' Leo said, 'I'd like to carry on reading my porn mags and smoking crack in peace.' I looked horrified. 'I'm joking,' he said. 'I'm going round to see Grandpa to get some advice.' As I was leaving, he looked up and said quietly, 'It's not easy being fifteen, you know.'

'I know, sweetheart.' I came back in and kissed him. He allowed me to hug him and rested his head on my shoulder for a moment.

'It's quite hard being forty-three too,' I said softly, as I closed the door.

I hadn't seen much of Sammy recently. His determined sleuthing on Madge's behalf had been taking up most of his time, and I think he'd also been seeing quite a bit of a Spanish girl who worked in the Tapas bar round the corner. He'd always been secretive about his love life. I found him now on the stairs, with a tear-stained face and a tattered, yellowing newspaper cutting in his hand. Our staircase, it seemed, had become the designated crying area. I sat down next to him and put my arm around his shoulders. I didn't say anything; he would speak when he felt able to. As it turned out, I didn't need him to say a word, because when I looked at the cutting it told me everything I needed to know:

FATHER AND CHILDREN SUFFOCATE IN CAR

Reg Jackson, 31, and his two children, Rosie, 7, and Jimmy, 5, were found dead in their car from carbon monoxide poisoning early on Monday morning. 'It looked like they were all asleep,' said Joyce Hinkin, 35, who lived next door to the tragic family. The car, a white Ford Cortina, was parked in a quiet alleyway near the house. 'I was taking a shortcut back home with my shopping when I saw them,' said Mrs Hinkin. 'They seemed such a nice family. What could make someone do such a terrible thing?' Reg's wife and the children's mother, Madge Jackson, had gone out for the day, leaving her two children in their father's care. She is being comforted by friends in the hospital where she is being treated for shock.

I carefully took the cutting from Sammy's hand. It was dated Tuesday December 12 1969.

'Where did you find this?' I asked.

'It was in Madge's flat. I've been tracing them, going to various authorities, looking for birth certificates and I was getting close. But then, today, I was at Madge's having a cup of tea and I saw it pinned to the wall with lots of other pieces of paper. It turns out that she's known all along. Well, some part of her has, but she

167

must find it too painful to believe, so most of the time she forgets and thinks they're still alive.'

'How awful. Can you imagine?' I felt like crying. 'What about Armie?'

'I'm trying to find out what happened to him,' said Sammy.

Ruthie called round to apologise once again for her behaviour the night before. 'I've just bumped into Lou,' she said. 'She's got a new man and she looks fabulous.'

'Really, who?' I was balanced precariously on a chair looking for a vase on the top of the cupboard. I'd found a lot of dust instead and a broken hash water-pipe. Whose was it? Greg's? Leo's?

'Someone she met on ushag.com, an internet dating site.'

'Is it really called that?'

'It might as well be,' laughed Ruthie.

'Blimey,' I said. 'The internet is the most successful pimp of all time. The number of people who subscribe to those things is amazing.'

'Anyhow, it seems this chap knows you, he's called Les Fallick.'

'Les?' I paused, tracing a pattern in the dust with a finger. 'I used to know a Gus Fallick.'

'That's right, Lou said he'd changed his name.'

I couldn't help feeling if I were him, it wouldn't have been my first name that I'd have felt needed changing.

'Last I heard, he was living in Glasgow and was married with kids.'

'Yes, well he's divorced now and there seems to be a general re-cycling of husbands going on at the moment,' said Ruthie dryly.

'That can only be good for the environment, surely?'

'Mmm, I might have to put Richard outside the front door in a green box and see what happens. Apparently Les is still living in Glasgow so they only see each other at weekends, Lou goes up there when James has the kids and Les comes down when she has them. Meanwhile, during the week they have constant internet sex.'

Of course! The Internet would be the perfect tool for his silver tongue. I was delighted that he was still putting his remarkable talent to good use and doubtless, thanks to the Net, had been able to give pleasure to thousands of women around the globe.

Ruthie was feeling a little better about her cocaine habit; she'd discovered that it was a recognised syndrome: she was a MICCA – Middle Class Cocaine Abuser.

'It makes me feel much more comfortable to know that I'm a statistic and that I've got a name,' she said. 'Apparently there are loads of us. FF first got me started on this cocaine thing you know, even before the girls in the office; it was when she was writing her celibacy book. You know how she thinks she's a twenty-first century philosopher?'

I nodded wearily.

'Well, she was experimenting with cocaine for her Art, doing her Timothy Leary explorer of the mind thing. She found it tremendously useful for exploring the inner workings of her psyche or some such crap. Anyhow, she's given it up now she's back in the saddle: it's no good for orgasms; makes it hard to have one she tells me, which is good for boys, but not so good for girls.'

Ruthie pushed her hair out of her eyes and realigned her pleats; her Issey Miyake was looking crumpled, an outward manifestation of her inner state, the disintegration of a uniform she would soon no longer need.

'I really am going to stop now, Chlo. I've been reading up on it and so many people die in Colombia in drug wars that it feels immoral to be taking it. Apparently, for every gram of cocaine that makes its way onto a dinner-party table, one person dies. I've made myself visualise each line as a trail of blood that I'm snorting up my nose. It's really put me off.'

'Be a good magazine article, Cocaine Housewives,' I said.

'That's a great idea. In fact, I might write it myself as a freelancer for a rival magazine now that my mag's dumped me.' Ruthie looked cheerier than she had for weeks.

'Why did you get so into it?' I asked.

'It was fun and I needed some fun.'

'It didn't look as though you were having much fun last night.'

'In actual fact, it was only fun in the beginning. It quickly got sad and desperate. I'll have to think of another way to have fun.'

'I hope my way of having fun doesn't get sad and desperate too quickly,' I said, thinking of my trysts with Ivan.

Ivan and I were lying in bed at Encounters, eating falafel in pita with chilli sauce. A little of the sauce had run down Ivan's chin and I was licking it off. Mgelika was making me feel increasingly uncomfortable. He'd taken to kissing me wetly on each cheek in greeting as if we were old friends and had just knocked on the door for the third time, entering with his passkey before we'd had time to answer on the flimsy pretext that he thought we had called for him. Luckily, we'd been pausing for breath at the time and not actually at it. Encounters was history, we needed a new venue.

'Becky really liked you,' Ivan said.

'Greg liked you too.'

'Maybe he will stage his own death à la Chernyshevsky after all and then we can get married,' Ivan said. (Could I really imagine myself married to Ivan, a man who was not the father of my children?) We discussed whether or not our spouses' liking for each other made us feel more or less guilty. There was a part of me that was pleased Greg liked Ivan. It was a curious validation of my own good taste. It would have been worse somehow if the man with whom I was cuckolding him were someone he didn't respect; I needed his approval, even if he was unaware of giving it. Objectively, it was deeply immoral to have a relationship with each other's spouses, but it felt strangely natural to want the people who were important to us to like, and even approve of, each other.

'I want to spend the night with you,' Ivan said, drawing my head onto his chest.

'Me too,' I said. It was becoming harder and harder to get up, get dressed, and re-enter our married lives.

I drove home feeling melancholy. *Why aren't you my wife?* Ivan texted me. *I was just wondering the same thing,* I texted back. *We have to get away for a few days together,* he wrote. Even now my skin bore the memory of his touch; it was as if he touched me still. I clutched my mobile phone tightly; it had become the umbilical cord that bound me to Ivan when we couldn't be together, permitting us the luxury of contact at any time. Textual intercourse; it was the next best thing. I guarded my phone jealously, never letting it out of my sight; it was the source both of my pleasure and, should it fall into the wrong hands, my potential downfall.

I phoned Dad.

'Who is this please?'

I laughed; he always had the ability to cheer me up. 'Why do I feel so sad after I've been with my lover?'

'A common phenomenon,' he said.

'How can I even be discussing this with you? You're my father.'

'You must have been very badly brought up. It's post-coital *tristesse*. Surely you know about that; it's a recognised syndrome, there's a French word for it and everything.'

'That makes me feel better. One thing Dad, why am I bothered by Ivan's slight coldness towards his wife?' I told him about our dinner at FF's.

'Is that so surprising? He is having an affair with another woman after all, so his marriage must hardly be perfect.'

'True. It just worried me for some reason.'

'There's a saying: You can know a man by how he is in his cups, how he is with money and in his anger. Perhaps it should add: how he is with his wife.'

'Yes, well that's what concerns me, although I suppose he could think the same thing about how I am with Greg.'

'You're not planning on running away with him are you?' Dad asked. I could hear a note of concern in his voice.

'No, of course not.' Was I?

'Good. See you later then, darling.' He was coming for supper.

How long could I go on like this? I lost myself in a reverie of possibilities. What if I were to divorce Greg? I didn't think I could bear those lonely Wednesday nights and alternate weekends assigned to fathers. There was a joke, Q: *What does a Danish woman think when she meets a man?* A: *Is that the man I want my children to spend every other weekend with?* I wasn't like that; as a Jewish mother, I was programmed to keep the family together at all costs. What if Greg were to disappear instead? You read stories like that in the papers all the time, quoting bewildered and abandoned wives. 'He only popped out for a pint of milk, said he'd be gone ten minutes and that was the last time I saw him, it's been seven months now.' It was what his own father had done, after all. Perhaps such behaviour was genetic. I was horrified by my disloyalty but comforted myself with the knowledge that I wasn't nearly as bad as Camus, who wrote that all normal people sometimes wished their loved ones were actually dead. I didn't want that, I had merely fleetingly wished for Greg to disappear. Of course I didn't really mean it and these black thoughts were merely a sign that I loved Greg, weren't they? The thing was I just wasn't *in* love with him anymore. I absent-mindedly sang along to the car radio which Kitty always kept tuned to a pop station. It was a song about being a bitch and a lover, a sinner and a saint. I was in trouble: pop songs had become pregnant with meaning for me once again. The words summed up exactly what it was that I'd been trying to tell Gina at her last session: a fundamentally good person is capable of bad behaviour. It was an analysis that applied perfectly to me too.

As I turned into our road, I spotted Sammy helping Madge tie more rags to the railings outside her flat.

'I hang these here so Jimmy and Rosie will be able to find my house,' Madge said. 'They love all my silks and satins, they call them their treasure.' She ran her fingers up and down the rich golds, reds and purples of the fabrics that shimmered like flags in the breeze.

I put an arm around her shoulders, and was again aware of her bony lack of flesh. I held her for a brief moment, surprised by her smell – she smelt fresh and clean, of rosewater. She lifted her head and looked at me with her clear, green gaze.

'Be careful what you wish for, Chloe,' she said at last.

Was she inside my head? 'I didn't really wish it and anyway, I'm not as bad as Albert Camus,' I almost blurted back. Had she wished for a similar thing herself? Could she once have hoped that Reg would vanish and leave her free to love Armie?

Madge smoothed my hair out of my eyes with her soft hand. She looked old, her expression heavy with the sorrow of having so long taken refuge from the truth in madness. The passage of time means nothing to memory, which brings events closer to us or pushes them further away at its whim. Time is elastic, a thing of our imagining, and has meaning only in subjective experience. Seconds, minutes, hours, days, weeks, months and years signified nothing to Madge. Her children's deaths were an event that had just occurred. Thirty-five years, the time that had elapsed since then, had done nothing to diminish her pain or her loss. She was no more able to face reality now than she had been all those years before.

Now she took me by the hand and led me inside her flat. It was cleaner and neater than I expected: one big room with a bathroom off it. Papers and clothes were stacked neatly in piles and a lonely cup and plate were draining next to the sink in the kitchen area. A tea towel celebrating a faded summer long ago in Bognor Regis hung neatly from a hook on the wall. A small single bed, a sign that all hope of intimacy had been abandoned forever, stood beneath the window. It had been carefully made and was covered with a threadbare blue and yellow patchwork quilt. By the bed was a small, framed photograph. From where I was standing, I could just make out the smiling faces of two children, neatly dressed in round-collared coats. An ironing board occupied the centre of the room; on it stood two piles of white knickers, one ironed, the other waiting its turn. Madge followed my eyes.

'It's very important to be clean. Very important. Children need a clean home.'

Out of the corner of my eye, I saw a movement; it seemed to mirror the pure white of Madge's laundry. It was a dove.

'He's got a message for me,' said Madge. The dove flew over to her and settled on her shoulder; she stroked the back of its head with a forefinger and its chest puffed out with pleasure. Twitching its small, black-eyed head from side to side, it emitted deep-throated cooing sounds.

'What's it saying?' I asked.

'Can't you hear?' she answered softly. 'He's saying, "find Armie."'

I glanced at Sammy, who had come in quietly and was looking out of the window and holding himself very still and quiet in that Buddhist way of his. I was beginning to feel that I had stepped into a remake of *Mary Poppins* with all this talking birds business, and was half-surprised that Dick Van Dyke didn't come whooshing down the chimney and emerge sooty-faced and singing from the fireplace. But who knows, perhaps the birds really did talk to Madge … Sammy and I left her with the promise that we would help her find Armie, and set off arm in arm down the road together. As we walked, we quietly chanted one of Dad's old army marching rhymes to keep us in step:

> Left, left, I had a good job and I left
> Right, right, it serves me jolly well right.

It occurred to me that I should have taught Ruthie this before she behaved in a manner that had led to her redundancy. Unfortunately, it was too late now.

'Can we invite Madge for Christmas lunch?' asked Sammy.

I'd barely thought about Christmas and it was just over a week away. I'd have to go into whirling dervish mode to organise presents and food in time.

'Yes,' I said, 'of course. Let's just check with the others first.'

We had a family confab at supper that night and everyone agreed that Christmas was a time for waifs and strays and Madge should be invited.

'What shall we eat this year?' asked Dad as he did every year. 'A goose?'

'Yuk, no thanks,' said Leo.

'Too fatty,' said Greg.

'In my country we always to have the carp fish on the night before the Christmas,' said Bea.

I shuddered, recalling the oily carp that swarmed like piranhas tearing at flesh in the reservoir near Sammy's tepee in Spain. It was a local sport – throwing stale bread into the water and watching the carp's feeding frenzy.

'If we're going to be such Jews for Jesus, why don't we go the whole hog, so to speak, and have roast suckling pig,' Dad suggested.

'Very funny. No, we'll have turkey as usual, but I'll roast a ham too if it'll make you feel more irreverent,' I said.

'And I make the carp fish for the night before,' said Bea firmly.

I usually enjoyed Christmas, but I wasn't looking forward to it this year, as it would mean that Ivan and I wouldn't be able to see each other for at least a week. We'd be too firmly in the bosoms of our respective families. His son, in his final year at university, and daughter, who worked in Paris, were both coming home.

In the event, Madge didn't come. She told Sammy she had to stay in her flat in case Jimmy and Rosie came home and he couldn't persuade her otherwise. After lunch (turkey and roast ham with all the trimmings), while the others lay bloated in front of the living room TV, I crept back down to the kitchen to call Ivan.

'I want to hold you in my arms,' he said.

'Me too. I'm really missing you.'

'Come and meet me now, just for an hour,' he said.

'It's impossible. It would look far too suspicious.'

A noise behind me made me jump. It was Greg.

'OK then, Happy Christmas, talk to you soon.' I said far too brightly, and hung up.

'Who were you talking to?' asked Greg.

I felt the colour draining from my face and tried not to shake. I had to think fast.

'When? Oh, you mean just then? That was only FF calling to say hello.'

'What would look too suspicious?' Greg said.

'What do you mean?' I feigned ignorance.

'I heard you say, "it would look too suspicious".' He wasn't going to let this go.

'Did I? Oh, yeah, um, she said why didn't I get some botox for the New Year to look younger, so I said I couldn't because you'd be far too suspicious and notice immediately.'

Not perfect, I grant you, since Greg rarely noticed anything about my appearance, but it seemed to appease him. He shrugged in an uninterested sort of way and put the kettle on for tea.

'Can I go and stay in your tepee in Spain?' I asked Sammy later that evening while I was making cold turkey sandwiches. He was playing the same few notes over and over on a small wooden pipe.

He paused, took it out of his mouth and ran his thumb up its smoothness.

'Mango wood,' he said. 'It's sacred to Hindus because Prajapati, the Lord of Creatures, was changed into a mango tree.'

'Really,' I said impatiently. I wasn't in the mood for Eastern mysticism.

'When Hindu believers die, their bodies are burned on pyres and the firewood of choice is mango wood because it is supposed to have an everlasting heat.'

'Lovely.' I looked at him expectantly, 'Well, can I go and stay?'

'Of course,' he answered, raising his eyes to meet mine. 'Alone?'

'Don't ask,' I said, 'it's much better if you don't know.'

Chapter Sixteen

Gem lettuce with garlic and walnuts

Two heads of gem lettuce, washed and dried
Ten unpeeled cloves of garlic, roasted in oven with olive oil and
allowed to cool
Generous handful of walnut pieces

Arrange lettuce in a bowl, squeeze garlic out of their skins and
into the bowl, add the walnuts and dress with olive oil and
balsamic vinegar, salt and pepper.
Serves two as an appetizer. Especially delicious when each feeds
the other by hand.

The light played on the Alpujarra Mountains, transforming them
into a giant's eiderdown which rested in soft billows beneath the
sky. Eight white windmills seemed to graze the horizon as they
turned gracefully in the breeze, generating power for the valley
below. The sky was a deep cloudless blue and ripe oranges and
lemons hung heavily on the trees that proliferated on the hillside.
Ivan and I had met at the airport that morning and now, at last,
we were alone together. It had been easier to escape than I'd
anticipated; I'd broached the subject of my going away to Greg
while he was busy exchanging emails with his parking fine chums.
I explained I needed peace and quiet to finish a paper I was writing. He'd waved me away saying, 'Fine, fine, whatever you want.
Can't you see I'm busy?' I'd chosen a week when Kitty would

be away on a school field trip and Jessie was back with FF. Since the boys could manage very well on their own for a few days, my absence would cause minimal disruption to all. The lying was hard, although Greg's indifference had helped to alleviate my guilt. And, as Ruthie said, it was all part of Rule Seven: *Make sure you're strong enough to bear the guilt of deception.*

In the distance, the snowy peaks of the highest mountains were visible as Ivan and I wound our way up in our small rental car. Conversation had been temporarily suspended and I silently watched his profile as he drove. 'I can't talk when I'm driving,' he had said. For, just like Greg, and all the other men I have ever known, he could do only one thing at a time. (Like most women, I can drive, talk, shout at squabbling children in the back seat, balance a ball on my nose and clap my flippers together all at the same time). Unlike Greg, however, Ivan did permit me to touch him while he drove, so I stroked the back of his head – that warm place where the top of his spine meets the base of his skull – and then ran my hand over his long trouser-clad thigh, bringing it to rest just where it met his crotch. It lingered there, heavy and warm with possibility. Ivan turned to look at me and wordlessly pulled over into a small space by the side of the road. He took my hand and pulled me up a mountain path and, after removing only as many clothes as necessary, he made love to me right there and then against a tree, our need for each other a powerful aphrodisiac. It was quick, urgent and exciting; a tasty hors d'oeuvre before the more sensual main course that we would share later.

That wasn't like Greg at all. I couldn't remember the last time he and I had had sex anywhere other than in our bed at night with the lights off. We never started fully dressed anymore. I remembered our first couple of years together, the hurried trail of clothes along passages and stairs leading to the bedroom. Often we didn't get that far and would make love on the stairs, my back pressed against the sharpness of a step, Greg's knees covered in telltale carpet burns; we bore the marks of passion on our bodies with pride – our love-battle scars. With an extra-marital lover, of course, Rule Eight applied: *Do not leave any visible marks.* Biting and scratching had to be kept to a minimum, lest their traces betray your secret.

Ivan and I arrived in Bubion and made our way up a steep hill on the edge of the village to the land where Sammy's tepee stood. The windows, of which Sammy was so proud, gave out onto a view of a snow-capped mountain. The valley beneath us was green and lush in the benign Spanish winter and a river was just visible below, languidly making its way in the direction of the coast some forty kilometres away. From the side of a rock, a small waterfall hurried to join it, filling the air with the hypnotic sound of rushing water. Ivan stood beside me, his arm around my waist and hugged me to him. I loved the way his tallness dwarfed me, I felt delicate and fragile in his arms. We ran down the hill, arms flailing with the unselfconsciousness of children, to the village shop. I felt suddenly embarrassed when I saw Jorge, the shopkeeper. What would he think, seeing me with this strange man? He'd met me with Greg and the children on numerous occasions and knew me as Sammy's sister. In my schoolgirl Spanish, I introduced Ivan as a colleague and explained that we had some business here for a few days. Jorge nodded and smiled, talking rapidly in his strong Andalusian accent where the endings of words can only be guessed at. Comprehension was made even more difficult by the fact that he had only two teeth – incongruously white and shiny – in his crumpled, grey-haired face, and always had a cigarette clamped firmly between his lips. His trousers were belted high on his waist and he wore a cardigan over his customary short-sleeved shirt as his one concession to winter. Jorge's shop was an Aladdin's cave: balls of string jostled for space on shelves next to plastic toy dinosaurs, frying pans, spicy sausages and fragrant cheeses. He had never disappointed us; if what you wanted wasn't available in the shop itself, he would disappear into his *almacen*, the adjacent storeroom, and produce whatever it was that you needed from there, a magician conjuring a coin from behind an ear. We bought *Jamón Serrano,* bread, cheeses, and honey with nuts and, like squirrels readying themselves for winter, scurried back with them to our nest.

The inside of the tepee was cold but colourful. Mexican rugs and blankets covered the floor and a soft fur rug engulfed the large double mattress that occupied the centre. Ivan efficiently lit the small paraffin fire and the gas lamp and we huddled beneath the blankets fully dressed, slowly removing our clothing as the combined heat of the fire and our desire warmed us. My body tingled where he touched me.

'Can I call you Givan?' I said. 'It's just that my boyfriends' names have always begun with G.'

'You can call me whatever you like, as long as you go on making me feel like I'm feeling now,' he laughed.

We fed each other hunks of bread, cheese and sausage, and sipped strong red Rioja as we lay cocooned on our mattress.

'When I was a teenager,' Ivan said, 'I read a novella by a nineteenth-century writer called Reshetnikov. It was about a peasant boy's love for his girlfriend. When she died prematurely, his sorrow and anguish at his loss was so great that he wanted to dig her body from the grave and bite her nose off her face. It sounded barbaric, but understandable, this need to consume someone you love. I always wondered if I would ever find someone I felt like that about and now I have.' He leaned over me and kissed my nose, grazing it playfully with his teeth.

I knew what he meant. I too had the desire to possess him entirely. Ivan was so delicious, I wanted to eat him up and so I did, in the process defiantly contravening Ruthie's Rule Nine pertaining to fellatio – *only swallow the first time and then you never have to ever again, but they always think you might.* I wanted to know everything about him, to make him mine, and to belong to him.

After we'd made love, Ivan drew my head on to his chest and told me how he and his family had lived in a crumbling pre-revolutionary building a few streets away from Nevsky Prospekt in the heart of St Petersburg. It was a communal flat, which they shared with another family. Listening to him made me feel I was living in the pages of an epic Russian novel. There were eight of them and one bathroom. He described their flat, which still bore the marks of a former era, the faded glamour of Tsarist times visible in its high windows and ceilings with their curlicued borders. It was on the third floor and through the window you could see one of the many canals that had earned St Petersburg the title of

Venice of the North. Ivan's father was a painter, and the rooms they occupied smelled strongly of oil paints, a smell he would forever associate with childhood. Jars with brushes and smudged pieces of rag covered every surface in the kitchen, incurring the wrath of the disagreeable neighbours with whom they had to share it. I found it hard to contemplate sharing your home life with another family.

'We used to go to a small *dacha* in the country whenever we could,' said Ivan. 'It was just a simple wooden shack, but it gave us some privacy and meant that we could make a noise without fear of complaint. We would make a fire and cook *shashlik* in the open air.'

'Let's do that here,' I said sleepily.

He wanted to get up and start collecting pieces of wood and kindling to build his fire immediately, but I pulled him back to me and distracted him with kisses, reminding him of a different hunger. Afterwards we lay together and I started to tell him about the holidays I had had with my parents and Sammy as a child, but after a few moments I realised from his breathing that he had fallen asleep.

For the next two days, I felt I was on holiday from my life. Ivan and I walked through orange groves kissing, we skidded stones over passing brooks; I watched the rise and fall of his breathing as we slept entwined or spooned into each other's bodies, his hand moving between my legs in the middle of the night rousing me to continue the lovemaking that sleep had briefly interrupted. In the morning, we awoke to the peremptory horn of the bread van as it made its way through the village selling freshly-baked loaves, and in the evening we walked through the streets of nearby Granada and sat together by candlelight in the small tiled dining room of Los Manueles, feeding each other gem lettuce with garlic and walnuts.

'We could be so happy together, Chloe,' Ivan said feeding me a walnut with his fingers.

'I know, but think of how much hurt we'd cause.'

'Lots of people get divorced.'

'But I have this thing about families staying together. I think parents owe their children that.'

'Don't you owe it to yourself to be happy too? I would devote myself to making you happy.' He ran his hand down the side of my body, just barely touching my breast. Could I imagine myself living with Ivan? I was beginning to, but when I thought what would need to happen to make that possible, I felt a big lump of sorrow in my throat. Mine and Greg's lives, woven together over the course of the past seventeen years, would have to be dismantled, our house sold, possessions divided. I could imagine my ghastly forced jollity as I tried to 'sell' the idea to the children of how much fun it would be for them to have two bedrooms, two houses ...

One morning I woke abruptly to the pale light of dawn, with a sense of unease. I thought I'd heard someone calling my name, but Ivan was still fast asleep beside me. I curled into his body and tried to go back to sleep. I could hear the sounds of early morning: a cock crowing, ubiquitous Spanish dogs barking, a woman calling to her child, *'Angustia, ven acqui.'* The bells of a nearby church chimed. It was seven o'clock. I got up quietly, picked up my mobile phone and went outside, shivering in the morning air.

'Dad.'

'That's funny darling, I was just thinking about you and how much I'd like to hear your voice.'

'What are you doing?'

'Pootling on the piano.'

'Why do you think Mum died, Dad?'

'As you know, they never really found the reason. I know it sounds odd, but I think she simply didn't want to go on living any longer. She had a terrible and unreasonable fear of ageing. It's such a waste. She missed so much of you and Sammy and, of course, of her grandchildren.'

'Do you think you'd have stayed together?'

'Hard to say, darling. I think so. Difficult as she was, I did love her, I just loved Helga too. Greedy of me, I know. That's the trouble with you and me, we want it all.'

Ivan's face appeared at the entrance to the tepee. He looked like a schoolboy, yawning and rubbing his eyes, his hair standing on end.

'I've got to go, Dad. I'll be back tomorrow. Love you.'

Ivan chased me back to bed where we remained all morning, playing happily with each other's bodies before drifting off into the delicious doze of sated lovers.

Later that day, when we'd dressed and I'd watched Ivan perform his bizarre ritual of stretching his socks before pulling them on (he didn't like the sensation of tight fabric around his feet and ankles. The thought flashed that this was precisely the sort of mannerism that could, with time, become irritating), we drove down to the coast at Salobreña and stopped for a drink at La Roca, a bar perched on a rock in the sea. The rock was a reclining centurion in profile, lying in the water, chest curving out beneath him, nose patrician.

'Can you see him, my rock man?' I asked Ivan.

'No, I can see a crocodile on a log.'

He described it to me and I, in turn, outlined my prone soldier with a finger. We watched the sun, an orange fiery ball, as it sank below the horizon and disappeared from sight. To the right of it, a small fishing boat stood motionless, silhouetted in its vanishing glow and two figures, distant pin men, were visible on board. We were a romantic couple on a seaside postcard made flesh. Ivan took my hand over the table. 'I love you,' he said.

'Me too.'

'Say it.'

'*Liubliu tebia*,' I said.

'*Po-angliiski,* say it in English.'

I opened my mouth to speak and paused, fearful, as if uttering these words might invoke a thunderbolt. I did love him, of course I did. I stroked his cheek with a finger and bent forward to kiss him by way of a reply. He held my face with both his hands and looked at me intently.

'Say it,' he repeated.

'I love you,' I mouthed soundlessly while crossing the fingers of one hand behind my back in the hope that this unique combination would ward off any impending thunderbolts.

Chapter Seventeen

Edie's Perfect Tuna Casserole

One can Campbell's Cream of
  Mushroom Soup
1/3 cup milk
6 1/2 oz can of tuna; drained
  and flaked (this must be tuna
packed in oil)
2 eggs, hard boiled and sliced
1 cup peas; cooked
1 cup potato crisps, slightly
  crumbled

Preheat oven to gas mark 4/180° C. Blend soup and milk in a
quart (litre) casserole dish.
Stir in tuna, eggs, and peas. Bake 20 minutes. Top with crisps;
bake for 10 minutes longer.
Serves 4

When I arrived home, Greg was asleep on the living room sofa
with the television blaring. Irritation rippled through me, each
wave breaking further up my body with the rising cadence of his
snores. Notwithstanding the fact that I'd been away with another
man, I'd somehow wanted him to be waiting to welcome me home,
to save me from myself and the path I seemed intent on taking.

I closed the door quietly and found Dad in the hall, pacing up
and down and shouting at someone on the telephone. It was the
day before the Albert Hall performance and he had to make last
minute adjustments to some of the songs. They were perform-
ing his *Prince and the Pauper* musical and, according to him, the
identical twins playing the lead roles couldn't even sing in tune.
On the hall table, I noticed a small glass with the sticky remains

of something sweet in it. I picked it up and sniffed it suspiciously. It was Baileys, which could mean only one thing; Edie McTernan was in *da house*. This explained why Greg was asleep at five p.m., early even by his standards. I had forgotten she was coming for Dad's Gala Evening. I contemplated bolting straight back out the front door, finding Ivan and making him run back to Spain with me, far, far from all this, but Dad finished his call and led me firmly off to the kitchen, a jailer dragging a recalcitrant prisoner into a cell.

Edie was standing by the kitchen table wearing an apron. She never travelled without at least two, identical, freshly laundered and ironed. They were always decorated with miniature shamrocks to show her allegiance to the motherland, a country where she had never spent more than a few days at any one time. She would take off her coat, tie one tightly around her waist and get to work on some area of dirt that had offended her, muttering 'they live in filth' loudly enough for us all to hear. Leo was next to her, seated at the table, his head leaning back and his eyes closed. Edie was holding a pair of scissors near his eyes.

'What are you doing?' I screamed.

'Trimming his eyelashes,' said Edie.

I snatched the scissors from Edie and, with difficulty, resisted the temptation to snip vengeful bald patches into her bottle black hair.

'They make him look like a girl,' said Edie huffily.

'Leo, what on earth were you thinking?'

'I thought if I looked more masculine, it might help me get a girlfriend,' Leo shrugged.

'They're wasted on him. He looks like one of those what-do-you-call-thems, transvestials. In my day, men were men,' sniffed Edie.

'This is still your day,' I said.

Dad, seeking to calm matters, poured some more Baileys into Edie's glass, which made her giggle girlishly. It was a pleasure to watch Dad at work: he brought out the flirtatious girl in every woman he came in contact with, whatever her age. He loved the company of women and they sank back into his easy charm as though into a warm, scented bath.

'You should have a glass yourself, Bertie,' Edie said coquettishly, downing hers in one. 'No alcohol you know.'

I kissed Leo and hugged him to me, seeking to anchor myself home after my absence.

'Any presents?' he asked, as he has done since he was two whenever I arrive home after an absence of more than a day. His eyes quickly registered the small carrier bag in my hand, bearing a slogan much beloved of my children *El Mundo de los Caramelos* (World of Sweets).

'Only the usual Spanish sweets darling, I didn't have time for anything else.'

Sammy walked into the room, spotted Edie, and kept straight on walking, out through the French doors and into the garden to hide in his tent.

'No one told me you were home,' Kitty's reproachful voice spun me round as she ran into the room and hurled herself into my arms.

'How was it? Did you have fun? Were you warm enough? What was the food like?' the questions rushed from my lips as I held her to me.

'Fun-ish, but Molly was a bitch as usual and whispered about me on the coach on the way back. I'm glad I'm home. You look really pretty, Mummy. What did you do in Spain?'

I felt a stab of guilt as the image flickered of Ivan naked and intent above me.

'Nothing much, tell me about your field trip instead.'

Kitty started to answer but was quickly interrupted by Edie, who launched into a long story about her neighbours Barbara and Derek and the minutiae of their lives. It seemed Derek had back problems and Barbara was finding it hard work coping with all the lifting and carrying that life necessitates, and last Tuesday, or was it Wednesday, just after the milkman had called for his money and before the washing machine man had arrived to have a look at her Hotpoint, a 1970s model that was playing up and it's no use telling Edie that she needs a new one, these things should last forever, Barbara had come round for a cup of tea and to pour out her troubles to Edie and Edie had told her that it was all right for her, at least she had a man around the house, unlike Edie, who had been left on her own all those years ago.

'Go and wake your father,' I hissed at Leo. I didn't see why I had to play the dutiful daughter-in-law while he shirked his responsibilities.

'Let the poor boy sleep,' said Edie, patting my hand. 'He looks exhausted, running the house on his own all week. He's got an awful cold too; has he been wearing his vest? You really ought to look after him better.'

Like a salamander catching flies on its sticky tongue, I only just managed to catch the words *fuck, right* and *off* as they were about to fly from my lips. My mother-in-law continued her monologue and the room emptied around her; first Leo, then Kitty, then Dad just barely suppressing a yawn, and finally I stole away, leaving Edie's incessant chatter to fall on the bewildered ears of Bea and Zuzi who continued to sit at the table as though frozen.

'Promise me you will have me put down if I ever get like that,' Dad whispered as we ran away, sniggering like naughty schoolchildren bunking assembly.

I crashed noisily through the living room door.

'Lo for thy kingdom lies yonder, sayeth he,' Greg said as he jumped and sat bolt upright.

'Oops, sorry darling, didn't know you were asleep.' He tried to turn over to go back to sleep, so I sat on him.

'Where is my mother now?' Greg asked fearfully; I half expected him to get on a chair and cower, a man afraid of a mouse.

'Holding forth in the kitchen. Come on, we have to go in there.'

He groaned, 'I can't, it will kill me.' I hit him. Quite hard.

'By the way,' I said, climbing off him, 'hello, I'm back.'

'Does that mean I can go away now?' he asked, flicking an anxious glance in the direction of his mother's voice, a long, continuous, enervating hum which carried from the kitchen.

He looked at me appraisingly, 'You look well. Nice time?'

'Yes, a good break. I mean, I got lots of writing done,' I said, recalling the reason I'd given for going away.

He kissed me; a quick, dry, dutiful kiss near, but not quite on my mouth. This reminder of our chaste existence went some small

187

way towards relieving the guilt that had threatened to overpower me after my reunion with my children. We went to the kitchen.

'On the Thursday, no, it can't have been Thursday, because that was the day I went into the town centre and had a cup of tea with old Mr Yates who used to do the flower beds. Oh, there you are, Greg, you remember Mr Yates?' Edie hailed us as we entered the room. 'He's got five grandchildren now, Benny, David, Colin, Georgina and, oh, what was the other one … tip of my tongue, tip of my tongue. It'll come to me in a minute. I was just telling these two about Barbara and Derek,' Edie was still in full flow. Bea and Zuzi were both wearing the glazed look of boxers who have been punched repeatedly in the face and are unsure how they've managed to remain standing. Dad had made a brave effort to return to the front line, but was already looking around wildly for some means of escape.

'Has Dad told you about what's happening at the Gala Evening?' I asked Edie, trying to shut her up by passing the conversational baton to him.

'Yes and it reminds me of the father of a boy in Greg's class. This was a few years B.E.'

Here her voice dipped to a hushed whisper as she alluded to Greg's father and his disappearance. 'There was a boy in his class, Richard was his name I think, and his father—'

A small cry of despair involuntarily escaped Greg's lips; he sounded just like Janet when I locked her up in the cat box to take her to the vet, trapped and desperate, unsure whether she would ever be free again.

Our arrival had had the effect of breaking Edie's stultification spell over Bea and Zuzi, and jolting them back to life. They took in their surroundings like Rip Van Winkle awaking from his long sleep. Bea looked at Zuzi and brushed a strand of hair from her eyes with a tender finger.

'We have the news to announce,' she said.

Edie opened her mouth to continue, but Greg arrested her with a hand gesture and said assertively, 'Wait. Let's hear Bea's news.' Bea was visibly nourished by the attention. She waited until we were all seated around the table and there was silence.

'Me and the Zuzi are getting married and we would like all

you for to come to wedding.' Bea took her betrothed's hand and flourished the ring that glinted on her wedding finger. Zuzi flushed prettily, her eyes cast down, the fair maiden whose hand has been won fair and square.

'That's nice dears,' said Edie, 'I hope you've both found nice young men. Are you having a double wedding?'

'They're marrying each other, mother,' said Greg.

'Don't be silly,' said Edie, 'they're both girls. Honestly Greg, you do talk the most terrible nonsense sometimes. Did you know,' she went on without pausing for breath, 'these days, most marriages end in divorce.'

Greg opened his mouth to speak again, but I gave him a look to silence him. What was the point?

'This calls for champagne,' I interrupted Edie's divorce statistics and foraged in the fridge for a bottle. 'You and Zuzi will obviously be wanting to find a nice place of your own now,' I continued, circumstances making an opportunist of me. 'I'll help you find somewhere.' I avoided their eyes as I unscrewed the wire hood and removed the foil.

'You do not want us for to stay here?' Bea asked.

Kitty rushed over to Bea and sat on her lap. 'She's only joking, aren't you Mummy?' Kitty said, and turned to Bea. 'She knows I couldn't bear it if you left us *ever*. When I'm grown-up you can move in with me and take care of my children.'

I lost control of the 'pop' and the cork hit the ceiling instead of exhaling, as it should, with a faint hiss in my hand.

'We stay,' Bea reassured Kitty, stroking her hair. 'Is our home where we have shared the happy times and the love.'

She and Zuzi exchanged an intimate, fond look. I know I should have stood firm, but, as for most working mothers, the fragile stability of my life revolved on the unsteady axis of paid help. Furthermore, I was aware of the potential damage not only to Kitty, but to Leo and Greg, that my recent behaviour, if dis-covered, would cause, and I didn't want to do anything further to upset the balance.

'Well, let's see,' I said, silently frustrated but retreating in defeat from my attempt to oust Bea and Zuzi, 'let's see what happens after you get married. I wonder how happily-ever-after you two will live.' Would it be any different for same-sex couples? Same sex, different sex; the truth was, I suspected, after marriage, there's precious little sex. Unless, of course, it's with other people. I wondered sadly whether their love boat would crash on the rock of daily trivia.

'I've made my tuna casserole,' said Edie, pulling a foul-smelling dish from the oven. It was her speciality, a culinary delight from *her day,* the 1950s; tinned tuna cooked in concentrated mushroom soup with potato crisps crumbled over the top. Kitty and Leo gagged slightly as Edie laid a generous steaming portion in front of each of them. For Dad, Edie's culinary efforts were the final straw and he made a great show of checking his watch, registering extreme surprise at the time and hurriedly putting his coat on.

'Have something to eat before you go,' I said mischievously.

'Wish I could darling, but I've got to meet the director.' He deftly parried my thrust and kissed me triumphantly. 'See you all tomorrow, six-thirty, don't be late.'

'We have to go too,' said Leo and Kitty, jumping up. 'We said we'd help Grandpa.'

'But I've just got back,' I complained.

'You'll see them in the morning, sorry, but we arranged this weeks ago,' Dad colluded, and whisked them to the tuna-free safety of the world beyond. Bea and Zuzi also succeeded in cutting and running amid the general goodbyes, and of Sammy there was no trace.

'That's a shame. Never mind, Greggie, you can have theirs too,' said Edie, setting Kitty and Leo's portions in front of Greg. He valiantly forced a few mouthfuls down. If Janet had been any kind of normal cat, he would have been able to decant food slyly into her bowl where she would have gobbled it up gratefully, but she wasn't and so, when Edie wasn't looking, and with the dexterity that comes of years of practice, he scooped most of it onto a napkin on his lap.

'Not for me, Edie,' I said firmly. 'I'm on a diet.'

'Ooh, you have to take care after forty, Chloe,' Edie said. 'If you're too thin, you'll look scraggy; we older women have to stay a bit plumper for the sake of our faces. You know what they say: *visage or derrière.*' She nodded her head with pleasure as though

inviting appreciation of her mastery of *foreign words*. Her pro-
nunciation of *derrière* rhymed with *terrier*, but considering that
Southern Ireland was the furthest she had travelled abroad, it was
a wonder that she knew any French words at all. Edie despised
foreigners but liked to mimic some of their ways, thinking this
lent her an air of sophistication and, as she would put it, *savvy
fair.*

I resented being lumped into a group of older women with Edie
and sharing the first person plural pronoun with her. I did not
belong there; I belonged with the *we* of twenty-five to forty-year-
olds. That was my set. Or did you, after forty, automatically join
an amorphous gang of forty-to eighty-year-olds?

'I'm really not feeling well,' said Greg. He took his own health
far more seriously than he did that of any of his paying customers
and now he looked as if he might be about to cry, but I suspected
this was less to do with his physical state and more to do with the
sheer misery caused by his mother's presence.

'You go and lie down dear, Chloe and I will clear up and have
a nice long chat.'

I looked at Greg as he left the room; he winked at me, a wink
of victory. If my eyes had been capable of it, they would have fired
poison-tipped arrows straight into his scheming heart.

I have always understood the word 'chat' to imply a convivial
exchange of news and views. This is not what happened now.
Certainly there were news and views; but any exchange thereof
was absent. Instead, I was the sole recipient of a barrage of information; the words that left Edie's mouth came at me in a steady
stream and I felt whipped by them as by driving rain; whichever
way I turned, more were waiting to lash me ever harder. I found
my means of survival in the sending and receiving of surreptitious
text messages to and from Ivan.

'Sorry about this,' I said to Edie, as I tapped, 'one of my patients.'
So, as Edie talked, Ivan and I engaged in textual intercourse, and
as a consequence of our increasingly sexually charged messages,
the last of which, from him, had read *I keep seeing your face as
you came when we made love in the tepee this morning*, Ivan and I
agreed to meet in fifteen minutes. You wouldn't have thought it

was possible to sit opposite your mother-in-law and have an erotic exchange with the man you were betraying her son for; but not only was it possible, it was actually happening. *I want you NOW,* wrote Ivan. Our time away together had only served to increase our addiction to each other.

'I'm so sorry, Edie,' I said getting up, 'I have to go and see this patient. He's in a state of some agitation and can't wait until tomorrow.' It was all perfectly true, except for the patient part.

Ivan's car was parked on the edge of the park at the entrance furthest from our house. He stood, a tall misty silhouette, haloed by the phosphorous glow of a street lamp.

'Did you know,' I said as I went into his arms, 'it's illegal to tie a giraffe either to a street lamp or to a telegraph pole in Georgia.'

'What about a beautiful woman you want to make love to? Can you tie her to one?' he smiled.

'Only if she lets you.'

I burrowed into his coat and inhaled his scent of intimacy and desire.

'I want to be with you, Chloe, I want us to be together.'

How had we arrived at this point so quickly? I said nothing but pressed my body into his. He kissed me. I loved these kisses; how our lips meshed together and our tongues lost themselves in each other's mouths in a way that was simultaneously a journey and a homecoming. I loved the feel and smell of him and the excitement of our bodies together. But could I sacrifice everything for this? His mobile rang. It was Becky.

'Yes, what is it?' he asked her, his voice cold. 'I told you where I put it.' He hung up abruptly, without saying goodbye; he closed his eyes for a moment as though to clear himself of irritation and turned to me. He must have noticed my expression as he said, 'I would never speak to you like that, Chloe. You don't know what she's like, you don't know what it's like to live with her.'

I felt uncomfortable. A sudden twist of the lens had brought into focus an image of him which cracked the Hollywood movie of our affair; a side of Ivan had been revealed that I would prefer neither to see nor to know. We sat in his car and as he kissed and caressed me, my discomfort ebbed away. He was right: I didn't know what she was really like; no one could ever know what went on between two people. In the distance, through the car window, I could see Madge's familiar form walking along the railings circumventing the park. I could just make out the white dove that she carried, cradled in her arms like a baby.

Ivan drove to a secluded spot, a dark mews that bustled with the trade of its garages by day and gave shelter to lovers by night. We made love in his car like teenagers, keeping most of our clothes on for warmth and discretion. There was no doubt about it; an illicit affair was a time machine that restored you to your youth, or at any rate gave you the illusion that it did. When we made love, I wanted to do it again before we had even finished doing it the first time, with all the greediness of a chocolate fanatic who craves the next bar while her mouth is still busy with the first.

'We'd be so good together, Chloe,' Ivan whispered in my ear. 'Just think about it.'

'It's too soon for all this,' I said, feeling tearful.

'It's OK, it's OK,' he soothed, stroking my hair and wiping my sudden tears away with a finger. 'We can go on like this. Just promise me you'll think about it.'

I felt afraid, as if I had swum into deep and unfamiliar waters leaving the safe dry land of my normal life too far behind. I could see Greg, Leo and Kitty's hands waving to me from the remote shore, and hear their increasingly thin cries entreating me to return as their distant figures grew ever smaller and I shrank to nothing more than a distant spot on their horizon. I struggled to return but was caught up in a current so strong that try as I might, I couldn't swim back to them. The vision made me ache with misery. What I wanted was everything – no more and no less; my husband and my lover. Was it really so greedy of me to want them both? After all, isn't it unrealistic to assume you can find everything you need from life in one person? In France, extra-marital affairs are an accepted part of life, with *cinq à sept* (or *sink a sept* as Edie would doubtless say, to rhyme with except), the hours set aside for the daily meeting of lovers, an institution. But I couldn't make us all move to Paris and become French and it was already some hours after seven and time that I returned home.

'Heart, mind and body,' said Ivan as I was getting out of his car. 'Those are the areas where you need to fit each other. You tick all three boxes for me, Chloe.' I was flattered, but I couldn't help feeling that this need to categorise and draw up lists was a uniquely male tendency: the way that men referred to beautiful and desirable women as a '10' and always wanted to know your top five records or books or your favourite film. What would happen if the tick in one of Ivan's boxes grew fainter with the passing of years, leaving first a dark smudge before ultimately morphing into a large black cross?

'Didn't Becky once tick all your boxes?' I asked.

'Never really the heart box,' he answered. He looked at me and rubbed his thumb over my mouth in a way that was both tender and a promissory note to be held on account until our next sexual encounter.

'I'll see you tomorrow night,' he said, 'at your father's gala.'

The Times was sending him to *cartoon* the event. I felt that newly familiar thrill of excitement and fear that occurred when my two lives collided.

I walked quickly home, searching in my pocket for my mobile phone to send Ivan some sweet punctuation to our tryst. I couldn't find it. I closed my eyes and saw at once, with shocking clarity, where I had left it. In plain view on the kitchen table with all of Ivan's earlier messages intact and ticking like a time bomb should anyone think to open them. I felt panic rising in me, keeping pace with the accelerating click of my every step. Greg was asleep; he had escaped his mother by going to bed. Edie wouldn't know how to access messages. It's all right, it's all right, no one will have seen it, I repeated to myself like a mantra. I ran the remaining fifty yards home.

'Is that you, Chloe?' Greg's voice came up from the kitchen to greet me with all the reassurance of a siren shrieking. I took my coat off slowly, and looked at myself in the mirror. Did I look like a woman who'd just had sex? Guilt seemed etched in my every pore, my eyes shone, my hair was sticking up at the back as it always did after the friction of enthusiastic intercourse. I brushed it down, straightened my clothes, took a deep breath and went downstairs.

'Please let him not have looked at my phone and I promise I'll never do it again,' I lied to the God in whom I didn't believe. Greg was sitting at the table with Sammy. My phone lay on the table between them; it throbbed there, radioactive, malign, mocking. 'Really,' it seemed to say, 'page one: keep your phone with you at all times. How hard is that?'

Greg's eyes seemed full of a silent question, but perhaps that was simply my guilt.

'Where have you been?' Greg asked. Was there an edge to his voice?

'Had to talk a patient down from the ledge,' I said. 'She's freaking out because she's getting married.' I was talking too much and too fast. I resisted the temptation to clamp my lips together with my fingers and with an effort of will forced myself to shut up.

'Not like you to make a house call,' Greg said. Was he suspicious? Had he read my messages?

'It was either that or stay here listening to your mother,' I retorted. He couldn't argue with that.

Sammy went off into the garden to his tent. His face told me that he knew exactly what I'd been up to. No doubt he felt that his continued presence implied a collusion he was unwilling to enter into.

'Oh, here, you left your phone,' Greg handed it to me.

'Thanks,' I said carelessly, using all my self-control to keep my breathing steady. 'I'm off to bed. Coming?'

'I'll be up in a minute.'

It was far too suspicious to take a shower in our bathroom, and with Edie asleep in the bedroom next to my consulting room, the basement bathroom was off limits too. I had to make do with washing myself as thoroughly as a flannel would allow, a flannie wash Kitty used to call it when she was little and didn't want to have a bath. Her childish phrase rang in my head incongruously. I felt whorish, a working girl between tricks, out of a car with one man and into bed with another. Still, I reasoned, at least one thing was certain; Greg wouldn't want to have sex.

Greg rubbed his foot up and down my calf; he reached for me and took me in his arms. Tonight of all nights, and after so long. I wish I could say I found it difficult to make love to my husband after having left the arms of my lover, but even after all this time it felt like a perfectly natural thing to do. Was Greg reclaiming his territory as he loved me? Was he spraying his scent all over me in the hope of keeping me for his own? Whatever the reason, it was comforting to be in his arms. Why couldn't I just stay there and be happy instead of wanting something more or something different? *If one were to look on life as a simple gift, one would perhaps be less exacting.*

'Are you happy, Chlo?' Greg asked as we lay in each other's arms afterwards.

I wanted to ask him why we hadn't had sex for so long, but was nervous of where the conversation might lead. Did he know what I'd been up to earlier and that I hadn't been to Spain alone?

'Happy-ish,' I said. 'I just wish we could be like we were in the beginning, full of the wonder of each other. What about you; are you happy?'

'I'm fine. This is what life is. It can't all be breathless excitement at every turn.'

I looked into his familiar blue eyes, inhaled the Greg-ness of him, nodded and fell asleep in his arms. I was only allowed to rest there for a few minutes before he began his usual night-time thrashing, talking aloud and invoking unseen deities.

'A strange thing,' I thought affectionately as I spooned him, 'but mine own.'

Chapter Eighteen

Zhivago's Revenge Recipe

1/2 oz pepper Vodka	3 drops Tabasco
1/2 oz cinnamon Schnapps	1 shot-glass

Pour ingredients in order into a chilled glass. Stir.
Best served ice cold.

We posed by the front door on our way out to Dad's gala evening and, pressing a camera into his hands, asked a passing stranger to record for posterity the tableau of our première finery.

'You're still a very attractive man, Greg,' Edie said, looking him up and down as we walked to the car. 'You'd better keep your eye on him, Chloe. I remember when he was just sixteen. This was quite a few years A.E. of course and—'

The rest of her reminiscences were drowned out by Kitty and Leo, who began squabbling over who should sit where. Sammy's face wore an absent, detached look, the result of too many words engulfing him with the force of a tidal wave.

'You've got your mountain face on,' I said.

'The peace of the Alpujarras,' he said. 'I'm missing my tepee.'

'I'm missing your tepee too.'

'Yes, but I suspect your reasons are rather different to mine,' he said.

We'd barely rounded the corner by the park, when Kitty leaned over me from the back seat. I thought she was going to stroke my hair as she used to when she was little and sitting behind me in the car.

'Your skirt's too short at the back, Mum,' she said. 'It's disgusting, you can nearly see your bum.'

Hmm, maybe I should have worn long after all. The knowledge that Ivan would be there was making me feel nervous enough as it was, and there's nothing like the disapprobation of a twelve-year-old for destroying the fragile confidence of the older woman.

Dad was standing outside the foyer when we arrived, seal-sleek in black tie, his silver hair combed neatly back, only the hair of his eyebrows escaping wildly in all directions giving an indication of how he was feeling. Helga, tall, elegant and newly arrived from Berlin, stood by his side. She was still beautiful in her seventies, and shone with a self-assurance born of a lifetime of admiration. For my own sake, I wished that Dad had brought her into our lives more; I would have liked a mother figure, having been prematurely deprived of one. But this wasn't about me, and her absence from the humdrum routine of daily life was precisely the point. Tonight was the first time she had appeared on his arm at a public event and the sight of them together made me hang back. I had only ever seen my father partnered with my mother. He looked more at ease beside Helga, not poised for flight as he had always seemed next to Girlie, fearful of the fluctuating emotional weather she brought with her and which caught all who came near in its unpredictable downpours or sudden bursts of sunshine. Helga had an aura of steadiness about her, discernible in her soothing hand on my father's arm and the affectionate and absorbed inclination of her head towards his.

The paparazzi were out in force, ladders clutched competitively to their sides, heads swivelling hungrily as they sought their prey. Tickets for the event had sold-out the first day they went on sale and the presence of London's leading celebritocracy was eagerly anticipated.

I was moving towards Dad and Helga when I heard an irritated voice behind me. 'Isn't that Kitty McTernan's mother? What on earth is she doing here?' I turned to see Mr and Mrs Fractions, Molly's parents. My presence seemed to affront them, as if in some way it diminished their own at this fashionable event. I knew that Mrs Fractions was still smarting from Kitty's and my Chocolate Cake Coup.

'Phil's bank are sponsoring the occasion,' she told me, before I could say anything, implying an ownership of the event and tacitly inviting me to explain my own presence. She glanced around the growing crowd as though seeking someone more worthy of her attention than me. 'But then I've always followed Bertie Zhivago's work. I'm a huge fan. As a matter of fact, I've met him several times.'

Very occasionally life affords you the perfect, sweet opportunity for revenge. All those years of feeling scorned in the playground had been worth it for this, an unusually warm January evening in London's Shaftesbury Avenue, when I was able to savour the moment, before saying these five simple words: 'Bertie Zhivago is my father.'

Mrs Fractions looked me up and down as though seeing me for the first time. 'I didn't know that.'

'Yes, well it's hard to make the connection,' I said caustically. 'What with there being so many Zhivagos around these days. Although,' I allowed grudgingly, 'since Kitty's surname is McTernan, you probably didn't know that mine is Zhivago.'

I was about to warn her to take better care in the future to determine whom it was that she was snubbing, but was saved by Dad's arrival at my side. He put his arms around me, turned me to Helga and said, 'Here's my beautiful daughter, Chloe.'

Out of the corner of my eye, I could see the Fractions opening and closing their mouths like goldfish.

'Dad, Helga, this is Phil and Jane, they're parents of a girl in Kitty's class.' I was so used to thinking of them as Mr and Mrs Fractions, I couldn't remember their actual surname.

'How lovely to meet you both and how kind of you to come,' Dad said. It was quite clear he had never met them before, or if he had, had no memory of any such meeting.

Jane looked as though she might faint with gratitude and shame and although my act of generosity in introducing them had initially been intended as a vengeful rubbing of their noses in the excrement of their own discourtesy, I was pleased that I had done it. Their noses were about to be rubbed further anyhow, I realised, as I heard Dad shout, 'Ruthie, over here my darling. Let me kiss you, you look wonderful.' Jane watched, horrified, as Dad clasped Ruthie, whom she had also deemed unworthy of her attention, to him, looked at us both and said, 'You two are as beautiful as when you were eighteen.' Ruthie looked radiant in a tight red dress that clung lovingly to her curves, Richard, Atlas and Sephy by her side.

'Just saying no to the Bolivian marching powder seems to be doing you the world of good,' I whispered as I kissed her. She squeezed my hand, took in the Fractions whose astonished gaping mouths were reduced to perfectly round zeros, and greeted them as magnanimously as a queen might her loyal subjects. Revenge was sweet and we swished past them to make our way down the red carpet and into the foyer to the flashes and calls of the paparazzi.

Leo, a man/boy in a tuxedo, willing slave to the great God iPodicus, walked the walk of the homeboy on his native streets of Harlem to a rhythm only he could hear. Kitty pulled my skirt down from behind. 'Honestly, Mum, you're so embarrassing.' Family patterns repeat themselves unavoidably, however much you may try to escape them: like my mother before me, I simply didn't dress as a mother should. Or, perhaps, no mother can ever dress or behave in a way that will satisfy her daughter. I looked at Kitty, enjoying the sight of her earnest little face; she seemed caught motionless, briefly suspended in time between childhood and womanhood; simultaneously I could see the baby she had been and the beautiful woman she was soon to become. A familiar profile caught my attention. (In truth, I'd been surreptitiously on the look out for it ever since we'd arrived). Kitty followed my gaze and gave me a brief hard look, at once knowing and quizzical, a woman's look. It was Ivan. I felt my breath quicken, as much with the fear of what Kitty might know or suspect as with the pleasure I always felt at seeing him.

I found myself standing between my husband and my lover as they shook hands and engaged in the sort of gruff, confrontational joshing that men enjoy.

'I see, like me, you can still safely wear your shirt tucked into your trousers,' said Ivan, patting his own crisp, flat, white shirt.

'Not many of us left. I weigh the same as I did twenty years ago,' Greg answered smugly.

'You're on a tightrope with no safety net, Chloe,' Ruthie murmured beside me, 'just keep your nerve and don't look down.'

The evening was a curious confluence of the many parts of my life: my husband and children at my side; my father and his hitherto hidden mistress; my mother-in-law; my brother; my best friend with her family; my lover and his wife; the school bully's hateful parents, and now, in a rising crescendo of whistles and cries of 'Over here,' 'Lizzie, look this way', 'Just one more', I could see my Famous Friend making her way towards us as flash bulbs exploded and voracious photographers captured her image on cameras thrust towards her like weapons. FF was in her element, the attention a welcome sun that warmed her upturned face; her eyes were half-closed, her lips parted as though in ecstasy. This was to be her first public outing with Jeremy and she wore sexual fulfilment on the easy swing of her hips as she declared to the world that her celibacy was a thing of the past. She might just as well have arrived as Lady Godiva, naked on a horse to illustrate that she was back in the saddle. Jessie trailed behind them, her eyes searching the pavement as if she might find some answers or meaning to her own neglected existence in the cracks between the flagstones.

'He's even stolen my name,' she told me as they joined us, 'she calls him Jezzie.'

'Hello darling,' said FF, kissing the air around my head.

'I see you've had time for another little procedure,' I murmured.

'Lipodissolve. It literally dissolves the fat away. They don't do it here yet; I had to pop over to Paris for the day. It's brilliant, you can do it in your lunch-hour and go straight back to work' – she glanced at Jeremy who had his back to us – 'and to play. You should try it on your sticky-out tum.'

'What tum?' I said complacently.

'What happened to it?' FF narrowed her eyes and studied me closely.

Jeremy turned round. I took a proper look at him and gasped. He was none other than God's Gift; I'd forgotten his real name was Jeremy.

'Oh yes,' said FF, following my gaze. 'Jezzie told me earlier that you two know each other.' She leant forward and whispered in my ear, 'He thinks you've got a bit of a thing for him actually. Where did you meet?'

In the distance I could hear a car alarm, an irritating, repetitive shriek that seemed to herald either an end or a beginning of something. It filled me with a sense of apprehension.

I took my seat and breathed in the heightened aroma peculiar to a big and important event. The string section was tuning up and the orchestra shifted in their seats like restless circus horses pawing the earth; best frocks in peacock-bright colours rustled and people called to each other in voices that were accustomed to being heard. We were right at the front and I was holding Dad's hand. He nervously counted my fingers in a ritual we'd played together ever since I was a child. After each counting, I would hide another finger until none remained for him to count. He would feign astonishment at the disappearance of all my fingers and then relief as, one by one, I made them appear again.

His hands were warm and dry; an instrument that he had always used to play the steady notes of parental love. As a child they had soothed me to sleep, wiped away my tears and expressed his love for me; I had never seen them raised in anger towards me or anyone else. But, for tonight I was the reassuring parent whose hands soothed.

'Remind me never to do this ever again,' he murmured, 'it's bound to be a complete disaster.'

'You always say that Dad, and it's always a huge success,' I said, kissing his cheek. I caught Helga's eye as she pressed his hand to her lips from where she sat on his other side. We looked at each other and smiled shyly. Helga leaned across Dad and squeezed my arm. I felt a sudden urge to cry and explain my complicated life to her and ask for her guidance.

'You and Helga should get to know each other better,' said Dad. I smiled and nodded, but I had the disloyal feeling that if I did get to know her, I might like her more than I had my own mother.

I turned around and saw Ivan looking at me from the row behind. Becky was sitting next to him, her face pinched and miserable; her body kept carefully separate from his as if physical contact could wound her.

'He's not that nice to her,' Kitty said suddenly.

'Who isn't?' I turned to her beside me; she had been watching me watching them.

'That Russian man you keep looking at. He's not very nice to his wife.'

I affected casual indifference. 'Mmm, really darling.'

'He told her she was like a heavy wet towel round his neck. I heard him.'

'You're right, that isn't very nice,' I said. The same dissonant note that always played when I observed Ivan with Becky sounded loudly in my head. Could he really be so nasty?

'I think he fancies you,' said Kitty. 'He keeps looking at you in a funny way. You're not going to have an affair, are you?'

'Don't be silly, darling.' The reassuring warm chuckle I had intended came out all wrong and sounded like glass breaking.

'Only Lucy Gray's mum had an affair and her dad found out and then her parents got divorced and now she never knows where any of her things are because she has to live in two different houses.'

I hugged her so she couldn't see my face and was saved from replying by the curtain going up. A clash of cymbals signalled the overture and awakened me for the first time to the full enormity of my actions. I was risking the happiness of my husband and children for a man who wasn't very nice to his wife. How long would it be before he started being not very nice to me? If Kitty suspected me, what must Greg think? I looked at Greg, seated next to Kitty. Despite our rare intimacy of the night before, he had the distant familiarity of an often seen stranger, like the man you might pass on the way to the bus stop each morning.

The audience's applause brought me back to the present and I turned my attention to the stage. The stage was divided into two halves: one half was a royal court rejoicing at the birth of a baby prince; the other a pauper's home where the family was rueing the unwanted arrival of yet another mouth to feed. The contrast between the opulence of the royal household and the poverty of the other was exquisitely realised; all plush velvets, candles, sumptuous clothes on one side, and dirty, barren, poverty on the other.

The scene seemed to reflect my life, or at least the way I perceived it: the sensuous plushness of my relationship with Ivan, contrasted with my increasingly impoverished relationship with my husband. I was poor little Tom Canty, my nose pressed up against the bars of the palace gate, longing for a life of plenty and gaining it, only to find it brought me nothing but trouble. Like Tom, I had found that the thing I wished for was not quite as I had dreamt it. I longed for the simplicity of my old life, where I'd had no need to tiptoe in secretive shadows ever fearful of the glare of imminent discovery.

Dad had been clutching my hand tightly and now seemed to relax a little as he sensed the warmth of the audience's response.

'It may still be touch and go, but so far it looks like it's not going to be a total fuck-up after all,' he whispered.

'When will you realise it never is?'

'When I'm dead.'

'Stop it, Dad, don't say that.'

I lost myself in the music and movement. It was a relief to throw myself into the story on stage and escape my own.

At the interval, we all crowded into a VIP room for lethal and aptly named cocktails: *Zhivago's Revenge*. God's Gift was standing by the entrance and gave me the sort of knowing smirk that suggested we had unfinished business while simultaneously admiring his own reflection in the pane of glass behind me. What on earth could FF see in him beyond physical gratification? Although, given his self-absorption, it was hard to imagine he could be a generous lover. A young journalist was standing next to FF, translating every word she uttered into spidery shorthand soon to be immortalised in print. She nodded earnestly like a woodpecker and gave an excited little acquiescent 'mm' with each peck. FF was holding forth about her yet-to-be-written next book.

'Sex,' she was saying, 'is very important for a person's energy. It is our fuel; just as a full tank of petrol allows a car to travel a certain number of miles, so, too, satisfying sex gives us the energy to live our busy lives. Like a car, a human being has to refill regularly to run optimally.'

'But wasn't your last book about celibacy?' the journalist asked.

'Yes, but that is the first part of the process, a cleansing of the person – or of the engine if you will – at the end of one relationship, where you learn to love yourself again before taking on the fuel of the next new relationship.'

'I don't think it's like that at all,' I interjected. 'Sex doesn't fuel you for ages like petrol does a car, quite the reverse. I think it's like when you eat a huge meal and think you can never eat again, and then wake up the following morning to find that you are absolutely ravenous; you know, the more sex you have, the more you want.' FF was looking at me as if I were the Pope pontificating on the joys of sexual union. 'Anyhow,' I added hastily, 'what do I know, I've been married to the same man for a hundred years and have so little sex I'm probably technically a virgin again.'

FF was still looking at me curiously: if sexual fulfilment oozed from her every pore, who was to say that it didn't from mine? I could see Ivan a few yards away. He brushed past me and pushed a note into my hand.

Meet me in the box two doors down.

'What's that?' asked Kitty, creeping up on me.

'Nothing, a bit of paper, that's all.'

'*He* gave it to you didn't he?'

'Will you stop it?' I retorted, with the defensive anger so familiar to the rightfully accused when cornered.

'Where are you going?' said Kitty, as I moved away.

'To the Ladies.'

'I'll come with you.'

Kitty insisted on walking right behind me to the Ladies, ostensibly to keep my skirt pulled down so that it covered my bottom, but it felt more as though I were under police escort. I felt ashamed that her anxiety made her scared to let me out of her sight. I closed the door of my cubicle and heard an odd snuffling noise from the one next to it. Bending down to look under the partition, I was met with the sight of a nose with a straw up it sniffing something from the floor. The ring on the finger holding the straw looked familiar.

'Ruthie, what are you doing?'

The nose and the finger jerked out of view. I stood on the lavatory seat and looked over into the next cubicle. Ruthie was on her hands and knees, caught in flagrante as she tried to sweep up scattered white powder onto a square of paper.

'What the fuck are you doing?'

'Chloe! You frightened the life out of me. Look, I was just having a little sharpener and dropped the fucking stuff all over the floor. It seemed safest to simply hoover it up with my nose.'

'You promised me that you'd stopped.'

'I have really. I haven't had one for ages, it was just one teensy little line to go with my glass of champagne.'

'We'll talk about this later,' I said, glancing over to the washbasin area where Kitty was drying her hands. Sephy came in and a few moments later the two of them skipped out together, Kitty's surveillance of me temporarily forgotten.

As I made my way to the box to meet Ivan, I couldn't help but feel that my life had veered dangerously out of control. How could I even like myself, a woman whose own child suspected her of having a lover? That felt far worse than a woman deceiving her husband. The understanding of how my actions were affecting those I loved, combined with Greg's repossession of me the night before, was finally bringing me to my senses. It seemed portentous that Ivan's note inviting me to the box was the first one he had ever written me in English, and I knew with sudden clarity what I had to do and that it had to be done immediately, before I lost my nerve.

I sensed him before I saw him; standing to one side in shadow, and for a moment I wanted nothing more than to float in the scent of him. He stepped forward to touch me and I pulled myself back with an effort.

'This can't go on, Ivan,' I said. 'I just can't do this any more.'

'Shh, shh,' he soothed, stroking my face.

'Don't,' I said, 'please, we must stop.'

'I want you, Chloe,' he said, trying to pull me to him. 'I want you all the time.'

'It's over,' I said, folding my arms in front of me. 'I can't see you any more, I just can't. It's different for me; your children have left home, but mine haven't. They need their mother and father, they need to be part of a proper family. I can't do this to them, it's just not fair. Please understand.'

Ivan looked at me; he shut his eyes tightly and when he opened them again, something had closed in his face.

'I am not a man who likes to beg,' he said. I looked at him and it was as though we had suddenly become strangers to each other. He took a step away from me and I turned and ran from the box, fat messy tears gouging muddy footprints through my make-up. All I had wanted, I thought, self-pityingly, was to live a little, and now misery was unpacking its bags and making itself at home for a lengthy stay in my gut. I ducked behind a pillar at the sound of Greg's voice. He was explaining the story of *The Prince and the Pauper* to Edie with the sort of controlled patience that is barely contained exasperation:

'It's a case of mistaken identity. Tom's not doing it deliberately, he tried to tell everyone that he wasn't the prince, but they refused to believe him and now he's trapped.'

'But can't they see he's not him?'

'No, he and the prince look identical.'

'Oh, is that why the palace guard made the real prince leave the palace, because in Tom's rags, he looked like Tom.'

'That's it mother, now you've got it.'

'Only I wondered about that, it didn't seem like a very wise thing for a guard to do ...'

I stayed hidden until after the bell and made my way back to my seat in that brief interval of darkness between the lights going down and the curtain going up.

'We were looking for you, darling,' Dad whispered.

I squeezed his hand and then took it and made his fingers start to count my own.

When the closing number of *The Prince and the Pauper* rang out, I sneaked a look at Ivan. He was rigid and staring resolutely ahead, his sketchbook gripped in his hand. The illusory palace of my languorous, lovemaking with Ivan was lost to me, a flicker of light receding to a pinpoint before vanishing altogether. I was back with Tom Canty in Offal Court, destined for a life of emotional starvation and sensory deprivation. Well, that may be putting it a bit strongly; but even though I knew I'd done the right thing, that's what it felt like. The twin boys playing Edward VI and Tom Canty took the stage hand in hand and sang:

> *Never judge a book by its cover,*
> *Never say you see what's not there,*
> *Never give your heart to another,*
> *Never eat a crust you can't share.*

They sang in perfect harmony: Dad's earlier fears about their talent had been unwarranted. The house thundered with applause as the curtain came down and Dad went up on stage to take his bow.

'Thank you everyone,' he said. 'I must confess when I was first told that there was to be this gala performance to mark my fifty years in musical theatre, I thought, my God, they must all know something I don't.' He paused. The audience looked up at him, their faces full of affection.

'You must all have noticed,' Dad continued, 'that any recognition or celebration of a lifetime achievement in showbiz is a prequel to death. I'm sorry to disappoint you all, but I'm afraid I plan to stick around for quite a few years to come.'

The audience roared with laughter and applause and stood up. I looked at the small figure of my father, alone on the big stage, and shivered. I put my arm around Greg. 'Stop it,' he said, shrugging me off, 'it tickles.'

Chapter Nineteen

Helga's Quick and Easy Apfelstrudel

450g sweet apples – peeled, cored and thinly sliced

1/4 cup golden raisins

1/4 cup dried currants

1/2 tsp. ground cinnamon

2 tbsp. white sugar

2 slices stale brown bread, crumbled into breadcrumbs

400g package filo pastry dough (life is too short to make your own)

1/4 cup butter, melted

Preheat oven to gas mark 6/200° C.

In a bowl, combine apples, raisins, currants, cinnamon, sugar and bread crumbs. Stir well.

Spread several sheets of pastry dough generously with melted butter and lay the buttered sheets one on top of each other on a baking sheet. Spread the fruit mixture evenly over the top sheet, then roll the sheets up to form a log shape. Brush the top with melted butter. Bake in preheated oven for 30 minutes, until pastry is golden brown and fruit is tender.

I must have drunk at least two bottles of champagne at the after-show party. Greg and the children had left almost immediately, dragging a reluctant Edie behind them. She was knocking back Baileys with wanton delight and was on her fifth or sixth – one more and she would have been singing 'Danny Boy'. She had pinned a woman against a wall and was showering her with inconsequential chatter. The woman's eyes were darting around desperately.

'Stay,' I'd said to Greg as he went to the woman's aid.

'I've seen Bertie and congratulated him. I can't be bothered with the rest of them, a bunch of self-obsessed luvvies all doing the moi moi moi thing. Anyhow, I want to go home and write to the council about their proposed plan to increase speed bumps in the area. The way they're going, we might as well all give up cars and become bloody show jumpers instead.'

'Hey, you're a fun guy.'

'Just because you want to stay, doesn't mean that I have to want to.'

'No, well, you never do anything that you don't want to do. God forbid that you should do anything to please anyone else.'

'For God's sake, Chloe, do you just want to have a fight?'

'It might be nice if I could occasionally be at a party with my husband instead of always on my own. I may as well not be married at all,' I said, my voice getting a little too loud.

'I'm really not in the mood for this. I'll see you in the morning.' He'd turned away from me and left.

Ivan hadn't come to the party at all; we'd exchanged a last lingering, pain-filled look in the theatre foyer. He'd pushed his body up against me in a way that felt both full of longing and reproach as he bustled Becky out.

'I thought we were going to the party,' I heard her say.

'You go. I'm not in the mood.'

'No, no, I'll come home with you, darling.'

I'd seen him smile tightly and turn away from her. Poor Becky, she seemed to try so hard and get so little back. And yet, once they must have been happy, lost in each other, drowning happily in kisses and caresses and whispered words of love just as Greg and I had been. How corrosive time was to a relationship, slowly nibbling away at affection and desire until all that was left was habit and obligation. Was it a question of having married the wrong person? Or would you end up feeling detached from whomever it was you had married?

At the party, I saw Lou in a corner with a bald man. It was Gus Fallick, or should I say Les. He'd had hair when we were together and I would never have known him but for the familiarity of the way his neck inclined towards Lou. Our brains store the intimate memories of a lover's gait and movement, the way they laugh and kiss, long after the intimacy has expired. What would I remember most about Ivan, I wondered. The way he urgently took possession of me, his quiet smile after we'd made love, the intentness of his gaze when he talked to me? Les was whispering in Lou's ear and she flushed as he spoke, her chest rising and falling quickly. I was about to go over and find out if he recognised me, when I saw Lou leave the room, followed almost immediately by him. They were on a mission, his verbal gifts were obviously still working their magic. Memory told me that he must have laid the groundwork in whisper form and now completion would follow urgently in some dark and discreet corner. What if I'd married him? Would that have been any better or worse than marrying Greg? But then of course I wouldn't have Kitty and Leo, so for that reason alone, I could never regret marrying Greg. I thought of Ivan and remembered how we'd parted earlier that evening. I clenched my fists tightly, digging my nails into the palms of my hands in an attempt both to externalise the pain and to stop myself crying. I had condemned myself to my marriage.

'What is the point of husbands?' I asked Ruthie as she walked past.

'That's a tough one, I'll have to come back to you.'

I gulped the rest of my champagne, helped myself to another glass and took a canapé of bread and dripping from a waiter dressed in rags – all the Prince canapés, the caviar on small black squares of pumpernickel, had been gobbled up and now all that remained were the Pauper ones.

I went over to Dad, who was surrounded by a crowd of well-wishers.

'It was wonderful Dad, I'm so proud of you.' I hugged him and then quickly took the opportunity to slip away when someone came up to talk to him, fearful of disgracing myself by bursting into drunken tears all over him and ruining his finest hour. There are times when you can't expect your parents to kiss you and make everything better.

'Come on,' said Ruthie, who had spotted me swaying towards the exit. 'I'll take you home.'

'The thing is, Ruthie, people often decide that it's time for them to get married and then marry whomever they happen to be with at that moment,' I said, as though we were already in the middle of a conversation, in that intense way when alcohol appears to have lifted the scales from your eyes and revealed the truth to you in all its crystal clarity. 'So you don't necessarily marry the right person, you just marry the person who's there. You know, the one that you might be going out with at that moment when you decide that it's time to get married.' I was not only repeating myself, but also slurring slightly and hiccuping.

'I mean, you could just as well have married the person you'd been going out with before, but you weren't thinking of getting married then, so you didn't. You didn't marry them. But now, suddenly, you decide that it is time to get married, so you do, you just marry the person you happen to be going out with then at that moment.'

Ruthie kindly pretended that I was talking sense and said, 'There is some truth in that. I think everyone does reach a time when they decide they should settle down, but unless you're unlucky enough to choose a violent or mad partner, you probably have just as much chance of finding happiness with one person as you do with another, which is why arranged marriages aren't necessarily such a bad thing. You know, I've come to the conclusion that it doesn't much matter whom you marry as long as they're from an appropriate pool of people.' She looked at me keenly. 'We'll be all right, Chloe, really we will. We're both just having a bit of a crisis; it's only a blip. Carry on seeing Ivan if it helps you get through it, but just be discreet about it.'

'But I finished it with him, I told him I didn't want to see him anymore and now I feel so sad. I've spoilt everything and I'll never ever be happy again.' I started crying in great noisy gulps.

I'm not entirely sure what happened after that, but I think Ruthie must have got me home somehow. I woke up the next morning, Sunday, alone in an empty house. I phoned her to fill in some gaps.

'Do you have any idea where my husband might be?'

'He's in the park with Richard, all the kids and his mother, looking like one of those stone statues on Easter Island.'

'Stern, immovable and permanent?'

'That's the one.'

'Would you say that this stone-like demeanour is a result of his mother's presence or of his wife's behaviour?'

'I would think a little bit of both.'

'Fuck. I might have to run away from home.'

I got up and drifted round the house. The kitchen was spotless – a silent reproach – Edie had been at work with her apron on. I didn't know what to do with myself in this unusually silent weekend house, so I crawled back into bed and flicked through the Sunday papers. Ivan's cartoon of Dad stared out at me from the pages of the *Sunday Times*. He'd drawn him dressed in ermine seated on a throne in the theatre's Royal Box: *Bertie Zhivago's long reign as King of the West End Musical* read the caption. Something caught my eye; I looked more closely and could see that Ivan had drawn the silhouette of a couple standing together in a neighbouring box, an homage to our parting.

Sometime later, Sammy came in and sat on the edge of my bed.

'Is everyone back?'

He nodded. 'Yes, the kids are doing their homework and Greg's just taking Edie to the station.'

'I didn't say goodbye to her.'

'It's okay, Greg told her that you weren't feeling well.'

'What did she say?'

'She sort of snorted disbelievingly and reminded Greg of his old girlfriend, Mary O'Grady, a "nice strong girl" who's got six children, the last of whom she delivered herself at home before going and collecting the others from school and making her husband his dinner. Fish pie, I think she said it was.'

Greg and I moved around each other warily for the rest of the day, avoiding eye contact and conversation. I felt miserable and ached to think I wouldn't see Ivan again. I couldn't very well confide my sadness at the loss of my lover to my husband or children. That was the trouble with secret lives; they had to remain secret and you had to bear the consequences of that. Forced to bear my grief silently, I found it easier simply to be angry with Greg.

By the following evening, the silence between us was growing oppressive.

'What exactly are my crimes apart from sleeping for most of Sunday?' I asked Greg, when I had come back upstairs after an exhausting day of dealing with other people's psyches. I wasn't much up to the task; keeping my own in order seemed to be taking all my efforts these days. Greg was sitting in an armchair in the living room; his body curved away from me, just as Becky's had been from Ivan the night of the Gala. But with Greg, it was as if proximity to me might infect him with disease. He held the newspaper up like a shield. Beneath its lower edges, I could just make out his mouth, pursed tightly. Without lowering the paper, he said, 'If you don't know, there's not much point in my telling you.'

OK, so I'd been a little bit drunk and had raised my voice at him in public. It seemed to me that he was over-reacting. Greg had a thing about not washing one's dirty linen in public; he liked to present a picture of family harmony to the world. I thought it was rather bourgeois of him, but then I came from a long line of shouty, let-it-all-hang-out Jews. Of course, before I worked myself up into a state of righteous indignation at what I considered to be this unwarranted anger, I should remember that I had been conducting an extra-marital affair for the past several months, thus forfeiting any right to indignation. As I sat there under Greg's silent reprimand, I felt like a scolded adolescent.

'So, as usual, you're not going to talk about it? You'll just ignore me instead?' It made me feel better to go on the offensive.

He didn't answer.

I was worn down by him, by the house, by our lives. The residue of Edie's floral perfume still hung in the air hours after her departure. I felt imprisoned by Greg's mood in the same way that my mother's moods had once held me captive as she lay disappointed in her darkened bedroom. I needed air.

'Fine,' I said, 'I'm going out.'

'Do what you want, you always do anyway,' Greg said.

I slammed the living room door as I left.

'Where are you going?' asked Kitty as I took my coat off the hook by the door.

'Out.'

'You're always going out. You're never here anymore. I may as well not have a mother.' She looked me up and down. 'And you're dressed like one of those women who's trying to look like a teenager again; like divorced women dress when they're looking for a new husband.'

'Oh darling.' I knelt down and took her in my arms. Her small body was stiff and unyielding.

'Are you and Daddy friends yet?' she asked.

'Nearly, but sweetheart, it's normal for people to argue; it doesn't mean that they don't love each other.' Although, I thought, I wasn't sure I did love Greg anymore. I seemed to have succeeded in ruining everything.

'Come with me, let's pop over and see Grandpa; it'll cheer us both up.'

It was a relief to leave the house and run home to Daddy. Everyone needs a sanctuary and mine had always been wherever my father or Ruthie were. Helga had extended her stay and after greeting me warmly, she whisked Kitty off for an apple strudel lesson, leaving Dad and me alone in his music room. I told him that I'd ended my affair. He didn't say anything; he simply hugged me and sat down at his piano.

I watched his hands as he played one of his songs and thought about Ivan and the way his hands had played my body. I must have let out a moan of anguish because Dad stopped playing and turned to look at me.

'Are you all right, Chlo?'

'I just wish I could have another go at everything.'

'What do you mean?'

'My life. I want to rub it out and start again; I seem to have made an awful mess of this copy. I'd just like the chance to try again. Do you think I'm having a nervous breakdown? Jung had one, you know, he called it a confrontation with the unconscious. I think mine is more of a collision with the conscious; I can't seem to stand my life any more.'

'Everything has a purpose, illness can be creative,' said Dad, 'although I can see that may be hard to appreciate now.'

*

Greg and I didn't seem able to say anything to each other without one of us taking it as a rebuke or a criticism. Consequently, we spent the next week baring our teeth at one another like animals that are forced to share the same cage. The marital scoreboard might just as well have been hanging up in full view, all of our respective misdemeanours over the past seventeen years illuminated in neon lights. I found myself calculating how many days remained until Kitty left school (five and a half years; five multiplied by 365 equals 1,825, plus half a year (182) equals 2,007. Call it 2,000). In about two thousand days I could leave him and my children's home would only be broken after they'd left it; but by then I'd be forty-nine, Ivan would have forgotten me and no one else would want me.

Greg spent his time busying himself with his various battles with the council and in correcting the misdemeanours of everyone he encountered – fellow drivers and shopkeepers alike – and shouting at the children. Now and again I would catch him watching me thoughtfully as if contemplating speech. Was he planning to confront me about his suspicions? I replayed my memories of my times with Ivan over and over. Not surprisingly, everyone felt the tension; Bea and Zuzi kept their distance and even Jessie chose to stay at her mother's.

Chapter Twenty

Abe's Potato Latkes with Jamaican Hot Sauce

For the latkes:

1 1/2 lb. russet potatoes	2 tsp. baking powder
1 lemon	Good pinch salt
1 onion, grated	Pinch pepper
1 egg, beaten	Vegetable oil or *schmaltz* for
2 tbsp. flour	frying

Preheat oven to gas mark 1/140° C. Squeeze the lemon and add the juice to a large bowl of ice water. Peel the potatoes and roughly grate them into the bowl; let stand for half an hour. Drain the potatoes well, squeezing dry with a kitchen towel. Place the grated potato in a large bowl and add onion, egg, flour, baking powder, and salt and pepper.

Place a few tablespoons of the vegetable oil or *schmaltz* in a heavy duty frying pan and heat over medium heat. Scoop 1 tbsp. of the potato mixture into the skillet for each latke, cooking four of them at a time. Cook until golden and puffy, about 1 minute. Turn and brown the other side for about 30 seconds. Place on a rack and keep them warm in the oven. Add a bit more fat to pan for each batch.

For the Hot Sauce:

1/2 pound red habanero chillies, seeds and stems removed
1 white onion, chopped
2 cloves garlic, chopped
1/2 cup cider vinegar
1/2 cup lime juice (or lemon juice)
2 tbsp. water

1 medium papaya, boiled until tender, peeled, seeded, and finely chopped
1 tomato, finely chopped
1 tsp. thyme
1 tsp. basil
1/2 tsp. ground nutmeg
2 Tbsp. dry mustard
1/2 tsp. turmeric

Combine the chillies, onion, garlic, papaya, and tomato in a food processor and purée (you may have to do this in batches). Remove to a shallow bowl. Combine the vinegar, lime juice, and water in a saucepan and heat until it reaches a slight boil, then sprinkle in the thyme, basil, nutmeg, mustard, and turmeric. Pour this hot, spiced mixture over the reserved purée and mix thoroughly. It will keep up to eight weeks in the refrigerator.

It was ten o'clock, Sammy was out, so were the au pairs, and everyone else was in bed and asleep except me. It had been four weeks since Dad's gala, four weeks since I'd seen or spoken to Ivan and I still couldn't stop thinking about him.

'What do you expect,' Ruthie had said that afternoon in the park café. 'It's only been twenty-eight days. You aren't allowed to call him or see him for sixty days; that's the rule.'

'What rule? You mean there are more rules?'

'Yes, lots. These are the rules pertaining to break-ups, don't you remember them? No phoning, no writing, no meeting. And if you feel yourself weakening, you have to phone me so that I can protect you from yourself.'

'What am I, a teenager?'

Ruthie didn't answer, she just gave a sort of expressive snort instead. It was true; I might just as well have been a sixteen-year-old.

My fingers were itching to text him and ask him to meet me immediately. I walked through the sleeping house and went down to the kitchen where I poured a glass of wine, hoping either to give myself the courage to call him or to knock myself out so that I couldn't. I rarely drink alone. I rested my head against the window and looked out into the garden. The bare branches of the cherry tree we'd planted for Mum were just visible in the moonlight. I caught sight of a reflection in the glass and, for a moment, thought I saw my mother's face, but soon realised that it was my own. I was looking more and more like her as I grew older. Mum had only been twelve years older than I was now when she died. None of us know how long we have to live; what would I do if I knew I had only twelve years of life left? How would I choose to live out the remainder? I reached for the phone to call Ivan but as soon as I touched it, it started to ring.

'Ruthie, thank God, I was just about to call him.'

'Come over. Now,' she ordered.

On my way out, I saw a small envelope lying on the floor by the front door. It was addressed to me and had been hand delivered. It was from Ivan, as though my longing for him had reeled him in to me. I opened it up to find a cartoon of him and me. I was sitting in my shrink's chair listening to him talking. He was holding his hands out towards me. Underneath he had captioned it in Russian: *Ne mogu bez tebia. Davai budem, kak my byli v nachale. Ia tak tebia liubliu.*

How could he have taken the risk of posting it through the letter-box? I walked with it resolutely to the bin, but at the last moment, I stuck it in my coat pocket instead.

Ruthie and I sat in her kitchen where she watched me drink another large glass of wine very fast before bursting into messy tears. I'd never mastered the art of crying prettily – a lone tear, a quiet sniff, a lace handkerchief pressed to the eye. No, I was an untidy, puffy-eyed and red-nosed weeper. Ruthie made a surreptitious trip to the loo, so I guessed she had some cocaine. I could see it in her face anyhow. What a mess we were both in.

'I wouldn't normally push drugs,' she said, 'but would you like a line of coke? It might cheer you up.'

I was still crying noisily, wiping my nose on my sleeve, hiccupping and gulping. I shook my head.

'No thanks, when I tried it years ago, it made me cry and I seem to be managing that perfectly well at the moment.'

I poured myself a shot of vodka instead and followed Ruthie to the safety of the bathroom, where she dried the marble next to the sink and laid out a fat line of white powder. As she deftly sniffed up her line, I knocked back my shot of vodka in one. The vodka seemed to have the same effect on me as the coke did on her; we both perked up enormously.

'I feel marvellous, never felt better, I really feel wonderful,' I said. 'Come on, let's get out of here and find somewhere to go and dance. Where shall we go? I know, let's go to Abe's all-night deli and see if his brother Herbie's band is playing. Come on, hurry up, let's go.'

'God, you're like a demented teenager. What was in that vodka?' Ruthie muttered as she restrained me long enough to dab *touche éclat* all over my tear-stained face before following me out.

Abraham 'Abe' Green was a six-foot-four Rastafarian with waist-length dreadlocks who ran an all night Jewish delicatessen just a few doors down from the Volga. He wore a rainbow-coloured, crocheted skullcap, a mini-version of a Rasta hat. Abe insisted that he was a nice Jewish boy whose Portuguese-Spanish forefathers had arrived in Jamaica in the sixteenth century and, indeed, his pale green eyes suggested complicated ancestry. His speech was littered with 'Oy Veys', 'ay yai yais' and 'Please Gods'. In his spare time, he was studying to be a rabbi and the breadth of his knowledge of Jewish texts coupled with the authenticity and deliciousness of his cuisine had led to him being quickly clasped to the collective bosom of the local Jewish community. ('He may be a *schwartze* with hair too long, but he's our *schwartze*').

'Well, well, well,' he greeted us as we walked through the door, 'to what do I owe the unexpected pleasure? You don't phone, you don't write, you've found somewhere better that you haven't been here for so long?' He could certainly do guilt like a Jew.

'How's business?' I asked.

'Gefilte Fish!* Feh, how should it be?'

Abe had an endearing habit of using the names of Jewish dishes as expletives in the place of swear words. Ruthie and I sat down.

---

* Gefilte Fish: Fish balls made with ground fish, matzo meal and eggs, cooked in fish broth. Served cold with horseradish.

I felt restless and couldn't keep still. Why had I brought us here? The last thing I wanted was food. I was drunk and wanted to be drunker. The room was full of elderly Jews having a little snack before going home to bed (God forbid they should die of hunger before they reached their own fridges), and Rastas with the munchies. Abe was berating a couple who, their meal long over, still lingered at their table: 'You want to sit, go home and sit, you want to eat, stay and eat.' Hard wooden chairs, a studied lack of ambience and stark Formica tables all reinforced the rule of the house: No Loitering. Eat and Go! Abe liked *turnover*. He brought a plate of pickled cucumbers and chopped liver to our table.

'I'm sorry, but I'm just not hungry Abe. Have you got any booze?' I asked.

'Booze? What do we Jews know from alcohol? Shish, what is it with you people, all sitting and no eating, what am I, a park bench?' He paused, 'A little Israeli Sabbath wine, I got.'

Ruthie and I looked at each other and pulled faces. Just how desperate were we? 'Is it dry?'

Abe shrugged, lifted his hands, palms turned up towards the heavens and pulled his face into an expression familiar to Jews since time immemorial; it was the sort of look that said, 'What do you want, a miracle?'

'Me, I'm thinking you don't so much need alcohol. You look edgy, what you need is a little smoke to calm you down and bring your appetite back and then a little snack.'

We went to his back room with him and watched as he expertly rolled a one-skin joint with some grass.

'In this matter, your Rasta genes clearly supersede your Jewish ones,' I said.

'Genes, shmenes, they're complementary, two halves that make a perfect whole: Rasta grass to give you an appetite, Jewish food to feed your munchies. Yin and Yang, you should pardon the expression. The Rastafarian Jew is the most highly evolved human being on the planet,' Abe said smugly.

Ruthie and I nodded at his wisdom, which struck us with added force after the sixth toke on the little joint he had rolled.

I played idly with one of Abe's snow globes; he had a collection of some two hundred, tumbling dustily from book-crammed shelves.

My favourite was of two Hassidic Jews, bent against the wind in their long black overcoats and black hats. Their long beards and forelocks seemed to sway in an imaginary wind. Now, as I looked at it, I felt like I was being sucked into the small glass dome and into the eighteenth-century Polish *shtetl* that was their home. Was that why I had felt so at home with Ivan, I wondered, because of the East European connection, an indelible race memory that was my birthright? There seemed to be something so familiar about him, a cultural sense of belonging that I didn't have with Greg. I pressed the globe to my face, feeling the cool of the glass. I'd never noticed before how slowly each little silvery snowflake fell, almost in slow motion really. Everything had been going too fast moments before and now it had all become so very s-l-o-w …

'When are you going to bring me some more of your chicken soup, Chloe?' Abe's voice asked. It sounded like he was speaking from the bottom of a very deep well.

'Soon, I promise.' My answer seemed to come some time later, as if the sounds could only be heard a long time after they had left my mouth. Or was it my mouth? It felt like my mouth, but what did 'my' really mean? And what, after all, was a mouth when you came down to it?

('You smoked Abe's grass?' Greg asked me the next day. 'You smoked Abe's grass?' he repeated, shaking his head in disbelief. 'Are you insane? I would never take more than two tokes on an Abe joint and I'm a master. You're lucky you didn't get locked-in syndrome.'

'What do you mean?' I said.

'When you can't move or speak at all. Jesus, Chloe, what's the matter with you?')

'Greg was here yesterday.' Abe's eyes were shut and he was swaying slightly as though he were praying. 'He was talking to Moishe in the kitchen and asking how much *schmaltz* he put in his kneidlach. Moishe's aren't as good as yours though.' He slapped his hand to his forehead, 'Tzimmes*! What a schmuck! I was supposed to keep that a secret.'

'Safe with me. I'm the Queen of Secrets,' I said.

* Tzimmes: a dish of carrots baked in butter and honey.

Abe looked at me sceptically as he put a CD into a ghetto blaster. 'Listen to this, Herbie's done a new mix of the Shema.'

We tapped our feet to Herbie's reggae version of the Jewish prayer. I got up and started dancing and I have a faint but terrifying memory of leading the other two out into the restaurant in a sort of conga line, our right hands covering our eyes as is customary when saying this particular prayer, while we sang *Sh'ma Yisrael Adonai Elohaynu Adonai Echad**. The mood seemed to catch everyone and the rest of the customers joined in.

Never let it be said that we Jews don't know how to have fun! By then, Ruthie and I had become ravenously hungry and so we sat down and fell on the familiar food of our forefathers: salt beef, chopped egg, bagels and, Abe's variation on an old favourite, potato latkes with Jamaican hot sauce, all washed down with sweet red Israeli Sabbath wine.

'Have they settled the terms of your redundancy?' I asked Ruthie, chopped liver escaping from my mouth.

I heard the hiss of a collective intake of breath. Everyone around us froze in a pantomime of shock. Forks stopped en route to mouths, glasses failed to reach their final destination, and here and there a couple of people could be seen spitting three times over their left shoulders to ward off the evil eye.

'What? What? What did I say?' I asked the room at large.

A smartly dressed man in a business suit leant forward from the next table and gripped me tightly by the arm, 'You should forgive me, but you think that's a word we like to hear when we're eating?'

'What, redundancy?'

The room gasped again and turned away from us. I saw Volodya coming through the door and waved to him. I'd secretly texted him when Ruthie wasn't looking and asked him to meet me here. He had a coat on over his pyjamas and was carrying his tattered copy of *Doctor Zhivago*.

'Which bit are you up to?'

'Lara's gone off to the station and Yuri's said he'll follow and meet her there.'

---

* Hear, Israel, the Lord is our God, the Lord is One.

'Do you really not know what happens?'

'No, shush, don't spoil it.'

'How can you be Russian and not know?'

'What can I say? I was away that day at school.'

I emptied my pockets. Dirty tissues, fluffy pieces of unchewed gum, coins, a screwed up parking ticket ... Finally, I found it, the card from Ivan.

'What does it say?'

Volodya looked around. The couple at the next table were watching with some interest. I got up, took Volodya by the arm and led him outside. He held the card under the light of a streetlamp and screwed up his eyes so that he could make out the words.

'It says, *I can't bear it without you. Let's be like we were in the beginning. I love you so much.*'

I started crying again. Quite prettily this time, just a couple of tears tracing a dignified path down my cheeks.

'Don't be like Yuri Zhivago, Chloe, go to the *vokzal,* the railway station; don't throw away your chance of happiness.'

'You liar, you do know what happens,' I hit him on the shoulder.

Volodya shrugged noncommittally.

'Anyhow, what happened to all that *be careful* stuff?' I said.

'Sometimes you just can't stand in the way of love.'

'I love Russians,' I said, throwing my arms around him, 'you're so irresistibly passionate and romantic.'

Well, I reasoned to myself, it hadn't done Yuri Zhivago much good had it, ignoring his love for Lara in the end? He'd ended up without Tonya and without Lara, dying alone and lonely in Moscow. It seemed like a sign, as though the universe were showing me the way forward. I kissed Volodya and went back inside the restaurant.

'Nu, well, what did the piece of paper say?' asked the heavily made-up matron who'd been sitting next to me as she passed on her way out.

'Not telling,' I said.

She waved a hand at me in disgust. 'Spoilsport.'

'Come on, Ruthie,' I said, sweeping her up and paying Abe. He pressed a small plastic bag into my hand containing some of his grass.

'For Greg,' he said.

I blew him a kiss as I led Ruthie off down the road. 'Let's go and you can have a little more of that white powder of yours, while I smoke Greg's grass.'

'You've turned into an animal,' she said, 'a wild, drug-guzzling beast.'

It was all a bit of a blur after that, although I seem to recall smoking a joint while lying on Ruthie's kitchen floor and watching her sniff a line of cocaine that circumvented one of the table legs.

'Who says they have to be straight lines?' Ruthie had said. 'Boring, boring, boring. I want to live a little, to make squiggles, circles, squares and to invent whole new shapes for cocaine and the snorting thereof.'

God but we were clever, creative, interesting, witty and marvellous and we had such a lot to talk about. Pity I couldn't really remember much of what we'd said, but I think that we solved quite a lot of problems, our own and other people's.

'That's it!' Ruthie had exclaimed at one point. 'I'll squirt superglue into the locks of David Gibfuck's car. That'll teach him to make me redundant. The cunt! He won't look so clever when he can't get into his snazzy Saab and has to walk or take public transport like the rest of us who are unemployed because of him, and who also don't have jobs because of him.' She stabbed the air with a finger for emphasis. (Drugs make you talk a lot; they just don't necessarily make you talk sense).

I have a disturbing memory of composing a very long text message to Ivan which may or may not have said something along the lines of *I'm so sorry about our parting, you must know that you are very important to me and that you have awakened my spirit in the past few months. I feel that we are soul mates with a unique connection. You have made me feel again, touched my senses in a way that they haven't been touched for years, opened my heart and ...*

'The essence of the text is brevity,' Ruthie had said as I tapped away.

'Yes, yes, but I just have to tell him a few things. It's very, very important; I can see it all so clearly now.' My finger had taken on a life of its own. *I felt a little overwhelmed by everything that was happening between us and thought that it would be best for both of us if I ended our relationship. I see now that this was a terrible mistake. Ever since, I have felt deep despair and sorrow. I so want to see you my darling and to feel your arms around me.* Just before I pressed send, I added, in a dope-fuelled rush of lust: *I also want to feel you moving inside me once more so that we can soar high together on the plains of carnal bliss.* It made me blush to think of it the next morning. In vino veritas? Perhaps. In narcotics nonsensicus? Clearly.

Now I lay in bed flushed with shame and reached out a tentative hand to pat the bed next to me. Empty. I looked at my watch. One o'clock. What did that mean? What sort of one o'clock – a.m. or p.m? I could see light filtering through the still closed curtains. Oh God, I'd slept half the day away. What time had I come home? I could remember Ruthie opening yet another bottle of wine at seven-thirty in the morning, before sending Sephy, who had just got up, round the corner to buy newspapers and cigarettes. (We'd both decided in the course of the night that smoking was a very grown-up thing to do).

'How come they sold you cigarettes?' Ruthie asked when she returned.

'Easy,' she answered, 'I just told them that my mum was too drunk to come and get them herself.'

This had the effect of sobering us up immediately and I'd somehow made my way across the park, which appeared to be hosting an early morning convention for park-bench drunks. They lolled wordlessly, clutching beer cans like security blankets. For once, I knew just how they felt; I was amongst my people. I stood in the chill dawn of a winter Sunday and looked at my front door. I had forgotten my keys, and after standing in a numb, bemused state for some minutes, threw a pebble in the direction of our bedroom window. It missed, but the loud and indignant squawk of the pigeon it hit (one of Madge's flock?) brought Greg to the window, mute and grim-faced. He came down and let me in without saying a word.

*

My mouth was dry, I had pins and needles in my arms and legs and my brain felt bruised. The house was silent. I found the phone and pulled it into my den of disgrace beneath the covers as I dialled.

'Ruthie?' I whispered hoarsely.

'I'm so sorry,' Ruthie said. 'I'm afraid your friend Ruthie is dead. A drug overdose, I believe. I am merely her walking corpse.'

'God, Ruthie, I'm so sorry about last night.'

'Actually, I'm not,' she said. 'I'm pleased, it was the big bang I needed to end on; you know, the enough-no-more point I needed to reach. After you left I sat and thought about how it wasn't big or funny or even very clever. I tipped the rest of the stuff down the loo, confessed to Richard and went to a Narcotics Anonymous meeting in Notting Hill Gate.'

'See anyone we know?'

'My lips are sealed; I have taken the NA oath.'

'You're no fun.'

I felt full of shame that I had encouraged Ruthie to do coke when I had been trying so hard to wean her off it. It made nonsense of the discreet conversation I'd had with Richard only the week before. I'd gone over there one afternoon when I'd known Ruthie would be out. Richard was in his study, buried in a book about Ancient Greek writings inscribed in stone. I'd explained to him that Ruthie was in trouble and had a coke habit. He'd looked rather bewildered and I realised I would need to frame it in a context that he could understand.

'Cocaine's been around for centuries,' I said. 'Perhaps, the Ancient Greeks were just as partial to the white powder as the Ancient Egyptians?'

'Yes, indeed,' said Richard, brightening up at once and pinching the bridge of his nose as he always did when he was about to explain something. 'During the ancient Olympic Games, there is evidence that the earliest athletes found all sorts of ways to enhance their performance; alcohol, stimulants and opiates which they probably chewed. As you know, of course, the ancient games stopped for good in A.D. 395 and Olympia was vandalised beyond repair.'

I didn't know, but I nodded anyhow. He paused for a moment, shaking his head sorrowfully as if the destruction of Olympia were a breaking news story.

227

'When the Olympics in their current incarnation were reborn in Athens in 1896,' he went on, 'some competitors did use cocaine and other stimulants to give them extra edge.' He carefully put his book down, first marking his place with a leather bookmark, and walked over to his desk. On it stood his gleaming concession to the modern world: a silver Apple laptop computer. He entered the words Cocaine Abuse into the search engine. 'Thank you for telling me, Chloe,' he said. 'I know Ruthie hasn't been happy recently.' I'd asked him not to shop me but I'm not sure whether he was listening and I'd left him researching the subject of drug addiction and making meticulous notes in the slim black notebook he always carried with him.

'What did Richard say?' I now asked Ruthie nervously, coming back to the present and wondering if he'd grassed me up.

'He seemed so relieved that I'd finally come clean about why I've been such a madwoman for the past few months. He hugged me and told me he loved me and that he'd do whatever was needed to help me sort myself out.'

'So there may be a point to husbands after all?'

'Well, let's not get too carried away. Although, I may have to concede that mine is not entirely without purpose at this precise moment.'

'God,' I said, as memory of the previous night flooded me. 'You're so lucky you're already dead, I want to die too.'

I retrieved my mobile phone from the safety of a locked drawer, where, out of a sense of self-preservation and notwithstanding my drunken, stoned state, I had hidden it. There were my messages to Ivan, intact and mercifully saved in *drafts*. Thank God I hadn't sent them. I had woken up with new resolve and knew I mustn't contact him. My affair with Ivan was over. Finished. The End. The phone beeped in my hand making me jump. Ivan? No, a message from Greg: *Text when you deign to get up*. Oops, it was clear I was firmly in the dog house. I texted him back: *I am awake*.

The woman who looked back at me from the bathroom mirror was someone I had never seen before. She was a stranger: older than me by some years, dark circles encompassing eyes that glimmered with desperation, and hair hanging greasily around a ravaged, puffy face in which the traces of any previous beauty appeared to have been all but extinguished.

I ran a bath, made my way through the empty house, whose every brick seemed to scream reproach, and collected an array of vegetables and cold wet tea bags that I placed carefully along the edge of the bath. Cucumber on its own wasn't enough; in my current condition I needed a fuller selection of crudités to soothe my swollen eyes. I added essential oils to the water, got in, lay down and prayed that natural remedies could counteract the damage wrought by alcohol and drug abuse. It was all very well your mind thinking that you were still a teenager, but your body was there to tell you that you were a middle-aged woman and simply couldn't take the pace any longer. Nothing seemed to help. I felt agitated and unwell and needed a doctor, but I doubted whether my own personal physician would be sympathetic to my plight. Perhaps FF was right – sex was like petrol and I was running on empty, soon to sputter, gasp and die.

Chapter Twenty-One

Chloe Zhivago's Humble Pie

The expression Humble Pie dates back to William the Conqueror's times when the lord of the manor dined on the venison meat of the deer, while the servants had to content themselves with the heart, liver, kidney and other innards, known as 'nombles' or 'umbles'. Since then, 'Eating humble pie' has come to connote a voluntary acceptance of humble status or humiliating treatment.

I am not an offal fan – in my opinion, one rarely needs to be quite that humble – so I cheat and use beef instead, making my own particular humble pie, more fit for a prince than for a pauper:

1 1/2 lb. good stewing steak cut into cubes
1 tbsp. flour, seasoned with salt, pepper and a tsp.. of cinnamon
1 medium onion, chopped
1 cup red wine

4-5 carrots, cut into chunks (I use Chantenay carrots)
1/2 cup flour
1 tsp. Marigold vegetable bouillon or an Oxo cube
Several tears of apology

Pastry:
6 oz flour
3 oz butter
Salt

A little cold water
1 egg yolk
1 beaten egg to glaze

Mix tbsp. flour with seasonings in a plastic bag; add beef cubes and shake to coat evenly. Heat a little oil in a pressure cooker and brown beef with the chopped onion. Add carrots, 1 cup water and the wine in pressure cooker. Add Marigold bouillon (or if you prefer a darker look, the Oxo cube). Cook on high until cooker comes up to pressure, then reduce to medium and time for 10 minutes. Add cold water and tears of apology to 1/2 cup flour and mix to a smooth paste. Add carefully to beef and carrots and stir well.

While beef is cooking, cube the butter and rub into flour and salt with your fingertips until it resembles breadcrumbs. Rub the egg yolk in then add enough water to bind the mixture. Cut in half and roll out on a floured surface, then place in a 23cm greased pie dish, trimming the excess edges. Pour in beef and carrot mixture, roll out remaining pastry and cover, brush with beaten egg, cut vents with a sharp knife. Bake at gas mark 4/180° C for 30 minutes.

Needless to say, my most recent transgression didn't endear me to my husband. I couldn't blame him really. In spite of my repeated attempts to apologise, he stopped talking to me altogether and one evening I found Kitty in her room packing a bag. She handed me a letter addressed to Greg and me, written in purple ink:

Dear Mum and Dad,
I cannot take this any longer. I don't know when I will be back. Why are you fighting? Two people who have been together for so long should grow closer not further apart. This is why I must love you and leave you.
Love from your daughter.
xxx Kitty xxx

Even Greg was chastened by Kitty's attempt to run away from home. Her grasp of our situation highlighted the childishness of our behaviour. It was ironic; Kitty had been the trigger for my ending my affair with Ivan, but it hadn't much improved matters; if anything, Greg and my relationship had got worse. In a curious way, having an affair had maintained a sort of equilibrium in our marriage.

That same evening, Leo came in drunk and vomited on the hall floor. He staggered towards me, tears streaming down his face and hiccuped.

'I hate myself,' he slurred. 'I really, really love you, but I hate myself.'

'What have you been drinking?'

'Vodka,' he said. He hugged me before lying down on the floor where he instantly fell asleep, only to wake moments later as he began to vomit again.

'We can't let him go to sleep,' I said to Greg as I turned him on his side into the recovery position. 'He'll choke.'

Greg and I helped him into the shower. I hadn't seen Leo naked for years, not since before puberty when he'd still had a little boy's body. It's true what they say: oaks do grow from acorns. I was so shocked that I couldn't help staring. Where had my baby boy gone? I remembered the moment that he was laid in my arms for the first time, a tightly wrapped bundle, proffered by the midwife. 'Take your son,' she had said and I swelled with pride, unable to believe that my female body could have created this small and perfect male creature; it was quite simply the cleverest thing that I had ever done in my life. Now, in the blink of an eye, here he was, a drunk, vomiting, naked man. But, for all that, he was still defenceless, still in need of my protection, still my baby boy.

'I jus' had a few drinks, Mum.'

'His sugar levels will be all over the place,' said Greg. 'He'll need to go to hospital.'

'I'll take him,' I said. 'You stay here with Kitty.'

In the hospital, Leo vomited on a stranger's shoes before falling onto the hard cold floor. This was too much even for the hardened, wounded brawlers who frequented the A & E department. They all looked at me reproachfully: what kind of a mother lets her son get so drunk?

'I imagine you must be pleased about this,' the staff nurse said as she led Leo briskly to a bed and put him on a drip to stabilise his blood sugar.

'Yes,' I agreed wryly. 'I'm absolutely delighted.'

I sat at my child's bedside through the night and watched as old drunks were brought off the streets and into safety. One of them in particular caught my eye, a tall man in a suit, which, although shabby, had a faded elegance about it. He was well-spoken and courteous to the nursing staff, speaking in the measured tones of someone pretending to be sober. I watched as he smoothed back his silver hair and laid his hat down carefully on the end of his bed in an action that was at once fastidious and familiar: it was clear he was no stranger to the hospital, and indeed, a moment later, a smiling nurse walked past him, gave him a mock salute and said 'Evening, Major.' I couldn't help wondering what his story was and what had led him to this. A lifetime of heavy drinking that had begun as an adolescent foible and somewhere along the way had unwittingly become a career decision. I turned to Leo and saw in his eyes that shame was beginning to replace inebriation. He was watching the drunk stranger too. I didn't need to say anything; I could see that he was learning the lesson for himself. Sometimes you need a crisis to move onto a new phase in your life. Perhaps I had needed my affair with Ivan to enable Greg and me to move forward. I wasn't sure how, but as I sat there listening to my son's steady breathing, I resolved more firmly than ever to put Ivan in the past and to focus on the future with Greg.

Nevertheless, life in Grumpy Towers remained difficult and my tentative attempts to inch my nose and paws out of the *maison du chien* and win back Greg's favour had so far fallen on deaf ears. He pretended everything was fine when the children were around, but when we were on our own he spoke to me in the distant tones of a not altogether friendly acquaintance.

'How are things at home?' Ruthie asked me in the café one morning.

'Bad.'

'Sex?'

'None.'

'Don't you think you should talk to him about it? I mean, after all, you are Mrs Talking Cure – it's what you do for a living?'

'I know, but the trouble is I feel that I forfeited that right by having an affair,' I said sadly.

It was hard to feel indignant with Greg for not doing with me what I'd so readily done with someone else. It was also hard not to long for Ivan and his kisses, especially as he'd started sending me text messages over the past few days. So far I'd resisted replying, but I had to confess that, whatever my resolutions, I still wanted to.

There was nothing for it, I'd have to woo my husband back, and the first step was to eat humble pie; both literally and metaphorically. And make some for Greg to eat too. The way to a man's heart is indeed through his stomach and not, as one all too often wishes, with a knife through his chest.

'What are you up to, Mum?' Kitty asked, as I peeled vegetables.

'What do you mean? I'm cooking supper.'

'You've got your faraway face on,' she said unhappily. 'I thought it had gone, but it's come back again.'

She'd caught me thinking about Ivan. Kitty might just as well have still been in my womb sharing my emotions through the umbilical cord that had once bound us; she could always sense emotional change in me. I was saved from further scrutiny by her phone beeping. Her face softened as she read the message.

She held the phone up for me to read: *I wish I could see you.*

'Who's that from?' I asked.

'Max, I'm going out with him.'

'Since when?'

'Yesterday.'

It was all so marvellously simple: Max had phoned Kitty and asked her to go out with him. She'd told him to hang on while she dumped Joe, who had been her boyfriend for the past fortnight, and now Kitty and Max were going out. Although, they didn't actually seem to *go* anywhere at all. In a few days or weeks one of them would dump the other, usually by text or phone and start going out with someone else, perhaps the dumped boyfriend's best friend. It was useful baby training slopes for relationships. What a pity it got so complicated as the years went on. Perhaps I should just tell Greg he was dumped and go off with Ivan. Judging by the regularity with which Kitty and her friends dumped boys and took up with new ones, was it any wonder that no one seemed to expect relationships to last and that the pattern for so many these days was serial monogamy? If only it were that straightforward and relationships could be like light bulbs: simply replaced when they'd burnt out.

My phone beeped. It was Ivan: *I wish I could see you.*

'Let's see,' said Kitty holding her hand out.

I hid the phone in my hand.

'I showed you mine,' she said.

'Sorry darling, it's a patient,' I lied.

Kitty gave a disbelieving snort and left the room, bumping into Leo as he came in.

'Fuck off, Leo,' she said, shoving him.

'Fuckoffyourselfyoulittlebitchwhatdoyouthinkyouarefucking doingdon'ttellmetofuckoff.' I looked at him, astonished less by the violence of his response, than by the extreme rapidity with which it was delivered.

'Hellomumwhat'stheproblemwhyareyoulookingatmelikethat?'

'Don't talk to your sister like that! What's going on? You have been a man of few words these last two years and now it's like listening to a volley of bullets from a machine gun.'

'Yeahwellthat'sbecauseI'mgoingtobethewhiteTwistahe'stheman ,thenumberonerapacrobat,thefastestrapperintheworldandI'mgoi ngtobethewhiteenglishversionandsoI'mpractisingtalkingasfastas Ican .'

'God help us,' I muttered.

'I can't win,' Leo said with exaggerated slowness. 'You go on about me grunting and now when I talk, you complain about that as well. You just don't understand anything. I've finally found the one thing I want to do with my life.' He stormed out, slamming the door as he left.

The scene was set for a peaceful and conciliatory family dinner. Greg and the children sat wordlessly around the table while I served supper. For once it was just the four of us, which only served to highlight the tensions. Greg started the meal with his nose in the paper, tetchily scolding the children for chewing too loudly and not using their knives and forks properly. Without the distraction of talk and laughter, it was all too easy to be irritated by one another's table manners. Sensing this, the children quickly gobbled their food and left the table as soon as they could, while

Greg and I continued to eat in silence. But as the pie began to work its magic, he relaxed, put the paper aside and met my eyes for the first time in what seemed like ages. I paused, a full forkful of pie on its way to my mouth.

'You know how I love watching you eat humble pie,' he said.

I laughed, got up to get him another helping and, passing it to him said, 'Not as much as I enjoy making you eat it.' I reached out a tentative hand towards him. 'Let's try being kinder to each other,' I said.

Later, I reached for him in bed, rubbing up against him, hoping that we could find our way back to each other physically as well.

'Too tired,' he said, moving away and turning over with his back to me.

I lay awake for some time, listening to the wind and rain outside and watching the fluorescent hands of the alarm clock as they inched towards two a.m. Sometimes you can feel far lonelier with someone beside you than you ever would on your own.

The following morning, there were three messages from Gina on my practice answer machine. Each one was more hysterical than the last, the cries of a bride panicking in the final hours before her journey to the altar. She was getting married that afternoon. I sighed and called her back.

'Do you think it's possible to be happily married, Chloe?' she asked in a voice tight with fear.

'I think the thing is not to expect too much and to take note of the good times, not only the bad.'

'I'm not sure I can go through with this.'

'I never thought I'd cite Dolly Parton as the fount of all knowledge,' I said. 'But I once heard her interviewed about how she managed to remain cheerful when she'd had so many bad things happen to her and she said, "I decided to choose happiness". It can be as easy as that. So Gina, choose happiness, you have a lovely man, you love him, and he loves you. I'll see you at the wedding.'

Gina was getting married in her parents' home, which turned out to be a grand mansion on the edge of Holland Park. The clean white lines of more than a hundred arum lilies flanked the stairway that led to the front door. A uniformed maid took my coat at the door and I joined the throng for a pre-ceremony glass of champagne. I wasn't feeling well and the boom of well-bred voices threatened to deafen me. I was also dying for a pee and made my way up the stairs. As I was pausing to decide which of the many doors facing me might lead to a lavatory, I heard voices and the sound of a door opening. Gina appeared in a froth of white lace, laughing as she tamed a few curls that threatened to escape from her wedding hairdo. Behind her, I could make out the figure of a man tucking his shirt into his trousers.

'Don't you know it's bad luck for the groom to see you before the wedding?' I asked smiling. She looked at me in silence. The penny dropped.

'Ah, that's not the groom,' I said. 'I see.'

'We were just saying goodbye. I'm not actually married yet.'

I held a hand up to stem the flow of her explanations. It wasn't the moment for therapy, so I wished her luck and told her she looked beautiful. That's what you're meant to say to brides and in this case it was the truth: she radiated that singular beauty of a woman who has just been sexually satisfied.

I found the bathroom and scrutinised my face in the mirror. I wasn't looking my best. I sat on the edge of the lavatory, wet one of the many appliquéd guest towels that are the trademark of the middle-classes-acting-posh and held it against my forehead. Shakily I made my way downstairs where the ceremony was about to begin.

The drawing room must have been over thirty foot long; at one end tall French windows opened out onto a large garden where trees were just beginning to come back to life. Here and there, among their still bare branches, tender green leaves were emerging, and early daffodils were celebrating in the flowerbeds. Chairs had been laid out on either side of the room, creating an aisle down the middle. More lilies crowded the room and I realised their aroma was making me feel nauseous. Gina stood waiting on her father's arm, ethereally bathed in the early spring sunlight that poured in from the window behind her. I smiled at her reassuringly as I took my seat. She appeared as if she might be about to cry. She was looking not at the handsome groom who turned to watch her as she walked towards him, but at the man I had glimpsed earlier, who was seated half way down. When she passed him, her body seemed to lean towards him as though magnetically drawn by their attraction to each other; she faltered for a moment, recovered herself and, squaring her shoulders, walked resolutely on. As her father handed her to her groom, she reminded me of nothing so much as a prisoner who, having just been sentenced, turns from the dock to be led into custody by the waiting jailers. I knew then what she hadn't yet understood: her affair with the shirt-tucking man, now brooding in his seat, was far from over. It is so much easier to see the truth about someone else's situation than it is about one's own. This flash of clarity about Gina and her lover made me realise that the same was true of Ivan and me. I had to see him again.

Later, as I was trying to slip away unnoticed, a sharp-featured woman in a fuchsia suit hurried up to me and laid a hand on my arm.

'You must be Chloe Zhivago,' she said. 'I'm Gina's mother. Thank you so much for everything you've done for her. I don't think we'd ever have got her up the aisle without your help.'

She looked over at Gina, who was standing next to her new husband and smiling for the photographer. Photographs are not emotionally reliable, they show only what can be seen on the surface; they can and do lie. This one would smile out down the years from a well-thumbed wedding album, a captured moment of fraudulent newly-wedded bliss; it wouldn't hint that the bride had been in the arms of another man less than an hour before her wedding. Even as I watched, I could see Gina's eyes slide away and rest on the dark figure of her lover who was leaning against a door and watching her closely.

'I hope they'll be very happy together,' I said to Gina's mother. I felt an impostor in this particular fairytale, the bad fairy who placed the curse on Sleeping Beauty that made her prick her finger on the spinning wheel, as though my helping Gina into a life of matrimony was an act not of giving, but of taking away.

The scent from the lilies followed me down the stairs and I stood on the street for a moment feeling dizzy. My phone, which I'd switched onto silent, vibrated in my pocket, an angry insect intent on attracting my attention. I ignored it, walked into Holland Park Gardens and found a bench in the Japanese Garden; I needed a moment alone. Whatever my relationship with Ivan meant for the future of my marriage, I knew I had to see him again. I sat and watched the still water of the Japanese pond from which a white rock rose and stood silent sentry – the gatekeeper, perhaps, to a more contemplative and spiritual way of being. My phone vibrated again, drawing me back to the present. It was Ivan.

'Come and meet me, Chloe,' he said. 'Just let me have one whole night with you. I've missed you so much.'

'I know, me too.' His voice warmed me. I wanted nothing more than for him to hold me in his arms and tell me his stories of Russia. That was what I loved the most, even more than the lovemaking, that feeling of being transported out of my own world and into another where life once again vibrated with possibility.

As I turned the car into our street, I saw Madge hurrying along the pavement, laughing and talking to herself. Madness had become her refuge from the unbearable sadness of her reality. Although, I reflected, as I watched her turn and admonish a pigeon, while madness may have served to shield her from her memories, it appeared to bring her little joy. There are, I reflected, some things it is impossible to recover from: the death of a marriage – yes; the death of your children – never.

Fortunately, the house was empty, and within twenty minutes, I was washed, changed, made-up and back out on my way to meet Ivan in a country hotel. Ruthie had tut-tutted at me down the phone, but had conceded defeat and agreed to have Kitty and Leo to stay the night with her.

'It's classic,' she said, 'the one last fix of the addict who's gone cold turkey. Just make sure it's not an overdose.'

I'd left a message on Greg's voicemail burbling some nonsense about staying on at Gina's reception after all and that I wouldn't be back until the morning as it was out of town.

I travelled by train to our meeting place, an Oxfordshire pub with a Michelin star. Ivan was waiting for me, lying naked in a four-poster bed in a bedroom designed for lovers. I turned away from him as I undressed, made shy by our absence from each other, and slipped quickly between the sheets and into his arms. I nuzzled up against him like a cat that wants to be stroked; it felt so wonderful to be touched again that it was all I could do to stop myself from purring out loud.

'I've missed you so much,' he murmured after we'd made love.

'Me too,' I answered, although the truth was that now, after the act, I felt detached; the high from my fix of him was not as intense as I'd remembered. Sex had left me feeling strangely empty and I needed to chat in order to find closeness with him again.

'Tell me a story about Russia,' I said. But I could tell from his breathing that he'd fallen asleep.

I got up, walked over to the window and looked out into the night. It was much darker and quieter than I was accustomed to and I could hear Ivan's breathing as he slept. In the distance the forlorn yipping bark of a lone fox calling for its mate broke the silence. I got back into bed and turned my phone back on. It rang almost immediately. It was Greg; his next words were the thunderbolt I'd always feared was waiting to strike me.

'Chloe, I've got some bad news, I'm afraid.'

'What's happened, are the children all right, what is it?'

'It's your Dad; he's had a heart attack. It's okay, he's in hospital and his condition is stable.'

'Oh God, and I'm not there with him.'

This was it, my punishment, the outcome of my wickedness. The price of the pleasure in the man beside me had to be paid for with the illness of my father and my absence from his side. I told Greg I'd be back as soon as I could and woke Ivan to explain.

'I'm sure he'll be fine,' he said sleepily.

Waves of dread coursed through me, starting in the pit of my stomach and travelling throughout my body until fear throbbed in my fingertips and at the ends of my toes. Ever since I was a child I have lived with the terror of my father's mortality. I wanted to rush to him, to be in my own home, to see my children and my husband. What was I doing in a hotel room with someone else's husband?

'I have to go home now,' I said.

'It's late,' he said, 'we'll be back first thing in the morning.

Anyhow, Greg said he was stable, let's enjoy our night together, you promised me a night.' He took my hand and tried to pull me back into bed with him.

'I can't, I have to go and see my Dad now, he needs me.' The soft bed with its warm sheets was now a cruel contradiction to the dark well of fear that threatened to overpower me.

'I need you too, Chloe,' Ivan sighed heavily; the sigh of a man who doesn't like to have his fun spoiled. Real life and illicit love affairs were uneasy bedfellows.

'Sorry darling,' I took his hand. 'You do understand don't you?'

With obvious effort, Ivan smiled tightly and said, 'Of course, come on, the last train's gone, I'll drive you back.'

As we drove, something curious struck me; earlier while we had been making love, I'd been thinking of my husband.

Chapter Twenty-Two

It was late by the time I arrived at the hospital. At the entrance, a couple of patients stood smoking, undeterred either by the drizzling cold or by the drip stands that stood guard beside them. Clinging onto life even as they sought their own destruction, they pulled fiercely on their cigarettes until the ends burned hot, long and red. You'd have thought they were trying to suck new life out of them, rather than accelerate their own demise. How ill did you have to be before the threat of death overcame addiction, I wondered. I watched an amputee in a wheelchair as he lit a fresh cigarette from the butt of an old one. He had the emaciated frailty of the lifelong smoker and was literally on his last leg. He caught my eye and gave an apologetic, 'What can you do?' kind of shrug.

The lights were dim on the ward and behind the desk a nurse whose breasts threatened to spring out from her tightly-buttoned uniform talked quietly on the phone. She looked more like an actress from a TV hospital drama than a trained medical professional. Anxiety, I thought, doesn't prevent one from observing detail; it simply renders it absurd.

'Where can I find Bertie Zhivago?' I asked.

'Visiting hours are over,' she answered, looking pointedly at the upside-down watch pinned onto her fugitive bosom.

'I'm his daughter.'

She flicked her eyes over me as though searching for any distinguishing characteristics that might support my assertion.

'Do you want a bloody birth certificate?' I snapped, fear overcoming decorum.

'Bed Number Twelve,' she said, pretending not to hear me as she busied herself with files. 'Don't stay long.'

The patients were grouped in fours in bays, most of them lying inert. I peered in to the first bay and someone gave a throaty, mucous-filled cough. The odour of sickness combined with that of the anxious offerings of flowers and fresh fruit to create a cloying aroma of misery and despair: illness's frequent companions. Helga was dozing in a chair next to Dad's bed, her chest rising and falling in unison with his own. He looked small and frail and his skin appeared grey against the white of the hospital sheets. I went to take his hand, but it was punctured with intravenous needles that pumped drugs into him. Wires were taped to his chest, leading to a monitor whose screen flickered with the graph of his heart's laboured workings.

He stirred and opened his eyes. Dad always seemed able to sense my presence: we shared that invisible bond that only a mother is supposed to have with her child.

'I'm sorry, darling,' he whispered. 'I'm being a bit of a nuisance.'

'Yes, it's all me, me, me with you,' I smiled as I squeezed his shoulder. I was shocked by how thin he felt. I wanted to fling myself onto his chest so that he could comfort me for being upset because he was ill. But he needed my comfort, so I carried on joking, talking with difficulty through the hard lump that had formed in my throat.

'What happened?'

'I was sitting in the study just starting to get the birds down for a new tune when a great big horse kicked me in the chest – at least that's what it felt like. Next thing I knew I was in here all wired up.'

'Thank God Helga was with you,' I said. If he'd been alone, how long would he have lain there unaided while I was out of town with a man who was neither my husband nor my children's father? Helga opened her eyes and smiled at us.

'I'll leave you two alone together for a bit,' she said in that brisk, cheerful tone that people adopt when they're trying to pretend there's nothing to worry about.

'I'm feeling much better,' Dad said, 'now that I've got my two favourite grown-up women here.' Helga patted Dad's cheek, hugged me and went in search of air.

'I really like her, Dad,' I said. 'She's so loving.'

'She likes you too. I'm very pleased; it's important to me that the two women I love should like each other.'

'Where's Sammy?'

'He and Greg left about an hour ago,' Dad said.

'Did Greg talk to the doctor?' I asked.

'I'm not sure I've actually seen a doctor. A twelve-year-old girl in a white coat came and took my pulse and said something about keeping me in over the weekend. Greg had a little chat with her.'

I marched over to the desk. Soap Star Nurse was still on the phone, and, judging from the way she was toying with the top button of her uniform, she was probably talking to her boyfriend. I stood in her eye line and stared her down.

'I'll call you back in a minute, I have a possible F.A.R situation,' she said and hung up.

'Fucking Awkward Relative,' I said. She blushed. She wasn't to know that I'd done my clinical practice in a hospital, had a doctor for a husband and was familiar with all the many acronyms hospital staff were so fond of using. I was pleased to have her on the back foot.

'Has my father seen a doctor?'

'Yes, Dr Ashby saw him earlier. She's the registrar on duty.'

The twelve-year-old, clearly.

'What about the consultant?'   .

'He's not here on the weekend.'

'Is the registrar still here?'

'No, she's off now, but she's on call. She was happy with his progress.'

'I see. If he needed a doctor, how quickly could he see one?'

'Well, it's the weekend now, so it would usually take a few hours to get a doctor, I should think.' I felt a sudden rush of blood to my head, a rage precipitated by her pitying smile, which seemed to suggest that she knew how to deal with difficult people like me.

'You say that as though a weekend were an unexpected event: oh it's Friday, goodness me, a weekend is upon us, that's a surprise,'

I said. 'You do know that this is something that happens every week?'

She moved objects around the desk, taking particular care to ensure that the telephone was perpendicular to a plastic tower of in-trays from which human lives in the form of patients' folders spilled untidily. Perhaps she hoped that her methodical organisation of inanimate objects would soothe me.

'I'm not sure that illness knows it should take Saturday and Sunday off and only trouble its victims from Monday to Friday,' I wasn't yet ready to relinquish my point.

'I'm sorry, that's how the hospital works,' she said. 'Your father is quite comfortable at the moment.'

I leaned forward over the counter. 'How would you feel if that was your father lying in a hospital bed having just suffered a heart attack? This isn't just some old man that no one cares about, you know, someone who's *had a good innings*. Everyone deserves the best care, but this is my father, a very loved man, with friends and family, and if anything happens to him on your watch I will hold you personally responsible.'

My eyes had filled with tears and I was on the point of losing control, but I could see by her expression that I'd got through to her and I was glad. Dad was no longer just another patient to her, he had become a real person with a life; he had become, in short, an individual.

She leaned forward and put her hand on mine. 'Don't worry, we'll look after him.'

'Thank you, I'm sorry for my F.A.R-ish behaviour.'

We were united now, daughters of fathers, so she smiled and said, 'I'm sure I'd be just the same if I were you.'

Dad was reading the newspaper and looking quite chirpy by the time I returned to his bedside.

'How was your trip to the suburbs?' he asked.

'Ha ha, very funny. Am I really so transparent?'

'You're my daughter.'

'I'm not sure. It was strange to see him and you're right about what happens to your inner city; mine's in danger of becoming so derelict that it may soon have a demolition order slapped on it.

Crumbling tower blocks, smashed windows, the lot. I mean, look at the recent events: son ends up in hospital with alcohol poisoning, husband is waging a one-man war against local government, daughter is most probably only moments away from teenage pregnancy and father has heart attack.'

'I don't think you can be held responsible for my heart attack or Greg's eccentricity, although obviously Leo and Kitty's misdemeanours are your fault by virtue of the fact that you are their parent.'

He took my hand and stroked it. 'Greg is a good man, Chloe, and he loves you. You know what Simone Signoret said?'

I shook my head.

'"Chains do not hold a marriage together. It is threads, hundreds of tiny threads, which sew people together through the years. That is what makes a marriage last – more than passion or even sex!" I think she's right, that's what bound me to your mother and binds me now to Helga.'

Helga came back just then with a plastic cup of some tasteless, brownish liquid that had the audacity to pass itself off as tea.

'You are looking better Bertie. I think Chloe may be the best nurse.'

Dad smiled and patted my hand. 'I'm going to sleep now,' he said, 'so why don't you two girls go home and get some rest as well?'

Helga and I looked at each other. I could see that she didn't want to usurp my place, but it was also clear that she didn't want to leave Dad.

'You stay, but phone me if you need to,' I said.

She smiled gratefully. 'I'll feel much happier sleeping next to him in this chair.'

It was difficult relinquishing Dad's care to another woman, I was so used to having him to myself. But I was needed at home.

I turned my phone back on as I left the hospital and it immediately beeped. *Phone me, Chudo. Ivan xx*

I had the distinct sensation that Ivan was slipping away from me. His face and voice, usually sharp and present in my head, seemed blurred. It was as though I'd had a long fever which had burnt out, leaving me weak and exhausted. He felt remote and strangely irrelevant, as if he belonged to another life. I quickly called him.

'How is he?'

'He doesn't seem too bad, rather pale and weak, but very much himself,' I said.

'Come back to the country with me,' his voice went low and husky, 'I'll tie you up and make you come in five different ways.'

'Um, yes, well, I really need to be near my father.' Sex talk didn't go with hospitals somehow, or with parental heart attacks come to that. 'Look, I've got to go, let's speak tomorrow.'

My tryst with Ivan had almost been that fatal overdose after all, but with my father and not me the victim.

I experienced a rush of affection when I saw Greg. It was well past midnight and he was sitting on the sofa in the flickering light of the television screen. The children were asleep on either side of him, their arms flung out with the carelessness of babies. Seeing the three of them huddled together brought tears to my eyes. Greg stood up, taking care not to wake them. We looked at each other, he sighed and pulled me to him. I wept on his shoulder, silent sobs of fear for my father and of sadness and regret for what had happened to Greg and me.

'It's all right, darling,' said Greg, stroking the back of my head. 'They said it was a minor heart attack and that he'll be fine with rest.'

'He just looked so thin and frail. I can't bear the thought of losing him.'

'I know darling, I know.' He held my chin and tilted my face up to his. 'But the children and I will always be here to look after you. It's true what you said; we do need to be nicer to each other.'

I was crying now as much for Greg and me as for my father.

'Everyone goes through rough patches, that's just how life is,' he went on. 'It doesn't mean it's the end, sometimes it's just the middle, a point along the journey.'

He was so much more grown up than I, I realised, remembering that this was one of the things about him that had first made me love him. And I had loved him so much. When we'd first started living together, I would rush home excited when I saw his car parked outside, happy that he was home and waiting for me. I was the one who was meant to have the tools to understand human behaviour and yet Greg, despite his foibles, was so much steadier than I.

First Kitty, then Leo stirred and sat up. Kitty pushed Greg and me closer together.

'Kiss each other,' she said.

'Ugh,' said Leo. 'Must they?'

'Why not? You did, you pulled in the park,' Kitty said.

Leo kicked her.

'What does that mean exactly?' I asked.

'He kissed a girl.'

'We used to call that "getting off with".'

'Yeahwellthingshavechangedit'snotlikeitwasinyourday,' said Leo, lapsing into fastest-white-rapper-in-the-world speak as he glared threateningly at Kitty.

We all looked at each other and smiled. I began to feel that some of the madness of the previous months was ebbing away.

'I'm sorry, Greg,' I said.

'What for?'

'Everything.'

Our family idyll was disturbed by the sound of Janet the cat being sick in a corner and the distant strains of raised voices from the top floor of the house. Bea and Zuzi were clearly having *words*.

The next day dawned crisp and bright. Bea was angrily buttering bread for sandwiches in the kitchen, her thick brows knitted in a mixture of irritation and concentration. Kitty was standing on a chair behind her, brushing her hair and coaching her in her marriage vows, formulated for same-sex couples.

'Where did you find that?' I asked, indicating the typewritten pages in her hand.

'Special website, MrsandMrs.com,' she answered with the technological savvy of a twenty-first century child.

'You say, "*I Bea Havlova take you Zuzi Palakhova to be my lawful partner*".'

Although it was months before their happy day, the preparations for what had become known to us as The Lesbitian Wedding, were occupying more and more of everyone's time. (Leo, learning to carve wood with Sammy while I was cooking supper one evening, had constructed a fantasy where Bea and Zuzi were not from the Czech Republic after all, rather they were natives of the isle of Lesbos and should henceforth be known as Lesbitians.

'Nopointlettingallmyclassicaleducationgotowastemum,' he'd said.

'It makes it sound like they're Martians,' I'd protested.

'Welltheyaretomewhatawasteofpussy,' he'd said, shocking me.)

Leo now entered the kitchen and reached blindly into the fridge for some orange juice. I don't think I'd ever seen him up so early on a Saturday morning before.

'You are very bad boy,' Bea complained, 'standing on chair looking into our room through glass at top when we are in the bed.'

Leo smirked with discomfort and said nothing.

'You didn't?' I asked.

He shrugged noncommittally.

'WellmaybeIdidandmaybeIdidn'tthat'sformetoknowandnotreallyanyoneelse'sbusinessbutmyownit'scertainlynotthesortofthing asonwantstodiscusswithhismother.'

'He and Atlas also are looking all the time in the telescope from the Ruthie's roof into the window at us.' Bea said, jabbing her knife in Leo's direction.

Oh dear, it was all very well being wishy-washy liberals, but I suppose we really should draw the line at staging live girl-on-girl sex shows in our own house for our adolescent son and his friends. Although, in Atlas's case it had clearly been therapeutic: Ruthie had told me only a few days before he'd recently been considering that he might be heterosexual after all.

I escaped the embarrassment of my son's burgeoning sexuality by seeking shelter in the living room. I found Zuzi there, her hands clasped around a cup of tea as though she needed to draw every drop of warmth from it she could. A closed copy of *Doctor Zhivago* was on the table beside her. She'd finished it at last. She was looking ahead bleakly in a glassy-eyed sort of way.

'Marriage for me is always seem like fairy tale. My Bea, she love me now, but do she love me enough? What if she find other girl? What if I am not for her, her Lara?'

'That's a risk everyone has to take. Choose to be happy.' (Once again the gospel according to Dolly Parton was proving a useful counselling tool).

She put her cup down and began twisting the sapphire engagement ring on her finger. Sapphire rings for Sapphic brides.

'In Czech we have different saying: *Do not always expect good to happen, but do not let evil take you by surprise.*'

I could see I was going to have a problem with the Czech psyche as far as Dolly and my little *be happy* mantra were concerned. Eastern Europeans were like Jews when it came to living on the brink of disaster and expecting the worst.

'Have you ever been with a man, Zuzi?' I asked.

'Few time, but for me is horrible. It make me sick how they smell.' She wrinkled her freckled nose in disgust.

That was what I loved the most about men, the smell of them. Not all of them, just the ones you were attracted to. There'd been a lot of research into pheromones recently and I'd been following it in an attempt to blame something other than my faithless heart for my affair with Ivan; he'd been leading me by the nose. What was it about the olfactory systems of gay men and lesbian women that made them attracted to the same sex? I made a note to myself to tell Ruthie to get Atlas to sniff both men and women and see which he preferred. That way he'd work out once and for all where his sexual proclivities lay. I began to get quite excited as I thought about all this; it would make a good paper for *Psychological Review*. For the first time in ages, I felt excited by my work.

Zuzi was still looking glum.

'You see, Yuri Zhivago, in beginning, he love the Tonya, the one he make for his wife and then he go to the war and fall for the Lara and he hurt the Tonya so bad. Maybe I am the Tonya and not the Lara and when Bea find the Lara, she leave me behind.'

'There's a Jewish saying too,' I said, quoting one of Dad's many aphorisms. '*Do not ask questions of fairytales.*'

For some reason, this made her face brighten and she went downstairs to see Bea: everyone, it seems, needs to believe in a happily ever after.

*

Dad was wide-awake and scratching blackbirds onto a sheet of manuscript paper when Sammy and I went in to see him later that morning. Helga told us the doctor had said he could go home in a few days. She looked exhausted, wisps of hair were escaping in all directions and her clothes were creased; not even her recently applied lipstick could hide her fatigue. We sent her home to change and rest.

'Helga's going to move in with me,' Dad said. 'She says she wants to look after me. I don't need looking after, but I'd like her to stay, and for us to be together properly. Aristotle said, "No one would choose a friendless existence on condition of having all the other things in the world". He's right. In the end, the minor irritations of day-to-day cohabitation are more than compensated for by the love and companionship you find in each other's company. If nothing else, this heart attack has taught me that.'

'I'm pleased,' I said. 'We really like her, don't we Sammy?'

'Yes,' he agreed, but I could tell from the way his eyes wouldn't meet mine that, even after all these years, he felt we were being unfaithful to Mum.

'It's about time you found someone yourself, Sammy,' Dad said.

'I am seeing someone; a Spanish girl. She's called Nieves.'

'Good,' Dad said. 'I don't like to think of you being lonely.'

At the other side of the room I could see the pretty nurse I'd lashed with my tongue the day before. She caught my eye and smiled. I went over to her.

'Thank you,' I said, 'he's so much better.'

'He's a pleasure to look after, I wish everyone was like him,' she said as a man in a nearby bed called out irritably, 'Nurse, nurse, nurse,' his voice growing louder with each summons.

I went back to Dad. In the bed next to him lay an old man, pale and unmoving. His family was seated solemnly around his bed, preparing to face the worst. I watched the face of one of them, a woman of about my own age who must have been his daughter. She looked up as though my gaze had touched her, and as our eyes met we gave each other a shy smile of recognition. We were both daughters who shared a special bond with their fathers. I wanted to get Dad out of here as quickly as possible and to the safety of the outside world as if her father's obvious fate were contagious.

'I'm going to have a sleep now and you two must have lots to do, so off you go,' Dad said, giving us both his signature triple kiss.

On the way downstairs, Sammy said, 'I traced Madge's Armie.'

'And?'

'He went back to Jamaica.'

'What will you do now?'

'I'm not sure what I can do; I suppose I'll see if I can get information from the Jamaican authorities and tell Madge I'm still searching.'

The smokers were continuing their silent vigil by the hospital entrance, wrapped tightly against the chill in dressing gowns with jumpers on top. As we passed them, my phone rang. It was Ruthie.

'Bea's just phoned me; Zuzi's vanished,' she said.

'What do you mean?'

'She left a note telling Bea to meet her at a railway station and saying something about testing the strength of her love. She didn't say which station though.'

It was *Doctor Zhivago* come to life: Lara going on ahead and Yuri Zhivago promising to follow her. Or, perhaps she was intending to throw herself in front of a train like Anna Karenina instead?

'Oh for fuck's sake,' I said, 'hang on a minute let me think.' Station. *Vokzal.* I remembered: once in that cosy post-coital exchange of stories that Ivan and I so enjoyed, he had told me that the Russian word for railway station derived from Vauxhall Station. The story goes that Tsar Nicholas I was on a state visit to London in 1844 and was taken to see the trains at Vauxhall. He mistakenly assumed that 'Vauxhall' (which in Russian was *Vokzal*) was the generic term for a railway station. It was a guess, but it felt like a good one in the context of all the Russian literature that the Russo-Czech 'Club of the Books' had been reading over the past few months.

'I'll go,' I told Ruthie, once again caught up in keeping Bea happy, 'I think I know where she'll be. Put Bea in a taxi and tell her to meet me at Vauxhall Station.'

*

As I hurried up the street to the station, I saw Bea getting out of a cab and running inside. I hung back; this was their story, not mine. While I waited, I phoned the hospital to check on Dad and was told he was asleep. Soon, Bea and Zuzi emerged from the station's archway. They had their arms around each other and were laughing and crying at the same time. A monkey's wedding, that's what Sammy and I used to call it when we were children and the sun shone and it rained simultaneously.

'How did you know she'd be here?' Bea asked me.

'*Vokzal*,' I answered with a shrug.

P.O.B. Passenger on board, I texted Ruthie as I swung out into the midday traffic against the murmur of backseat sweet nothings in Czech.

'I am tell her she too sensitive for Russian literature, she take it too much to the heart, all the emotions, it is too much for her and make her to run away,' said Bea from where she and Zuzi sat behind me, 'but this is why I love her, for the tender heart.'

I glanced at them in the rear view mirror. Zuzi had her head on Bea's shoulder and Bea was stroking her arm.

'I am her Lara,' said Zuzi. Their innocent belief that love was enough made me want to cry, it took so much more than love to get through a life in partnership with someone else.

I pulled up at some traffic lights and looked in my mirror again. I could see Bea placing her hand proprietarily over the slight flare of Zuzi's belly. 'Was Zuzi pregnant?' I wondered. 'But where had they got the sperm from?' I had a disturbing vision of them robbing Leo of his nightly emissions as he slept. As the lights changed, I realised with frightening clarity that it was I who was pregnant and not Zuzi. I mentally counted back and remembered that my last period had been ten days before I had slept with both my lover and my husband on the same night. I hadn't used contraception with either of them. That made me two months pregnant and meant that I couldn't be certain who the father was.

'You all right?' Greg asked when I opened the front door. 'You're looking very pale.'

I couldn't talk to him about it now, I needed time to think.

253

How could I have another baby? How could I go back to the beginning and start again? The sleepless nights, the nappies, the twenty-four-hour police surveillance required by the parent of a toddler. Back to never finishing a sentence or reading a book. Then I remembered the sweet milky smells, the small creature stretching and pulling funny baby faces, the short little arms stretched straight upwards that only reached as far as the top of its head. The arrival of a new person, whole and complete. You shouldn't have a baby to save a relationship, but at the same time it could be another chance for Greg and me. Except it may not be his child. In which case, it would be an end and not a beginning at all. I'd said to Dad that I wanted another go, wanted to rub this life out and start again, so was this a sign that I should start a new life with Ivan? Could we have a child and live happily ever after? What was that Jewish proverb? *When two divorced people marry, four people get into bed.* More like eight if you count the children, or nine, if you were to count the new baby too.

FF was sitting in my living room holding forth to the assembled company about the importance of sex in a relationship. There was quite a party going on in there. She looked beautiful despite the preposterous pink and white hat she was wearing that looked like an upside-down ice cream cone. Jezzie sat on one side of her, while Jessie appeared frozen to her seat on the other. Jezzie was smirking in an I'm a hell of a guy sort of way as she alluded to his sexual prowess, and Jessie looked as though she had forced her mind out of her body to escape her exquisite embarrassment. Three Eastern European lesbians, summoned earlier by Bea in her hour of need, were hanging on FF's every word, particularly at the point where she began a detailed discourse on how few men really understood women's bodies and how if it weren't for the fact that she liked being fucked, she'd be a lesbian herself. A tall serious-looking woman with short bleached-blonde hair scribbled something on a piece of paper and passed it to her right under Jeremy's nose, saying, 'If you are changing your mind about this, please to phone me.'

Trust FF to pull a lesbian. I could just see what her next book might be: *Sapphic Love: the true female orgasm* or something like it. Jeremy's confident smile wavered for a moment and Jessie, looking as though she might be sick, finally found the strength to get up and leave the room.

'Jezzie and I are going to get married,' FF whispered to me. 'I think I'll announce it to everyone now.' She raised a fork to chime against the side of her glass to get everyone's attention.

'Don't do it now,' I said, my hand staying hers as I looked over at Bea and Zuzi sitting closely together with their arms around each other. 'Let Bea and Zuzi have their moment.'

FF paused and looked at me. 'You're right,' she said. 'I am horribly self-centred sometimes aren't I? I don't know why you put up with me.'

I didn't know why I did either, but perhaps it was because while I was with her I couldn't help but be entertained. The fact that sometimes even she knew when she'd overstepped the mark also redeemed her. Everyone should have an absurdly beautiful friend; it was like having a work of art: whatever the difficulties involved in acquiring and keeping it, ultimately nothing could detract from the pleasure of its contemplation.

FF looked at me now and said quietly, 'It's over, isn't it?'

'What?'

'Your affair with Ivan.'

'I don't know what you mean.'

'Come on Chlo, you know I have witchy powers. I suspected for ages and then the night of Bertie's Gala I knew for sure. But it's finished now, I can see.'

Was it finally over? Perhaps it was. What was it that Ruthie had said? Sometimes other people can tell things about you that you don't yet know yourself.

'Are you really going to marry Jeremy?' I asked, changing the subject.

'Yes. The beginning of a marriage is such heaven, isn't it?'

'I don't know,' I answered. 'I've only had one and I'm still having it.'

I knew what she meant, though; the first part of a relationship was heavenly. That's what I had loved about my affair with Ivan. But the sad truth was that there was no guarantee that it would go on like that and, more likely than not, we would slide inevitably into that state somewhere between contentment and indifference that is the fate of most married couples.

I saw Greg coming towards me, his face solemn. Had he decided to confront me about Ivan?

'Chloe, Helga just called. Bertie's had another heart attack. He's in intensive care.'

Chapter Twenty-Three

Dad's face was barely visible beneath the oxygen mask. Helga stood at the foot of his bed in conversation with a doctor. I was relieved to see that he was over forty and looked like a consultant. He turned as Greg, Sammy and I approached, his expression grave.

'This is Mr Zhivago's son, daughter and son-in-law,' Helga explained, coming to stand next to me. 'Mr McTernan is also a doctor,' she added, placing a hand on Greg's arm.

The doctor gave Greg a tight smile; the smile of a professional who knows he can tell it like it is to a colleague.

'Mr Zhivago has suffered a severe myocardial infarction and is very weak,' he said. 'We're treating him with medication; he's on a GTM infusion and has a hyperium IV. We're monitoring his blood for oxygen levels and carrying out serial ECGs.'

'What about surgery?' Greg asked.

'His arteries are not suitable for a by-pass, I'm afraid, and he's too old for a transplant. We'll have to watch and wait.'

More than his words, I didn't like what I saw in the doctor's expression. Neither did Greg; he drew me to him. It was dark outside, and the room was quiet save for the sound of Dad's breathing. A nurse moved around him, taking his blood pressure and monitoring his various drips. She didn't seem to want to meet our eyes.

We sat through the night, the four of us, and watched the laboured rise and fall of Dad's chest. I think we all knew that it would be his last night and didn't want to miss a moment of it. We didn't talk much, just held each other's hands and wiped our tears away. We took turns holding Dad's hands too, moving silently around the bed, swapping a foot for a hand; it was as though by touching him we were tethering him to life. Helga sang softly:

> Bertie is from England
> Zhivago is his name
> Lives in Temple Fortune
> On High Market Lane
> Building number twenty
> The doorbell's just the same

It was the verse Jürgen had memorised so that he could find Dad after the war.

At one point in that still, dark and timeless night, I sat vigil alone for a few minutes. I took Dad's hand and stroked it, held it to my face and kissed it. There was so much I wanted to tell him. I wanted to beg him not to leave us, I wanted to laugh with him one more time, to enjoy his warmth, wisdom and humour and to thank him for all the love he'd given me all my life. But I couldn't do any of those things; I didn't want him to know that he was dying. So I said the only thing that I could, words that didn't seem up to the job of expressing how I felt about him:

'I love you, Dad.'

He stirred and suddenly pulled his oxygen mask from his face.

'I love you, too,' he said. He looked at me and added, 'You know what I'm proudest of?'

I didn't trust myself to speak, so I shook my head.

'My family; being a father and a grandfather,' his voice sounded surprisingly normal. He smiled at me so sweetly, patted my hand and closed his eyes. I replaced the oxygen mask gently and smoothed his soft, silver hair on his clever, witty head, which was so packed full of knowledge, sayings, music and blackbirds. Where would it all go? Surely it had to go somewhere and couldn't just be extinguished like a light at the flick of a switch? Helga came back and sat on his other side. Our hands met as we stroked his head.

I thought of him, a young man far from home, in an Italian forest with an enemy soldier's gun at his temple, his life still ahead of him, yet fearing death was upon him. I thought of all the vicissitudes of the path that had led to this point, with that same German soldier's widow beside him, loving him at his end, when death finally did look certain. How curious it would be if we knew at the outset how our lives would play out. I sat there, with a new life just beginning to stir within me, the first flutterings of a baby that felt like bubbles, soon to be popping within me. All my life I had dreaded the loss of my father and now it appeared as though there could be no escape. All the chicken wishbones I'd wished on, the dandelions I had blown, the salt I had thrown over my left shoulder while I incanted *please let Daddy live to be ninety-four in perfect health*, an age I had plucked from the air because it seemed so impossibly old and distant. None of it had worked. Why was I always pregnant when one of my parents was dying? It was a cruel reminder of the inevitable cycle of life, each birth had to be paid for with a death. When Mum died, Kitty was growing inside me and I used to think about how her birth would mean a rebirth of part of my mother. I had the raw material, the DNA, to recreate my mother in some way, although not to replace her, for there can be no replacing. Now as Dad lay fading in front of us, I was growing another new life inside me, a new member of my family who would have something of my father in him or her. I knew then that whatever happened I would have this baby, whoever the father was. I also knew that it would be a boy.

The consultant returned early the next morning. He took Sammy and me aside.

'I want you to realise how serious your father's condition is,' he said. I think until that point I'd been praying that our love for him would be enough to keep Dad with us. Sammy and I hugged each other as we wept.

'We have to get the children here,' I said to Greg.

'Won't it be too upsetting for them?' Helga asked.

'They'd never forgive us if we didn't let them see him.'

I'd asked Ruthie to stay at our house with the children and I went out to call her, my voice breaking as I told her the news. I walked back along the corridor; the hospital was coming to life. Here and there, nurses and doctors were chatting and laughing; I was offended by their normality. 'How will I bear this?' I asked, the question repeating itself in my head. I could understand now why Madge had chosen madness; grief is too painful and can chase you to a different place.

Ruthie arrived with Kitty and Leo, whose faces were weighted with a sorrow they seemed too young to support. They were bravely trying not to cry. We stood there, all of us around him, watching and waiting as the consultant had advised, but each knowing that we were saying goodbye. Suddenly, Dad sat up and removed his mask completely. He looked around at us.

'Hello everybody,' he said. He was delighted to see us all and sounded like he had just opened a door to welcome us in. For an instant I dared to hope that he was recovering, then I remembered hearing about those moments of lucidity that often precede death. Dad looked at each of us in turn, as though memorising our faces, lay back, closed his eyes and breathed out, a long sigh of letting go. He had left us. In the end, his passing reflected his being; it was dignified and quiet.

I don't know what made me go in search of some scissors so that I could cut off small locks of Dad's distinctive silver hair as a keepsake. The same need to hold on, to possess a piece of the loved one that had fuelled the peasant boy's desire from Ivan's Russian tale to bite off the nose of the dead girl he loved? I held Leo and Kitty to me. In that moment, apart from the unbearable sorrow of losing my father, a grief that threatened to crush me forever, I knew that I would stay with Greg and that my affair with Ivan was, as FF had observed, quite over.

Chapter Twenty-Four

I did see Ivan once more. It was a few weeks later, after the funeral, after the initial searing pain of loss had settled into a dull, continuous ache. Each morning after I woke up, I had a brief moment of normality before I remembered that I was waking up to a world that no longer contained my father. Then the familiar, steady ache would settle in for the rest of the day. We'd held the funeral two days after Dad's death, Sammy and my Jewishness kicking in atavistically. Jews bury their dead as soon as possible. I used to think it was due to the heat of the desert, but in fact, Ruthie had explained to me, it's because once a person's soul has returned to God, it's considered shameful to allow their body to linger in the land of the living.

'Births, marriages and deaths, that's when religion comes into its own,' Sammy had said as we sat in Dad's flat a few days after he'd died. We'd all gone there from the hospital; it had felt like the obvious place to be, as if it were a way of remaining in his presence and keeping him alive. The flat still smelt of him, and the piano was open as he had left it, motes of dust dancing in the rays of a spring sunshine that insolently shone in on our sorrow. The room was still and quiet, as if the piano knew that my father's hands would never make it sing again. We'd stayed in the flat pretty much ever since the funeral, sitting *Shiva** as was customary. Ruthie had brought food and looked after us as we sat and cried and shared memories of Bertie.

---

* Shiva – a seven day period of formal mourning observed after the funeral of a close relative.

'Jews do some things well,' Sammy went on. 'I mean, you can see why they tear their clothes. It helps to have an external expression of your inner state. That's just how I feel. Torn. Don't you?'

In accordance with Jewish custom in times of mourning, Sammy was unshaven and wearing a ripped shirt.

He looked like I felt, bereft, an orphan. It doesn't matter how old or grown-up you are when your parents die; you still feel abandoned and alone. When they die, part of you dies with them, your younger self, your childhood. There's no one left to tell you what you were like as a baby, what your first words were or what your favourite toy was. All those memories are buried with them. I was no longer somebody's daughter. The safety net had gone, no generation lay between us and the grave now. At the end of that terrible first week, Helga had left for Germany leaving us orphaned and bereft all over again.

'You do understand, don't you?' she'd explained, 'I need to be with my children in Germany. But I will come and visit you often; we will always be part of each other's lives.'

A few weeks later, Sammy and I had gone to the flat to begin the business of sifting, sorting and packing away in boxes a life that was now over. I found some of our childhood there, hidden in drawers in the form of old yellowing school reports and little nonsense notes of love that I'd written to Dad and he to me. He'd kept them all, tucked away in a wooden box in the back of a cupboard. Daughters, if they're lucky, learn the business of loving from their fathers. The notes almost undid me; they made me realise all over again how much I had lost.

'You should be really grateful for all those years you had a Dad,' FF had said to me the day before as she stood in my kitchen, holding out her hand for me to admire the engagement ring Jeremy had given her. 'I didn't have any of that.'

FF's father had died when she was ten. 'Here, I've got you something to cheer you up.' She handed me an envelope. Inside was a voucher for a session with Rasa Rastumfari, the legendary colonic irrigator. I suppose she meant well, but did she honestly think a clean colon could remedy the loss of a beloved father?

Sammy found me in Dad's bedroom weeping over a photograph

I had found. It was a picture of me, aged fourteen, sitting next to my father, my head resting on his shoulder. He was half-turned towards me smiling. I remembered the day it was taken, the day after Grandma Bella's funeral. Just moments before, Dad and I had been weeping in each other's arms. Sammy was carrying a cardboard box that he'd found in the same cupboard, portentously labelled, My Youth. He sat beside me and ran his past through his fingers.

'Ginny Best's vagina,' he said suddenly, holding something up.

'I beg your pardon?'

'These photos. I took them of her vagina. Actually, strictly speaking they're of her vulva, not her vagina. Must have been when we were both about nineteen. Not bad,' he said, bringing the photo closer to him.

'The vagina or the photo?'

'Both. I was a good photographer.'

He used to spend hours in the bathroom, which he'd turned into a darkroom, with me hammering impatiently at the door.

'What should I do with them?' he asked me now.

'Send them to her?' I suggested. 'Throw them away?'

'Do you want to see them before I do?'

'I think not, don't you?'

The vagina/vulva episode lightened our mood, so that when Ivan texted me a few moments later, asking if he could see me, I told him to meet me in a café round the corner.

It is death and not love that changes everything. How handsome Ivan looked when he arrived. A handsome stranger. I could see why I had wanted him, though the connection between us now felt quite broken. At first, we didn't openly acknowledge that we were saying goodbye; we didn't have to, we both knew. I sat opposite him and ran my little finger along the scar in his eyebrow reading the Braille of his face with my hands to memorise it.

'Becky and I are getting divorced,' he told me. 'I hate the way I am to her, she deserves better.'

'Is she all right?'

'I think she's relieved.'

We sat in silence for a few moments.

'I'm so sorry about Bertie ...' he began.

My eyes filled with tears. 'I have to go,' I said, 'Sammy is waiting for me.'

'If you need me or things change ...' he said as I was leaving.

I put a finger to his lips before replacing it with my mouth as I kissed him, as he had once done to me when all of this began.

At the door, he handed me a piece of paper. A verse was typewritten on it in Russian.

'One more note,' he said with a sad smile. 'Forgive me for borrowing someone else's words to tell you how I feel. These are the words of the greatest Russian poet, Aleksandr Pushkin.'

He held me to him one last time, turned and left.

> *Ia vas liubil: liubov' eshche, byt' mozhet,*
> *V dushe moei ugasla ne sovsem;*
> *No pust' ona vas bol'she ne trevozhit,*
> *Ia ne khochu pechalit' vas ni chem.*
> *Ia vas liubil bezmolvno, beznadezhno,*
> *To pobost'iu, to revnost'iu tomim;*
> *Ia vas liubil tak iskrenno, tak nezhno,*
> *Kak dia vam bog liubimoi byt' drugim.*

This time, I wasn't going to ask Volodya to translate. Instinctively, I knew that this was both too private and too sad. Instead, I logged on to Dad's computer back at his flat and found a translation myself on the internet:

> *I loved you: it may be that love has not completely died in my soul; but let it trouble you no longer; I do not wish to sadden you in any way. I loved you silently, hopelessly, tormented now by shyness and now by jealousy; I loved you so sincerely, so tenderly, as God grant you may be loved by another.*

Pushkin had written it in 1829. Nothing's new in love, it seems, and there is some comfort in that.

I didn't see Ivan again after that. I couldn't. The knowledge that the new life growing inside me might belong in part to him made it impossible for me to see him. The only way I could cope was to compartmentalise; to deny his existence and tell myself that none of it had happened and I was nothing more than a married woman, pregnant with her third child.

'Should I tell Greg about Ivan?' I asked Ruthie one afternoon on the phone.

'Rule Two, remember?' she said. *'Never confess. If you can't do the time, don't do the crime.'*

'But I do have to tell him that I'm pregnant.'

'Yes, that you do have to do.'

Greg came through the front door looking very pleased with himself and waving a piece of paper at me. 'Read this,' he said.

Dear Sir/Madam,

With regard to your Penalty Charge for entering the Congestion Charge Zone without paying the fee.

I was careful to await the time of 18.30 before entering the Congestion Charge Zone.

In your letter you inform me that your system is synchronised to the 'Rugby Atomic Clock'. I made sure to note that 18.30 was the time recorded on both my watch and my car clock before entering the zone. Your first letter claims that I entered two minutes and forty-six seconds before 18.30 – presumably according to the 'Rugby Atomic Clock'. I must say that I have always regarded myself as a highly punctual individual and have always considered it very important to ensure that my various time-pieces are accurate. I shall be sure in the future to check my watch against the speaking clock before setting out on a journey into central London's Congestion Charge Zone in the evening.

However I made two other two points in my letter:

[1] I believe a difference of less than three minutes to be within the limits of acceptable variation between chronometers.

[2] If Transport for London wishes motorists to adhere to the Congestion Charging times as accurately as the Rugby Atomic Clock, then I believe that clocks recording the accurate time should be in place at every road junction within the Congestion Charge zone.

Therefore, I again respectfully request, in view of the two points that
I have presented above, that you cancel this PCN.
    Yours sincerely,
    Greg McTernan

'Very good darling,' I said. 'I'm pregnant.' (Well, when *is* the right moment to tell someone that?)

'That'll give them something to think— What?'

'I'm pregnant.'

He looked at me, a long, hard, calculating look. 'But we've hardly had sex recently and you used your cap didn't you?'

'You're a doctor, you should know it only takes one go. And no, I didn't use my cap. Don't you remember? It was among the many items you hid last year and neither of us have been able to find since.'

'Oh yes,' he said sheepishly. 'You could have gone and got a new one.'

'It hardly seemed worth it,' I said, a little more sharply than I'd intended.

He seemed about to say something, but changed his mind. 'What do you want to do, Chlo?'

We were standing in the kitchen, Greg was leaning against the fridge, next to the photograph of all of us taken outside the house as we set off for Dad's gala. Dad had been right after all; it had been a lifetime achievement award for a life that was almost over. Next to it was the order of service from his funeral. It had the photo of him that had been above his piano, the one where he was so fondly watching Leo and Kitty as they opened their presents. Who could have known that this photograph, taken so spontaneously at a time of joy, would one day come to symbolise the sorrow we felt at losing him?

I turned to Greg. 'Did Dad ever talk to you about dying?'

'Not so much about dying,' he answered quietly. 'But about after he was dead.'

'What did he say?'

Greg paused, turned on the kettle and busied himself with getting mugs out to make tea. 'He was worried about how you would cope. He told me to look after you and I told him that I would always look after you because I love you too.'

I looked into his eyes and recognised the expression in them. It was the way he used to look at me when we were first together.

'I remember you,' I said, poking him playfully to chase away the tears that were filling my eyes. 'You're my boyfriend Greg, that boy I fell in love with all those years ago. I feel like I haven't seen you for ages.'

'I'm the same person and so are you. Nothing's changed,' he said, stroking my face.

If only that were true.

'What do *you* want?' I asked Greg, running a hand over the as yet barely perceptible swelling of my stomach.

'I want you to be happy; I want us to be happy. I want you to understand that I love you,' he put his hands on my shoulders and drew me towards him. 'I want whatever you want.'

'I want to have the baby,' I said.

'Then we will, even though it means that we'll have to go on working until we're seventy.'

Kitty and Leo were excited by the news, once they'd got over the disgusting fact that their parents still had sex. I wasn't sure how I was going to tell Jessie that I'd need her room back for the baby. She was back to spending every weekend with us, and frequently a night or two in the week. When I tried to broach the subject with FF she waved her arm dismissively and said, 'Don't worry darling, she can bunk in with Kitty.' She was far more concerned with telling me that it was extremely unlikely I'd ever get my figure back this time; after a third child and at my advanced age.

'You should have a caesarean and a tummy tuck at the same time,' she said. 'That's what everyone is doing these days.'

Perversely, I was almost more afraid of telling Bea I was pregnant than I had been about telling Greg. As it turned out, my concern was well-founded.

I found her standing in front of the hall mirror, plucking her eyebrows.

'I do not look after the babies,' she said firmly.

Perhaps it was for the best. We couldn't go on having both her and Zuzi in the house; this would finally give me the perfect way out and the opportunity to find someone new who might actually do some work.

'This is not my job,' Bea continued, turning from her scowling image to face me. 'For this you need my Zuzi, this is the work she is done in Czech Republic, she is the trained baby nurse.' Before I could respond, she'd called Zuzi down and, far from getting shot of them, I found myself agreeing to employ them both; Bea for Kitty, Leo and, of course, Jessie; and Zuzi for the baby. Now I would have two wages to pay instead of one and an extra child in the house; in fact, two if you counted Jessie.

'A hundred,' Greg said when I told him.

'A hundred what?'

'Now we'll have to work until we're a hundred, not seventy.'

Only to Ruthie could I sometimes confess my sadness at losing Ivan and my anxiety about my baby's paternity, which kept me awake most nights.

'You wouldn't be the first, Chlo,' she said, trying to comfort me as we lounged on the sofa in my living room one afternoon several months later. I was seven months pregnant and she was now officially and happily unemployed, relaxing until she decided what she would do next. We'd taken to having an afternoon rest together and slavishly watching Richard and Judy.

'I did a piece on DNA paternity testing for *Smart* once,' she went on. 'Did you know that roughly thirty per cent of men taking the tests discover that they are not the biological fathers of the children they've been bringing up as their own. Rule number ten, by the way – *never agree to a DNA test.*'

'It amazes me,' I said, 'how some people change partners so effortlessly. You read about these women who get divorced and then a second later they're shacked up with someone else and having their baby. They all seem to do it so lightly.'

'Who are these women?' Ruthie said, looking at me a little more pointedly than I would have liked. After all, I had chosen the path of righteousness, sacrificing my lover for my husband.

'Oh you know, they're in all those magazines, "Chav Weekly" or whatever they're called.'

'Maybe they don't have that family thing that we have, you

know, the compulsion to preserve the unit whatever the cost.'

'Mmm, I suppose that's a good thing, though, isn't it? What else is there really that's as important as family?'

'Are you and Greg having sex again?' Ruthie asked.

'Constant,' I answered, 'it's so weird, it's as if nothing happened.'

She gave me a shrewd look. 'Once a week?'

I nodded.

'That's about right,' she agreed. 'For marital sex that is pretty constant. What was all that abstention about then?'

'I don't know. Greg says it was just a stage in our lives before we moved on to the next stage. I told you about the GrayAway I found in the bathroom, didn't I?'

Ruthie nodded. 'He's stopped using it, hasn't he? I like his greying temples.'

'Me too,' I said. 'Strangely that grey frosting was one of the things I found so attractive in Ivan.'

'Do you think you'd ever have another affair?'

'Never say never,' I quipped.

Ruthie sat up and looked at me in horror.

'Only kidding, next time it's your turn,' I said.

We sat for a few moments in silence, enjoying the laziness of the afternoon until the doorbell interrupted us.

It was Madge with a bunch of roses she'd picked in her small garden, tied with a strip of gold satin from her fabric collection. Their rich scent made you want to burrow deep with your nose in the petals.

'I want to thank you for helping me,' she said.

'It wasn't me, it was Sammy,' I said.

'Well, both of you have made me feel better.'

'Sammy's still trying to find Armie for you.'

She nodded, and we looked at each other for a few moments. I invited her in, but she shook her head and turned to go. I watched her walk across the road and into the park where she was at once surrounded by a small flock of pigeons.

'I miss Bertie,' said Ruthie, when I came back in.

'Yes,' I answered quietly. 'Sometimes it's the smallest things that undo me. I was on the tube yesterday and there was an elderly man opposite me; the sight of his hands made me cry, they reminded me of Dad's.'

Old man's hands that symbolised love, parental hands that soothed brows and stroked cheeks.

We were silent awhile, playing our own memories of my father in our heads. I looked at Ruthie. She was healthy again, her cocaine addiction in the past. Between us, Richard and I had barely let her out of our sight for the past few months.

'Do you remember the box?' I asked. 'I wonder whether anyone ever found it.' A tartan biscuit tin buried in a garden more than thirty years ago. It had been a rainy Saturday afternoon in July and we'd spent most of it getting ready to get ready (the best part) for a birthday party that night. As the rain fell, we'd sat inside and discussed what we wanted from life. Who could have known then what living happily ever after would come to mean? It certainly wasn't quite what either of us had envisaged at the time.

And now, all these years later, it was time to bury something else, something unbearably sad that spelled the end of an era. Dad's ashes. On a grey, cloudy day, on what would have been his seventy-ninth birthday, we gathered in the garden by the cherry tree where Mum's ashes were already buried. Helga had come over from Germany. She'd been so thrilled that I was pregnant and I'd asked her to be an honorary grandmother.

'That means a great deal to me, Chloe,' she'd said.

We'd squeezed each other's hands, unable to say more. She stood tall and erect with her arms around Kitty and Leo on either side of her. She'd become their grandmother too. Kitty sang one of Dad's songs and Leo read a poem he had written. They looked so desperately sad, and stumbled over their words as tears ran down their young faces. It seemed unfair that they should have to know this sorrow at such a young age, and yet this was life's inescapable cycle of love and death. One day, as for all children, if the natural order of events were observed, they would have to bury Greg and me. I looked at Greg, slim and handsome, his blue eyes rimmed red as he stood solemnly beside me. The passage I'd chosen to read was about fathers and daughters, but it applied to all of us in relation to Dad. It was from a novel I'd read recently, *Decorations in a Ruined Cemetery* by John Gregory Brown: *There's something like a line of gold thread running through a man's words when he talks to his daughter, and gradually over the years it gets to be long enough for you to pick up in your hands and weave into a cloth that feels like love itself.*

Ruthie reached for my hand. Sammy opened the urn and poured the ashes into the earth and, as they fell, an unexpected ray of sunlight shone through the clouds and illuminated the ground. A blackbird alighted on a branch of the cherry tree, its head twitching inquisitively from side to side. It opened its mouth and sang; one long, high, ringing note as though a call to wake us up. Janet, who still ate only rarely, eyed it hungrily and Sammy looked up and scanned the clouds.

'I thought I saw Dad's face there for a moment,' he said sadly. 'Wouldn't it be great if he was watching us?'

Perhaps in some curious sense he was. What if a relationship does not end with death after all and can continue even if someone is no longer physically present? For a moment, I had a brief glimpse into some other world not as seemingly absolute as the one we inhabited. Dad's voice was still in my head and sometimes I felt his presence beside me. The baby kicked me under my ribs, making me cry out. Greg and the kids put their hands on my stomach. We knew that we'd never get over our loss, but that time with its inexorable passage would, possibly, one day make it a little more bearable.

Epilogue

Chloe Zhivago's Thai Green Placenta Curry
(not for the squeamish)

2 tsp. coriander seeds
1 tsp. black peppercorns
2 fresh green chillies seeded and
chopped
1 inch piece of ginger finely
chopped
3 tbsp. chopped coriander leaves
and stems
2 large cloves of garlic

3 tbsp. chopped spring onions
1 lemon grass root roughly
chopped
2 tbsp. vegetable oil
400 ml coconut milk
4 kaffir lime leaves
850g fresh placenta
1 small bunch fresh basil leaves
1 tbsp. fish sauce

Grind the coriander seeds and peppercorns to a powder in a coffee grinder or mortar. Add the fresh seasonings (chillies, ginger, coriander leaves, garlic, spring onions and lemon grass) and grind to a paste. (If you want to cheat, you can buy Thai green curry paste ready made from an oriental supermarket and miss this stage). Fry this seasoning paste in a saucepan with the vegetable oil for a couple of minutes. Add the coconut milk and lime leaves (which you have de-stemmed and de-veined) and simmer for 10 minutes. Cut the placenta into bite-sized cubes. Add to the sauce with 1 cup of water and simmer until tender (about 20 minutes).

Add chopped basil leaves and fish sauce to the curry to taste. Serve with rice.

Serves 6.

Chloe Zhivago, 44, cradled her newborn third child, a boy, in her arms. 'Can we call him Bertie?' she said, looking at her husband, Greg. He nodded, leaned towards the baby and pulled back the blanket to reveal a tiny foot. The little toe lay crookedly on top of the fourth. Greg kissed the baby's foot, covered it up and said to his wife, 'I'm not sure I could have borne it if he hadn't been mine.' The baby stared at his parents with all the wisdom of an old man in the body of a freshly minted infant. Chloe looked like she was about to say something, but Greg silenced her with a kiss. 'Here, eat this,' he said, feeding her with a spoon. It was chicken soup with kneidlach. 'Delicious, darling,' Chloe said. 'It's got the secret ingredient, hasn't it? It's perfect.' In truth, it wasn't absolutely perfect, but pretty damn near.

Author's Note

Ivan would, of course, have used the Cyrillic alphabet when writing his notes to Chloe, as did Pushkin when he wrote his poem. I decided that it would be best for all the Russian in this novel to be transliterated into the Roman alphabet so that the non-Russian speaking reader would be able to get a sense of the music of the language. I have used the Library of Congress System (without diacritics).

Acknowledgements

I would like to thank my brother, Conrad Lichtenstein and dear friend, Claire Ladsky who were the first to read the manuscript of this book and offered so much valuable help and encouragement. My friends who sustained me while I was writing it: Simon Booker (who kindly explained to me that writing isn't just typing, it's all the hours away from the keyboard too), Lola Borg, Richard Denton, Neil Grant, Alla Svirinskaya and Colleen Toomey. Thanks also to Tania Abdulezer, Jochen Encke, Marc Faupel and Neil Geraghty who kept my body and soul functioning and to Amy Jenkins and Philip McGrade for valuable writing insights. I'd also like to thank many people called Gill – Gill Morgan, Jill Robinson and her Wimpole Street workshop, and Annabel Giles (not Gill exactly – but a Gile thing going on in her surname) who were there at the beginning of this. Gillian Gordon for her inspirational dream-writing workshop and Gill Hudson who gave me an office in which to write. Thanks too to Henrietta Morrison for the generous use of her office in Poland Street where much of this book was written. I am grateful to heart surgeon Mr Shyam Kolvekar for his advice. Enormous thanks are due to my agent, Clare Alexander, who guided me with a steady, wise hand throughout and to my editors, Jane Wood and Anika Streitfeld – I couldn't have had better women on my team. And to Sally Riley who has sold Chloe Zhivago and her gang all over the place. A great debt of gratitude to my husband, Simon Humphreys and my children, Oscar and Francesca, without whom I would be nothing. And to Edwin Lichtenstein, my darling Dad, who read the first three chapters – all that I had then written – before he died. He told me I should carry on. I hope he would have been proud.

Olivia Lichtenstein, London, June 2006